Possession

A Novel

By A.C. Hessenauer

This novel is a work of fiction, though certain settings and character traits draw inspiration from real-life individuals and places. Names, descriptions, and major plot points have been utilized and altered for the purposes of the narrative.

ISBN 979-8-218-55641-9

"Monsters are real, and ghosts are real too. They live inside us, and sometimes, they win."

-Stephen King, The Shining

For the one who helps me fight my own monsters.
Who reminds me, whenever I forget, that I never really needed
help, anyway.

Possession Playlist:

1. *I Miss You* -blink-182
2. *If You Don't, Don't* -Jimmy Eat World
3. *deja vu* - Olivia Rodrigo
4. *Teeth* - 5 Seconds of Summer
5. *vampire* - Olivia Rodrigo
6. *DARKSIDE* - NEONI
7. *Breezeblocks* -alt-J
8. *I'm Not a Machine* -Bishop Briggs
9. *lacy* -Olivia Rodrigo
10. *Autumns Monologue* -From Autumn to Ashes
11. *The Fiction We Live* -From Autumn to Ashes
12. *Panoramic View* -AWOLNATION
13. *Sleep* -My Chemical Romance
14. *Everlasting Light* -The Black Keys
15. *When The Darkness Comes* -Jeris Johnson
16. *Insane* -Black Gryph0n & Baasik

1.

Clay

Clay Martin was already angry when he saw the notification pop up on his phone. He saw the sender and quickly scanned the email preview. He had to consciously remind himself to unclench his jaw. Clay turned the screen off, returning his attention to his boss, but as the meeting dragged on, he couldn't help but look back at the screen again; it was like his eyes returned to it of their own volition. He hit the button on the side of the phone, peering at the notification, squinting like he hadn't seen it before. Like he didn't already know exactly who it was from and what it was about.

"Clay!" He jerked and swung his gaze up to see John glaring down at him, "Is there something more pressing demanding your attention?" He felt the tide of anger start to rise again and cleared his throat.

"No, no, of course not. Sorry." He locked his phone again and set it down quickly on the glossy wooden table. John was such an asshole. He just needed to get through another 20 minutes of this, and then he would be free. Well, it was Friday, so free for a few days at least. Clay refused to look at his phone again, keeping his gaze fixed on John's pudgy face. *He may be able to control my eyes, but he can't control my brain.* Clay disassociated for the remainder of the meeting.

As soon as the meeting ended, he grabbed his phone, shoved it in his pocket, and headed out of the conference room to his desk. Grabbing his jacket, he swung it on and shoved his glasses case and laptop into his bag, not bothering to turn the laptop off. He turned to leave and practically ran into Jane. Clay sighed internally. "Hey," he said, trying to keep his face and voice neutral.

"Hey!" She smiled back widely. "So, any plans for this weekend?"

"Um, yeah, I'm meeting up with some friends tonight." He lifted his arm and shrugged his sleeve down a bit, pretending to check his watch. "I need to get going, actually. Don't want to be late."

"Oh, yeah, okay." Jane smiled again, clearly not as cheerfully this time. He felt a brief pang of guilt. Jane was a nice person, but he just wasn't interested, and he didn't want to be stuck talking to her after hours on a Friday, not with that email waiting to be read in his pocket.

"Have a great weekend!" He replied, giving her what he hoped was a friendly smile back.

"You too," she said, nodding, as she stepped aside and let him pass down the narrow walkway between the cubicles. He rushed out to his car, jogging down several flights of stairs all the way to the parking garage below the office. He found his car quickly and jumped inside. He sat there momentarily, sighing, as he loosened his tie. Then he turned the car on, the AC blowing hot air in his face. He should drive, he thought, and get out of here as soon as possible before traffic gets any worse, but he slid his hand into his pocket instead, pulling his phone out. He pressed his thumb to the fingerprint image on the screen, and in his haste, it took several tries before he was able to unlock the phone.

Clay immediately clicked on the email notification and quickly scanned the rest of the message. As his eyes skimmed over the lines of text, a few words jumped out at him: *'Ten-year reunion... Hammond Castle... ultimate escape room... private weekend getaway... once in a lifetime experience... I know you'll all be there... I'm counting on it.'* Then he signed it with just his first name. He had to give it to him; Alex was always selling.

Clay rolled his eyes and tapped the "CC" at the top of the email to expand the list. He carefully read the addresses. Some had the names typed out, but most didn't. Still, he thought he could sort out who they were. There was only one he really cared about, and she was on the list. He counted. *Only six of us listed. That's interesting.*

Clay sighed loudly, his finger hesitating over the 'Reply all' button. His heart was hammering; it felt like it had migrated to his throat. He pushed the button to shut the screen off and flung the phone onto the passenger's seat. He quickly checked his mirrors and threw the car into reverse. The wide-angle backup cam confirmed that the garage was clear behind him. He backed out and made his way out of the parking garage into traffic.

Clay decided he wouldn't give Alex the satisfaction of responding immediately; he'd let it ride for a while. Maybe he'd wait until Alex texted, or even called, to see if he had read the email, but he already knew what his answer would be: he would go. He wouldn't be able to stay away. He came to a dead stop behind a long line of cars at a red light. "FUCK!" He yelled loudly, slamming his hands on the steering wheel, startling himself in the silence of the empty car. He turned the radio on. His hand was shaking. He took a deep breath and tried to calm his heart rate down. He tried not to picture her face.

2.

Bee

Phoebe "Bee" Blake reread the email for what might've been the tenth time. She'd lost count. She sighed loudly, running the tip of her thumb back and forth over her lip as she read. Her nails were cut down to the quick; nothing to chew on. Hammond Castle was in Gloucester, Massachusetts. The first thing she did was Google the location. She had never been there before, never been to the East Coast at all, in fact.

She felt a strange reluctance mixed with excitement and anticipation. Of course, she would go, wouldn't she? She couldn't imagine them there without her, as much of a pain as it would be to get the time off. She would probably have to beg Goldsmith. It was either that or beg her co-workers to swap with her. Then she'd end up working two weeks straight, most likely, with no break. Still... it would probably be worth it.

She sighed again, her blue eyes widening at the thought of the outfits she could wear, but God, she'd have to fly by herself. She was a nervous flier and hated navigating airports while constantly feeling like she was late, but Alex had said in the email that they could fly right into Logan in Boston. He would even send a car to pick them up and drive them to

Gloucester. All she had to do was get the time off, book the ticket, get herself to the airport, and get herself on the plane, and the rest would be easy. She grabbed a strand of her copper hair and twirled it absentmindedly. She was already thinking of the outfit she'd wear on the plane and which bag she would pack.

She smiled to herself, picturing their faces when they saw her get out of the car. "Bee!" A voice called off to her right. She turned swiftly, shoving her phone back into the pocket of her royal blue scrubs. "We need you in seven. Can you come help?" Bee smiled, flashing her white teeth.

"Of course!" She responded brightly, heading down the hall to room seven. "I actually have a favor to ask you, too."

3.

Cam

Cameron Summers rolled her eyes and smiled as she read the email. Her partner, Grace, leaned over and whispered to her.

"Do tell..." Grinning at her in a conspiratorial way.

"Oh god," she replied. "It's nothing work-related, just one of my old friends from college... being a bougie idiot. Listen to this," she licked her lips and began to read, "*This year marks the 10th anniversary of our graduation from MSU, and it seems only proper that we hold a reunion of sorts. To that end, I've booked Hammond Castle for a weekend, the elaborate seaside home of the eccentric inventor John Hays Hammond Junior, who holds the title of second most US patents (second only to Thomas Edison). Hammond Castle has been turned into the ultimate escape room challenge for the weekend. We will work together to solve customized challenges in order to escape. You will arrive on Friday, for a night of whale watching on a private charter, with a seaside gourmet dinner and drinks to follow. The challenge begins on Saturday and concludes on Sunday evening. Plan to stay until Monday. This is a once-in-a-lifetime opportunity. I know you will all be there. In fact, I'm counting on it.*"

"He lists all the travel details below. He's going to send a car to Logan to pick us up individually. He's such a show-off." She rolled her eyes at Grace. "You're rich... we get it already."

"Yeah, well, that does sound awesome though. You're obviously going." Grace replied matter-of-factly.

"Oh please, there's no way. Not with the trial coming up. Sorry to disappoint, Alex." She chewed on her bottom lip, scanning the other email addresses on the message. Everyone else would probably go. She knew Bee hated to fly, but she wouldn't miss it. Lan and Austin were the only two she wasn't 100% sure of. Lan might not be up for a whole weekend stuck with them. Austin might not go out of spite.

"Oh, come on, Cam, it's one weekend, you can freaking take a weekend off." Grace rolled her eyes this time.

"Yeah, and I would have to travel on Friday and wouldn't get back until sometime on Monday, which means I'm missing two days of work. It's not just a weekend."

"You're going," she said, glaring at her. "I'll make sure of it. You work too hard as it is. Besides, you miss them. You still talk about them. Just go have fun and relax for once."

Cam tucked her phone away and quickly got to her feet as the judge entered the courtroom. "Fine," she whispered out of the corner of her mouth while tucking her blonde hair behind her ears, "What do you want to bet I beat his stupid escape room by lunch Saturday?"

4.

Darcy

Darcy Cole dipped her paintbrush into the bright red on the palette she clutched in her right hand. She gently and carefully added the vibrant color in subtle touches to the tree leaves. She blew a puff of air up and to the right, aiming at her bangs that had fallen into her eyes. She tossed her head back until they settled out of her line of sight. She hummed along to the music as she painted.

This commission needed to be done by Sunday. She thought she only had a few hours left of intensive work. After that, she could relax. It would just be the finishing touches from there. The commission would more than cover her plane ticket to Boston. Alex had offered to pay for everyone's ticket, but she wouldn't give him the satisfaction. Besides, she had done well recently. She was growing a following on Instagram and had a bunch of local commissions lined up. Her showings in a few restaurants downtown had helped. She knew her life was simple to some, but it was quiet, peaceful, and it suited her. She may not be able to host fancy escape room parties in castles, but she could take care of herself, and she owned her own home. That was all she ever wanted, really.

She jumped slightly as she felt something brushing against her leg. Her cat, Rufus, pressed against her, meowing loudly. She looked at the clock on the wall. She'd lost track of time once again; it was way past dinner time; Rufus was probably starving by now. She set her brush and palette down. She would have to finish the rest later. Her humming continued as she entered the kitchen, pausing momentarily at the fridge; an old photo hung there, secured by two magnets. The faces that smiled out at her were younger, certainly, more carefree. *Has it really been 10 years?* She eyed each of them in turn, smiling to herself. It would be good to see all of them again, although the thought made her feel somehow a little nervous at the same time.

She shook her head to clear it and grabbing a can of cat food, went over to Rufus' bowl, feeding him as he mewled loudly. "I'll have to ask someone to look after you while I'm gone," she told him softly. She looked around her cozy little cottage. She would be reluctant to leave it, especially for the bustle of a huge city like Boston. *But the castle would be lovely,* she thought. There was no reason not to go. Maybe it would even inspire a painting or two. She quickly grabbed her phone and hit reply all, typing out her message before she lost her nerve or, worse, forgot.

Good. She hit send. It was done. Now for the others to respond.

5.

Lan

Lan Nguyen folded his shirt sleeves back, turning them several times. He slid on a pair of gloves, sighing deeply, taking only a second to prepare himself before entering the apartment. He looked around at the complete mess in front of him. The conditions of the apartment were awful, but nothing he hadn't seen before. He nodded to his partner across the room. "What did we catch?"

David grimaced back at him before responding, "A deal gone bad. Either that or a fight broke out amongst the ranks. My bet is on the former." Lan surveyed the room, nodding.

"Everything already bagged and tagged?" he asked in a clipped tone. It was late, and he could use some fucking sleep.

David nodded, "Yep, got it covered, partner."

Lan nodded briskly, "Sorry I was late. I got tied up with..." David was already waving a hand, cutting him off.

"Don't even worry about it; I know what you got tied up with." He eyed him narrowly, "You don't look so good, man; I think you need a vacation."

Lan chuckled ironically. "Yeah? I'm not going to the stupid escape room thing, so you can stop bringing it up." His stomach churned slightly at the thought of it.

"You need to, Nguyen," David replied. "Don't make me go to the boss... tell him you need time off..." he let his voice trail off.

"Are you threatening me, asshole?" Lan asked, chuckling again.

"I dunno, man," David continued, grinning now, "You haven't looked too good for a while now... might be you need more of an *extended* vacation, if you know what I mean. I'm just looking out for you; we're partners, after all." Lan rolled his eyes, laughing now.

"Fuck, you're really not going to let this go, are you? I wish I never read the damn email."

"Just go, man. Take a few days off and clear your head. What's the worst that could happen? You're a fucking NYPD detective. You scared you're going to get beaten by an escape room?"

"An escape *castle*, technically," Lan said. "And no, that's not it." That wasn't it at all. It wasn't the escape room part that bothered him; it was who he would be trapped in there with.

He swallowed, loosening his tie around his throat. He didn't know if he could face seeing him again after everything that had happened. The thought made him feel a little nauseous.

"Well, either way, you're going." David pointed at him from across the room. "Don't make me fucking rat you out to get you to leave. Book the flight already."

Lan sighed deeply before nodding. "Fuck. Fine. You're a bastard, you know that?"

David smiled broadly. Nodding his head and turning. "Yeah, yeah, you can thank me later when you're drinking martinis on that asshole's yacht. Now let's get out of here. I've spent enough time in this dump."

Lan followed him out the door, ripping his gloves off as they went. He would do it, he decided. He would go. David was right; he could use a break. A few days away from the city would be good for him. It wouldn't be that bad. He could get through it. Hell, overall, he would enjoy seeing them again. Besides, like David said, what was the worst that could happen?

6.

Austin

Austin Maynard breached the surface of the water, filled his buoyancy vest with air, and pulled his mask down. He took a deep breath before wiping off his face. He kicked over to the boat, quickly removed his vest and belt carrying extra weights, and handed them to the set of open hands waiting for him.

He pulled his fins off his feet and handed those up, too, before grasping onto the ladder and hauling himself out of the water and onto the boat. He was beat. His whole body felt sore and heavy as he left the water and felt the pull of gravity once more.

"How was it?" His buddy Brad asked as he found a spot to sit.

"Visibility was really poor," Austin replied. He shook his head. He hadn't enjoyed that dive. It had been like descending into a black hole of nothing. He usually wasn't fazed during dives; he was able to stay calm and keep his breathing even. Every movement and action had to be calculated. He had struggled to maintain his composure for the first time. The complete lack of light and visibility had been disorienting. Somehow, they had still managed to find the lost receiver they were searching for. It had likely been pure dumb luck, really, given the conditions. "I couldn't see anything down there," he added, looking up at Brad, "Not my favorite dive by far."

Brad nodded solemnly. "Yeah, that sucks, man. Bet you're glad it's over."

Austin nodded his agreement. "Yeah, I am," he said bluntly. Are we heading back in?" He looked over at the rest of the crew, who were discussing something, and pointing down into the water.

"Yeah, I think we're heading back in a minute." Brad looked at him thoughtfully. "Hey, did you book the flight yet?"

Austin sighed wearily. Time was ticking by. He'd looked up flights from Detroit to Boston and had his finger poised over the button to book, but he couldn't seem to bring himself to do it, somehow. He'd even talked to his parents already about taking the kids for him for the long weekend; they were more than happy to... it wasn't that.

"Yeah... I dunno, man. Not yet, I guess."

Brad grinned a little, nodding his head and looking off into the distance over the water. "Hey, what if I went in your place? Do you think anyone would notice? It's been a while, right?" Austin chuckled, shaking his head. Brad continued, "I bet I could convince them I'm you."

"Yeah, and I just grew another foot or so since they last saw me, huh?" Austin asked.

Brad just laughed, chucking a buoy out of his way and taking a seat. Brad was quite a bit taller, not to mention they looked nothing alike in the first place.

"I dunno, I think I could pull it off somehow." He grinned, wiping his hands over his face. He said, more seriously, "You know I'll be around if anything comes up with the kids while you're gone. Your parents have my cell number."

Austin swallowed, nodding and looking down at his feet. "Yeah, I know." He nodded again, "Thanks, man, I appreciate it." It hadn't been easy since Miranda left. Brad had stepped in to help him out on more than one occasion. Austin slicked his brown hair back; it was getting too long again. He grabbed his DNR hat, slipped it on, and adjusted the brim over his face.

"When is it again?" Brad asked him.

Austin pretended he had to think about it. "Ah, it's coming up in about three weeks now. End of August." If he didn't book soon, the price of the flight was only going to keep going up. The kids would be fine, too. It wasn't really that close to the start of school; still proper summer for another week or so.

Brad just nodded thoughtfully. "Well, go and have fun. How many chances do you get to do that anymore?"

Austin nodded back, gazing out over the waters of Lake St. Clair. That was true, in a way. But would he? Have fun? Or would it be awkward and uncomfortable? Would it be painful? To see Cam again, especially? His stomach lurched slightly at the thought, and it had nothing to do with the waves rocking the boat back and forth. The idea of seeing her again filled him with a unique mix of excitement and doubt. He sighed loudly, then said more to himself than to Brad, "I'll have to book the flight soon."

7.

Bee

Bee had never been so relieved not to be moving. She stood still outside the terminal, relishing the feeling of the flat, steady ground beneath her feet. She breathed in deeply. The air was dense and humid. She imagined she could already smell a hint of the ocean. She quickly scanned the road in front of her again. There were multiple lanes, with cars and buses moving swiftly in and out. Pure chaos. She was glad Alex had sent someone to pick her up. Having made it through the flight, she could now finally just relax, sit back, and enjoy the weekend.

She smoothed a hand over her dress and adjusted her grip on her roller bag. As far as the whole escape room thing went, it wasn't exactly her thing. She liked a good puzzle, though, especially when it came to helping her patients. Maybe she would end up enjoying it more than she thought initially.

She was starting to feel impatient now. It had been a long day, and she still didn't see anyone that looked like they could be there for her. Alex had insisted the driver would be there waiting for her when her plane arrived. A long, dark town car pulled up next to the curb right in front of her. She could practically see her reflection in the shiny black metal. A man leapt out of the car and came around the front of the vehicle to approach her. He wore dark sunglasses and a black suit.

"Ms. Blake?" he asked, somewhat breathlessly. She nodded, a smile breaking out over her pale features. "Ah, good," he replied, "My deepest apologies, Miss, I was delayed in traffic."

Bee shook her head and responded, graciously, in her opinion, "Oh, no need to apologize whatsoever; I'm just so glad you're here." He gave her a quick smile back and was already reaching to take her bags for her. He loaded everything efficiently into the trunk and swiftly moved to the door for the back seat. He swung the door open for her and stood patiently waiting for her to enter the car. She smiled again in thanks and climbed in.

On the way to the castle, Bee hummed lightly to herself in the backseat. Traffic, indeed, was dreadful; he hadn't been lying about that. It took them well over an hour to get to Gloucester. She was expecting the car to pull up in front of a gorgeous castle, but instead, as they drove down a road that ran right along the waterfront, the car abruptly turned into a parking lot of what looked like a restaurant right on the water. Bee looked around in confusion.

"Um," she said slowly, "Are you sure this is the right place?" She looked behind them, through the car's rear window, and saw a wooden sign with a whale tail next to a little wooden shack.

"Yes, Miss," the driver said, "This is the right place. You'll be meeting up with the others for the private whale-watching tour first, then dinner is right next door this evening. I'll be taking your things over to Hammond Castle in the meantime. But please, if there is anything in the back you'd like to keep with you for the evening, I can open the trunk up."

"No, no, that should be fine," Bee responded, adding, "Thank you. I have my purse with me; that should be fine."

The driver nodded as he gazed back at her in the rearview mirror. "Perfect, Miss, let me get the door for you." He swiftly approached her side of the car and pulled the door open. He stood still as a statue, looking straight ahead as he waited for her to exit. Bee climbed out of the car as gracefully as possible, smoothing her dress down as she went. She looked up to the right, and a smile curled the corner of her lips. She saw the group approaching from the dock. They must have been down looking at the boat.

Alex led the way at the front of the group with a broad grin on his face. He was wearing dark aviator-style sunglasses. He was followed by Austin, Darcy, and another man Bee didn't recognize. Bee couldn't help herself; she started to jump up and down in excitement. Darcy smiled broadly and ran to her. Bee met her halfway, grinning as Darcy wrapped her arms around her and squeezed her tightly, laughing.

"Welcome!" Alex called out, laughing a little himself. "Glad to see you made it through the flight Bee." He grinned, pulling her in for a hug as soon as Darcy released her. She patted him on the back.

"I did," she said, taking a step back and straightening her designer jacket.

"And not a wrinkle in sight." Alex grinned. "You look fabulous, darling."

Bee laughed and posed. "When are you going to put me in one of your movies then? Hmm?" Alex had started off making low-budget documentaries but had quickly gone on to direct a reality show that had become wildly popular. It was God awful if Bee were being honest, but it had allowed him to make a name for himself. He had made a fortune in reality TV and had tried his hand at directing movies from there. Most of them had done okay. He was still waiting for his huge box office hit. Bee had no doubt he would do just as well directing movies as he had directing reality shows. He just needed a little more time.

Alex grinned. "You could convince me..." he looked her up and down, eying her dress. "What is that? Versace? Looks like you've done well enough for yourself. All on your own? Or did you bag a handsome doctor?"

Bee smiled back demurely, removing her sunglasses and giving him a winning grin. "Nothing but the best for this trip, love. And no, no doctor, yet." She turned to Darcy. "How are you, Darcy? I feel like I haven't seen you in ages."

Darcy smiled warmly back at her. While they couldn't be more different in many ways, she and Darcy had always seen eye to eye. Darcy was someone you could always be honest with. Bee never felt she had to sugarcoat or hide anything from Darcy. She never felt that she could. She trusted Darcy quite implicitly. It would be so nice to spend time with her again this weekend. Really, it was going to end up feeling too short.

"I've been doing well," Darcy responded quietly. "I'm just so glad to see everyone again. It's been far too long."

Bee nodded swiftly, "You're right; it really has. We shall all have to make more of an effort to see each other more often."

Alex laughed darkly. Bee whipped her head to look at him, a bit startled. "Wait until the weekend is over... see how you feel then." She frowned at him. *What on earth was that supposed to mean?* He took his sunglasses off and grinned at her in the disarming way he had. "You remember Rahul," he said matter-of-factly, gesturing towards the man who accompanied them.

"Rahul..." Bee started, then trailed off as she extended her hand towards him. She squinted at him as though that would help her remember who he was. He had black hair and warm brown eyes. He was Indian and handsome... God, she never forgot a face, but she couldn't think for the life of her where she would have met him before. "I– I'm not sure that I do," she grimaced at him in an apologetic way, "I'm so sorry... we've met previously?"

"Of course!" Alex laughed, shaking his head and clapping Rahul on the back fondly as he reached out and met her grasp. He shook her hand firmly, smiling warmly at her. He had such lovely brown eyes. Very kind. And his smile actually met his eyes... so many people didn't smile with their eyes anymore, Bee had noticed. They didn't really look at you, really see you. Everyone was too busy or too self-centered nowadays. Rahul was looking at her as though he actually saw her. Alex continued, "You remember, he was on our floor at MSU. Freshman year. His room was just around the corner from mine. Don't you remember?" Alex asked her, a puzzled expression on his face.

"Oh." Bee felt herself flush. How stupid of her... she hoped she hadn't hurt his feelings. There were so many people living there in Bailey. And really, they had been the cool group on the floor. Everyone had wanted to hang out with them. He must have been around, but honestly, she couldn't remember him at all. He looked utterly unfamiliar. Well, add to that it had also been ten years. People could change a lot in ten years. "How silly of me." She smiled warmly back at him. "Of course, at Bailey."

He returned her smile, but something flickered briefly in his expression. Great. She had offended him then, after all. She would try to chat with him later to smooth it over. She looked over at Darcy.

Darcy was watching her closely, her head tilted to one side, a curious sort of expression on her face. She raised an eyebrow at her, but Darcy just stared at her a moment longer before looking away, squinting out over the water. She shaded her eyes and stood watching a sailboat coming into the bay. *Where were Darcy's sunglasses?* She always was the most forgetful little thing. Always had her head in the clouds, daydreaming about something. Bee wondered how Darcy was really getting on. She knew she was all on her own, unless that had changed.

"Well," Alex said suddenly, clapping his hands together and grinning at all of them. "Shall we head back onto the boat? Everyone expected tonight is here now; you were the last, Bee. Always fashionably late." He winked at her before putting his sunglasses back on.

Then he turned and led them towards a boat that was tied up at the dock. A walkway had been unfolded to allow them to board the ship. Tourists walked up and down the wooden boardwalk above, watching them. People inside the restaurant watched them through the windows, and from the covered balcony that jutted out over the water. Alex saw her gazing over at them and said, "They'll be kicking them out soon enough." He caught her puzzled expression and added, "I booked the whole restaurant for us this evening. They'll be closing to the public soon."

"How lovely," she responded back. Of course he had. That wasn't even close to necessary, not for the small number of people in their group, but Alex liked to make a scene wherever he went. Rahul had fallen in beside her. She saw him grin a little to himself at her response. Did he catch the note of sarcasm in her tone? She grinned a little back, watching him out of the corner of her eyes. His smile broadened as he turned to look at her. *Interesting...* so he thought Alex was a bit of a show-off too. Most people did. It was hard not to make fun of him a little for it. Bee grinned at him conspiratorially and said quietly, "Because that was completely necessary for all eight of us to be able to dine there tonight."

Rahul grinned, chuckling quietly. "Oh, you know Alex; can you say you're surprised?"

She grinned again. "No, of course, you're right. I can't say I'm surprised at all, but I can't help making fun of him a bit for it either. Apparently, the private whale-watching tour and the private castle weren't enough." Rahul nodded in agreement. "But" she added hastily, "I, for one, certainly won't complain about it. It does sound like a fantastic weekend all in all."

Rahul nodded again. "I agree; as pretentious as all of this is, I can't say I won't enjoy it." He smiled at her again, pushing his dark hair back out of his eyes. He really was handsome, wasn't he? Bee sighed internally. Too bad she couldn't remember him or a thing about him. Alex was still talking up ahead, explaining how he had booked the charter for the whale-watching tour. They usually took around 80 people on a given run, but he had felt it would be much more enjoyable to have the boat to themselves, naturally.

"They'll be serving beer and wine and refreshments for us inside the cabin," Alex continued, "The others are already on their second drink by now if I had to guess." Bee smiled at that. She wouldn't say no to a drink herself, not after getting through the flight and getting herself here in one piece. As they made it to the top of the ramp leading onto the boat, there was a little gap between where the green carpeted walkway ended, and the edge of the boat began. It wasn't very wide, but wide enough to make her pause. Rahul stepped over it swiftly and turned back. He held out his hand to her, and she smiled at him, taking it gratefully, steadying herself as she stepped over the gap and up and over the edge of the boat.

"Thank you," she said with a huff as she landed on the boat and immediately gripped the railing. The crew behind them started to dismantle the walkway to prepare for departure. "Chivalry is not dead, it seems," she said brightly.

Rahul chuckled. "Not while I'm around, at least."

"Come on, you two," Alex said, stepping up to them, "Let's get a drink in your hand and get you settled in. We'll be heading out shortly. There's some paperwork for you to sign. Just a little waiver, you know. They require that sort of thing."

"Of course," Bee said politely. Alex turned and led them through an open doorway into the interior of the boat. The boat was lined with wooden tables on either side of a little hallway. There were windows on either side of the interior room that allowed a view of the water. Bee smiled as she saw the others all seated at a few tables in a row. Austin sat on the far end of the middle bench, his back to the window behind him, leaning against it. Dark sunglasses hid his eyes. He held a beer in one hand and sipped at it. Bee was glad to see he was here. She hadn't been sure he would come.

Next to him was Clay; he sat facing her, grinning broadly back at her as she smiled and nodded to him. He held a beer in his hands as well. It looked like he had already pulled the label off, just like he always used to. Cam and Lan sat at the table behind them. Lan with his back to them. Cam grinned at her and waved both hands in excitement. Bee waved back. Darcy had been walking ahead of Alex and slid into the bench seat next to Cam. Cam waved to her, beckoning her to come join the two of them. Alex stopped in front of the two tables, and Rahul slid into the bench seat opposite Austin and Clay. Bee definitely wanted a chance to talk to him more, but she squeezed behind Alex and made her way over to Cam and Darcy.

Cam squealed and reached for her, hugging her with one arm, squishing Darcy between them. Darcy laughed, her big dark eyes sparkling. Bee kissed Cam on the top of the head, leaned over, and kissed Darcy as well. They all giggled. "Ahh!" Bee exclaimed, "This is going to be so much fun! I've missed you girls."

"Well," Alex said, spreading his arms out wide, "The gang's all here!" He grinned at them, "I knew you would all make it, and, hopefully, you won't regret it. I can't wait to get the weekend started. But, first," he held up one finger, "There is the small matter of paperwork," He held a hand out as a young woman approached him with a stack of clipboards in her arms. He plucked one out and held it up to show them.

"You each have a waiver here to sign. This is required by the whale watching tour and the company putting on the Escape Room weekend for us. I figured I would have you just sign everything all at once. We'll pass them out. There's one for each of you with your name at the top." He and his assistant quickly read the names and passed the clipboards around to each of them.

Bee took hers from Alex, skimming over the text on the first page. Normally, she was a stickler for never signing anything without reading it thoroughly, but there were pages and pages here. It seemed to go on forever. There was no way she was going to sit here and read all of this. She glanced around at the others. Some were flipping to the back page and signing it. Clay had signed his and was already handing it back to the assistant.

Austin seemed to be skimming through each page, as was Rahul. Lan made a cursory effort to look through the document and seemed satisfied as he turned to the last page and read that before beginning to sign his name. Darcy was watching Alex, a thoughtful expression on her face. She stared at him for a few seconds before turning directly to the last page to sign. Cam was leafing through still, frowning.

"Really, Alex?" Cam said finally. "This seems like a bit much. I get the waiver for the whale watching tour, but the escape room..." She stopped leafing through and sat frowning, reading to herself under her breath.

"Ah, come on, Cam," Alex responded, "We get it, you're a lawyer; thanks for the reminder." Lan chuckled. So did Clay, turning to look at Cam, grinning at Bee as he did so. "And I mean, feel free not to sign it... I'll just have to kick your ass off if you don't." Cam glared up at him.

"I forgot what an asshole you are, Alex, thanks for the reminder." That got a louder chuckle out of the group.

"There's that charm I remember." Alex grinned at her unapologetically. Cam gave him a deadpan look before slowly rotating her hand and giving him the finger. Then, as the group laughed, she begrudgingly lifted her pen and signed her name on the line. Bee blew out a breath and quickly signed her name as well. Alex's assistant came and gathered the clipboards from everyone before promptly disappearing from the inner cabin.

"Good!" Alex said, grinning at them again. "Now that we got that out of the way, let's get the rest of you a drink, and we'll be heading out shortly. Our tour guide will speak to us from up on the top deck. She is an expert on whales in general and the whales in this area in particular; she knows each of them by name. Fun fact: Humpback whales can be identified by the patterns on their tails." He waggled his eyebrows at them. "Enjoy!" he added before bowing slightly and disappearing from the cabin himself. The woman behind the bar at the back of the cabin came over and quickly took their drink orders. Cam asked for a glass of pinot grigio, and Bee asked for the same. Darcy shook her head. She was holding a water bottle and was apparently fine with just water for now.

Cam turned to Bee. "So, what's new? I feel like we haven't talked in ages." She tucked her blonde hair behind her ears.

Bee smiled at her. "Oh, you know, just the same old same old... nothing new lately."

"You're still working at the same hospital?" Cam asked.

Bee nodded. "Yep, same hospital. We did have some turnover a while back, though, so I got some new co-workers, which actually turned out to be a nice change. How about you? You're still with the same firm?"

Cam nodded, smiling tightly. "Yes, not much has changed there. Hoping to make senior partner. Eventually." Cam rolled her eyes. Bee had forgotten how pretty her eyes were; a pale green color.

"Well." Bee smiled graciously. "I have no doubt you will someday. Although I'm sure it must feel like it's taking forever."

Cam nodded, sighing. "Pretty much. We'll see what happens. Hopefully, taking this trip didn't set me back much."

Bee raised her eyebrows in surprise. "Really? Taking a weekend trip could do that?"

"I can't even imagine..." Darcy trailed off, staring out over the water.

Cam nodded again. "Unfortunately, yes. It's high stakes. And they are always watching any move you make. Judging you. Deciding if you are 'committed enough'," she made air quotation marks and rolled her eyes again. "Honestly, it's ridiculous," Cam stared at the back of Austin's head, "But I wasn't about to miss this."

Bee looked pointedly at Darcy, who looked back at her, raising her eyebrows, her dark eyes wider than usual. Darcy was a bit unusual looking. She had an almost classic, timeless beauty in a way. Her dark brown eyes were abnormally large, nearly too big for her face. She wore her dark hair in a long bob with French bangs. She was the quietest of the group, but she would open up one-on-one. Bee would have to find time to chat with her alone later on in the weekend.

As far as she knew it had been years since Cam had seen Austin. Possibly, she thought, they hadn't seen each other since graduation. Cam hadn't gone to the wedding. Bee joined Cam in staring at the back of Austin's head. She still didn't know all the details of what had happened. She knew Miranda had left him a few months ago but didn't know why. Those poor kids... She was curious if the others knew anything further than she did. Miranda was noticeably absent, the only one missing from their group this weekend. Only six of them had been on the email, plus Rahul, apparently. She should have realized Miranda wasn't invited. And she understood why, in a way, but still, to leave her out completely also felt odd.

Alex had reappeared suddenly, and as he walked down the hallway, Bee felt a lurching in her stomach. The boat had started to move. *Here we go,* she thought. Hopefully, the meclizine she had taken for the flight hadn't worn off yet. The last thing she wanted was to get seasick and ruin the whale watching, or worse, her dress. She groaned slightly and turned to see Darcy grinning, her head swiveling back and forth as she looked out the windows on both sides of the boat. "I'm glad someone is enjoying this," Bee murmured.

Just then, she heard a woman's voice, amplified through loudspeakers built into the ceiling. She welcomed them to the whale-watching tour and quickly shared a little of her background. She gave them an overview of the types of whales they were most likely to see on the trip. It would be about a thirty-minute ride to get out to the area where they would likely see whales. *Ugh,* Bee groaned again, internally this time. Well, she would just have to make the most of it. Distract herself with talking to the others and hopefully the time would fly by. Lan turned around to face them and grinned at her. He had been sitting with his back to the girls, chatting with the guys.

"You doing okay so far Bee?" he asked, his grin widening as she rolled her eyes.

"What do you think, Lan?" Bee replied. "Distract me for a while."

Lan grinned and nodded, "Okay, and how do you suggest I do that?" The other guys had turned and were listening in on their conversation now.

"Tell me what you've been up to lately. Any new ladies in your life?" She grinned at him, raising an eyebrow. Lan flushed. His whole body seemed to stiffen imperceptibly.

"None to speak of." He responded a bit tersely, Bee thought.

"Really?" Bee raised an eyebrow at him. "A tough New York City detective like you? Still single? Hmm... I would have thought you could take your pick." That got a few chuckles out of the group. Lan continued to blush. *Odd.* She didn't remember him being self-conscious like this, or shy. Not when it came to women.

Lan shrugged, putting on an air of nonchalance. "I guess not. Not to say there hasn't been anyone, of course, but no one recently." He met her gaze evenly. Bee nodded.

"Well then, that makes two of us." She smiled at him reassuringly. She saw Rahul's eyes flick up to her briefly before he looked away, out over the ocean.

The tour guide interrupted, making any further conversation impossible. She announced they were approaching Hammond Castle on their right. The group stood one by one and headed out to the right side of the boat to get a closer look. Apparently, Hammond Senior built the first "castle" further down the shore, and his son, Hammond Junior, had built the second, more elaborate castle.

"Hammond incorporated a mixture of architectural elements found throughout Europe, taking inspiration from medieval castles, gothic cathedrals, and a Renaissance-era French village. He filled it with artifacts from his travels as well. After Hammond's untimely death, the castle was turned into a museum open to the public in the 1930s. Hammond castle is available for private events, such as weddings, or, apparently, escape room weekends," the tour guide added with a chuckle, "and is full of Hammond's inventions, for which he held over 400 U.S. patents. He was second only to Edison and had actually met Edison, who mentored him for a while in his youth. Hammond was particularly known for his work in radio and radio waves, and many of his patents were used in the Zenith brand radios back in the day. Hammond Castle is rumored to be full of secret passageways, secret rooms, and a series of underground tunnels."

Lan chuckled, leaning over towards Bee. "How much of this do you think Alex asked her to add in for dramatic effect?"

Bee grinned at him. "I wouldn't put it past him. It certainly reeks of Alex." Lan rolled his eyes at her.

"Knowing him, we were just given our first clues for the escape room tomorrow." Lan tapped his forehead. "Nice try, Alex; I'm one step ahead of you."

Bee grinned, nodding her head. "We'll see how long it takes us to escape... hopefully well before Sunday. Then we can spend the rest of the weekend partying."

The castle seemed to be right on the shore, with a beachfront view. Bee couldn't tell for sure, but it looked like an odd mixture of buildings, several wings branching off of the main building. It looked like it was made from stone blocks and really did look like a castle. She had looked up some photos ahead of time. The castle grounds had looked gorgeous; it was surrounded by trees, with a garden area and a courtyard that must be somewhere in the castle's interior.

She particularly liked the photos of a huge balcony-type room with open stone archways for walls. It had looked out over the sea. She strained to locate it now, but the castle was too far away to make it out. She scanned further down the peninsula and noted that right at the point, a large lighthouse sat at the edge of the sea. A large blue light flashed at the top in intervals as it spun. It must be very bright at night, given it was still visible during the day.

Bee felt someone approach on her other side and turned to see Clay leaning against the railing, smiling at her tentatively. "Hey, Bee. It's good to see you," he said softly. *Oh, Clay.* She had wondered how long it would take him to come talk to her. She was a bit surprised actually, that it had taken this long.

"Clay," she said, smiling back at him warmly. "It's really good to see you, too. I hope you've been doing well. Work been going okay?" She asked him politely. Clay worked for some sort of marketing company. Something to do with online ads and clicks and viewing time. She quite frankly didn't understand it fully. He seemed to be good at it, from what she could gather, but he had never seemed to enjoy his work very much, at least as far as she could tell. Clay smiled a little grimly, and looking out over the water, he took a sip of his beer. He swallowed audibly before responding.

"Yeah, it's been going okay. My boss is a jerk, but other than that, it's not that bad." He turned his dark eyes back to her, and they flickered back and forth over her features, studying her. "How about you? You still like being a nurse?" He asked her eventually. Why did she feel like he had been about to say something else?

She smiled, peering back over at the castle. It was falling behind them now as the boat picked up speed and moved away from the harbor out into the open ocean. She gripped the railing tightly with both hands. "Whoa," she said, giggling a little as she lost her balance for a second. Clay reached out and placed a hand on her back, steadying her.

"Are you okay?" He asked her, concern creasing his brow.

She nodded, turning back to him. "I'm fine; I just need to hold on to the railing. I'm sure I'll get used to it soon." She smiled reassuringly at him. "And yeah, I do still enjoy it. It's not the perfect job by any means, although I'm not sure anything is...but it's not the worst way to spend your days."

Clay nodded, smiling back at her. He moved his hand off her back and gripped the railing again himself. Lan slid behind them and headed back into the cabin. The others turned and started to follow him. "I'm going to head back in; we might as well enjoy our drinks while we wait for the whales to show up."

Clay nodded. "What happens if they decide not to?" He grinned at her. "I can't imagine Alex would take that lying down."

Bee laughed, glancing through the window at Alex as he gestured animatedly to Lan and Cam. "No, I think you're right about that. He wouldn't stand for it." She thought for a moment and stopped grinning. "I feel bad for the crew, actually, if that happens." Clay raised an eyebrow at her and nodded solemnly.

"True," he replied, eyeing Alex as well. "He must be a son of a bitch to work under when things don't go to plan. Although, I'm sure he could probably be just as amazing to work for at times...when he's in a good mood." Bee nodded thoughtfully. That summed up her impression of Alex pretty well. Back in college, he could be the life of the party, or he could ruin everyone's day when he was in a foul mood. He was unpredictable, too. You never knew what you were going to get with him. So far, he was playing the part of the gracious host.

Hopefully, he kept his spirits up throughout the weekend. They headed back into the cabin to join the others.

Bee sat back and relaxed, sipping her wine while she watched the others, laughing and talking. The moment felt surreal suddenly. It was hard to believe she was really here. All of us back together again, finally, she thought to herself. At least for a while. Well, almost all of us.

She flashed back to a memory of one of the last times they had all been together at MSU. Austin and Cam, flirting, as usual. Lan and Alex, drunk off their assess, nearly getting them kicked out of that last bar. Clay's look of disappointment when she wouldn't come back to his apartment with him. She remembered shaking her head at him, saying nothing, before she turned and practically ran to catch up with the other girls. She sighed to herself.

Bee snapped back to the present as the voice squawked suddenly through the loudspeakers. "Whales, two o'clock!" The boat banked swiftly, causing them to lurch a bit. Everyone froze for a second and looked at each other, then they began to scramble to their feet. It took Bee a beat to orient herself again. They had said to think of the ship like a clock, with 12 o'clock being the front of the ship. Two o'clock meant off to her right-hand side. Some of the others, led by Alex, had already started off in that direction. She followed them, starting to feel excited. She had never seen a whale in real life before.

As she exited the cabin and approached the rail, the wind gusted, and she felt a spray of droplets pepper her face and hair. Some of the others laughed and squealed a bit at the cold spray. Bee grabbed onto the railing and couldn't help but gasp slightly. The whales were massive. As long as the boat itself, at least. She gaped, mouth dropped open, as they curved their backs, diving deeper into the water. They just kept going and going. These couldn't be humpback whales like she had been expecting, but she had no idea what they were.

It looked like there were maybe three or even four of them. They were resurfacing, though, one or two at a time, making it hard to tell exactly how many there were. She strained to hear the guide over the exclamations of the group. Apparently, they were Finn whales and were a very rare sighting. Well, she thought, her mouth pressing into a grim smile; Alex was getting his money's worth after all.

They followed the group of Finn whales for some time; eventually, they decided to head upstairs, to the boat's upper level, so they could see farther out and get a different view. They brought their drinks with them. Bee grasped the railing as often as she could. There were two long benches against the side of the boat up top, but that was it. She gratefully claimed a spot on one of the benches. Rahul came and sat down next to her. She noticed he waited until the girls had all found a spot to sit. Well, all except Cam; she seemed to have no difficulty standing, somehow keeping her balance without even holding onto the railing. Austin seemed similarly blessed with good balance. He stood out in the middle of the boat, swaying back and forth slightly with the boat as it moved. That made sense: she knew how much time he spent on the water at work.

Rahul made small talk with her, asking what she did for work and how she liked her job. That sort of thing. All the usual questions one might ask a new acquaintance. It struck her again; that surety that she didn't know him. She frowned over at Alex as she contemplated this.

They also saw a humpback whale a few minutes later, which made the trip further out into the ocean worth it, she supposed. She kept waiting for it to jump up out of the water, like in *Free Willy*, but of course, that never happened. Bee shuddered as she glanced back in the direction she thought led to shore. She had a feeling she was probably better off not knowing how far out they were now. The bay had been one thing, and that had been quite far enough. But they must have traveled a half hour, or even forty-five minutes, out into the open ocean at this point. She hoped they would turn back soon. Rahul must have noticed her shuddering.

"Are you cold?" He leaned over to her, looking concerned. "Do you want my rain jacket?" She looked him up and down, and he followed her gaze. "I left it down in the cabin; I'll go get it for you. I wasn't sure how soaked we might get. It will help block the wind, at least." He was gone a second later before she could reply. He really was a gentleman, she thought. Such a nice change from the type she usually went for.

Clay sat frowning across from her as Rahul returned with the raincoat. Clearly, he didn't love that. Well, he was going to have to get over it, unfortunately. She thought back to their days at State; how he was always offering to walk her back to her apartment. And before that, in the dorms, she'd open her door to leave for class to find him waiting for her in the hallway. How he'd memorized her class schedule. How she'd tried, guilted herself into going out with him that one time. It had felt like dating her brother.

She smiled up at Rahul gratefully as she settled into the jacket, wrapping her arms around herself. A strand of her copper hair fell over her eyes, momentarily blown by the wind. She quickly swiped it out of the way. "Thank you," she said simply as he smiled back. "You're right; that does help with the wind." He nodded and sat back down next to her.

"Good. Anytime," he said, turning and squinting off in the distance over the water. "Are we done watching the whales now? I think I'm ready to head in; I don't know about you."

Bee nodded, her gaze turning to Alex. "I couldn't agree more. I suppose it all depends on what our gracious host has planned for us this evening."

Rahul grinned. He rested his elbows on his shins, hands clasped together as he leaned forward, watching Alex as well. He went past the 'Do Not Enter' sign, which blocked off access to the front of the boat, where the captain must be, stepping easily over the rope with his long legs.

"Yeah," he chuckled, "that's not going to stop him." Bee laughed as they watched him enter the captain's cabin, their guide's voice cutting off abruptly. "That man does what he wants when he wants," Rahul added. His smile was less broad now. Most of the warmth was gone.

Bee nodded thoughtfully at him. "Isn't that the truth."

Rahul smiled at her, catching her studying him. "Well, I like to be truthful," he responded glibly, then seemed to sober up. "Whenever I can, that is." He concluded, looking down at his hands. He cleared his throat. Did he seem uncomfortable suddenly? She placed a hand on his arm reassuringly.

"Well, I like that." She smiled at him warmly. "A man who tells the truth, I mean." He smiled at her, looking a bit cheered. But yes, she thought there was something bothering him. "At least, most of the time. About the big things." She clarified. "I mean, if my hair looks a mess or my outfit is awful, you can feel free to keep it to yourself. My grandma always said a little white lie never hurt anyone. And I firmly believe that to be the truth."

He smiled warmly at her once again, his eyes drifting up to her hair, which was surely a tangled mess, whipped back and forth by the wind. Why hadn't she thought of that and put it up? "Your hair looks beautiful." He grinned at her broadly. She laughed and ran a hand over her hair, pushing it to the other side of her head momentarily before the wind whipped it back and half over her face again.

"See," she said laughing, "you learn quickly."

He shook his head. "No white lie needed. Truly, you look beautiful."

Bee felt herself flush slightly and was glad she had her sunglasses on still. Although it was starting to get a little dusky out. "You're too kind." She laughed, making light of it. Although, he certainly looked serious. He watched her with his dark eyes, attempting to peer into hers through the mirrored sunglasses. She shivered slightly again and looked around them, scanning the water. "When are we heading back?" She asked no one, and everyone in general.

Cam turned to her and sauntered over. "I think Alex just went to let them know we're ready to head in. He wants to get the ball rolling on the evening. Sounds like we're in for some ghost stories about the castle. Oooohhhh." She made a silly fake ghost noise and waggled her fingers at Bee.

"What?" Bee asked, her brow furrowing. "What do you mean ghost stories? What has that got to do with the escape room?" Cam shrugged, already looking bored with the topic.

"I dunno, something about telling us the history of the place, and apparently that involves some ghost or demon-thing that's said to haunt the castle. I can't remember the name of it." She shrugged again. "In any case, it's just Alex trying to hype the place up and psych us out. They're going to read the main prompt or whatever for the escape room tonight. It sounds like we'll basically be locked into the guest wing, and first thing in the morning, we have to start to find our way out."

Bee groaned. "Ugh, that all sounds awful. Why did I agree to come this weekend? Do we even get breakfast?" Cam shrugged. "What about coffee?" Bee was feeling seriously annoyed now. This was so not a vacation.

"I don't know, Bee," Cam said, sighing and plopping down on the other side of her on the bench. "I'm sure they're going to feed us. But I don't understand yet how this will all work. We'll figure it out."

"Okay," Bee said, sighing and folding her arms. "But you know how much I hate ghosts and things like that. I really don't think we need to add anything like that into the mix. The whole escape room thing is enough."

Rahul chuckled next to her. "Sounds like it's part of that whole thing, though." She whipped around to glare at him. Somehow, he could tell, in spite of the sunglasses. He held his hands up. "I mean, I don't really know what the theme is, or whatever. But regardless, I'm sure it won't be that bad."

Bee followed his gaze as he looked past her to see that Alex had emerged from the captain's area and was making his way back over to them. He was rubbing his hands together, grinning, like he was up to no good. Bee groaned again. "I'm going to need another drink," she said bluntly.

Cam laughed. "Amen to that."

8.

Cam

It was odd having the group back together again. Aside from Miranda, of course. Cam didn't want to admit it to herself, but she was half disappointed Miranda wasn't invited. As awkward as it would have been, a small part of her would have enjoyed watching Austin squirm.

Aside from whoever this Rahul character was supposed to be, as well. She was pretty sure she would have remembered an Indian guy hanging out with them in the dorms. She would have to ask Darcy if she remembered him. Darcy might be accused of having her head in the clouds, and rightly so, to an extent, but she noticed things, too. Things that other people often didn't. Maybe she would have a chance to chat with her separately at dinner. They would have the whole restaurant to themselves for the evening. No need to stay all bunched together for the entire night. Maybe she would get a chance to talk to Austin, too, for that matter. She had noticed how carefully he seemed to be avoiding being in a position where he might have to speak to her.

She frowned, watching him as he disembarked the boat. Maybe she was being unfair. He had moved like a natural, of course, on the boat, darting all over the place, never staying in one spot for long. Maybe it wasn't on purpose. He seemed a bit restless. Could he be nervous to see her too, after all these years? No. She chided herself. He didn't give a shit about her. Not really. And he probably never had. And why would he? She mused, watching him as he stooped to pick up Bee's sunglasses she had dropped.

There was something about Austin. There always had been. He was so goddamn gorgeous. And she couldn't explain it, but something in his movements, even the way he walked, was suggestive. He walked like he was tightly wound and about to spring, exuding an air of quiet dominance. Moving with feline grace, he oozed sensuality mixed with a tinge of something else. Something almost... dangerous.

Lan broke her out of her reverie, suddenly popping up behind her right shoulder. "What's this I hear about a demon ghost living in the castle?" He quipped, grinning at her. "No one told me I had to escape from a *haunted* castle. I thought it was just a regular, plain old, normal castle filled with secret rooms and underground passages. You know, the boring kind."

Cam laughed in spite of herself. "You have a point, Lan." She mused out loud, watching Alex now. "It begs the question; is a ghost demon really necessary to add to the mix?"

Lan grinned back, chuckling. "That's Alex for you. Never enough drama is there?"

Cam chuckled. "You mean in his stupid shows or in real life?"

"Both." Lan grinned. "Speaking of his stupid shows, I'm surprised he isn't filming this right now."

Cam rolled her eyes and laughed dryly. "God, can you imagine?" The comment gave her pause, though. He wouldn't do something like that, would he? There's no way they would ever consent to that. Well, she wouldn't, at least. Some of the others might. Bee, for example. Cam wouldn't be surprised if she were willing to star on some reality show of his. Get her fifteen minutes of fame.

They quickly crossed the distance over to the restaurant and entered through the doors being held open by staff who nodded and smiled as they greeted them. The lights were dimmed inside, filling the room with a warm glow. It was a welcome change after being battered by the chilly wind all afternoon. Cam felt herself shiver slightly as she rubbed her hands together to warm them. Lan watched from her side. He nodded over at the bar, where a lone bartender waited for them, raising one eyebrow, "Is it still gin and coke? Or has the fancy lawyer upgraded her tastes?"

Cam grinned. "You remembered. I'm impressed."

"Of course I did, Cam." Lan smiled back at her. He tapped his forehead, "Mind's like a steel trap."

"Sure it is... maybe when it comes to alcohol. And yes, I am a fancy lawyer now, but not too fancy for gin." Lan laughed as he walked away from her, heading towards the bar.

Cam turned and followed the others across the now-empty restaurant and out onto the covered balcony. A large table had been set up in the center, close enough to the railing to allow them the best view of the ocean and curving shoreline off in the distance. A few of the others stood at the railing, looking out over the water. There were heated lamps nearby, which she was grateful for. The sun had started its descent towards the horizon, and while it wasn't dark yet, the air held a slight chill that had been absent earlier in the afternoon.

Austin was already seated at the table. She eyed the empty chair next to him wearily; a jolt of something close to fear coursed through her stomach. She couldn't do it. Not yet.

She had come on this trip knowing she would confront him. Now that Miranda had left him, there was no reason not to. No reason to hold her silence anymore.

The thought of the number of nights she had jolted awake from a dream where she was with him left a wave of rage and regret in its wake. In her dreams, she was always so desperately, deeply in love with him as though no time had passed. As though things were back to the way they had been before. As though she had never told him she loved him, and he had never rejected her.

She had to know why, once and for all. As the years had stretched on, that one question lingered. She would wake with his name still on her lips, her cheeks still damp from the trails tears had left behind in her sleep. She would be confused, for just a moment, unsure where or when she was. Then she would remember. The rational, conscious part of her brain was more than over him; had moved on years ago. It made her angry, furious even, that some small, secret part of herself kept him tucked away. Loved him still. It was weak of her. And she despised weakness of any kind.

She would confront him this weekend. She could imagine it; picture herself asking him if he had ever really cared at all. But she wasn't ready yet and this certainly wasn't the time or the place. It might be tricky, with the whole escape room thing, to get him alone, but she would find her opportunity, and she would get an answer.

She realized he was watching her, studying her intently as she stood frozen and eyed the empty chair. Their eyes met for a beat too long. She turned her head, grimacing involuntarily in disgust, and went around to the other side of the table. She took a seat and looked back at him coolly. He was still watching her. His blue eyes pierced into hers with almost a hurt, pleading expression on his face for just a split second. The nerve of him. Then she heard someone clearing their throat, and Austin looked over her shoulder. She turned to her right to see Lan standing there, holding a drink out to her.

She smiled up at him gratefully and took the cold drink; the glass was already slick with beads of condensation. "Thanks, Lan." She managed, her voice coming out softer and huskier than she had intended.

"Of course," he replied easily, his brows furrowing. "Everything okay?" ?He asked quietly, dropping down into the seat next to her.

She turned to him for a second, her gaze drifting back to Austin. He was slumped back in his chair now, his arms folded across his chest. His brown hair, which always managed to look somehow perfectly, imperfectly tousled, swept back from his forehead. He appeared to be half listening to Alex, who had sat to his right and was whispering animatedly into his ear. She purposefully turned her back on him.

"Not really," she said gingerly, sighing, releasing a long stream of air. "I guess I just..." she trailed off, "I guess I wasn't as ready for this as I thought I was, that's all."

Lan raised one eyebrow at her inquisitively, his gaze flickering momentarily across the table. "Ah," he said, stretching out the single syllable until it carried meaningful weight. "Well, I can commiserate with that, actually."

"Can you?" Cam asked, raising an eyebrow back at him. "Well, do tell." She gestured with an open palm swept between them and took a sip of her drink. The drink would help. A little, at least. Lan seemed to blanch a little at her words.

"Well, I, uh," he mumbled, then paused and took a long

pull from his beer. "There's not much to tell," he finished lamely. "Just, let's just say, I get the feeling of not being ready for this. That's all." Was he blushing now? Cam peered at him, causing him to grin and then laugh a little. "What?" he asked, shrugging his shoulders.

"What are you not telling me, Detective Nguyen?" Cam asked, smiling back. "You know how good I am at finding out secrets..." She grinned around the rim of her glass as she took another sip. "You can't hide anything from me. Might as well confess now and save us both the trouble." Lan shook his head and rolled his eyes.

"Oh god, Cam, forget I said anything, okay? Really, it's nothing. Just trying to commiserate." He gave her a tight-lipped smile and glanced around the room, clearly looking for a change in topic.

"Sure you were," Cam replied evenly. "Who is it, though?" She mimicked him, looking around the room curiously. "Obviously not Darcy."

Lan chuckled again, shaking his head. "No," he agreed, "not Darcy." She continued to scan the room. "Let it go, Cam," he said quietly.

"Hmm..." her gaze fell on Bee, standing over at the railing. That Rahul fellow was chatting her up again. "So it's Bee." Lan snorted, shaking his head again. "I mean... you'll have Clay for competition, but hey, if you're into feisty little redheads," she shrugged, "I get it."

Lan chuckled again. "Sorry, Cam, but for once, your radar is off... and like I said, there's nothing to tell in the first place." He shrugged as though he was bored. "Waste of your time."

"We'll see about that," she replied, smiling sideways at him as she turned at the sound of Alex calling for their attention.

He stood now at the head of the table to her left and waved the others over to the table to have a seat. He waited until everyone was seated before continuing.

"Welcome," he said, his hands clasped together as he smiled broadly at his friends gathered around the table. "Welcome, and thank you all for coming. I can't tell you how much it means to me that you are all here. I appreciate you taking time out of your busy lives to be here this weekend. Tonight, our agenda calls for a delicious five-course meal, created specifically for this group and for this night only, by Chef Edgar. Let's give him and the staff a round of applause." The group clapped, following his lead.

"A little premature, don't you think?" Cam murmured to Lan. He chuckled and inclined his head to her. "I think I'll reserve my judgment and applause for after the meal." She clapped lightly, though, along with the group.

Meanwhile, Alex continued. "We will be receiving our prompt for the escape room, or escape castle, I should say, shortly, before we head over to Hammond Castle. That way, we can all contemplate it on our drive over and have it fresh in our minds as we enter the grounds for the first time. I promise you will have copies for your reference, and we will go over all the details of how things will work for this weekend."

He leaned over and picked up his glass, raising it high. The others followed suit, raising their glasses in a toast. "To you." Alex grinned charmingly, taking a few seconds to gaze around the table at each of them. "To old friends, to old memories... and to making new ones." He paused, then raised his glass and nodded to them. "Cheers." A chorus of cheers and salutes were uttered all around, followed by the sound of glasses clinking.

Alex smiled and set his glass back on the table. "Now, without further ado." He flourished towards the kitchen, where staff waited to bring out their first course. "Please, enjoy your meal." The group clapped politely again as he took his seat.

The staff promptly made their way over to the table and set plates of fancy-looking salads in front of each of them. Rolls were brought out as well, with whipped butter. They wasted no time in starting in on the meal. Cam didn't know about the others, but she was starving. She tucked into her salad and grabbed a roll and some butter.

The conversation at the other end of the table quickly turned to recounting old college stories, seemingly prompted by Alex from what she could tell. Clay was laughing hysterically before too long. Alex couldn't even speak as he tried to retell the story of the time Clay had shown up drunk to a tailgating party that some of their parents had driven up for.

He had been carrying the cheese and crackers platter that the girls had made at their apartment and asked him to bring over. He had come staggering up to the group, clearly drunk off his ass, and had literally thrown it at the table. Cam started to chuckle herself, remembering the look on her parents' faces. Thank god Clay's hadn't made it out that time. Or really any time, for that matter. Her laughter died off a little at the thought.

Clay hadn't really had an easy time of it growing up, Cam remembered. At State, he had to work a lot; long hours, mostly at the Caf, to help pay for his room and board. He was there mostly thanks to scholarships, and thanks to Affirmative Action likely as well. His parents hadn't made it up to visit him often, and he had gone home with one of the guys on more than one holiday break. She didn't think he liked going home very much back then. She wondered if he saw his parents much now.

She glanced sideways at Bee, her mind turning to their relationship. Well, their one-sided relationship, that was. Clay had always been infatuated with Bee, and he hadn't ever bothered to hide it. Cam had always felt a little sorry for him, that Bee never felt the same way about him. Bee was always dating some new guy, never with anyone for very long. She liked to have fun and go on fancy dates. Dress up and plan her outfits.

She liked guys who were a little rough around the edges, too. Clay wasn't like that. He was never exciting enough for her.

Cam frowned a little, pushing the remainder of her salad around on her plate. Was that how the others thought of her and Austin? Did they feel sorry for her, too? The thought made her cringe. But no, she thought, watching him again as he listened to the conversation, chuckling and shaking his head, theirs had never been a one-sided thing. He had reciprocated in a way Bee never had. That was part of the problem. She sighed loudly and picked up her glass, draining the rest of it.

When she set her glass back down, she realized she had caught not only Lan's attention but Austin's and Bee's as well. Bee gave her a small smile, a look of concern flashing across her features. "Well," Bee said, filling the awkward silence as was her way. "I, for one, can't wait to hear this prompt for the escape room." She turned and leaned forward, glancing expectantly down the table in Alex's direction. He seemed to have been listening in and heard her comment.

"Ah." He nodded at Bee, setting down his fork as the staff approached the table to whisk away their salad plates and replace them with what looked like a fancy reductionist version of surf and turf. "Yes, absolutely," Alex continued, "we will get to that shortly." He nodded towards Clay and Darcy. "We were just chatting about the old days, how some things never change." Bee nodded, smiling. "It made me curious," Alex continued, with a wicked sort of grin on his face as he glanced back and forth between first Bee and Clay and then Cam and Austin. *Where was he going with this?* Cam tried to take a nervous sip from her now-empty glass. "I'm sure we all remember that night at Henley Park." His words hung in the air, draped in a very heavy, pregnant silence. No one seemed to move, everyone frozen in place.

"That's not really a question." Cam managed to say stiffly, her gaze fixed on Alex. His gaze continued to rove around the table. The same stupid grin fixed on his face.

"What do you mean?" Alex asked, his attention turning to her finally after another long pause.

"I mean, that wasn't a question; it was a statement. You said you were curious... curious about what?" Cam waited for him to respond. She could hear her pulse hammering in her ears. Why would he bring up that night, of all nights?

"Oh," Alex responded. He leaned back, a thoughtful look on his face. He rested his hand on his chin, then ran a knuckle back and forth over his lips as he watched her. "It was nothing really. It just makes me curious, that's all. Seeing all of you again after so many years. It makes you wonder, doesn't it, if things might have happened differently. Might have gone differently, that night, in particular, if we were all the people we are today... instead of who we were back then."

Cam stared at him, her pulse hammering harder. She swallowed, her mouth feeling dry. "What an odd thought to have," she said finally. Then added, "And an even odder thing to say."

Alex looked at her bemusedly, twisting his head to the side. "Is it really, to you? Hmm..." he trailed off, studying her, "Somehow, I doubt that very much."

"That's enough," Austin said. Cam turned to him with wide eyes. His voice was deep and gravelly. Full of warning. He was glaring at Alex. His arms rested on top of the table, on either side of his plate. She could see his fists were clenched.

Alex grinned back at him, appearing not in the least concerned. "Eat." He gestured, waving a hand at all of them. "Before it gets cold." He took a bite and chewed slowly before turning to Darcy, as though nothing had happened. "Still doing your little doodles, Darcy?"

Darcy looked over at Cam, her dark, wide eyes even wider than usual. She swallowed audibly before she spoke. "Yes," she said simply. "I'm still painting." She kept her gaze locked on Cam. Cam shook her head at Darcy and turned back to her plate. Alex could be such an asshole sometimes. *Little doodles...* why pick on Darcy, of all people? And why on earth would he bring up that night?

She took a bite of the surf and turf concoction. It was delicious, but she felt like she was losing her appetite already. She could feel how stiffly she sat, her back ramrod straight, shoulders raised. She couldn't help but feel on edge now, alert. Cam forced herself to relax in her seat. Looking up, she met

Austin's gaze this time, his eyes fixed on hers. She flushed as they exchanged a long look before he returned his focus to his plate as well.

Cam lifted her glass again, only to remember that it was empty. Lan noticed and took it from her gently. "I'll be right back," he mumbled, rising quickly. He seemed happy to have an excuse to walk away from the table. Cam looked down at her lap and closed her eyes, composing herself.

Alex continued to chat with Darcy, asking questions about her paintings. Lan returned with her drink. Another gin and coke. She sipped it slowly as she cleaned her plate. She glanced around the table at the others. The mood had certainly been subdued. No one else seemed to want to meet her eyes. Other than Rahul, that was. He seemed perfectly happy and content. Unaware that anything was amiss. Again, she was struck by the thought that he wasn't one of them. She would have to find a chance to talk to some of the others later. The next course was brought out, and the conversation continued. Cam tuned out as the others made small talk. She continued to sip at her drink. The next two courses passed by without further incident, and finally, dessert was brought out: a lovely-looking cheesecake. Cam wasn't sure she could eat another bite at this point, as enticing as it looked.

Alex chuckled, pulling her attention back to his end of the table. "Well," he said, leaning back in his chair. "Clay has certainly never been adept at hiding his feelings." He looked down the table at Bee. "Isn't that right, Bee?"

Bee flushed deeply, her gaze going to Clay automatically. He looked away from her quickly and stared down at his plate, a confused, angry expression on his face. *What was Alex up to?* The group fell silent, and Cam waited to see if Clay would respond. But it was Clay, after all, and he said nothing, stewing silently and sipping his beer, a dark expression on his face. Was Alex trying to put everyone into a foul mood? What was the purpose of that?

She thought back to Lan's comment earlier about filming them. In a way, it would be just like Alex, too. Bringing all of them together, dredging up shit between them that should stay long buried. She shook herself slightly. There was no way. The boat had been windy as hell. There was no way he was recording anything out there. They would have all needed to be mic'd and even then, but the restaurant... that was another possibility. She looked around the covered balcony, studying the ceilings, and didn't see anything remotely resembling a camera.

Cam kicked herself internally. She knew she should have taken the time to read through every word of that waiver he made them sign. She should have gone over it with a fine-toothed comb. She knew better than to sign something without reading it. How stupid could she be?

She flashed back to the moment and realized the table had gone quiet again. Alex was grinning at Austin now. Looking between him and Lan, back and forth. "She couldn't make it out, for tonight. But I'm hoping she'll join us tomorrow."

Cam watched them in confusion. Neither of them was moving. Lan and Austin looked at each other, then back at Alex. "Who?" Cam heard herself say quietly. "Who couldn't make it?"

Alex turned to her, that shit-eating grin on his face. "Miranda, of course."

Cam stared at him. It took her a moment to process what he was saying. Miranda was coming after all? She looked over at Austin, eyes wide, understanding now. He sat stiffly in his chair, his jaw clenched tight. He had a hand gripped around his beer glass. He was staring daggers at Alex. "Why didn't you tell me?" He said evenly, in a low voice. Alex grinned back at him.

"I am telling you. I'm telling you now."

Cam shook her head in disgust. As much as part of her enjoyed seeing Austin upset, it was a really shitty thing to do. It hadn't occurred to her to ask Alex if Miranda was invited. Why would it? They all saw the email; she wasn't on it. And it made perfect sense why. Clearly, she'd made the mistake of assuming Alex was being a tactful, thoughtful human being, as he'd invited her after all. Alex's gaze turned back to Lan again, smiling still. *Why did he keep looking at Lan?*

She turned to look at Lan herself. He'd turned away from Alex and looked down at his plate, resting his hand on his chin and covering his mouth. He appeared lost in thought.

"Well," Alex said, clapping his hands together so loudly and suddenly that half of them jumped, including Cam. She whipped her head back around to him. "Shall we listen to our prompt now?"

"Listen?" Bee asked, a confused look on her face. Alex smiled graciously and pulled out his cell.

"Yes! I thought it would be much more appropriate if the prompt were read to us, with some sound effects thrown in, of course, for dramatic effect," he grinned at them and shrugged. "I am a director, after all."

"As though you'd ever let us forget," Cam mumbled under her breath. Only Lan heard her and smirked a little.

"I'll play it for all of us now, and we have copies printed out for everyone as well." He glanced around the table again, making sure everyone was ready and listening. Then he pressed a button on his phone and set it out towards the center of the table.

After a few seconds of silence, a man's voice began to speak.

"Welcome to Hammond Castle! I'm the groundsman; I've been serving the estate for more years than I care to admit." The old man chuckled. "I must say, you're lucky to have made it here safely in this storm. This is no little squall. This here's a nor'easter! Won't be safe to leave the castle for some time, possibly a few days! But rest assured, we have plenty of space for all of you to stay comfortably for the night. Right this way."

Cam heard the sound of footsteps, exaggerated, as though walking on a stone pathway or marble floor. "I'll take you around the garden and through to the main entrance. That'll give you a quick chance to see some of the grounds before we head inside. You'll not lack for things to look at during your stay; John Hays Hammond Junior was a collector of sorts; he gathered artifacts from all over the ancient world. The house is full of treasures and secrets!"

The old man paused and then continued, as though the imaginary guest seeking shelter was speaking back to him, "Oh aye, there are secret tunnels all right; they wind to and fro under the castle grounds. But mind you, don't enter those tunnels unless you absolutely must, and especially not at night! You don't want the Besomar to get you!" He paused again. "What's a Besomar, you say? Ach, you've never heard of a Besomar? The Besomar of Hammond Castle is a legend in these parts. Well, how do I describe it? It's an evil spirit of sorts. It's said to be sort of a mix of a vampire and werewolf." He paused briefly again. "Yes, I know, those are two different things, to us, that is. To the Slavic people, they were very similar, I suppose. The Besomar originated there. How one traveled here, to New England, that I couldn't say. But they're known to possess people, sort of. They can take control of you and bend your mind so as you don't know what is real and what is false. They feed off of negative energy; hatred, jealousy, envy, greed, and wrath."

He paused again for a long moment, but they could hear him breathing, huffing, and his feet clomping as though they were climbing up a set of stairs. "Yes, that's right, just like the seven deadly sins. That's how you invite a Besomar in; you open up your heart to wrath, to envy, you may as well hang a welcome sign out front for 'im. But the tunnels... especially avoid those after dark. In fact, don't go wandering around the castle at night, in general. Personally, I never spend any time in the castle at night. Once the sun goes down, if I were you, I wouldn't leave your room at all."

There was the sound of a door swinging open on rusty hinges. "You'll be staying in the lap of luxury and safe from the storm, and if you keep your wits about you, you'll have a lovely stay. Just be mindful of what I told ya." Another pause before he added, "and one more thing; Hammond Junior liked to create puzzles and games, and he was an inventor, of course. Before his untimely death, he made several modifications to the castle. There are hidden doors, hidden rooms, and clues scattered throughout the castle. If you ever find yourself stuck inside a particular part of the castle, just keep that in mind. There might be a way out, hiding in plain sight. And like I said, be careful of how you act... your actions, even your thoughts, keep them positive and pure. Stray into the dark side of human nature, and you'll fall prey to the Besomar. He's always watching and waiting. Remember, three strikes, and you're out." The recording seemed to end there, stretching into silence as they all sat staring at the phone, waiting for more.

"That's it?" Lan asked, his brow furrowed. "What is that supposed to mean? Three strikes and you're out?"

The others swiveled from Lan to look at Alex. He shrugged, saying nothing in response.

"So, what; if we commit a sin, one of the seven deadly sins... that's a strike?" Lan held his hand out, shaking his head, an incredulous look on his face. "What happens when we're out?"

"I dunno," Alex said slowly, shrugging again. "That's one way to interpret it." He grinned wickedly at Lan. "You planning on doing much sinning this weekend Lan?" Lan gave him an icy glare back. Alex just laughed, his voice pitched low, "I guess we'll find out then, won't we?" They sat in silence for several seconds.

"I don't like this whole Bes-bes..." Bee started to say, struggling to come up with the right name.

"Besomar." Rahul leaned over and added matter-of-factly.

"Thank you," Bee said, glancing at him briefly, "Besomar thing." She frowned. "I don't like it."

Alex shrugged again. "Sorry, Bee, it's part of the game."

Her frown deepened. "Well, can't we tell them we want to skip that part? Can't we just do the clues and solve the puzzles and things and skip the rest of it?"

Alex chuckled. "It's kind of a package deal Bee. This whole thing was created and put together very carefully for us for this weekend. It's too late now to be changing things and taking parts of it away." Bee sighed loudly. "Besides, it will be totally fine, it's all for fun, all pretend. There's nothing for you to worry about."

"Will that be it though, for like clues to start off?" Clay spoke up. "It doesn't seem like there was much there to go off of."

Cam was still focused on Bee, she sat frowning unhappily, twisting strands of her copper hair between her fingers. Cam smiled at her in what she hoped was a commiserating way. She remembered the first Halloween in the dorms together, when she tried to make the group watch a scary movie marathon that weekend. Bee had completely ruined the whole thing, squeezing her eyes shut and whimpering before anything had even happened just five minutes into the first movie. She and Austin had wanted to keep going, but Clay had insisted they turn the TV off. They ended up playing euchre and rummy and drinking cherry vodka. It had still been a good night.

Rahul leaned over to Bee, and Cam could barely hear him as he said softly to her. "Don't worry, I won't let anything happen to you." Cam tried to suppress a grin as Bee flushed and smiled at him gratefully. Cam turned pointedly away, letting them have their moment. She knew next to nothing about Rahul, but she had a good feeling about him so far. She approved, she guessed, for now. Bee had certainly dated worse guys in her time at State, and since, from what Cam knew. They used to make time to talk to each other on the phone, to catch up now and then, at least in the early years after graduation, but that had fallen by the wayside the past few years. Hopefully, this weekend would bring them closer again.

She turned her attention back to the others; they were all discussing the prompt still of course. Cam had to agree with what Clay had said. Other than the warnings about the Besomar, the tunnels, and the secret rooms, there really hadn't been much there to go on. She wasn't sure why they would need a copy in writing or that it would benefit them much, but she supposed there could always be something hidden in the text. She thought back to the escape rooms she had done previously. Only two, but both had involved words or codes needed to unlock something hidden in text at various times. Maybe certain letters would be capitalized or underlined or something, and that would spell out a clue or a code. She bet it would be something like that.

As they debated what clues the prompt might contain and joked about the Besomar, she found her gaze landing on Austin again. He had stayed silent throughout the conversation.

He swirled the last dregs of his beer around and around in his glass, staring down at it with a sort of blank expression on his face like he was far away.

Was he thinking about seeing Miranda tomorrow? She felt a jolt of jealousy twist through her gut at the thought. God, she was pathetic. She had come here hoping to confront him and get over him for good. Seeing him again after all these years was supposed to prove to her subconscious once and for all that she didn't love him anymore. That she really didn't even know him. Not who he was now. And that he had certainly never loved her. Yet here she was, feeling jealous of his ex-wife, of all people. It was ridiculous.

She had been wildly jealous of Miranda when she first heard they were dating, just a few months after graduation, then eventually engaged and getting married. She had felt betrayed. Not just by him but by her, too. They had been good friends, and Miranda knew how she felt about him. The fact that Austin had picked one of them, in the end, but somehow, it wasn't her... it hurt more than she would ever care to admit. She hadn't gone to their wedding; had made up some excuse about work. She couldn't bear it.

She turned to look at Lan as her mind returned to Alex's odd behavior. He had fallen silent as well but was watching the others, following the conversation as they tried to glean what they could from the prompt. He caught her watching him and gave her what looked like a half-hearted smile.

"You okay?" She asked him, tucking her long blonde hair behind her ear and out of her face as she turned towards him.

"Yeah." He smiled more warmly back at her, "Just tired, I guess."

She nodded, suddenly feeling weary herself at his words. "Yeah, same. I'm ready to get out of here. Although," she paused, thinking, "I'm not so sure I'm ready to go to the castle tonight. Kind of wish I had just booked a Hilton, you know?"

Lan grinned. "Yeah, I'm beginning to feel like that too. I doubt you have to worry about being possessed by an evil spirit if you commit a sin at the local B&B."

Cam giggled a little. "I dunno, some of those are run by some pretty severe old ladies. They might not like you sinning on their premises either, Lan Nguyen." She made a tisk-tisk sound and shook her finger at him. "No inviting young ladies back to your room at those establishments."

He laughed and gave her a real smile at that. "True, maybe I'll be better off staying at the castle after all."

Austin stood up suddenly. "I'm getting some air." He announced to the room before turning and making his way through the double doors leading back into the restaurant.

"Aren't we sitting outside already?" Cam heard Bee wonder out loud as she watched him go. She thought about going after him, but decided against it.

Alex got up and motioned one of the staff over to the table. It looked like they would be wrapping up soon. Cam stood as well and made her way over to the balcony railing. She looked out over the ocean and breathed in deeply.

Closing her eyes, she reveled in the feeling of the cool sea air rushing over her face. The smell of the salt water and the sound of the waves crashing below her had a calming, soothing effect. After a moment or two she felt herself relax. She could do this. She could get through this weekend and accomplish what she came here to do. It was only a matter now of how uncomfortable it would be to do it. But either way, she didn't plan on leaving the castle without putting an end to her feelings for Austin once and for all.

9.

Austin

Austin was starting to regret the entire thing already. He had felt okay at first on the boat. At least, until Cam arrived. It had been just him and Lan and Clay for a while, and Alex, of course. And Rahul. He kept forgetting about Rahul. It had felt just like old times; the guys back together again, laughing and joking around. Then Darcy had arrived, and he had felt hopeful, and genuinely happy to see her again. She was such a truly kind person; you couldn't help but feel relaxed around Darcy. She had that sort of effect on people.

Then Cam had shown up. He had just glanced down to see her walking up the gangway. He saw the look on her face when she saw him watching her. Her expression had been wary and somehow filled with something close to disgust. He had felt the bottom drop out from under him, like his stomach was dropping away as he crested the top of a hill on a rollercoaster. He didn't know what he had expected to happen when they finally saw each other again. Didn't know why he had agreed to any of this in the first place.

And now Miranda was coming tomorrow. It really couldn't get any worse. He could kill Alex for tricking him like this. He was seriously considering leaving at this point.

He had made it through the boat ride, making sure to keep his distance from Cam. He had managed to stay busy talking with the others. He just didn't know what to say to her.

Then there had been dinner. She had thought about sitting next to him, for a brief moment, at least. He had seen her contemplating the open seat beside him, a spark of something in her green eyes, but then she had given him that half-disgusted look again and sat as far away from him as she could get. So, she hated him. Fine. And could he blame her for it?

He made it through most of dinner without throttling Alex, somehow, and the escape room prompt had distracted him for a bit. But by the time they were finishing up dessert, he just couldn't stand sitting there any longer. He had to get out. He had mumbled some excuse about needing fresh air and left the restaurant. It didn't bode well for the remainder of the weekend. He was about to be trapped with these people and couldn't even make it through dinner.

He walked away from the restaurant a bit. He headed up the boardwalk at first, wanting to see the ocean, but that took him over towards the balcony, and he could hear their voices again, floating over to him. He turned and headed away from the restaurant into the parking lot. He started walking down the street a ways, taking deep gulping breaths of cool air. The sun hadn't set quite yet, but it was starting to get dusky. The scent of saltwater and the fresh cool breeze hit him, and he felt himself start to relax a bit. He felt so tense. So nervous and off-kilter. Like he didn't belong here. Shouldn't be here. It wasn't just seeing Cam again that had rattled him. It was Alex.

He had acted so oddly at dinner. The things he said. Bringing up Clay and Bee, for one thing. They never talked about Clay and Bee. Not in front of Clay like that. It was an unspoken rule. It was old news, and sure, they might joke about it privately from time to time, just one or two of them, but to announce it like that to the whole group? It was bizarre. And bringing up that night... Henley Park. Why would he do that? It had almost felt like he was trying to upset them on purpose. Or make them upset with each other. Bringing up old shit. It made Austin uneasy that he didn't quite know what Alex was up to. And he didn't like it.

Then the whole Miranda thing had been the icing on the cake. And he was done at this point. If Alex wanted to choose to be an asshole this weekend, fine by him. He wasn't going to let it get to him. Although a small voice in his head told him it clearly already had. Well, he wouldn't let Alex see it, at least then. Or Cam. Or Miranda, once she eventually showed up. And if she had any decency left, she wouldn't.

Austin turned around, not wanting to drift too far away from the restaurant; they would probably be heading out soon. He ended up walking back to the parking lot, and when no one was in sight, he turned and headed back up the street again. He ended up pacing like that, back and forth, for some time. An older couple passed him, out for a walk downtown. They smiled at him and nodded hello. He nodded absentmindedly back at them.

He thought of this whole Besomar thing. He had never heard of a Besomar before, and it sounded odd. What could a mix between a werewolf and a vampire even look like? And supposedly, it was some type of demon that somehow possessed people and could control their actions if they invited one in. The whole seven deadly sins thing was interesting; that would clearly be part of the theme. And then there was the part about them needing to be "pure" or "positive," not only in their actions but in their thoughts as well. That was odd too. How could they monitor what they were thinking? He decided the whole thing was silly, and it didn't make much sense.

Austin guessed they could monitor what they did easily enough. There would have to be cameras everywhere, but he figured that was typical for an escape room. Usually, you were only in there for what, though, an hour or so? Were they going to be on camera all weekend? Would someone be watching them 24/7, everywhere they went, even while they slept? The thought gave him the creeps a little. He would have to clarify that part with Alex. Not that he trusted him to give a straight answer.

Austin continued his route, pacing up and down the street, and returned to the parking lot again. He looked up to see Clay standing alone in the parking lot. He was looking up at the moon in the distance. It hung low, appearing impossibly huge and glowing pinkish red. Austin approached him, and Clay looked over in his direction. "What do they say about the moon being red again?" Clay asked.

Austin thought for a moment. "I don't know about the moon, but there's a saying about the sky being red. Red sky at night, sailor's delight. Red sky in the morning, sailors take warning."

Clay nodded thoughtfully. "That's probably all rubbish, though, right? With the sun setting and rising, isn't the sky usually red both at night and in the morning?" Clay grinned at him. "Doesn't make much sense to me."

"No," Austin said, "I guess it doesn't. Who knows where these old sayings come from anyway."

Clay nodded again, looking at him thoughtfully now. "You okay, man?"

Austin nodded, looking away. "Yeah, man, I'm fine." He cleared his throat and stared out towards the direction of the ocean. "How about you?" he added, remembering Alex's comment to Bee.

Clay nodded, looking off in the same direction, back towards the ocean and the restaurant. "Yeah, I'm okay. You know... I guess I forgot how Alex could be. Apparently, ten years is long enough to forget someone can be a real dick sometimes."

Austin chuckled a little. "Yeah, I guess so. Though, you'd think he could make it through the first couple hours at least. I guess it's going to be a long weekend."

"Yeah." Clay nodded, looking thoughtful again. "Is there an eighth deadly sin about being an asshole?" Austin laughed again, louder this time. "Cause if so, Alex might not be around all that long, after all." They smiled at each other, contemplating that thought.

"Hey, maybe one of us can provoke him into wrath and get him another strike. Or there's always pride... I think he can walk right into that one all on his own." Austin grinned.

He looked over at the restaurant doors as the others began to exit. Clay followed his gaze and said quietly. "That's true, no doubt. What're the other ones?"

Austin thought for a moment. "There's lust... envy..."

Clay chuckled. "Lust, huh? Great. That one won't be a problem at all." He turned to look back at Austin. "For any of us, right?" He clapped him on the back and turned towards the others as they joined them.

"You guys okay out here?" Darcy asked. She was smiling, but she looked concerned. Darcy had always been the peacemaker of the group, Austin thought. She hated to see any of them upset, especially with each other.

"It's all good, Darcy." Clay nodded reassuringly at her. He slipped an arm around her shoulders as she approached him, and they walked off through the parking lot toward the black cars waiting for them. "Did you see the moon?" Austin heard Clay asking her. He heard her exclaim as they stopped to admire it.

The others followed, filing past him in a line. He noted Bee walked with Rahul; they were laughing about something, giggling and whispering together like little kids. He grinned at them, watching them. He didn't realize Cam had trailed the others at the end of the group. She approached him now, and he was just standing alone in the parking lot, looking like he was waiting for her intentionally. *Oh jeez.*

She met his eyes, watching him as she walked straight for him. It looked like he couldn't avoid her any longer. "Hey," he said. *That was it? Hey?*

She slowed and looked at him skeptically, one eyebrow raised. Then he saw the corners of her mouth twitch and turn up a little. He grinned at her, and she smiled back, shaking her head. "Hey yourself," she said, chuckling a little. "It's only been what? Ten years? That's all you have to say to me, huh?" She stopped, crossing her arms and glaring at him.

He met her gaze steadily, and they just stared at each other for a moment. Finally, he said, "I have a lot more than that to say to you." He saw her eyes widen almost imperceptibly. That had caught her off-guard.

She had changed, that was for sure. For one thing, she was clearly much more direct than she used to be. More confident. But he still knew her well enough to be able to tell he'd surprised her.

She swallowed and looked away toward the others. "Well," she said calmly, meeting his gaze again, "I can't wait to hear it." He nodded, and she was the first to break eye contact.

He stood there, hands in his pockets, unsure what to do next. Then, for some reason, he tilted his elbow towards her, offering her his arm. He felt a brief moment of uncertainty, wondering why he'd done that when she stood there staring at him, clearly about to refuse and walk past him. But then she slipped her arm through his, and they walked towards the waiting cars together like it was the most natural thing in the world.

10.

Darcy

It had been a very strange day. Darcy felt tired by the time they finished up at the restaurant. She trailed behind Bee and Rahul, walking out to the cars Alex had told them were waiting for them. She smiled to herself at the sound of Bee's laughter. Rahul seemed to make her happy, which was certainly a nice thing. It was strange, though, Darcy thought, how Alex had been able to convince Bee she knew him. Had the others all been convinced too? Or were they just pretending? Were they just going along with it for now, like she was?

Alex had been acting strangely at dinner, too. Talking about Clay and Bee and bringing up that last night at Henley Park. His comment about her "little doodles" had seemed... deliberate. He knew she was an artist; that painting was how she made a living. Something about it hadn't seemed real to her. Almost as though he was playing a part. She felt uneasy. And mostly, she felt bad for the others. For Clay and Austin.

Darcy sat in the back of the long shiny car, biting her lip as she stared out the window. The others were laughing; someone had opened a drink from the mini bar and spilled it everywhere. She saw absentmindedly that it must have gotten on Bee's dress. She was laughing with her head tipped back, as they helped her clean it up. She was momentarily struck by how beautiful Bee looked, especially when she laughed. Her green eyes sparkling as she smiled at Rahul.

Darcy wasn't looking forward to Miranda joining them tomorrow. Although she missed her and wanted to see her again, she was worried it would all be too awkward. It hadn't even been that long since she left Austin. It must still be painful for him. Why would Alex invite her and not tell him? Darcy wondered, not for the first time, just what Alex had planned for them this weekend. Because somehow, she knew, the whole escape room thing was just the start of it.

Buildings and streetlights flashed by in a blur in front of her. The sun was sinking lower, and it was starting to get darker now. It turned out the castle was not as far away as it had looked on the boat ride out. They seemed to arrive there in no time at all.

The car came to a stop as she was still lost in thought. A face appeared in front of her as the driver pulled the door open. He smiled at her and offered her his hand. She just blinked at him, her dark eyes wide, as she snapped out of it and realized he was trying to help her get out of the car. Darcy laughed at herself and shook her head. "Sorry," she mumbled, and she took his hand and let him help her out of the deep seat.

She walked a few steps away, looking back at him as he leaned in to help Bee next. Then she turned and saw the castle up close for the first time. She came to a stop, staring up at the worn stone walls that stretched into the sky. It was surrounded by trees, moss, and curling vines that grew on everything. The sound of the waves pounding into the shore crashed over her back; the smell of salt from the ocean and the scent of damp earth filled her lungs. The moon was just visible behind the castle, glowing red, along with the entire skyline. The clouds looked like they had been painted pink and gold.

Darcy felt herself freeze; her breath caught in her throat. A stone fountain stood to her left, and in front was a crumbling statue of an angel. She held bundles of stone roses in each hand. Her expression was filled with sorrow. Vines curled around her feet. The wind picked up, lifting and swirling the leaves that littered the ground, the trees swaying back and forth. The whole landscape seemed to breathe in and out. A tunnel of green led further into the grounds, the depths of it lost to shadows.

Darcy took a step forward, then hesitated before taking another. She stared into the darkness and felt it almost pulling her forward... to come in. It must be the wind and the waves... whispering in her ears, but she felt her heart start to race.

Darcy felt herself take a stumbling step back, hitting something solid behind her. She jumped and turned, gasping a little. She saw Clay's face, his dark eyes peering into hers.

"Darcy?" he asked, gripping her arm. She looked down at his hand, then back at the tunnel of leaves. "Darcy!" Clay said again, his voice louder and more insistent.

"What?" she asked, her voice barely a whisper.

"What's wrong? Are you okay?" Clay studied her, his eyes roving over her face, his grip on her arm too hard. The others were starting to gather now. "You looked like you were going to pass out or something."

"No, I..." Darcy began. "I'm fine." Clay looked unconvinced. He glanced over at Austin, a look of concern passing between them.

Austin stepped closer, studying her as well. "You sure you're okay Darcy?"

She shook her head, clearing it. "Really, I'm fine. I'm probably just tired."

Alex appeared beside them. "All right, everyone," he raised his hands in the air above them, a grin on his face. "We're about to enter the grounds, and just like in the prompt, we have the groundsman here to give us a quick tour." Alex turned and gestured toward an older man in a fedora who stood watching them. He nodded and smiled grimly. He looked a little uncomfortable, Darcy thought.

Alex continued, "We will be limited to the grounds outside and a general common area inside the castle for tonight, which we will continue to have access to throughout the escape room challenge. We will also have access to our bedrooms throughout the challenge; those areas will not lock down. It's our job to unlock any further areas from there." He grinned at all of them. "Are we ready?"

They looked around at each other. No one spoke. Darcy saw Clay glance down the long dark tunnel of green that had captivated her a moment ago. He looked back at her, his face full of apprehension.

There was a chorus of murmurs, people nodding. Darcy heard Lan say, "Let's do this!" Which got a few nervous-sounding laughs. But Clay and Darcy just stared at each other until Clay finally turned to Alex, his mouth starting to open as though he was about to say something. Then Alex turned and clapped the old man on the shoulder, a big grin on his face.

The old man turned and waved them forward. "Right then, right this way, follow me." And then they were moving. Clay fell in behind her, and whatever he had been about to say was lost. They entered the dark tunnel. Darcy hesitated for just a second before she plunged in after them.

The man's voice didn't sound anything like the man in the recording, Darcy noticed. Clearly, that had been an actor, and this was probably the real groundsman. He didn't speak much throughout the tour, only when he was asked a direct question. They wound their way through the tunnel for a ways initially. The walls, she assumed, were stone underneath, but they were completely covered in ivy. As they came to the far end of the tunnel, the man turned on a small flashlight to help light their way. She saw a statue of a woman set into the wall on her right, half covered in the overgrown ivy. Her blank eyes peered out at them, watching as they passed.

They eventually emerged from the tunnel into what must be a garden. Twisted tree trunks lined the low stone walls on all sides, sparse at first but becoming more numerous, until they formed the wall of a thick forest. She saw another tunnel off to her left; the start of a pathway that wound through the forest, the roof of the tunnel formed by overlapping tree branches. Large roots were visible, rising out of the soil. She could still hear the pounding of waves here, only slightly fainter. The sound was soothing, creating a counterpoint to the rapid pounding in her chest.

The far stone wall caught her eye; instead of spikes at the top, there was a series of what looked like heads from this distance. She made her way slowly over to them, peering at them in the dim light. She heard the others chatting in the background. They had stopped next to the fountain in the middle of the garden. "Nah, there's nothing on the other side of the grounds, not for some distance at least..." she heard the groundsman say, "... yes, the tunnels are real. They run underground, all throughout the property. It's a maze down there; easy to lose your way."

They were heads after all, on the wall, with short spikes at the top. She peered at them in fascination. Each face was slightly different, eyes downturned, lines of moss growing down over their eyelids.

Darcy heard footsteps behind her, the crunch of leaves as someone approached. She turned to see Clay watching her from a few feet away. He nodded to her, and she nodded back. "Come on, we're moving on." She looked behind him and saw the group had started off towards the castle. She looked back at the heads for a second and then turned and followed him. The Castle walls looked much the same as the stone walls lining the garden. They were covered in moss in places, strands of ivy twirling and twisting up them, framing the peaked windows. A gnarled tree grew off to the left, quite close to the wall; the leaves on its branches were already starting to turn burnt orange and red.

They came to a set of wooden double doors. The groundsman removed a clinking set of old-fashioned-looking keys from his pocket and found the right one surprisingly quickly. Inserting it into the lock and turning it, he stepped back and held the door open for them to enter ahead of him. Darcy followed behind Clay at the end of the group.

They stepped into a wide-open space. Darcy took in the room with a little thrill of excitement. Her lips parted into a smile, but she slid one hand under Clay's arm, grasping onto it. He looked down and over at her briefly, and then they continued into the room together.

The far-left wall was lined with ornate stained-glass windows, and a curving spiral staircase wound in front, leading to a second floor. The walls were covered in books on the left-hand side of the lower level. To their right, on the far side of the room, was a massive fireplace. Oversized leather couches and armchairs framed the fireplace, with a large square coffee table in the middle. The bank of windows on that side of the room were crisscrossed with black iron bars, and they ran from floor to ceiling, their tops pointed just like the windows on the left.

Candles were lit on the coffee table, but there was no fire in the grate. Darcy shivered a little. The room felt inviting and cozy, despite the castle itself giving off an air of dark foreboding, but it was cold. Wall sconces lined the space, glowing with a dim, warm light. "This is the common area you'll have access to for the weekend." She heard the groundsman say. His voice echoed slightly in the large space.

"I'll take you through and show you to your bedrooms in the guest wing. I'm told access to all other areas will be locked down until you can open them." He gestured over towards Darcy's left; she turned to see a large wooden table lined with chairs. "Food will be brought in for you, three meals a day; you'll find it waiting for you here. Times are 8:00, 12:00, and 6:00." He glanced around at them. The others nodded their understanding. "Right this way then, if there are no questions." No one spoke up, and he continued on, leading them through a narrow doorway past the dining table.

They filed through behind him. Darcy let go of Clay's arm as they passed through the doorway. Once they were on the other side, she noticed he stayed close to her. He seemed to take in his surroundings warily. Darcy glanced over at Cam. She looked thoughtful but excited as she surveyed this new space. Bee was looking up at the ceiling, a smile on her face. Were she and Clay the only ones that felt nervous?

A set of stairs faced them, but her gaze went to the floor first; they stood on large black and white slabs in a checkered pattern that looked like a chessboard. To her right was a set of massive wooden doors, which Darcy assumed to be the main entrance. Paintings and more stone statues lined the wall to their left. A railing with an overlook ran the length of the long rectangular room upstairs to their right, running over the top of the double doors. They followed the groundsman as he led them up the stairs.

Darcy gripped the railing as she climbed the stairs after the others. She lingered at the back of the group once more, head swiveling as she tried to take everything in. They came to the top of the staircase; a closed door faced them down a short hallway, but the groundsman led them off to the left, down a longer corridor. This hall was lit by twin pillar candles that jutted out from ornate golden holders every six feet or so along the walls. Doors lined either side and stood open. About halfway down the hallway, the groundsman stopped and turned to face the group.

"This is the guest wing," he announced, "Where you'll be staying for the duration of the weekend." Darcy turned and peered over her shoulder into the closest bedroom. She caught a glimpse of more of the tall gothic-style windows. Her eyebrows raised as she noted the black cross-pane bars that covered these windows as well.

"Rooms have not been assigned to you, but your bags have been placed inside rooms for you; if you'd like to switch, you'll choose amongst yourselves. You'll each have your own private powder room." The groundsman continued. "If there aren't any further questions, I'll take my leave of you." They looked around at each other. Suddenly Darcy felt more apprehensive at the thought of them being left alone here, but she assumed they would have a way of contacting the outside world if necessary.

"What about in an emergency?" She heard Cam pipe up. "Is there a way to contact you or the... whoever is in charge of all this?" She looked over at Alex.

"In a true emergency, you can dial 911," the groundsman answered. "There's a landline phone that's been installed in the common area downstairs."

Alex added, "All cellphones will be confiscated tonight. My assistant will stop by this evening and take them with her for the duration of the challenge." There was a murmur of protests at this. "Like George just said," Alex went on, unphased by their exclamations, "There's a landline phone available for emergencies. We can't have people cheating and looking up answers online." He shrugged.

Darcy saw Austin moving at the far end of the hallway; he paced up and down the hall, away from them and back again, peering into bedrooms. He looked as uneasy as she felt.

Alex spoke up next. "The escape room team will be monitoring our movements as well. Only if absolutely necessary, they will intervene or can assist." Darcy saw Austin still, peering sideways at Alex as he spoke.

"Where are the cameras?" He asked.

Alex grinned at him, a wicked look on his face. "Nowhere you'll ever find them." Austin glared back at him, half his face in shadow in the dim lighting. "This is a professional crew," Alex added, "I've recruited only the best to join my team."

"Okay," Cam snorted, "We'll need a little more information than that. Are they everywhere? In the bedrooms?" She gestured to an open door beside her. "Are you filming us all the time?"

Alex grinned at her. "There are cameras in the bedrooms, yes," he said slowly. Several of the others groaned, and murmurs of protest started up in earnest this time. Alex held up his hands. "Hang on, hang on, let me finish. There are cameras in the bedrooms, but they will be off by default. They may only be turned on when a group of people are gathered in a bedroom."

Lan snorted. "Define group," he clipped.

Alex raised an eyebrow at him. "Why, Lan? Are you planning on entertaining a guest?" Lan flushed and looked away immediately. Alex stared at him momentarily, then continued. "Let's say the team sees several of us enter a bedroom. In case we are looking for clues, discussing a puzzle, that type of thing, they might turn the cameras on briefly to monitor. They won't be spying on you changing, or going to the bathroom, okay?" There was another general groan. Alex waved his hands. "There are no cameras in the bathrooms, to clarify." The grumbling died away.

They were silent for a moment, and then the groundsman cleared his throat. He still stood there, looking rather uncomfortable now. "Any further questions for me?" He looked more than ready to leave.

Bee spoke up, "You mentioned the tunnels under the castle are real, but obviously," she chuckled, "This whole Beso..." she stopped, unable to remember the name.

Rahul chimed in from just behind her. He leaned against the wall, his hands in his pockets. He certainly gave off an air of looking casual and unbothered. "Besomar," he added, head ducking forward.

"Yes, Besomar, thank you," Bee said, her gaze flickering to the side momentarily. "This whole Besomar thing was obviously made up for the escape room prompt." She smiled at the groundsman encouragingly.

"Ah, that," he sighed deeply. "No, Miss, that wasn't made up for the escape..." he gestured, clearly unsure what to call all of this, "... weekend." He finished.

Bee's face fell flat like her smile had been wiped off. "What?" She said, looking crestfallen. Her gaze met Darcy's for a second as she scanned the group. She rallied a little and tried to smile again, "What do you mean? It wasn't made up for just this weekend? They've used it before for other groups, then?"

The groundsman looked at her, confused. "I... I don't think they've done any other escape weekends here, Miss. But no, that's not what I meant. The Besomar is a local legend. The locals have heard stories passed down of the demon that haunts the castle grounds for decades. They say it lives somewhere down in the tunnels, deep underground. It's said to only emerge at night or in darkness. It avoids sunlight. The way I've heard it described is sort of like a vampire, but some describe it more as some sort of wolf." Bee frowned at the groundsman; this was clearly not the answer she had hoped for. He caught her expression and cleared his throat. "But those are just stories, of course, Miss, nothing more to them than that."

"But the prompt said it possesses people, takes control of them," Cam piped in. "Is it able to move around on its own then? It can be its own entity without a host?" Lan was frowning now, too, looking at Cam. She saw him eyeing her skeptically and added, "in the stories, I mean."

The groundsman sighed again, his gaze drifted through an open bedroom door. "Well, let me see. The stories make it sound like it possesses people, yes." He nodded to himself, "I suppose it can move around on its own, though as well. But I'm no expert, Ma'am. To be honest, I don't put much stock into any of the stories. For as long as I've been around, I've never seen anything happen myself."

Cam nodded, she was staring at the ground now, looking thoughtful.

Bee seemed to feel better at his words; she gave Darcy a small smile, and Darcy smiled back reassuringly in return. She knew that part would continue to bother Bee, but hopefully, she would feel more at ease now.

Alex spoke up again suddenly. "Yes, well, thank you, I think we should be all set for now." He nodded to the groundsman, clearly dismissing him.

The older man, George, Darcy reminded herself of his name, nodded to them. "Good luck," he said, and with a look of relief on his face, he took off down the hallway, heading back to the stairs.

They stood there, looking around at each other. Then Bee said, "Well, should we check out the rooms?" There was a stasis for another few seconds, and then everyone scattered, heading into the nearest bedroom. Darcy stood there watching as Rahul started to follow Bee into the bedroom to their right. He froze in the doorway, seeming to think better of it, before backtracking into the hall again. He noticed Darcy watching him and grinned, flushing slightly. He nodded at her before turning and heading back down the hall and disappearing into another bedroom.

Darcy turned and entered the doorway behind her. She couldn't help but feel impressed, and excited seeing the room in full. It contained a massive bed covered in a thick emerald velvet comforter. A bank of gothic-style windows was framed by long curtains on either side. There was even a small fireplace, with two armchairs and a small side table sitting in front of it. There was a basket of wood stacked off to the side. The room felt warm, inviting, and luxurious. Darcy made her way over to the windows and peered outside; they faced the back garden from what she could tell.

Clay peeked his head into the doorway and called to her. "Nice! This room is even bigger than the one I was checking out." She turned to face him, a grin on her face.

"It is really nice, isn't it?" He smiled at her and stepped inside. She saw he was holding her worn-out floral travel bag.

He lifted it and gestured to it with his other hand. "Same one from college, huh?" She smiled at him and then at the bag fondly.

"Yeah," she laughed a little, "I guess it is! I've had it forever; I couldn't part with it. I suppose I'll use it until it splits open."

Clay chuckled, "Looks like it might." He was right; it was packed to the brim. She had shoved as many clothes in there as she could. She always overpacked for trips. You never knew what you might be in the mood to wear. "I was going to see if you wanted to trade rooms because your stuff was in there, but this one looks better. You want to come see and decide for yourself?"

Darcy smiled at him, "No, I'm fine with this one, thanks Clay."

"Sure," he said, "No problem." He set her bag down off to the side.

"How are the others doing?" Darcy asked him.

"Well," Clay chuckled again, glancing back into the hall, "Bee and Cam were fighting over rooms for a minute." Darcy grimaced, but he waved his hand. "I think they were just joking around, having fun. Although... there was a mention of a sleepover, so we'll see where they end up." Darcy laughed.

"Just like old times in the apartment; half the time, I'd come home and find them both asleep out in the living room." She grinned at him and flopped into one of the armchairs. "It's nice, isn't it? All of us being back together again?"

Clay's smile faltered. He walked over and joined her, sitting in the other armchair. "Yeah," he said thoughtfully. "It is. And it isn't, at the same time. You know what I mean?" Darcy nodded at him. She bit her bottom lip and stared into the empty fireplace. "It's such a weird feeling," he continued, "Like we're right back where we were ten years ago, but at the same time, so much time has passed, and things have changed. We've changed, you know? I just... it feels weird." He shook his head, "I don't know."

Darcy nodded at him again. "No, I know exactly what you mean."

"And this place..." Clay continued as he leaned forward, his voice lowering. "I don't like this place. It gives me the creeps."

Darcy met his eyes, frowning. "There is...something about it." She looked around the room. "It's beautiful, elegant, and... interesting. But it has a sort of..." she struggled for the right word, "Ominous, feeling to it as well."

"Yes." Clay was nodding as she spoke. "Yes, there's something off about it, isn't there?" He looked at her, running a hand over his mouth and sighing. "I felt it when we first arrived. Didn't you?"

Darcy watched him, frowning again. "I felt..." she thought back to that moment, and the tunnel that seemed to whisper to her. "I felt something. Yes." She nodded.

"Hey guys!" A voice startled Darcy from the doorway. Rahul peeked inside the room. "Sorry to interrupt," he said a little sheepishly, seeing he had startled her. "Um, the whole room thing has been sorted out, and everyone's meeting back downstairs for a drink."

"Okay, cool, thanks man," Clay said. Darcy nodded and smiled.

"Okay, see you down there." Rahul nodded back and disappeared into the hallway.

Clay looked at her and shrugged. "I guess we should head down there then. Glad to hear they have drinks in this place..." he got up and started for the door. Darcy stood and followed him. She paused and turned back to look at the room, and as she turned, she could have sworn she saw a flash of movement through the tall bank of windows opposite. She stopped and peered out the windows but saw nothing other than tree branches against the swiftly darkening sky.

11.

Lan

Lan found a spot on one of the brown leather sofas in front of the fireplace. He felt slightly better now, with another drink in his hand. Still, he had to admit, the weekend wasn't off to a great start. And he doubted things would improve tomorrow.

The specter of Miranda's arrival hung over them now. A reunion including Miranda would be bad enough. The fact that they would literally be locked in together made the whole thing laughable. He held the cold glass of beer up to his forehead. He needed to calm down. He had managed to give himself what he could tell was about to be a whopper of a headache. He had been so tense all day that he had to continuously remind himself to relax his shoulders and unclench his jaw. Little good that had done. Now he would be stuck with a tension headache on top of everything else. Or even worse, the stress may have triggered a migraine. He didn't get them often, but when he did, they were pretty awful.

"You okay, man?" He heard Austin's voice across from him. He brought the glass down to his lips and took a sip, wiping the moisture from his forehead.

"Yeah." He nodded, giving Austin a tight smile. "I'm fine. Just a little headache, that's all." Austin nodded, sighed, and sank down into one of the leather armchairs. Lan noticed he didn't have a drink in his hand. Cam and Bee made their way around the couches and found spots next to each other, closer to the fireplace.

Bee shivered and rubbed her hands together. "A fire would be nice, wouldn't it?" she said absentmindedly, looking around the room. "Such a cold place. I'm glad I packed some sweaters."

Cam nodded in agreement. Lan could still hear the pounding of the surf outside. He thought he could hear the addition of the wind howling now as well. The windows rattled slightly in their frames.

Austin stood up. "I'll see if I can get a fire going," he said. He shrugged his leather jacket off and slung it over the back of the armchair. He started grabbing firewood from a bin next to the fireplace, which apparently contained something to use for kindling, too, then knelt and set it in front of the grate. He pulled a fancy-looking silver lighter out of his pocket and lit the kindling first. He created a little bundle and blew into it, forming a sort of nest around the tiny flickering flame. Lan watched him work. Weirdly, he'd never learned how to start a fire properly; had never had an opportunity really to try it.

"Thanks, Austin." Lan heard Bee murmur to his right. He glanced over at the girls and saw Bee was typing out something on her phone, probably texting someone. Cam was watching Austin, a frown on her face. She noticed him watching her and catching his eye, she rolled hers and sighed, leaning back against the couch.

"Yeah," Lan said, "thanks, Austin. You're such a boy scout." He heard Cam snort and looked over to see her grinning at him. She had a drink in her hand—probably gin and coke again if he had to guess.

Austin snorted as well, "Thanks Lan, you're such a dick." Cam laughed harder at that one. Lan himself couldn't help but chuckle.

Lan thought back to that night at Henley Park, how Cam had staggered past him, sobbing. He'd followed her, keeping a distance, watching as she sat in the grass on a hill overlooking the river below. The sky had been full of stars that night, twinkling brightly above a miraculously cloudless sky. He didn't think he had ever seen so many stars. Even the swirling edges of a star cluster was visible. Eventually he had gone and sat beside her. She had been inconsolable, unable to speak. But she leaned her head on his shoulder after a while.

They sat that way in silence for what felt like an hour or more. Until finally, she spoke, her voice barely a whisper, "I can't imagine there's nothing better in store for me in a universe filled with a billion worlds like this one." He'd smiled in the dark and squeezed her hand. And she told him what had happened then, how she had finally worked up the courage to tell Austin how she felt. And how he'd rejected her.

Lan shook his head, watching Austin's back as he stacked the logs in the grate over the little fire he'd made. "Only when it comes to you, asshole." Austin looked at him over his shoulder, and Lan grinned at him. Austin shook his head and went back to tending the fire for another moment or two. Eventually he seemed satisfied, and he went and took his seat again in the armchair.

It wasn't long before the room seemed considerably warmer, and the fire added much-needed light to the space as well. Lan looked over at Austin. "Good job man," he said, nodding at the fire. Austin gave him a look. "For real. I can never start fires right; they just smoke and then die. Guess I never learned how to do it properly.

Austin raised an eyebrow at him. "Oh yeah? Well, I could've shown you just now." He nodded towards the fire. "Next time," he added. Lan nodded back.

"Maybe tomorrow, you could teach us," Bee said, smiling up at them as she tucked her phone into her clutch. "I never learned either. It's probably something that would come in handy."

Austin nodded at her. "Sounds good, Bee; we can start a new one tomorrow morning if we want." Alex strode up behind Austin's chair, lowering a full beer glass down in front of his face and holding it there until he took it. "Thanks," Austin murmured, tilting his head back and looking up over his shoulder.

Alex made his way around the side of the armchair and stood in front of the fire. He stared into it for a moment. "I'm really glad you could all be here; truly." He turned and looked at the group gathered around the fire. "I think this weekend will be good for all of us." Lan met his eyes before his gaze moved on to one of the others. Then Lan heard Darcy's voice coming from somewhere behind him.

"What is this?" She asked, sounding confused. Lan and the girls seated on the couch turned as one to look at her. She was standing over by the wall opposite, to the left of the door that led to the front staircase. There was what looked like a sort of office area, with a large wooden desk. Lan noted the landline phone sitting on the desk. Darcy leaned over the desk slightly, looking at a sign or something on the wall. "It has our names on it," she said looking over at them.

Clay was sitting at the dining table behind her, staring at the wall as well. He looked over towards the fire, where Alex stood, before getting up and walking over to join Darcy.

The others waited, watching. "You guys gotta come see this," Clay called over to them. Lan and Austin glanced at each other and stood up. After a moment, the girls followed.

Soon, they were all gathered in front of the desk, staring up at the wall. Lan scanned it quickly, seeing exactly what Darcy had described: a list of all their names. To the right of each name was what appeared to be a series of three light bulbs; all were unlit. Lan squinted at the sign, as though that would make it easier for him to understand what he was seeing.

"What the hell is this, Alex?" He heard Austin ask. Turning, Lan realized Alex was the only one who hadn't joined them over at the sign. Well, Rahul was missing, too, it seemed. Alex still stood by the fireplace, leaning nonchalantly on the mantel with one elbow. He turned to look their way and started to move closer.

"It's for the escape room tomorrow," he said, hardly glancing at the sign.

"What for, though?" Clay asked him, his brows creased with confusion as he stared up at their names.

Alex shrugged, "I dunno...any guesses?" He smirked at them. "Might as well start exercising your brains a little tonight."

The others turned back to the sign again, but Lan saw Austin was still staring at Alex. Alex just grinned back at him. Lan shifted his gaze to the list again. "Three light bulbs, next to each name..." he trailed off.

"Three strikes, and you're out," Cam finished for him, their eyes meeting briefly before they turned to Alex.

He held his hands up and started slow clapping for them.

"Good job guys." He grinned. "Maybe we have some hope of escaping after all," he chuckled.

Clay spoke up. "Seriously? How on earth is this thing supposed to work?"

Alex shrugged again. "Like I said, we'll find out tomorrow. I suggest you get all your sinning out tonight..." he winked at them. "Or maybe, don't, actually," he turned and sauntered back towards the fireplace. "You know, technically, the whole Besomar thing is still an issue tonight, I guess. You don't want to invite him in by accident."

"God," Bee said, shivering visibly and wrapping her cardigan around herself, "I don't even want to think about that. How the heck am I going to sleep tonight?" She grimaced at Cam, who sighed and patted her on the back. Bee surveyed the room, her brows wrinkled, "Has anyone seen Rahul?"

Her question was met with nothing but silence as the group looked around the room. Rahul was nowhere in sight. Clay spoke up. He had taken his seat at the table again. "He must still be upstairs. He came up to tell Darcy and I to head down here a few minutes ago."

Lan looked over at Darcy. She still stood on her own in front of the list of names, staring at it. He turned and continued over towards the fireplace, taking his seat on the couch with its back to the windows again. He didn't like the idea of facing the black windows; it was fully dark now, and they couldn't see out, while someone outside would be able to easily see them.

Cam sat down in roughly the same place as well, facing the fire. And Bee plopped down next to her. She seemed restless, though, and after a moment or two, she turned back towards the door that led to the stairs. Clearly wondering where Rahul was. *Was she so attached to him already?* Lan wondered absentmindedly. But then, Bee had always been that way. She made up her mind quickly and didn't often change it. She knew what she wanted, he guessed. Unlike some people. Lan's gaze drifted to Austin. He was back in the armchair as well, his beer glass still practically full. He was staring into the fire, a dark look on his face.

Lan sighed and looked away, realizing Cam was watching Austin, too. Again. She sat with her legs crossed, one foot bouncing up and down, up and down. She never could sit still, and she looked as nervous right now as he felt.

God, his head hurt even worse now. This wasn't looking good. He really didn't want to be dealing with a migraine tomorrow. Lan held his beer glass to his temples again. First one side, then the other. The glass wasn't as cold now, but it provided a momentary relief.

Alex had reappeared next to the fire. He walked over and took a seat on the far end of the couch Lan was sitting on.

He looked pointedly at each of them. "My, what a cheerful bunch we are tonight."

Bee sighed loudly, glancing back at the doorway again, just in time to see Rahul walk briskly through. He saw her peering over the back of the couch at him and he grinned at her and winked.

"You're right," Bee said, suddenly looking much happier than she had a moment ago. "We've lost our energy somehow." She looked around the room at them.

Darcy had wandered over to the library area and appeared to be scanning titles on the shelves. Clay was sitting at the table nursing a beer, glaring, as he watched Rahul make his way over to the couch beside Bee. "I know," Bee said brightly, "Let's play a game." A few people groaned at the suggestion. Lan was one of them. "Oh, come on," Bee said, "It'll be fun."

Cam gave Lan a look. Clearly, she wasn't excited about the idea. "I'm not sure what our options are for games."

"Hmm," Bee looked around the room, turning to find Darcy over by the bookshelves. She called out, "Are there any board games or cards over there, Darcy?"

Darcy was standing at the foot of the spiral staircase now, one hand held out to grasp the railing. Her foot was lifted in the air as she stood frozen halfway in the action of placing her foot on the first step. She didn't turn to look at Bee. Lan waited a long heartbeat, frowning over at her.

"Darcy?" Bee called over to her again. Her voice faltered a little. Lan stood up, and his head throbbed in protest at the sudden movement. He started over towards her, getting a glimpse of Bee's worried expression as she watched him walk past. Austin tracked his movements as well, frowning at him.

"What is it?" he asked, turning to peer around the armchair now towards the little library area.

"Darcy," Lan called out to her, a little louder this time. Still, she didn't move. Didn't flinch. Just stood there. Lan moved more quickly now, approaching her and calling to her one more time. "Darc, what's wrong?"

He reached her. Grasped her shoulder and peered around her to see her face. She stood frozen in terror, gazing up the spiral staircase. Her mouth gaped open. Her wide eyes looked unnaturally wider than they normally did. "Darcy," Lan said, shaking her shoulder a little bit. His heart started to pound in time with the hammer in his temples. *Was she having some sort of stroke?*

Finally, Darcy moved, gasping, she scrambled to grab onto his arm, her foot coming down on the edge of the step. She looked at him in fear and confusion. It was like she didn't recognize him; didn't know who he was. "Lan?" she whispered finally, squinting at him. "Did you hear that?" she demanded, gripping his arm hard, her nails digging into his flesh. "Did you see it?"

Lan shook his head, peering up the stairs, trying to look from the same angle she had been. "See what Darcy?" He looked back at her.

"I thought I saw... I thought I saw..." She trembled a little, her voice trailing off. She sounded horrified. She turned then, her eyes searching by the fireplace. She saw Austin, standing next to the armchair now, and Lan saw her release a rush of air, her shoulders slumping forward. She was breathing heavily. Bee and Cam were standing too, Rahul as well; he had started to make his way over to them.

"Oh god," Bee said, her hands covering her mouth. "What was it?" She looked almost as scared as Darcy.

Rahul watched them, then said carefully, "If this is some kind of practical joke, it isn't very funny."

Lan frowned over at him. "She's not joking," he said softly but firmly to him. "Something scared the shit out of her."

Darcy acted like she hadn't even heard them. She was still looking over at Austin, a puzzled expression on her face. Or was it Alex, she was staring at, Lan wondered. He realized Alex stood just behind Austin.

Clay spoke up, "Darcy wouldn't do something like that." He was glaring at Rahul.

Rahul held his hands up, "Okay, never mind. It just seemed odd that's all." He looked back over at Bee. She stood there, eyes still wide with concern.

"Why don't we all go to bed, get some rest, and be ready for tomorrow?" Cam spoke up.

"Oh, come on," Alex piped up. "It's way too early."

Clay held out a hand. "I found some cards." They all turned to look at him. He gestured towards the desk. "They were in the desk."

Alex sauntered over. "All right, there's just enough seats at the table, let's all play something. Have another drink." He looked over at Cam, trying to smile reassuringly at her. Cam just stared at him. "Come on. We only have a few nights together." He tilted his head to her. "For old times' sake."

Cam sighed. "Fine." She turned to Bee. "Do you want to play?"

Bee thought for a moment, then nodded to her. "I don't want to go to bed yet."

"Okay then," Cam said, clearly resigning herself. She and Bee made their way over to the table, and the others soon joined, claiming seats. Rahul sat on the other side of Bee. He put a hand on her upper back and rubbed her shoulders. She gave him a weary half-smile in return. Lan turned back to Darcy. She was still holding onto his arm. He would have vastly preferred going to bed himself. It felt like he had a band-like vise wrapped around his head now, squeezing his eyes. He wasn't about to leave Darcy alone though.

"Come on, Darcy," he murmured to her, "Let's sit down for a minute." He moved his arm, walking slowly, pulling her gently, and she followed, letting him lead her over to the table. She seemed a little shell-shocked. Whatever she had seen on the stairs had really spooked her. Lan got her to a seat at the table, bringing her over by Clay. She sat down slowly, her wide dark eyes staring blankly down at the tabletop. Lan caught Clay's eye, "Keep an eye on her for a second, okay?"

Clay nodded solemnly.

Lan turned and headed over to the staircase. He needed to check out the upper level and make sure no one was hiding up there. He made his way quietly up the staircase, the black metal railing cool to the touch. He neared the top of the stairs, peering over the railing. No one was in sight.

The upper loft level ran about half the length of the room, stopping before the fireplace area. He was met with a wall of books, and a carpeted empty loft. A single armchair sat towards the end of the loft. There was no one there, and there didn't seem to be anywhere for a person to hide. He walked up and down the length of the bookcases keeping an eye out for anything that looked odd. Maybe a false wall? Maybe if he pressed or pulled the right book, the bookcase would swing open, revealing a doorway. He recalled what the prompt had said about Hammond Jr being an inventor, about the hidden doors and secret rooms, but nothing stood out to him up here. He gave up after a few minutes and made his way back down the stairs.

Clay caught his eye immediately; he had clearly been waiting for his return. Lan shook his head at him. "Nothing," he said shortly as he returned to the table.

Clay nodded, his shoulders relaxed slightly, as he turned back to the conversation at the table. Lan took the open seat on the other side of Darcy, peering at her as he sat down. She turned and met his eyes; she looked like she was all there, this time. He gave her a stiff smile. "You okay?"

Darcy nodded at him, not returning his smile. "I'm fine. Sorry to freak everyone out," she said, looking over at Bee as she spoke.

"Don't worry about it," Lan replied, watching her closely. "Darcy, what did you see, exactly?"

Darcy looked at him, her eyes growing wider, flickering back and forth, like she was remembering. "Something that didn't make sense," she said finally. She gave him a tired smile. "It was nothing, Lan; I was imagining things."

He stared at her for a long moment. "Okay," he said finally. "But if you want to talk about it, let me know, okay?"

Darcy nodded at him, still smiling. She turned back to the table. The others were laughing and chatting, passing out cards.

Alex approached, set Lan's beer glass in front of him, and smiled. "Drink up my friend," he said smiling. "The night is young."

Lan groaned inwardly. He lifted his glass and held it out to Alex. "Cheers." Alex clinked his glass against Lan's, nodding at him.

"Cheers."

They drank together, Lan drained his glass this time. Alex laughed and clapped him on the back. "That's the Lan I remember." He pointed at him as he walked away, "I'm getting you another one."

Lan shrugged. He might as well, it couldn't make his headache any worse at this point. Alex was already gone, heading over to the mini bar beside the desk. Lan wondered if Alex had made them install it just for their purposes, or if it was already here.

He sighed, watching Darcy's face from the corner of his eyes. He wouldn't push her. She clearly wasn't ready to talk about it. And he wouldn't admit it to the others, but there had been a split second when he had first turned his head to look at her, where he thought he saw something moving on the stairs.

12.

Clay

Ten years later, but still the same damn thing. He had to laugh at the irony of it, at the very least. He hadn't honestly expected anything to happen between him and Bee this weekend, but he couldn't help but feel hopeful at the thought of seeing her again. Having a chance to reconnect. Instead, he had spent the first day of the trip watching her fall for some other guy. It was like college all over again. He knew what they said about insanity; it was doing the same thing over and over again but expecting a different result.

Clay felt somewhat relieved when the others were ready to head up to bed. He'd tried to keep a good-natured look on his face, but he was getting sick of watching them together, and he was starting to feel bitter. He wasn't looking forward to lying in a dark room alone in this castle, it was creepy as fuck, but at least he would have a break from watching Bee batt her eyelashes at this random guy. Clay didn't even remember him at all from State, so that's how much of an impression the guy left on him, but maybe she did.

He walked next to Darcy as the group left the main common area. He'd noticed Lan kept glancing over at her all night like he was keeping an eye on her. It made him nervous.

Alex, of all people, had managed to lift the group's mood, bringing up funny stories and inside jokes, reminding them of the good times at State. He hadn't brought up anything weird, thankfully, not like at dinner. At one point, one of Alex's assistants, who he introduced as Maya, had stopped by. She had a basket with her and asked that they all place their cell phones in it. They had parted with them reluctantly.

Austin made a stink about needing to keep his in case there was an emergency, because of his kids, but Alex had put his foot down, insisting it was in the waiver they signed, and he had no choice. Austin eventually handed it over to Maya. She had smiled apologetically and wished them all good luck. They'd played card games and had more than a few drinks. Clay wasn't wearing his watch, and since he'd given up his cell phone, he had no clue what time it was when they finally decided to call it a night.

Clay glanced over at Darcy again. She seemed to be off somewhere else, inside her own head. Which, to be fair, wasn't unusual at all for her. But she had a worn-out, tired look to her that he didn't remember noticing when they met up on the boat earlier. There were dark circles under her eyes, and she looked drained somehow. But it was late, he reminded himself. She was probably just tired. A good night's sleep would do them all good.

The group was quiet, somewhat subdued again, as they tromped up the stairs. Once they made it to the guest wing, it took them a minute to recall which room was whose. Alex called out to them from his doorway, causing them to step back into the hall.

"So, remember guys, breakfast will be at 8:00 tomorrow; try to make it down for breakfast so you are ready to go and not playing on an empty stomach."

"When does the actual escape room challenge start?" Lan asked.

Alex grinned at him. "It already has baby... we're locked in right now." Lan's eyebrows raised, and a few people murmured to each other. "But I figured we'd get going after breakfast; give everyone a chance to eat first. I'll have the written version of the escape room prompt out on the table for you to look over first thing."

The group broke up, each of them going their separate ways. Alex called out to them one more time. "Don't forget... don't leave your rooms at night... you don't want the Besomar to get you." He made a spooky ghost noise and retreated into his room, closing the door behind him.

Clay turned to go check on Darcy one more time. Bee brushed past him, heading down the hall to Cam; she grabbed

A.C. Hessenauer

her arm. "He's such an asshole." She rolled her eyes. "But seriously, I'm kind of nervous to sleep by myself."

Cam gave her a look, then one corner of her mouth tipped up in a lopsided smile. "I had a feeling that might happen. Do you really want to do a sleepover?"

Bee smiled, blushing a little. "Yes. I know you think I'm being silly, but seriously...I'm freaked out. Do you mind?"

Clay saw Rahul had paused in his doorway, watching them with one eyebrow raised. At least she wasn't asking him to stay with her. Clay smirked a little to himself. He continued down to Darcy's room. Her door was still open. He poked his head around the frame and found her; she was standing in front of the bank of windows, staring out at the darkness.

"Hey Darc," he said quietly, so as not to startle her. She didn't react at all though. He stepped into the room. "Darcy, are you good?"

She turned to him this time, a strange expression on her face. "Yeah, I'm fine Clay, thanks." He watched her for another few seconds, then nodded.

"Okay." He looked back towards the door. "I'm just down the hall if you need anything. Turn left, and I'm the third door on the right, okay?"

She looked back at him, her dark eyes solemn. She nodded slowly.

"Okay. Good night," Clay said.

"Good night," she said back, giving him a small smile. He turned and left the room, closing the door behind him.

Clay felt uneasy, but he didn't quite know why. The whole Besomar thing was ridiculous; just a silly folk story. But the feeling he got from the house? From Darcy's behavior tonight? He didn't like any of it one bit.

The hallway was mercifully empty as he made his way down to his room. At least he knew Cam would keep an eye on Bee tonight. And hopefully Darcy would go right to sleep. If everyone just stayed in their rooms and got some sleep, things would probably look better in the morning.

Clay quickly got ready for bed. He was glad they each had their own little bathroom attached to their room. They'd done enough sharing of bathrooms in college to last a lifetime; no need to return to that for the weekend.

Clay climbed into bed, thinking he would fall asleep quickly, but in the end, he lay there for quite some time. Staring up at the ceiling, listening to the waves pounding outside in the distance, and the howling of the wind. His ears strained for any sounds outside his room, within the castle walls. But he heard nothing. The walls must be thick, he thought. He thought of Bee, lying next to Cam down the hall. He wished he had the guts to get through to her somehow, make her see what she meant to him and what he should mean to her. Eventually he drifted off into an uneasy sleep.

13.

Cam

Cam stared down at the prompt in front of her, a frown on her face. She had expected to find certain letters underlined, or in bold, or something of the sort. Figured they could string the letters together to get their first clue. But there was nothing. It seemed to be normal text; just the script typed out of the recording they had listened to at the restaurant. She rolled her eyes at the description of the Besomar. She still didn't get what it was supposed to be.

Sighing, she turned her focus back to her plate. She had gone with eggs and bacon and some fruit. She sipped her coffee gratefully. At least they would eat well while they were here. The breakfast spread was impressive. But she didn't know what else she had expected, with Alex involved. She found herself wondering how much of the weekend he had orchestrated. Was this really some outside company he had hired putting this on for them? The groundsman, she couldn't remember his name now, had said they hadn't hosted any other escape weekends in the castle.

The others seemed quiet this morning; there wasn't much socializing going on as they munched on their food and looked over the prompt. Austin was sitting over by the fireplace, showing Lan how to start a fire. Apparently, Bee had lost interest and decided not to join them. Bee had woken Cam several times during the night; tossing and turning. She'd hit her in the face once when she flung her arm out. They'd had a good laugh about it this morning. Cam acted annoyed, but she didn't really mind. If she were being honest, she had felt a little uneasy thinking about being all alone in her room for the night. The castle was beautiful, but it did give her the creeps, just a little.

Lan and Austin settled down on the couches now; watching the fruits of their labor, sipping coffee. She could see the steam rising from their mugs from here. It was definitely colder in the common area this morning than it had been last night. She was grateful she had packed heavily and had a sweatshirt to throw on today.

They didn't seem to be speaking to each other much, she noticed, watching the guys staring at the fire. Lan and Austin had always had a strained relationship. They were competitive, she thought, in a way the other guys weren't. She wasn't entirely sure that Lan *liked* Austin, to be honest. He seemed to find him a bit too full of himself. He had always been more than ready to listen when she wanted to vent about Austin being a jerk. Had encouraged it, really. She knew he had always been somewhat bothered by how Austin had treated her. And maybe that was all it was.

Cam finished her food and grabbed her coffee, bringing it with her over to join them on the couches. Alex had told them to just leave their dishes out and that staff would come by and clean everything up later. So, they weren't truly locked in, she reminded herself. Staff would be coming and going, bringing them food and clearing the table. She plopped down into the armchair, claiming the seat closest to the fire. She sighed as she sat down, causing Lan to raise an eyebrow at her. Austin gave her a tight smile and a nod.

"You alright Cam?" Lan asked, taking another sip of his coffee.

She nodded at him and sighed again, looking around the room. "Yeah, I'm fine. Just ready to get going, that's all. We're wasting time. And I'd really like to beat Alex's stupid escape room by lunch." They both chuckled at that.

"Wouldn't that be something?" Austin grinned; he looked over at the table. "Where is Alex, anyway?" Cam followed his gaze and saw that he wasn't seated at the table with the others. She shrugged. She hadn't seen him leave the room. Her gaze went over to the board with their names on it. It was one of the first things they had checked when they came downstairs this morning. Alex had made a big deal about going over to the board to see if anyone had any strikes yet. The lightbulbs all remained off.

Alex appeared in the doorway, practically skipping as he entered the room. Cam sighed a third time. "Oh my... he is having way too much fun."

He grinned over at her. "And you're not having enough fun, Cam." He pointed at her, grinning, and added "Yet." He made his way over to the table.

She laughed, "Oh, I can't wait, Alex. Super excited over here." She watched him join the others at the table. He walked around, checking on everyone. People looked like they were getting ready to wrap up breakfast. "When can we get started, by the way?" She called out to him.

He strode over their way; leaning with one hand on the back of the couch facing the fire, he glanced at his wristwatch and looked over at the wooden door that led outside. "We're just waiting on our final guest to join us now."

Cam looked over at Austin. He froze with his coffee mug halfway to his lips. He caught her watching him and continued to take a sip.

"I got an update last night to expect her around 9:00. I figured we might as well wait for her before we start."

Austin was staring at the fire again, pointedly avoiding looking at anyone. He looked less than thrilled.

Lan cleared his throat. "Oh okay... I wasn't thinking she'd get here first thing."

Cam and Austin both turned to him, and their eyes met again. Cam didn't recall Alex ever saying anything about what time Miranda was supposed to arrive.

Lan stood up and walked over towards the table. He wandered around aimlessly for a minute before grabbing a seat.

They sat around for a while; Cam would have normally spent the time scrolling on her phone, but since it had been taken away, she paced around the room impatiently. Eventually, she made her way over to the little library area. She scanned the titles of books on the shelves on the lower level first. Then she made her way up the spiral staircase to the loft level. Once there, she began to pull books off the shelf at random. She peeked over the railing, down at the others. She was getting bored and anxious to get started. She checked her watch; it was almost 9:30 now, and still no Miranda. Alex was pacing back and forth behind the couches now, looking disgruntled. She went back to examining the bookshelves with a sigh.

Eventually, she heard Alex's voice; he was speaking sharply to someone. She peered over the railing again and saw he was on the landline phone. He must have called his assistant to see what the holdup was. "Alright, fine." She heard him snap. "Get her here as soon as you can." Then he slammed the receiver down.

Interesting, Cam thought. Was there some sort of logistical delay with Miranda's arrival, or was she causing the delay?

She heard Alex's voice again, louder this time. "Okay everyone." She peeped over the railing again. "We're not waiting any longer, we're going to get started. Miranda will join us when she gets here."

Cam made her way down the stairs to join the others; she held onto the railing, moving carefully down the narrow steps. Darcy smiled at her from the table. Cam walked over to her. "Ready?"

Darcy nodded. Alex waved them over, and the group gathered together by the door to the main entrance.

"Alright, so, we're finally getting started here. I suggest we start by looking around this room first and then move on to the main entrance from here."

Cam spoke up, "I was just sort of randomly checking the bookshelves; mostly upstairs. I took books off the shelf, just making sure none of them were somehow a secret switch or something." The others glanced over at the library area. "No luck so far," she added.

Clay nodded over to the desk. "There's a lot of stuff on the desk. I noticed last night when I was looking for the cards. Didn't look through it yet."

Alex nodded approvingly. "Okay, Clay, do you want to start with the desk then? Darcy, why don't you join him? Lan, maybe you too." He pointed to them in turn. It looked like he was making himself the unofficial leader. Cam looked around the room. The desk was their best option in here for a clue. There wasn't much else to look through.

"I'll come too," she said. "Maybe everyone else can start looking in the main entrance area? We might as well split up, cover more ground more quickly."

Alex nodded, and they split into two groups. Cam joined Clay, and Darcy by the desk. Lan still sat at the dining table, looking mildly bored.

Cam peered over Clay's shoulder at the desk. He was right; there was quite a lot there. The landline phone, obviously, sat in the right-hand corner. There was a pile of the copies of the prompt sitting next to it. There was a stack of old books in the other corner, an ancient-looking quill pen lying next to crinkled, yellowed sheets of paper, which were covered in script and drawings of what appeared to be medical images. She saw bones of various types, and a drawing of the musculature of the human face with labels. There was a handheld golden magnifying glass lying there as well. A small globe sat on the desk, and a candle holder with a half-burned taper that was unlit.

Clay started on the desk drawers, pulling them open one at a time and rifling through the objects inside. "Check for keys specifically," Cam instructed him. Darcy stood behind them, staring back over at the library area, a blank look on her face. Cam grabbed the top page of the handwritten medical pages and the magnifying glass and began to scan the text for any clues. She found nothing on the first page.

Sighing, she grabbed the second page. She studied the drawings. This page showed the lower portion of a human skull; the teeth were still intact. She noted the canine teeth appeared to be oddly elongated. There were more labels on this page. She scanned the cursive text and noticed with a little jolt that there was a letter underlined on this page. A capital letter "A" with a small line underneath it. She quickly scanned the rest of the page and found the letter "p" also underlined, lowercase, this time. That was all on this page. She quickly grabbed the next, reaching over Clay's head as he searched through the desk drawers.

Cam found an "o" next. Chanting "A-p-o" to herself in her head, she found an "l" underlined. And a second one after that. She found another "o" on the very last page, and that seemed to be it. "Okay guys," she said, "I've got letters underlined here...A-p-o-l-l-o..." she repeated out loud. "Apollo!" she said excitedly.

Clay stopped and looked up at her. "Okay, sweet. Apollo..." he looked around the room, getting to his feet. "What does that mean?" He looked back at the desk. "I didn't see any keys."

"There's a statue of Apollo."

They turned to look at Darcy. She was staring over in the direction of the spiral staircase still. She turned and pointed towards the door that led to the main entrance. "Out there."

"Nice," Cam said, smiling at her, "Good one Darcy. Let's go check it out."

They moved out into the main entrance hall, and Darcy led them over to one of the large statues that lined the back wall. The others seemed to be wandering around on their own, combing the room for clues. "We may have something," Clay called out to them. They came over and gathered around the statue Darcy was pointing to.

It was a stone statue of a naked man. Cam was glad Darcy recognized it; the statue stood in a line of similar-looking statues. She never would have known which was supposed to be Apollo; even though she'd certainly heard of the famous statue before. The statue had one arm raised aloft and appeared to be holding something in a closed fist. Darcy was peering at his hand; she reached up and poked whatever it was from underneath, and Cam saw a rolled-up piece of paper slide out the top of the statue's hand.

"Nice." She heard Alex exclaim from somewhere behind them. "What does it say?"

Darcy unrolled the scroll of paper and skimmed over it. She cleared her throat and read, "What can travel around the world while staying in one spot?" They looked from Darcy to each other and scanned the room around them.

"What travels around the world..." Lan repeated. He walked in circles in front of the main entrance. They thought and paced for a while, but no one seemed to be able to think of something that stayed in one spot. Eventually, Lan walked over to the front door, "Is this even actually locked?" He pulled on the large metal handles. The door shuddered slightly but didn't open. He examined the door handles more closely. "There's no lock on this side..." he leaned back and pulled harder on the handles, "... feels like it's padlocked on the other side." He turned to look at them and found Cam's eyes. "Looks like we won't be leaving through the front door then."

"There are plenty of other ways out of the castle," Alex spoke up, watching Lan from the other side of the room. "And following the clues is the only way we get out." He eyed Lan darkly.

Cam sighed, racking her brain again, repeating the clue to herself.

"Something on an airplane?" Austin suggested after a while. The others started throwing out guesses. "A package, or mail, travels all over..." he mused a few minutes later.

"I know!" Clay said, "A stamp. A stamp stays in the same spot on an envelope. There was a stack of old letters in one of the drawers in the desk. They had stamps on them." Clay and a few of the others rushed back into the other room. Cam followed them. They quickly found the stack of letters and started examining the stamps. They were mostly butterflies and moths, a few were of old boats. Nothing that stood out particularly.

"Maybe the clue is on the other side of the stamps?" Cam suggested; they started carefully peeling the stamp off of each letter. Cam glanced over at Lan as he sauntered up to join them. "I have to say, I'm not super impressed," she whispered to him. "These seem like pretty generic clues so far. Like what you'd find in any escape room."

Lan shrugged. "Yeah, I guess I'd agree. Although, I mean, there's only so much you can do, right? With puzzles and clues like this, they're bound to all be kind of similar."

There was a number written on the back of each stamp. Someone grabbed a notebook and pencil from the desk and wrote all the numbers down. "Okay," Alex said, "So I'm guessing we're looking for some sort of lock that needs a number code, or maybe a safe or something?" The others nodded their agreement as he looked around at them. "Maybe we spread out and start to look for something that needs numbers or a code to unlock?"

They spread out and started the search anew. Cam glanced over to see Rahul and Bee were sticking close together, wandering around somewhat aimlessly, chatting and laughing. Bee didn't seem to be that into finding the clues. *Big surprise.*

They wandered around for what felt like fifteen minutes or more, searching for anything with a combination lock or a keypad on it and coming up empty. Finally, Cam heard voices shouting in the distance. She had wandered back to the library area, taking random books off the shelf again. She bounded down the spiral stairs as fast as she could and ran out into the main entryway, passing Rahul and Bee as she went.

There was a small group huddled at the top of the staircase, around the door. It was open.

She joined them, slightly out of breath. "Awesome, good job guys." She looked down at the handle and saw an open combination lock hanging there.

Alex was smiling broadly. He looked around, asking "Is everyone here?" He eyed Darcy climbing the stairs below them, and Bee and Rahul trailing behind her. Austin and Clay were already there. "Okay, let's go, we've made it out of our first room."

The group filed through the doorway, Cam let the others pass her, waiting for Bee and Rahul to catch up. She glanced over at Austin; he was lingering on the other side of the doorway, his eyes on the far entrance to the common room.

He was looking for Miranda, Cam realized with a jolt. Waiting for her. His eyes met hers, and she felt a flash of fire travel through her gut. He gave her a half-hearted smile and held a hand out to motion her through the door ahead of him. Cam turned her back on him and walked through the doorway. She didn't smile back.

14.

Darcy

Darcy followed the others into the next room. She realized it wasn't a room at all but a long, wide corridor with multiple doors on each side. They quickly spread out, scanning the space. Only one door appeared to be open, she saw: at the far end of the hallway. She drifted towards it, eyeing the paintings on the walls as she went.

She entered the room to find a small study. A desk sat on the far wall, underneath a large bank of windows. The lights were off in the room, aside from one bright floor lamp. It stood next to the desk and arched high over it, flooding the top of the desk with a warm pool of golden light. Darcy saw what sat in the makeshift spotlight and froze.

She knew what it was from here without taking another step into the room; an ancient-looking Ouija board, its planchette sat off to one side, waiting. Darcy scanned the rest of the room: more floor-to-ceiling bookshelves. A pair of small accent chairs off to one side. Then she heard a faint tapping sound. Her ears strained, and she peered around the dark room, checking the corners. It was coming from inside the room... she heard it again. It became more frequent, picking up speed. Darcy felt herself shrinking, she pulled her arms into her chest, recoiling. What was in here? She felt movement, a rush of air behind her.

Clay moved past her, stepping further into the room. He looked around and she followed his gaze past the desk to the windows. "Oh, it's starting to rain," he said, almost absentmindedly. "Was this door already open?" He turned to her, a quizzical look on his face.

Darcy swallowed audibly and felt her muscles relax as she dropped her arms to her sides. She nodded slowly at him. "Yeah, the door was open." She looked back at the windows; she could see it now: fat splotches of rain pattered the windows—just raindrops. *God, what was wrong with her?*

Ever since they'd arrived at the castle, she had been feeling so odd. And the dreams she'd had last night were disturbing. She had followed someone, or something, roaming the hallways of the castle. It had been searching, hunting for something. And it had felt hungry, somehow. She shuddered. It was just her imagination; the creepy atmosphere of the castle was getting to her, and she was letting it. She stood up straighter and smiled more confidently at Clay. He was looking at her with a funny expression on his face. He smiled back, seemed to look reassured, and turned his attention to the desk.

Clay walked over and picked up something long and cylindrical that sat next to the Ouija board. Darcy realized it was a piece of paper as he began to unfold it. He looked down, his eyes moving back and forth as he read. A clap of thunder sounded in the distance. Darcy strained; she could just barely hear the waves against the rocks below the castle from here.

Clay looked up at her after a moment. "There are a bunch of riddles; questions, on here." He had a puzzled look on his face. "Some of them seem like classic riddles, but some of them are about us."

They stared at each other. Then Alex brushed past her, joining Clay at the desk. He was followed by Cam and Austin. Darcy turned to see Bee and Rahul behind her as well. Bee entered the room and hung back, just inside the doorway, leaning against the frame. Rahul stood behind her in the doorway, his arms spread on either side, propping himself up. He saw Darcy watching them and nodded to her.

"Okay, guys," Alex said. "It looks like we've got a set of riddles here. Who has the notebook?" They looked around at each other blankly.

"I think we left it on the desk in the common room," Bee spoke up. She glanced up at Rahul, and he nodded.

"I'll run and go get it." He disappeared back down the hallway.

"Okay, first one," Alex said, clearly not wanting to waste a moment of time. "Read it to us, Clay."

Clay looked up at him briefly, and began, "Okay, first one; What is so fragile that saying its name breaks it?" He looked up at them. Everyone fell quiet.

"I don't know," Alex said, shaking his head and looking frustrated. Rahul returned with the notebook, slightly out of breath. "Rahul, write a number one and leave a blank space. We'll come back to it."

Rahul nodded and started writing in the notebook.

"Okay, the second one," Clay continued, "I am a voice without a throat. I speak in waves but not in boats. I whisper secrets of the deep, in me both giants and tiny sleep. What-"

Cam interrupted him before he could finish; "That's an easy one, the ocean." The others thought for a moment and nodded; Rahul wrote the answer down.

Clay continued scanning the page and chuckled. "Um, this next one's kind of weird; some of these are about us." He looked up at Alex briefly as he spoke. "Who was only included because he was Austin's roommate?" The group was awkwardly silent. Then Clay mumbled, "Alex," glancing over at Rahul. Alex glared at him and then at Rahul as well.

"Nice." He frowned, looking out the window. "Wow, good to know. Thanks, Clay."

Clay's brows creased. "I mean, I assume that has to be the answer, right?" He looked around at them. "You and Austin were roommate's freshman year; you went in blind. After that, we got the apartment." He shrugged. "Who else could it be?"

Alex nodded. "Okay, fine. What's the next one?" He crossed his arms in front of his chest.

Clay cleared his throat and continued, "What can't talk but will reply when spoken to?"

"I know this one," Austin mumbled. "An echo." Clay looked at him with one eyebrow raised. "I've heard that one before." Austin shrugged.

"Okay, cool, um," Clay looked back down and continued reading, "Um...who is missing?" He looked up at them. "That's all it says for that one."

They looked around at each other. "Well, Miranda, obviously," Cam said after a moment. "But...wasn't she supposed to be here by now? How would they have known that?"

They all turned to look at Alex. He shrugged, "Heck if I know." He looked over at Rahul, "Go ahead and write it down; it's the best guess." He looked back over at Clay expectantly.

"Alright, ah..." Clay found his place on the page again, "I can run but not walk, have a mouth but can't talk, have a head but can't weep, have a bed but never sleep. What am I?"

Darcy smiled to herself. "A river," she said, her voice coming out almost as a whisper. They all turned to look at her. Clay nodded his head, looking impressed. "That was one of the riddles from the kid's version of *The Hobbit*," she explained. "I had an old cassette tape of it. I used to listen to it every night while I fell asleep."

"Sweet," Clay said. "Man, we're nailing these. Okay, last one," he looked down and the smile fell off his face. "Um, I..." he said. "I'm not going to read this one."

"What?" Austin chuckled. He'd sunk into one of the accent chairs and leaned forward now to see Clay. "Come on, man, we need to get the answer."

"I know the answer," Clay said, looking flustered. He rolled up the paper and set it down on the desk. 'It's Bee." He looked out the window, refusing to look at them. Rahul stared at him, then looked over at Bee. She gave him a grim smile, and he leaned down and wrote her name on the paper.

"Okay," Rahul cleared his throat, "We need to go back to the first one though. Can you read that one again?"

Alex leaned over and grabbed the paper. Clay tried to snatch it out of his hand, but Alex was too quick. He unrolled it and scanned to the bottom of the page. He looked over at Clay and chuckled.

Clay glared at him. "You're an asshole sometimes, you know that?"

"What?" Alex shrugged, "What did I do?"

"Obviously, you told them to put that in there. How else would they have known?" Clay's voice was rising now; Darcy saw him clench his fists. She sighed and jumped slightly as another crack of thunder pealed, sounding closer this time. The raindrops continued to pelt the windows.

"Oh yeah?" Alex asked, sneering at him, "And I guess I told them to put that one in about me being Austin's roommate, too, then, huh?"

Clay shrugged, "You tell me, man. This is your stupid weekend."

"Oh, it's stupid now?" Alex clenched his jaw, "Nice, and I'm the asshole."

"Come on guys," Cam spoke up, as she reached out and took the paper from Alex's outstretched hand. "Let's focus." She looked down at the paper, then up briefly at Clay, before continuing. "Okay, the first one was, what is so fragile that saying its name breaks it?"

They spent several moments in silence, during which Alex and Clay continued to glare at each other before someone finally came up with the answer.

Rahul spoke up from the doorway. His deep voice caused Darcy to jump a little. "I think I might know; could it be silence?" The others turned to him. "You, know, you break the silence by saying its name..." He looked hopefully over at Alex.

Alex nodded thoughtfully. "I mean, yeah, that makes sense. Okay, write it down," he directed.

Rahul wrote the answer down and looked down at the list in his hands, frowning. He glanced over at the Ouija board. "I'm assuming this involves the Ouija board somehow...but it seems like it would be super difficult and complicated to spell out all the answers on there. Do you think we combine them somehow?" He looked up at the others, expectantly.

Cam was nodding to herself, "Here, let me see the list," he handed it over to her and she scanned it thoughtfully. "Yeah, maybe we take the first letter of each answer? Use that to spell out a word. Maybe it's like, what's it called? An anagram? If we combine all the first letters."

"Good idea." Rahul was nodding, "Okay, do you want to write out the first letters on the next page? Start fresh with those."

Cam got to work writing out the first letter of each answer, flipping back and forth between the pages. Darcy wandered over to the second armchair and sat down gratefully next to Austin. She was feeling somewhat weak and tired; although she'd slept, the dreams had made her toss and turn. She'd never fully woken in between but could feel herself moving restlessly all night. She gave Austin a weak smile.

He leaned over to her. "How's it going, Darcy?"

She smiled at him again. "Good. I'm just a little tired today." She looked over at the Ouija board. "I had a lot of weird dreams last night." She stopped there, then continued, "about the castle." Austin gave her a long look, his blue eyes peering into hers.

"So did I, actually." He looked at her another moment before following her gaze to where it kept returning over to the pool of light on the desk. "What did you dream about?" He asked her, dropping his voice even lower.

The volume in the room was increasing; Cam and Alex were arguing about something. Darcy looked over at them, momentarily pulling her gaze away from Austin. "I... I'm not sure," she finished lamely. She studied him again; he had dark circles under his eyes. He didn't look so good actually.

"Are *you* okay, Austin?" She asked, studying him.

He raised his eyebrows in surprise. "Yeah, yeah, of course," he leaned back, chuckling a little. "I'm totally fine."

"Okay, okay," Alex held up his hands, then turned towards Rahul, leaning in the doorway again. "Why don't you take a turn looking at it, Rahul? Fresh eyes, okay?" He gave Cam a look, and she snapped her mouth shut, clearly about to retort.

Rahul nodded and leaned past Cam to grab the notebook back from Alex. He frowned, looking down at the letters on the page. "Pencil?" he asked, holding a hand out towards the room in general. Cam slapped the pencil down into his open palm. Rahul took it, tapping the eraser against the edge of the paper, before tucking it behind his ear. He stepped out into the hallway, pacing back and forth in front of the doorway. He was out there for several minutes. Darcy leaned back in her chair and gazed out the window, listening to the rain and the faint surf in the background.

"Ha!" Rahul exclaimed suddenly, popping back into the room again. "I've got it! This should have been obvious,

God." He shook his head, grinning around at them. "It's Besomar; the letters spell the name of the demon thing haunting the castle."

He held up the notebook for them, showing the word "Besomar" scrawled in large letters across the bottom of the page.

Darcy scanned the page; he was right; the letters spelled out Besomar, which made sense.

"So, what next?" He asked, looking over at the Ouija board. "We gotta summon this thing on that?"

As one, they turned towards the Ouija board.

15.

Bee

Lan peered over Bee's shoulder from the doorway, brushing past Rahul. She heard his voice chime in out of nowhere right next to her ear.

"Sweet."

She turned and peered up at him incredulously; he was easily a head and a half taller than her at least.

He grinned down at her. "You'll be all over that, right Bee?" He nudged her arm and chuckled.

Where had he been? She hadn't noticed he was gone until he reappeared. She gave him a pointed look, which he seemed to either not notice, or ignore. "Yeah," she murmured, turning back to look at the board sitting ominously in the pool of light. "I'm not touching that thing."

Rahul chucked from the hallway. "Didn't think so."

Alex nudged his way closer to the Ouija board. "Well, I'm not scared of a piece of cardboard. Although I don't see how this is going to do anything." He peered around the board and ran his hands along the edges, lifting it slightly off the desk to peer under it. Then he ran a hand in the air back and forth over the board. "It doesn't seem to be connected to anything..." he trailed off and shrugged, reaching over to grab the planchette. He looked over at Cam. "Ready?" He raised his eyebrows at her.

She hesitated for only a moment before reaching out and placing two fingers on the edge of the planchette. She touched it delicately; like she expected it to be hot. To burn her.

Alex grinned wickedly at her as she reached out her arm. Bee felt herself shudder a bit involuntarily. "Austin," he called over to where Austin sat in the armchair next to Darcy. Darcy looked paler than usual, Bee thought. But then again, so did Austin, as he turned to swivel his head towards Alex. Maybe it was just the lighting in here. They both looked awful like they hadn't slept in days.

"What?" Austin sighed.

Alex rolled his eyes a little. "Get over here."

Austin sighed again, and slowly got to his feet. He made his way over to the desk. He stared down at the Ouija board, then looked at Cam. She watched him expectantly. He reached over her shoulder and placed a finger on the planchette as well, leaving space for someone else to stand behind him.

Bee felt Lan push past her as he made his way over to the desk. "What," he said, "do we think this doesn't work without all of us or something?" He laughed as he said it like it was silly. But that certainly seemed to be the feeling Bee was getting as well. Why would Alex need anyone else to do it with him?

She felt Rahul start to move past her as well, but she reached out and placed a hand on his arm, stopping his forward motion. He looked at her, a puzzled expression on his face. "Don't," she said under her breath. "Don't touch that thing."

He gave her a look, but she didn't budge, staring back at him sternly. He raised an eyebrow, and she felt him relax, rocking back on his heels, as he shook his head and looked away.

Fine, Bee thought. That's fine if he wanted to think she was being silly. She wasn't letting him get anywhere near it. If they truly needed all of them to make this stupid thing work, well, then they'd just be stuck here. They wouldn't make it any further. They could hang out in the common area and drink until the crew came and let them out Sunday night, for all she cared.

"Come on Clay," Alex called out. Clay looked over at Bee, and she shook her head at him. She watched his gaze slide down to where her hand still rested on Rahul's arm. Then he met her eyes again, and turned, and joined the others. She sighed and glanced at Rahul. He gave her a grim smile back.

"Darcy," Alex said, his voice softer, as he craned over the other's heads to look at Darcy.

Darcy shook her head no at him. "Go ahead without me," she said softly. She glanced briefly at Bee before dropping her eyes to the floor. So, Bee thought, she wasn't the only one who felt nervous about that stupid board.

"Okay," Alex sighed, "Ready? Let's do this slowly." The group chanted the letters out loud, as they slid the planchette slowly over the board, pausing at each letter before moving on to the next.

Bee jumped as a bright flash of light lit up the room; she looked up at the bank of windows behind the desk. That looked like it had been right outside. "M", the group kept going, a few of them looking up briefly. Thunder ripped through the air, and she could feel it reverberating in her chest. "A," the chant continued, and the floor itself seemed to shake beneath her. She gripped Rahul's arm tighter, digging her nails into his arm involuntarily. "R," They finished, and she heard it now.

It wasn't just the thunder, the floor was actually shaking, vibrating beneath her feet. She heard Darcy gasp and saw her jump up out of her chair, scrambling backward towards them. She moved just in time as Bee watched a hole open up in the floor where Darcy had been standing a second ago, right in front of the armchair she had been sitting in.

Rahul grabbed her by the shoulders as she teetered on the edge of the black square beneath them. "Holy shit," he said, dragging her back a step.

"Wow." Cam took a step towards the square of darkness. "They weren't kidding about hidden rooms." She hit a button on her watch, and crouching down, she stuck her arm down into the darkness below them. "There's a ladder." She called up to them.

"We're going to need flashlights or something," Clay murmured, leaning over her shoulder. "It's pitch black down there."

"Let's go look back in the common area," Lan suggested. "I think there were some flashlights in one of the desk drawers." Lan and Clay shuffled carefully past them to go look for the flashlights.

Bee watched Alex; he was standing over by the desk still, frowning down at the Ouija board. "But..." he said, "how..." he ran his hands over the board again, frowning over at the hole that had opened up in the floor, then back at the board again. "But that's not right..." he muttered, speaking out loud to himself. He crossed his arms over his chest, and looked up, peering around the room where the crown molding hit the ceiling. *Was he looking for a camera?* Bee wondered. And what did he mean, that it wasn't right? She opened her mouth to ask him when Clay and Lan reappeared behind them.

She, Rahul, and Darcy shuffled out of their way as they moved past them into the room. They both had two flashlights in their hands. They each kept one, and Austin and Alex ended up with the other two.

A brief argument ensued between Lan and Alex over who should go down first. Lan won in the end, as Alex rolled his eyes and gestured for him to go ahead. Lan held his flashlight upside down in one hand, gripping the sides of the ladder as he made his way down into the darkness. Alex held his flashlight out over him, trying to illuminate the ladder as he climbed down. Bee held her breath for a moment. Then she heard him call out from the bottom, somewhere far below them. "Made it! Send the next one down!"

Alex insisted on going next, handing his flashlight over to Rahul to hold for him while he climbed. Then Cam and Austin followed. Bee looked over at Darcy, gesturing for her to go ahead next. But Darcy just shook her head slightly. Bee looked at Rahul.

"I'll go first," he said, grinning at her. "Meet you at the bottom." He tucked the flashlight in his pocket and made his way down. Grinning at her once more before his head disappeared below the wooden floorboards.

Bee waited until she heard him calling up to her. She gave Darcy a brave smile and nodded once at Clay, who stood patiently next to her. He nodded back at her. Bee knelt on the floor, then backed over the edge, swinging one leg down, flailing until she placed her foot down gingerly in the dark onto the first rung she could find. She took a deep breath and began her descent.

She peered down below her, between her arms and legs, and saw the glow of flashlights in the dark. They looked farther away than she had anticipated. She felt her heart rate start to pick up and shook her head at herself. She was being silly. It was just a dark room, and probably the first of many in this stupid weekend. She had better get over it fast. Besides, there was nothing down there waiting for her in the dark. Nothing besides her friends.

She felt her grip tighten on the cold metal of the ladder. She continued to move steadily downwards, only lifting one appendage at any given time from where she made contact with the ladder. She couldn't fall that way, she told herself.

About halfway down, her foot slipped out from under her as she went to move down to the next rung. She gasped loudly, her heart leaping into her throat.

"You okay Bee?" She heard Cam's voice calling up to her, and a second flashlight beam swung over her feet.

"I'm okay!" She called back. She needed to calm down, she could feel herself starting to tremble a little. "My foot slipped, that's all."

"Just take it slow," Cam called back. "You're almost there."

Bee took another deep breath and willed herself to continue moving. She went slower this time and was extra careful to only lift her foot when both hands and her other foot were steady.

She finally heard voices getting closer. She looked down again and realized she was almost at head level. She felt Rahul's hands reach up to her waist, and he steadied her as she descended the last few feet, until she was back on the ground. She dropped her hands onto her knees. "Phew," she breathed, looking up at Rahul and laughing a little, "Well, that was fun, wasn't it?"

"Good job," he said laughing, his voice echoing around them. It felt like they were in a large open space, from the way sound carried. Bee glanced around and saw flashlights bobbing away in the distance. Rahul followed her gaze. "They're searching for a light switch."

"Coming down!" They glanced up at the sound of Clay's voice calling faintly above them. Rahul found Darcy descending the ladder and trained his flashlight beam on her.

They waited together at the bottom for both Darcy and Clay to descend. Clay was about halfway down the ladder when light suddenly flooded the room. Bee squeezed her eyes shut, cringing as she opened them to let her eyes start to adjust.

"Wow," she heard Rahul murmur next to her. She turned and spun around the room, taking it in through half-open eyes. They were in some kind of cathedral-looking space. A massive room, with a high ceiling and what looked like a huge organ on one wall, its long brass pipes shining. She took in plush red velvet curtains lining the space and more ancient-looking statues. Double doors stood wide open at the far end of the room. "Check out that organ." Rahul chuckled to Lan standing next to him, swinging his now unnecessary flashlight around the room, "Do you think the phantom of the opera lives here too?"

"What the hell?" Alex threw his hands up, as he paced around the center of the room, moving in a circle. "Really?" he yelled up at the walls, at the ceiling.

"What?" Austin asked him, brow furrowed. "Who are you talking to man? Something wrong?"

Alex glared over at Austin. "Um, yeah, you could say that." He glanced over at Rahul and Bee. "You could say someone has royally fucked up and is going to be fired the second I'm out of this castle." He raised his voice, sneering as he looked around the room. "Enjoy your last hours of employment!"

"God," Bee murmured, "Come on Alex,"

Austin shook his head. "Really man? What got messed up?" Austin looked around the room, as though he would be able to see something out of place.

"The entire fucking thing, that's what." Alex gestured around the room. "We're not even supposed to be down here yet, I don't know what the hell happened. But someone is going to pay for it."

Rahul and Bee glanced at each other; he looked nervous. He cleared his throat and said, "Come on, man, it'll be all right. Maybe something had to be changed up for some reason. We're all having fun still, let's just keep going."

Alex stared down Rahul, looking like he was going to bite his head off. "Did I ask you for your opinion?" he said coldly.

Bee saw Rahul stiffen. "No," he murmured, looking away into the distance. "No, you didn't."

"Yeah," Alex sneered, "That's what I fucking thought."

"What the hell Alex?" Cam chimed in, approaching them from the far side of the room. "Why are you treating him like that? It's not his fault your stupid game got messed up."

"Okay, you know what, that's the second time someone's called it stupid. If you think it's so stupid, why did you bother to fly out here on my dime? Huh?"

"Don't be a dick," Cam retorted, glaring back at him. "I came because you invited me, just like everyone else. What are we supposed to do now? Lick your boots and tell you how grateful we all are? Get over yourself." She snapped at him.

"Get over myself? Really?" Alex held his arms out, his expression incredulous.

"Yes." Cam glared back at him. "You think you're better than the rest of us. You always have."

Lan held up a hand, stepping between Cam and Alex. "Hey, come on guys, let's calm down. There's no need to argue."

Alex just laughed, eyeing Cam before turning away from her. "Sure, Cam. You keep telling yourself that. I'm the problem, not your massive inferiority complex."

"Hey," Bee called out, "Why don't you back off, Alex?" She walked over next to Cam. Cam barely turned to look at her. She was staring after Alex, shaking her head in disbelief.

"Why is he acting so weird?" Darcy asked softly. She was standing near the ladder still, next to Clay.

Bee swiveled to look over at Darcy before following Alex's movements as he crossed the room. Was he being weird though? Or was he just being Alex? Cam was right, he had always given her the impression that he thought highly of himself, thought he was somehow better than everyone else. His fame and success had clearly only made it worse. He was probably used to everyone bowing and scraping to him on set. She rolled her eyes to herself. It didn't mean they were going to do that. She couldn't believe the way he had talked to Rahul.

Rahul had fallen silent and drifted away from the rest of the group. He was off on the far side of the room. As she watched, he disappeared through the open double doors.

She sighed and turned back at the sound of Lan's voice. "Well, can we keep freaking going? This is going to take us ages if we don't stay focused."

Cam sighed and turned to him. "I agree. Let's keep going." Bee heard her add under her breath, "So we can get the fuck out of here." Cam turned and looked towards the doors. "Do we want to see what's through the doors?"

Lan nodded and they made their way towards the double doors, following in Rahul's footsteps. Austin looked back at Alex before sighing loudly. He tucked his hands in his pockets and turned to follow them.

He saw Bee still standing there, and as he moved past her, he paused and held out his elbow to her. "Come on Bee, let's go." He looked over his shoulder slightly. "Let's give him a minute." Bee nodded and gave Austin a weak smile, before slipping her arm through his.

They walked in silence, and she watched him out of the corner of her eyes. She took in the dark circles and the haggard look he seemed to have taken on in the hours since they'd arrived. "How're you holding up?" she asked him gently.

She felt him stiffen slightly and glance her way. Then he smiled at her. "You know me, Bee. I'm fine."

She nodded thoughtfully as they passed through the open doorway. "Yeah, I do," she said, "and you seem like you're having a tough time."

He grinned slightly, shaking his head as he stared down at their feet. He didn't respond back.

"Well," she continued, "You know I'm here if you ever need anything." He nodded, his jaw clenching slightly.

"Thanks," he murmured gruffly. She nodded to herself. Austin wasn't the type to open up. He hated talking about feelings of any kind. But still, it needed to be said. She was worried about him. He didn't look right. It was a lot to process, having Miranda showing up this weekend. She cringed inwardly. She really was not looking forward to the moment she arrived.

They found themselves in yet another long hallway. This one seemed to be the mirror of the one upstairs; a series of closed doors lined the hallway on either side of them. Once again, they found only one door was open at the far end of the hall. Bee felt a flicker of déjà vu as they approached the open door.

They peered through the doorway together, finding Rahul, Lan, and Cam already inside. This room was much larger than the little study upstairs had been. It looked like some sort of workshop or something Bee thought. Long workbenches lined each wall. There were tools hanging on peg boards on the walls, wires, and things hanging from the ceiling. It looked like every spare inch of space was taken up.

"Oh God." She heard Rahul mumble. "This is going to take us ages to look through."

Cam stood in the middle of the room, hovering over a round table. "I don't think that's necessary," she said, "Look," pointing down. They moved over to her side and saw an old-fashioned typewriter sitting on the table. Next to it, there was a large piece of yellowed paper, with some kind of series of bars and dashes written out. Each line had a letter at the end.

Austin scanned the paper. "It's Morse code," he said, looking over at Cam, "I know a bit of it, for emergency situations."

"Like what?" Bee asked, wrinkling her nose. "How would this help you in an emergency?"

Austin cleared his throat. "So, it's kind of an old-fashioned or crude way of communicating over long distances. Boats, for example, out on the ocean, could signal to each other with a series of flashing lights. The whole code is made up of either dashes, a long flash, or dots, a short flash. You can do this with light, or sound, or even voltages." Austin explained.

"Voltages?" Cam frowned at him.

"Yeah." He nodded, looking excited now, "That's how telegraph worked actually. It used a series of voltages, sent in Morse code, to spell out a message."

"Okay," Cam said, nodding. "So, this isn't a telegraph machine, just a typewriter, but maybe we can somehow use the typewriter with the Morse code for this next part." She looked excited now, too. She picked up the paper and scanned it. "What are we trying to spell out, though?" She looked back at Austin.

He just shrugged. "I have no idea, there must be another clue here somewhere." They turned and looked around the room.

"Like I said," Rahul sighed, "This is going to take a while."

Bee grinned at him. He smiled back at her. It looked like the sting from Alex's tone with him earlier was starting to wear off. She felt bad for him. She walked over to him, "Let's look around together." He nodded at her, and they began to stroll around the room.

Bee scanned the materials on the workbenches. She didn't know what they were looking for, but she figured she would try to take it all in and see if anything stood out as significant.

She perused the room for some time, Rahul staying close to her. They pointed things out to each other. There were a lot of cool-looking parts and things, but nothing stood out in particular to her. Cam and Austin were sitting together at the small round table now, hunched over the Morse code, typing out different things on the typewriter.

She heard Cam laughing suddenly and glanced over to see her smack Austin on the arm. He started laughing too. She grinned over at them, watching them. Seeing the two of them laughing together took her right back to State. They had been inseparable, always laughing about some joke that none of the rest of them were in on. Bee sighed then, watching them, thinking of how much had changed.

Rahul caught her watching them and grinned. "Penny for your thoughts?" He said, leaning over the workbench on one elbow. "You looked sad, just then."

She smiled at him, his dark eyes watching her. He spoke flippantly, but he looked like he was actually concerned. Did he really care that much? About a passing look of sadness on her face? She found herself wondering yet again if this guy was for real.

"Oh, it's nothing," she said, smiling at him. "I just thought..." she looked back over at Cam and Austin. "The two of them," she inclined her head towards them, "laughing together again, it just brought me back, that's all."

He nodded at her thoughtfully. "You all have a lot of history between you, don't you?" She nodded in agreement, watching as Cam slid the typewriter over in front of her while Austin protested, grinning at her.

Bee turned back to him. "Yes, we certainly do." She smiled at him for a moment before she remembered, and her smile faltered. Wasn't he supposed to be one of them? One of their group at State? Why had he sounded just then like he didn't know them, back then? She frowned at him slightly, her brow creasing.

"What?" He looked at her quizzically, the look of concern returning. "What did I say?"

Bee just shook her head, frowning. The certainty in her gut that she had never met him before was growing even stronger now, and it made her nervous. Why would Alex lie about something like that? And why on earth would Rahul play along?

She took a step backward and turned away from him. "Nothing," she said over her shoulder. "Let's keep looking." Just then she heard something, a deep rumbling sound, then high pitched... it was music, eerie somehow, drifting in from down the hallway.

She saw Cam and Austin pause, their heads turning towards the doorway at the sound. Cam looked down at the sheet of paper in her hand, then back at the doorway.

The notes seemed jumbled together, like a child playing or someone who didn't know how to read music.

"God, what a racket," she heard Rahul say behind her.

"That's it!" Cam exclaimed, grabbing Austin's arm. "Music notes. Those correspond to letters, right? I saw a page of sheet music sitting out on the organ, it looked hand-written!"

Austin smiled broadly at her, "I bet you're right, let's go." They quickly stood and rushed out of the room. Bee shrugged and turned back to Rahul. He was still watching her from across the room, eyeing her thoughtfully.

"Bee," he started to say, "I think we need to talk."

She stared back at him, her heart beating a loud tattoo suddenly in her chest. She felt her cheeks flush slightly. "Talk?" She murmured. "About what?" She suddenly felt nervous, her stomach twisting in a knot.

He hesitated now, seemed unsure of what to say next. "About... about... there's something I want to tell you," he said, taking a deep breath.

"Okay." Bee breathed deeply as well. "Is now really the best time?" She glanced towards the doorway. "The others will be back any minute."

"I know," he said, eyeing the doorway nervously now, "But I..."

He opened his mouth to start to explain, and just then, she heard Darcy scream.

16.

Clay

Alex was being a complete asshole again, out of nowhere. One little thing went wrong in his plans, and he was furious, blaming everyone else and threatening to fire people. So, he was a dick to his employees, just like he'd figured he would be. *Big surprise.* He rolled his eyes as Alex sat down at the organ, picking up the sheet music lying there and studying it thoughtfully. That guy didn't have a musical bone in his body. And the way he had talked to Rahul? It was ridiculous. It was almost like he was acting like an asshole on purpose.

Clay had gotten that same odd feeling at the restaurant; almost like Alex was putting on a show. But why would he do that? Clay mused. Putting on a show for who? For them? It didn't make any sense.

Clay shrugged and walked away from where Alex sat at the organ. He was smashing out random-sounding notes now. The pipes above vibrated and clanged loudly. To be honest, Clay was over the whole escape room thing. It had been fun at first, but it was already getting old, and he could feel himself starting to lose interest. He glanced around the room, noticing

Lan peering behind the red curtains that lined the space. Stone archways opened up every few feet along the walls, the red curtains hung inside the arches. Lan was going from archway to archway, checking inside each one. One wall contained more stone arches, but inside each one was a glass cabinet filled with what looked like artifacts and artwork. Darcy was peering into the glass cabinets, studying the artifacts inside. Clay paced the room, peering up at the ceiling that arched high above them. There were different murals painted on the ceiling, he realized. Each square was framed with wooden joists and showed a different scene. He did have to admit that while he didn't love the feeling the castle gave him, it was a beautiful place.

He studied the ceiling for some time, then turned to a painting that hung on the wall next to him. In the painting, he saw stone archways similar to the ones in this room, but these archways looked like they were open to the air. They faced the ocean. He could see water and the sun, either rising or setting on the horizon in the distance.

The painting showed a woman with long dark hair, standing framed in one of the archways. It looked like she stood on the far side of the arch, her arms outstretched wide at her sides. It almost looked like she was about to jump, he thought. He stared in fascination. He studied the rest of the image more closely, and his breath caught in his throat. A pillar of stone off to the right, behind the woman, was edged in shadow, but the shadow looked like it had a shape, a form to it. He thought he could make out an arm, a hand, the shape of a head. Were those meant to be eyes, gleaming out of the dark?

He heard Darcy scream then, a long, drawn-out wail, that cut off abruptly at the end.

He jumped about a foot and whipped his head around the room, searching for her. He had just seen her a moment ago. "Darcy?" He called out to her. Alex stopped playing. Austin and Cam burst into the room from the doorway.

All the color was drained from Cam's face. "What was that?" She asked, turning to Austin.

He shook his head, scanning the room. "Where's Darcy?" he asked Clay, striding over to him.

Lan stumbled out from behind a curtain. "I think she was helping me, checking behind the curtains," he said breathlessly.

"Which one?" Austin asked urgently.

Lan shrugged at him, running a hand through his hair as he glanced around the room. "I... I don't know, I wasn't watching where she went." He stammered, shrugging.

"I'm sure she's fine," Alex said in a bored-sounding voice from his seat at the organ. "She's been jumping at every shadow and screaming at nothing since we got here. I wouldn't worry if I were you."

"Gee, thanks, Alex," Austin mumbled.

Cam moved over to the nearest curtain and started to look behind it. Clay noticed she held a large piece of paper in one hand.

"Start checking behind the curtains," Austin said urgently, moving to the other side of the room. They combed the room, sweeping the heavy curtains out of the way, one by one. They found no sign of Darcy anywhere.

Clay was starting to panic now. He had a very bad feeling about this. Where on earth could she have gone? There was no other way out of the room, and Cam and Austin had been heading down the hallway when they heard Darcy scream. That meant she hadn't left that way. They were debating what to do next when Clay heard a rough scraping sound reverberating from the far side of the room.

They turned toward the sound just in time to see Darcy burst out from between a set of curtains, stumbling backward into the room. She was panting slightly.

"Darcy!" Clay called. "What the heck happened?"

Darcy whipped around, taking a deep, shuddering breath. She smiled slightly. "I found a hidden room," she said simply.

Clay started to chuckle in relief and heard several of the others join him.

"I triggered a hidden doorway," Darcy continued. "I went behind a set of curtains further down there." She pointed down the line of archways to her left. "And I found a little metal figure nailed to the wall. It was a bit crooked and looked odd. I pulled on it, and a little hole in the floor opened up right below me. I ended up in a narrow passageway suddenly. I had to crawl on my stomach to get through, but it ended up in a normal-sized room. I think we can probably all fit in there. There's a whole table laid out with clues." She smiled, looking a bit proud of herself.

"Wow, nice Darcy," Cam said excitedly, "Imagine if you hadn't stumbled upon that passage, who knows how long it would have taken us to find it."

Darcy nodded excitedly. "Should we go check it out?"

Cam nodded. "Austin and I found something else; there's a typewriter down the hall with this sheet of Morse code next to it. We heard Alex playing the organ and thought the code we need to use might be the music notes from the sheet music."

Cam looked over at Alex, and his eyebrows went up in surprise. He looked down at the sheet music in his hand, and after a moment, he nodded up at her. "I think you could be right, Cam." He looked excited now too. "The notes seemed so random to me; they didn't make any sense. It definitely didn't sound like music." He walked over and handed the sheet to her. "Let's give it a shot."

Cam nodded. "Okay, let's check out the little room Darcy found first?"

Alex shrugged and nodded in agreement, and Darcy led them over to the curtain she had disappeared behind.

Clay didn't like the sound of the narrow passageway. He liked it even less when he saw it. He hung back at the tail end of the group. Waiting to make sure Lan and Austin could fit through okay before he even thought about going in there.

The others laughed and joked about the small space. Alex clapped him on the back and made some kind of joke about claustrophobia. Clay nodded and pretended to chuckle a little as Alex laughed, but he wasn't even really listening. He was in his own head, reminding himself to take deep, even breaths.

Bee stopped and looked back at him before she went in; he knew she shared his fear but on a milder level. She looked worried for him. Rahul had gone in with no trouble. He wouldn't be backing out now.

Clay lowered himself into the entrance of the passageway when it was his turn. "Oh, hell no..." he heard himself exclaim, his heart starting to race. Darcy wasn't kidding about having to crawl. More like slide. He slithered along on his belly, like a snake. His shoulders just barely fit. He was panting, his heart rate through the roof. He tried not to think, to just move. If Darcy hadn't already gone through before and come back out safely on the other side, he knew he wouldn't have been able to do this.

They clapped for him when he finally emerged into the room. Standing up, he felt Austin grab his arm to help him climb out of the narrow tunnel.

Bee came over and patted him on the back. "Good job Clay," she murmured.

Clay shrugged and nodded, attempting to get his breathing back under control. He still felt a dull edge of panic nearby, but thankfully, the room itself was large enough to put him more at ease, although he didn't like the fact that there were no windows. Clearly, this room was deep in the interior of the castle. A table was set up in the center of the room, with a large box in the middle. The far side of the room held a wall of bookcases and a few chairs. Otherwise, the room was empty.

"Okay, so," Darcy said, once they were all in the room, "There's a prompt here on the table, for this next challenge. I haven't read through it fully yet, but it involves these tarot cards."

The group moved to gather around the large table. Clay stood behind Cam, peering over her shoulder at the tarot cards spread out on one half of the table.

Above the tarot cards, their faces engraved with brightly colored drawings, were a set of plain cream cards with lines of text written in gold scroll. On the far side of the table, Clay saw larger cards with each of their names written out on them.

"What does the prompt say?" Cam asked, peering over at the piece of paper Darcy held in her hand.

"Here, you can read it," Darcy handed it over to her.

Cam scanned the page, and Clay read with her over her shoulder as she began to read out loud. "Okay, so it says, spread out on the table before us, we will find 20 tarot cards, along with nine regrets." She paused at that for a few seconds. "Our task is to match the tarot card that represents each of us, with our regret. We must answer honestly in order to reveal the code."

She lowered the prompt slowly and moved around to the side of the table, examining the tarot cards more closely. Clay followed behind her, eying the cards with the gold writing warily. A somewhat uncomfortable silence fell over the room.

"Okay..." Lan cleared his throat. "How do we know which tarot card represents us?" He looked around at them, then continued when no one responded. "I know nothing about tarot cards. What sorts of things are on there?"

"Hmm..." Cam spoke up, "Looks like they say all sorts of things. Most of them depict people, but not all. That should help us narrow it down, at least a little, right?" As she spoke, she flipped the prompt over. "Oh wait. There's more on the back. It lists the cards and a description of each. That's good." She scanned the list, and the others moved closer. Bee read over Cam's shoulder, and they began to discuss the cards.

After a few minutes of this, Cam concluded, "Well I'm assuming I must be Justice... I guess," she shrugged. "I'm going to pick that for now. I'll start looking over the regrets." She shrugged again and handed the paper back to Clay.

He scanned the list of cards. He had already scanned the pictures, and none of them stood out as describing him in particular. This part was going to be harder than he had thought.

He handed the paper to Austin after another moment or two. He decided he was pretty much going to be useless for this one. He may as well let one of the others sort it out.

Cam was picking up the regrets cards, reading them one by one and placing them back down on the table. She froze, reading the card in her hand, and looked over at Austin. She studied him before placing the card back down. He caught her looking at him and raised an eyebrow.

Austin coughed and ran a hand through his hair, looking uncomfortable. Then he handed the paper over to Alex and Rahul, and they began to point to the list and murmur to each other.

Austin moved over to the regrets cards with fake nonchalance. Clay watched as he picked up various cards until he came to the one Cam had set down a moment ago. He read it, eyebrows rising slightly. Then he bent the card in one hand and tapped it repeatedly on his palm as he watched Cam continue to read the regrets.

She looked up eventually, tucking a card and the Justice Tarot card into her folded hands. She saw Austin watching her. "I think I found mine." She raised an eyebrow at him. "Did you find yours?"

"I found my regret," he said evenly, and they exchanged a meaningful look.

Cam flushed and looked away. Then moved over to the far side of the table. "Good," was all she said.

She marched over to the larger card with her name and placed both cards, face up, above it. "Need help, Clay?" she said somewhat sharply. She moved swiftly back over to stand next to him, cheeks flushed, pointedly avoiding looking at Austin, who continued to watch her. Clay was very curious about what was on that card. He grinned a little but smoothed over his expression when Cam glanced up at him, eyes narrowing.

"Um yeah," he coughed, "I have literally no clue which card could be mine."

"Strength," Darcy murmured suddenly. She moved over the tarot cards, her hand hovering over them, as she murmured to herself. Her hand paused over the Strength card, and she picked it up, turning and handing it to Clay with a smile. "You're Strength, Clay. That's an easy one."

"Can I see the list?" Cam asked, clearing her throat, and moving over to join Alex and Rahul. "Strength," she read, "courage, bravery, vulnerability, and valor." She smiled over at Darcy and then at Clay. "Yes, I think that's a good fit. Nice one, Darcy."

Clay shook his head in protest. "What? Why?" He shrugged. "I don't think that describes me at all."

"I think it does," Bee said thoughtfully, watching him. Clay felt himself flush slightly under her gaze.

He shrugged again. "I don't see it."

"Well, we do," Darcy said, "Maybe you're braver than you realize." She grinned at him and turned back to the cards.

"Well, I think you're The High Priestess, Darcy," Cam read, "Intuition, instinct, inner knowing, subconscious, and ancient wisdom." She walked back over, searching for the right card. She plucked it from the table and handed it to Darcy.

Darcy smiled back at her and nodded. "I'll go with that for now."

"And, while I'm on a roll..." she continued to scan the cards, "I'm going to go with The Tower for Alex." She looked over at him and held out a hand, "What was it again? Chaos, upheaval...read the rest for me?" She gave Alex a wicked grin.

He gave her a long look and shook his head in disgust. Scanning the page, he read aloud, "The Tower: upheaval, chaos, destruction, surprise, shock." He shook his head, whistling as he finished. "Wow, gee thanks, Cam. I'm touched, truly." He placed a hand on his chest. "Oh, and what was it you chose for yourself? Justice, was it?" He scanned the page again, "Hmm, equity, equality, fairness, righteousness, morals, and ethics." He shook his head, chuckling. "My my, someone has a high opinion of themselves..."

"I'm a lawyer, Alex. I thought it fit if any of them did." Cam shook her head, rolling her eyes.

Alex pretended to think for a minute. "Oh wait, what about this one though? The Devil; obsession." He paused and gave her a pointed look before his gaze swung to find Austin. Then he continued, "Compulsions, addictions, vices, entrapment. Oh, and materialism. Well." He shrugged, "That last one, maybe not so much, that might be more up Bee's alley."

"Hey," Bee quipped, brows furrowing as she glared at Alex. Then she shrugged after a moment and laughed a little. "I do like nice things...don't I?" She sighed deeply and turned back to catch Cam's expression.

She was glaring open-mouthed at Alex, her cheeks flushed a deep red. "Also, you're an asshole, Alex," Bee added sharply. "And there you go again, causing chaos like the stupid crumbling tower you are." She picked up the card with the picture of a medieval-looking tower breaking in half and crumbling and moved over to place it by Alex's name. "Is there a card that says, 'I regret constantly being an asshole?' If so, we can put it over here for Alex."

Cam sighed and shook her head, scanning the regret cards. "I have an idea which one might be his, but I'll let him sort that out for himself."

"What about you, Bee?" Cam chewed her bottom lip, turning back to the Tarot cards. "Lan?" she added. "Shoot, Lan, you could be justice, that might work too, with you being a detective. I didn't think of that." She sighed. "This is going to be harder than I thought."

Darcy scanned the cards next to her. "I would pick The Emperor for Lan, I think." She said, picking one up and holding it out to him. "It says something about leadership, right?"

Rahul cleared his throat. Clay noted that Alex seemed to have finally decided to shut up for a while. "Yeah, so it says authority, power, leadership, confidence, and determination."

Lan shrugged, hands in his pockets. "I mean, I'll take it; there are worse cards, right?" He grinned and walked over to take the card from Darcy. He scanned the regrets cards next. Clay saw his eyebrows go up briefly before he swiped up a card and moved to the far side of the table. He was pretty sure Lan placed the regret card face-down. He eyed him for a moment then looked away as Lan looked over at the group.

"Can I see the list again?" Darcy asked, moving over to join Rahul. He held it down lower for her to read as well. She read briefly and smiled to herself. "Cam, grab The Moon for me, will you?" She cleared her throat, "Illusion, confusion, secrets, mysteries, and unknown." She tilted her face up slightly. "For Rahul," she added. She gave him a knowing look, which he returned with a look of surprise. He glanced briefly at Alex, who showed no reaction whatsoever.

"Okay, interesting..." Cam murmured in response. She grabbed the card and walked it over to place it by Rahul's name. "Rahul, we'll leave you to find your own regret as well. Who's next, oh wise High Priestess?" she asked Darcy, with a mock bowing motion as though she were worshiping her, she moved back to the tarot card side.

"That leaves only Bee and Austin, right?" Lan asked. He stood on the far side of the table, staring down at the list. "Oh, and Miranda, sorry, I forgot." He pointed to the table. "She's on here, too."

"Okay, that's right, thanks Lan," Darcy murmured, taking the paper from Rahul as he moved over to the table to scan the regrets. "Okay..." she said, moving closer to get a better view of the remaining tarot cards. Rahul slid over further to make room for her. "Sorry, it helps me to see the pictures." She eyed them, eyes scanning back and forth between the list and the cards on the table. She was quiet, thinking.

"Honestly Bee, don't take this the wrong way..." She looked over at Bee, a nervous look on her face.

"It's okay, Darc; be honest with me." Bee began to grin, and Darcy smiled back at her. "Be brutally honest; give me your worst," she giggled.

"Okay," Darcy giggled a little as well, "Okay, so I think you might be The Fool."

Bee placed a hand on her chest and rolled her eyes, "You bitch," she said, in mock seriousness.

Darcy held up a hand, "But wait, listen to the description, 'The Fool stands for new beginnings, youthful energy, fresh starts, and the start of a cycle.' The full description says, 'The fool's face is uplifted to the sun and doesn't appear to have a care in the world. Their clothing is flamboyant, and they hold a white rose for purity'." Darcy looked back at Bee, an apprehensive smile on her face.

"Okay, okay, I see it, girl, I see it..." she walked over, holding a hand out to take the card. "Give me that fool card." She smiled at Darcy, who gave her a brief one-armed hug. Bee scooped up the card and moved on to read the regrets.

Clay watched her thoughtfully. He wondered what her regret card might say. Would it be about him? He doubted it, somehow.

"Okay," Cam murmured, studying the remaining cards. "That leaves Austin and Miranda, right?" She looked over at Darcy. "What do you think, Darc?"

Darcy was quiet for a few seconds as she looked back down at the list. "Honestly, I'm feeling The Empress for Miranda. I know she's not here yet to give her input, but it says the keywords are nurturing, mothering, nourishment, abundance, and creation." She shrugged, glancing over at Austin. "I mean, I don't see any others that seem like a good fit, and she is the only one of us who is a mother."

Austin became very interested in staring at the bookshelf and ignoring the discussion. Cam looked over at him for a moment and then nodded to Darcy. "Okay, let's give it a shot." She scooped up the card, and Clay walked over to take it and walk it over for her. "Thanks, Clay." She gave him a small smile. He placed the card on the far side of the table above

Miranda's name and then moved back over to scan the regret cards.

He found his quickly, flushing deeply at the realization that Bee must have seen and read it already. He should have read the cards first and grabbed his before she could see it. Of course it was about her. Although it didn't mention her by name, he figured she could have inferred it was about her easily enough. The card read, *"The regret of love long felt but not returned."*

He frowned, walking hastily over to place it by his name. He supposed the card might just as well apply to Cam, as it did to him, but she had already chosen a regret first and left it face up next to her name. Clay moved slowly past, eying Cam's card after placing his. He debated for a moment but left his face up as well. It wasn't like everyone here didn't already know. Besides, he was supposed to represent strength, apparently. He didn't pause long enough to read it fully, but he thought hers said, *"The regret of unspoken words, and what might have been."*

Clay moved back around the table. He was curious what Austin's regret card said, but he still held it in his hands, folded into a cylinder, which he tapped nervously over and over as he paced around the room in front of the bookshelves.

"Okay," Cam interjected, "I don't think that fits, does it?" Clay realized he had been tuning out the conversation. The girls were debating which tarot card was Austin's. He eyed his nervous pacing again. Clearly, it was making him uncomfortable. Or he was just feeling the way Clay was starting to feel: anxious to get out of this room and move on.

Cam stared down at the cards, picking up one after the other. "I really don't know Darc..." she mumbled.

Rahul had scooped up a regret card Clay saw and moved over to place it next to his name. He lay his face down, Clay noted with a smirk.

Alex looked like he was deciding which one was his, too. He picked up a card after another moment's thought and walked over to set it down. "Well, I mean, we can always just try one, right? Worst case, we're wrong, and we choose a different one. It's a process of elimination from there."

Cam nodded. "Yeah, I suppose that's true, isn't it." She looked across the table at the other cards. "I guess we won't be sure which card is wrong... but we can just try swapping out one at a time from there until we get it right." She squinted over at the cards. "What are there, numbers on the back of the cards?" She asked, looking over at Rahul and Alex for confirmation. "Looks like there's a lock on the box in the middle that has one of those super long number combinations on it."

Rahul flipped over his tarot card and examined the back. "Yep, she's right," he showed the card to Alex. "There's a number on the back of mine. I bet we use these in the order they're laid out on the table for the combination. What do you think? Tarot card number first? There's a number on the back of each regret card, too."

"Yeah." Alex nodded, looking excited, "Let's try it that way first." He looked back over at Cam. "We need Austin's cards first."

"Okay," Cam said, looking back at the cards. "Austin, try The Chariot," she held out a hand for the list, and Darcy handed it to her. "It says strength, perseverance, endurance, and emotional stability." She looked back down at the card, then over in Austin's direction. She cleared her throat. "I think that describes you pretty well." She held the card out for him but looked away quickly when he met her eyes.

Austin took the card silently and paused as he moved past the regret cards. He hovered, then scooped one up. He moved slowly over to the far side of the table. He placed the tarot card with the chariot face up, and his regret card face down next to it. He walked over to Miranda's name and placed the second regret card face down. He stood off to the side, arms folded in front of his chest, staring down at his feet with his head bowed.

"Okay." Alex rubbed his hands together. "Finally, let's give this a shot. Does anyone have the pencil?"

Rahul pulled the pencil out of his pocket and handed it over to Alex. Cam brought the paper with the prompt over and they got to work writing out the long sequence of numbers.

Once they had the sequence written out in full, they slid the large box over with the combo lock. Cam carefully entered the code while Alex read it out loud for her. They waited patiently until the code was entered, and Cam tugged on the lock. It didn't budge.

"Dammit," Alex murmured, "Something's wrong."

"Yep," Cam muttered, "That means at least one card is wrong, maybe more."

They proceeded to attempt to swap out the tarot cards, one at a time, but nothing seemed to work. Time ticked by, and Clay moved over to have a seat in one of the chairs by the bookshelves. Darcy watched him and came to join him, taking a seat with a grateful sigh.

Frustrations mounted until Cam and Alex were snapping at each other. Clay glanced sideways at Darcy. "Just like old times..." he said softly.

She gave him a grimace and snorted a little laugh. "God, you're not kidding," she said quietly in response.

"Is everyone actually sure that their regret card is right?" Cam asked, running a hand through her hair. She pushed it off to the side, to cascade in shiny ripples over her shoulder. "How do we know it's the tarot cards that are wrong?"

"I think we all know what we regret, Cam," Lan murmured quietly. He glanced up and surveyed the others with raised brows. "Right? Anyone not sure?"

They slowly shook their heads, one after the other. Clay shook his head as well.

"Dammit, then I don't know what to swap out next. Maybe we should take a break from this one for now, go back out to work on the other puzzle." Cam huffed a sigh and turned to walk away from the table. She paced back and forth for a moment. The group was silent.

Alex leaned over the cards, propped up on both hands, scanning them and shaking his head.

Clay turned as Darcy got up from her chair next to him and moved over to the tarot cards again. She scanned them, face thoughtful. She held a hand out over one, then moved to another.

"We've tried almost all of them, at least the combinations that make any sense," Bee said, watching Darcy studying the cards.

"Have you tried this one?" Darcy asked, her hand hovering over a card, she reached for it half-heartedly, as though she were reluctant to pick it up.

"Well, no," Bee admitted, coming to look over her shoulder. "Why would we?"

"Can I see the paper?" Darcy asked, looking over between Rahul and Alex. Rahul scooped up the paper and carried it over to her. Clay could see from his seat that it was now covered in long strings of numbers.

Darcy took it from Rahul with a nod of thanks. She held the paper up and Bee peered at it as well. Darcy nodded and took a deep breath. "Okay," she began, her voice sounding nervous, "Change, transformation, transmutation, ending of a cycle, rebirth." She looked around the room at the others, pausing for a response. They stared at her. She looked back at the paper, then at the card, and nodded to herself. "Yes, I think that feels right," she said.

"Okay," Alex said, "Bring it over here, let's give it a shot."

Darcy picked up the card and brought the card and paper over to Alex. She slid a card up, out of the way, so she could place the new one. Clay couldn't see from his seat which card it was.

"For who?" Cam asked, pausing her pacing to peer over at the table.

"For Austin," Alex said, looking up at Darcy with an odd expression on his face. "Are you ready Cam?" he asked, glancing behind him. Cam returned to the table and prepared to enter the code again, as Alex crossed out a number on the sheet and wrote something else. Then, he read the new sequence out loud.

This time, when Cam entered the final digit and tugged on the lock, it popped open with a loud click. There was a general chorus of cheers and laughter, and Cam grinned, popping open the lid of the box. Clay stood and moved over to the table to see what was inside.

A large ornate gold key lay on a velvet cushion in the box. "Nice," Cam exclaimed, holding up the key for everyone to see, letting it dangle from the red ribbon tied to the end.

"Great job everyone," Lan called out, clapping Alex on the back and grinning. "That was not easy, I'm proud of us."

Cam smiled up at him and nodded in agreement. "That was awesome," she turned to look at Darcy. "Okay Darc, how do we get out of here?"

Darcy stood alone at the far end of the table, her face worried. Cam's face fell slightly when she looked over at her. She looked down at the table, scanning the cards, frowning. Clay saw her pause, her brows furrowing, as she stared down at Austin's new tarot card. The key in her hand was forgotten.

"What was the card?" Clay asked her, his voice pitched low. The room quieted as they watched Cam. She finally looked up at him, then over at Austin.

"Death." Darcy's voice came out barely a whisper from the far side of the table. "It was death."

They exited the hidden tarot card room swiftly from there. In silence. Clay thanked his lucky stars that the narrow passage that led out of the room felt just slightly shorter than the one that led in.

They exited through the curtain Darcy had originally popped out of and made their way down the hallway from there; Cam and Austin leading them to the laboratory with the typewriter.

Clay sighed to himself, annoyed with Alex's sudden change of mood; he now seemed excited and happy again, even elated. He clapped Rahul on the back and said something about how they were making good progress. All his earlier fury seemed to have evaporated. It reminded Clay too much of his own asshole of a boss for him to not be irritated.

They gathered in the laboratory room, around the circular table, while Cam explained their hypothesis on how this puzzle might work. Someone suggested putting a fresh sheet of paper into the typewriter. Once they'd sorted that out, Cam sat down in front of the typewriter and began to painstakingly type out the corresponding letter to each musical note. Alex read them out loud to her. They had to start over once or twice and it seemed to take forever before they finally said they had it.

Meanwhile, Clay busied himself searching around the lab. He figured if Darcy had randomly found the hidden room like that, there could be other hidden spaces or clues lying around anywhere. Not that he wanted to enter any other hidden tunnels.

There was just so much in the lab that it was overwhelming, though. Searching this room alone for anything meaningful would take them hours, especially with no clear idea of what to look for.

When the message was completed, nothing happened. They stood there for a moment; Clay felt like the wind had been knocked out of their sails a bit. Austin asked to see the typed note. He held it side by side next to the Morse code sheet.

"Okay," he said, "So, this is the message, right?" He held up the text Cam had typed out on the typewriter. "And this is the code we are going to use to send the message." He held the Morse code sheet up in his other hand. "What we need to figure out now is what we are using to send it, and where are we sending it, right?" He glanced around the room at the workbenches. "I don't see anything that looks like a telegraph machine in here, did any of you who looked around?"

"I don't think I did either," Bee spoke up, looking over at Rahul for confirmation. He nodded his head in agreement. "Not that I know what it looks like exactly."

Austin quickly described to them what a telegraph machine might look like. Heads shook back and forth as they thought over what they had seen that day. "Okay," he said, nodding to himself. "So, maybe we just haven't found it yet."

"We do have the key," Darcy spoke up, pulling the key out of her pocket. "Maybe this gets us into another room that has the machine in it?" She said hopefully. Austin nodded encouragingly at her.

"I bet you're right, Darc. We'll hold onto these for now, and hopefully we'll come across it soon."

"I thought everything was all messed up," Bee said, frowning a little. "If we went to the wrong room, and things are out of order, I mean..." she trailed off, "Will the clues even still work at this point?"

Alex sighed loudly and ran his hands over his face. "Honestly, I don't know the answer to that Bee. Though hopefully some idiot watching this right now does," his voice rose as he looked around the room at the ceiling level again. "But at this point, I guess we just keep going the best we can. Until we get stuck completely, that is." He glared over at Rahul as he said that last bit. Rahul shifted his weight back and forth, looking somewhat uncomfortable, but he remained quiet.

They all stood in silence for a moment, and then Cam said, "Wow, you guys," drawing their attention over to her. She stood on the other side of the round table, an old-looking leather-bound book in her hands. Her eyes flickered back and forth across the pages. "Listen to this, it's some kind of journal." She looked up at them, and seeing she had everyone's attention, she cleared her throat and began to read out loud.

"I arrived early in the evening, as the sun was just starting its descent. My sister-in-law, Marianna, ran out to meet me at the gate; it was as though she had been watching for me. She smiled at me, a genuine, heartfelt smile on her face, as she greeted me. As we exchanged pleasantries I naturally asked after my brother's health. Then I watched the smile wiped from her face, as though it took all warmth and feeling of happiness with it. "You will find him much changed," was her reply. And she refused to say anything more.

She led me into the castle, and it was some time until my brother appeared. Not until we sat down for dinner did I see him, although my arrival was announced to him earlier. He nodded and gave me a rather tight-lipped smile and embraced me as usual. He seemed distracted and perhaps tired. But there was naught to signal any great urgency to me or concern for his condition. My brother very often became this way when he was in the midst of working on some great puzzle, or challenge in his work.

I attributed Marianna's concern to this and shook my head to myself and chuckled even slightly. I remember thinking at the time that she should have known him better and had worried herself needlessly. She had written to me in such a state as produced in myself an answering state of haste and distress that had caused me to rush to his side. Yet here he was, his typical, albeit unusual self. How wrong I was.

Late that night was my first indication that something may be amiss. I had noted how little John ate during dinner, seeming to want only drink and to partake in the steak that was brought out to him; so under-cooked from my perspective as to leave behind a pool of blood on his plate, which he proceeded to lap up with bread. My stomach turned slightly at this, but I thought nothing further of it.

I had stayed up quite late into the night, reading in the library by candlelight until my eyes were burning with the strain and need for rest. I took one candle with me to guide me to my room, snuffing out all the others as I went. As I approached the wing that contained my room, candle held aloft, the light shone on a set of eyes in a far dark corner.

I jumped back quite suddenly at this, surprised to see an animal in the house as I did not know of any animals that were kept indoors. John had a dog, but it had passed on some years ago. Yet I was sure what I saw was a pair of eyes that might belong to a dog or a cat, such as that seem to glow or reflect back their own inner light when in darkness.

I was never more surprised to see that it was, in fact, John that I had startled coming around a corner. He told me he had been up late working on some problem or other in the contraption he was building currently, and he was in dire need of sleep. We bid each other good night, and I continued on my way. Although I looked back several times down the passage, I did not see those glowing eyes peering back at me again that night."

Cam stopped reading there, looking up at them all with wide eyes. "It sounds like it's his brother's journal." She flipped through the next few pages, keeping her thumb on the page she had stopped on. "There's quite a bit more here. I bet you this thing is full of clues."

"But wait, is it... real?" Bee asked, frowning as she walked over to Cam's side. "I mean, it can't be, right?" She studied the journal as Cam closed it for her, keeping her thumb tucked inside again as a bookmark. Bee ran her hand over the cover gingerly. "But it looks so old..." she murmured. She looked up at Cam, a grimace of concern on her face.

"Either way, let's take it with us," Alex said, "I think we should head back for lunch now." He looked at his wristwatch as he spoke. Clay hadn't noticed until just then that his stomach was rumbling, and he was actually quite hungry.

The group agreed to the suggestion, although Cam seemed reluctant to stop. She brought the journal tucked tightly in her arms, and Clay saw her looking backward more than once as the group began to head back to the common area. There was a lot of grumbling, from Bee in particular, about having to scale the ladder again.

They found lunch was laid out for them, ready and waiting, back in the common room. Clay took a seat next to Darcy at the far end of the table and began to eat eagerly. He was just taking a second bite of his sandwich when he happened to look up at the board hanging over the desk. He couldn't chew fast enough.

"Uh, hey Alex," he called over to him at the other end of the table. Alex had been laughing and joking around with Austin and Lan. Alex paused a grin on his face, and turned to look over where Clay was pointing. His face fell immediately; his grin replaced with a look of shock first, and then anger. Lan and Austin paused eventually in their fit of laughter and looked over too. They stared at the solid red light that shone dimly next to Alex's name.

"What the hell..." Alex muttered. He practically stammered as he walked over to the board and stood directly in front of it, peering closer at the red light. "You've got to be kidding me!"

Clay wasn't sure who laughed first, but he was pretty certain it was either Lan or Austin. He heard someone snort, stifling a chuckle, and then, before he knew it, most of the group was laughing. Cam almost spit out a mouthful of water when she finally looked over and saw what had happened.

Alex turned slowly to face them, and Clay rested his chin in his hand, masking the grin he couldn't quite remove from his face. But Alex, thankfully, wasn't furious like he expected him to be. He shook his head, smirking, and then shrugged. "Whatever man, give me a stupid strike. For what?" He shrugged again, looking around the room. "For being annoyed that my own employees are incompetent, I guess? Whatever," he repeated.

"Being annoyed isn't a sin though, is it?" Darcy said quietly at his side. She wasn't laughing. Wasn't even smiling, like the rest of them.

Cam cleared her throat loudly, before taking another sip of water. "No, you're right Darcy, it isn't. But wrath is if I remember correctly. So is pride." She met Alex's eyes evenly as an uneasy silence fell over the group.

Alex stared at her before responding. "Thanks, Cam." He turned away, back to the desk, then paused and turned back. "I guess I'll just be grateful it isn't you, flipping the switch." He turned and leaned over the desk and plucked the phone out of its cradle. He dialed swiftly, too fast for Clay to see which numbers he hit.

Alex spoke softly into the phone. The others began talking again slowly, chatting about the clues. Cam and Bee were arguing about whether or not the journal was real. Clay wished they would all just shut up for a moment, so he could hear what Alex was saying, but as much as he tried, strained, and attempted to block them all out, he could only catch a random word here or there. Not enough to string together into anything meaningful.

Clay sighed deeply and decided he might as well keep eating. He watched Alex and the board above him out of the corner of his eyes. His gaze kept returning to the light bulbs beside his own name. He glanced over at Bee as well, at Rahul sitting next to her. Did he have to have his chair pulled over, so close to hers? Clay fought to push down the rising wave of jealousy and rage he felt growing inside him. He wondered why his own lights were all out still, because it certainly seemed to him that at least one of them should have been lit by now.

17.

Austin

It was pretty funny, watching Alex's face when he saw one of his light bulbs was lit up. Austin was still trying not to laugh. And Alex more than deserved it.

Austin guessed that much of Alex's behavior since they had arrived had been staged or at least exaggerated. His anger, though, at the escape room sequence getting mixed up, had been real.

Austin found himself feeling more and more wary as the day went on. He told himself this was because of Alex and the odd mix-up. Because if Alex didn't know what was happening... well, who did? Austin's mind went back to the questions on the piece of paper in the Ouija board room. That one question kept nagging at him. Because Alex's reaction to the roommate question... that had seemed real, too. But it nagged at him mainly because it didn't seem like Alex. Didn't seem like something he would have ever brought himself to tell his crew, much less even admit to himself. Austin was sure it hadn't come from him. So how had it made its way into the game? It didn't make any sense.

Austin busied himself with pondering over that question while the others ate. He had sat down to eat, feeling famished, but after taking one bite of the sandwich, he suddenly felt a little queasy, almost sick. He had lost his appetite entirely and ended up pacing the room. He feigned he was looking for more clues, but really, he just wanted some space, and time alone to think. Because, of course, it wasn't only Alex and that odd question that was bothering him. It was much more than that.

His mind kept going back to the Death card, over and over again. *What on earth was that supposed to mean?* He felt a little tickle of discomfort every time he thought of it. It was like when you lost a tooth, and your tongue kept returning involuntarily to that spot, to feel how strange and foreign it felt. He tried to remember the description Darcy had read. It hadn't all sounded that bad. Something about transformation, and rebirth. That part could be good. Like a fresh start, or a new chapter.

He thought of Miranda. As the minutes and hours ticked by and she still didn't appear, he felt himself growing more and more anxious. And that was natural. There was nothing odd about that. He hadn't seen her face to face since she left for good. That last time she had come to the house, to pick up some of her things, he had purposefully prolonged a work call in order to avoid having to speak to her, but he couldn't get rid of the image of her face, as she peered at him through the door into the study one last time. How heartbroken she had looked.

Austin shook his head and cleared his throat. He took another sip of the glass of ice water he carried with him. It was more than that though. It was this place. This house. This castle... whatever you called it. It was... bothering him. Affecting him in some strange way.

Austin strode over to the bank of floor-to-ceiling windows on the far side of the couches. He stood there, watching the raindrops splattering on the glass. Listening to the roar of the surf as it pounded the rocks along the shore. He heard another faint rumble of thunder. Clearly, the storm was still going outside. He had thought the sound of the ocean would help lull him to sleep last night like it usually did. He typically never slept so soundly as he did when he could hear moving water, but last night had been awful. He had spent most of the night tossing and turning, in a half-awake, half-asleep, sort of semi-conscious state.

When asleep, he had been plagued by constant images, a recurring dream sequence in which he rose from his bed and proceeded to wander the halls of the castle. It had been night in his dreams as well. The halls and rooms had been dark; the only light visible filtered in through the clouds and left the imprints of the cathedral windows on the floor.

Austin had followed someone. He had glimpsed a figure, half in shadow, over and over again. He would find them disappearing around corners, or just ducking into a room down the hall. And somehow, he never seemed to be able to catch up. He had heard things, too. Strange scratching sounds, and the echoing click of claws on the stone floors seemed to follow him as he wandered through a maze of corridors.

Finally, at the end of a hallway, the figure had paused and stood framed directly in the slanted moonlight shining through a tall cathedral window onto the floor. The figure had turned halfway towards him. Austin had been startled out of sleep, pulling himself out of the dream. It had been his own face, staring back at him. And he had smiled. A smile that was evil-looking. Unnatural. And his eyes...

He had awoken drenched in sweat, his heart pounding in his throat. He hadn't been able to fall asleep again for the remainder of the night.

He thought back to the passage from the journal Cam had just read. It wasn't by any means exactly the same as his dream, but the description had been close enough to make him feel uneasy.

Austin sighed and plopped into the armchair near the fireplace. The fire he had started that morning was mostly ashes at this point, for lack of tending, but some embers still glowed orange. He knew he was being ridiculous; there was nothing special about this house. So, he had a night of bad dreams; it was nothing more than that. That and the power of suggestion were clearly getting to him. He stretched his legs out and cringed. He was so sore though. He had woken up that way, his legs especially achy, as though he had truly been walking all night. Even his feet hurt a bit. Maybe he was coming down with something. The start of a fever. That would be just his luck.

Austin looked up, startled by Cam's sudden appearance next to him. She was looking at him like she was waiting for him to respond. "What?" he asked in confusion.

"Didn't you hear me just now? I was talking to you for like a whole minute." She frowned down at him, her brows furrowed. Austin eyed the journal in her arms wearily. "Are you okay? You don't look so good." She peered at him, studying his features. He looked away, suddenly uncomfortable, and stared into the fireplace.

"Yeah, I'm fine," he said gruffly. "I mean, I didn't sleep great. I'm a little achy today; probably coming down with something." He shrugged to show her it wasn't a big deal.

Cam nodded thoughtfully at him, then she went and sat on the edge of the stone surrounding the fireplace. "Listen," she said softly, lowering her voice, "I started looking through the journal, just skimming through the pages, but this looks really interesting. It's all written by this brother, John's brother. I think his name is Garrett. It almost sounds like he is in love with John's wife though, the sister-in-law, Marianna, or whatever."

She brushed her blonde hair back, tucking it behind one ear, and peered down at the open journal again. "He keeps talking about how something is wrong with John. He thinks his brother is changing. It sounds like this," she waved a hand off to the side, "stupid Besomar thing." She paused, and looked up at him, waiting for a reaction. He just nodded back to her, and she continued. "And look, I know Bee is saying none of this is real, that it's a fake journal they created for the escape room thing. But..." she paused again, biting down on her lip like she always did when she was nervous about something. "I don't think it is. I think this journal could be real, Austin."

She watched him, her hazel-green eyes wide, and locked onto his. "It's kind of freaking me out." She looked around the room, gazing up at the ceiling. "I know I don't normally believe in this kind of stuff, but if this journal is real, I mean, maybe that's where the local stories come from, at least." She continued on, when he said nothing. "I think it's really important that we read this whole thing. I know we're going straight back to the challenge after lunch, but I'm going to read the rest of it. I'll stay up late tonight to read it if I have to. Will you read it with me tonight? If the others don't want to?" She asked him.

He thought for a moment and nodded again solemnly at her. She still looked nervous and uncertain. "Sure, Cam," he said, smiling at her. "It's a date."

A smile broke out at his words, her cheeks flushed slightly, and her eyes lit up. "Okay then, perfect," she said, sitting back and sighing. She closed the journal but kept it tucked closely to her in her lap. Cam looked around the room, watching the others still seated at the table. "Okay," she repeated to herself. She looked relaxed now.

"Good," she smiled at him again. "So, we'll focus on the challenges for now and worry about this tonight." She looked down at the journal, then back up at him. "I want to put it somewhere safe, it's too big and cumbersome to carry it with me everywhere." She chewed her lip again. "I guess I'll put it in my room, for now. Just to be safe." She looked up at him like she was waiting for him to approve.

Austin shrugged and nodded. "Yeah, sure, why not?" he agreed.

She nodded and stood up, heading out of the room towards the main foyer and the bedrooms beyond. Austin sighed, watching her go. She seemed to have forgiven him, just a little, after reading his regret. He knew she saw it, knew it must be his. *"The regret of a life that could have been, but never will be."*

His stomach twisted a little at the thought of staying up late, reading the journal together. What had he just agreed to, exactly?

He thought back to State. How many times had she invited him somewhere, or invited him over, just like that? Casually, like it was for some other reason, that they needed to be spending time together alone, in the evening. Too many times to count. And somehow, nothing had ever happened between them. Although there were times, he wanted it to, it just never quite felt right to him. He couldn't explain it really, not even to himself. Would the same thing happen this time? Did he want something to happen? He stared down at his hands, clasped around the water glass that was now dripping condensation onto the floor.

He paused, distracted from his reverie by his fingernails. They were so... long. How had he not noticed before? He must have forgotten to trim them for a while, but he could have sworn he had not that long ago.

"Hey man!" Austin was startled again, this time by Alex, practically jogging over to him. He vaulted over the back of the couch, placing one hand down and slamming down onto the cushions. "You ready to get going?" Alex studied him, then glanced back over at the table. "You still hungry? You didn't eat much."

Austin shrugged and chuckled. "I'm good, man; I'm not that hungry right now."

"You sure?" Alex asked him, "Gotta keep your strength up for tonight."

Austin looked at him from under his eyebrows. "Really?"

Alex just grinned at him.

"Okay, thanks, Mom." Austin rolled his eyes, and Alex started to laugh. "Did you turn into a mother hen, in your old age, or what?"

Alex laughed and leaned back on the couch. Stretching his legs out straight in front of him and arching his back. "Nah man," he grinned at him again as he relaxed. "Just saying, who knows what we're in for tonight, want to make sure we're all in good shape."

"Alright, well," Austin grinned at him, "I'm good. Ready to get going when you are."

Alex nodded and grinned back at him, standing up and clapping him on the shoulder as he walked past. "Good. I'll rally the troops." He strode over to the table. "Let's get a move on!" He called over to them. "Finish up, and we'll head back down and start trying that key."

The group finished up lunch without too much grumbling, although Austin could hear Bee complaining about the ladder again, and Rahul trying to reassure her it wouldn't be so bad the second time. Austin had to chuckle a little, given that seemed to be their only route at the moment, she was going to have to climb back up again tonight, too, when they returned for dinner and bed.

Cam had returned from stashing the journal in her room. Austin didn't know why she felt the need to put it there versus leaving it in the common room. She smiled at him as she entered the room. He placed his water glass back on the table and went to join her by the doorway.

"We left the papers with the note sequence and Morse code downstairs, right?" He asked her as he approached.

She nodded affirmatively. "Yes, I left them next to the typewriter."

"Okay cool." He nodded back. "I'm guessing we'll need them next after we figure out which door that key opens." Cam nodded and he saw her eyes wandering over towards where Darcy stood near the table. She stood next to Clay as he chatted to her and cleared up the table; he was stacking dishes and gathering napkins. Austin couldn't hear what he was talking about, but Darcy certainly didn't seem to be listening. She stared over at the spiral staircase, her dark eyes wide and concerned-looking. Then he watched as she turned to look at him. Darcy stared openly at him.

He saw Cam looking back and forth between them. She cleared her throat, and he tore his gaze away from Darcy's to look at Cam. "Has Darcy seemed a little... strange to you?" Cam was frowning at Darcy and back at him. "She's been acting sort of odd, don't you think?"

Austin frowned a little himself, and Darcy looked away, seeming to realize finally that Clay was talking to her. "Yeah, she's seemed a little off, hasn't she?" Austin agreed. He stared over at the spiral staircase himself.

"Let's go!" Alex called, moving rapidly behind them over to the doorway. "We've got a lot of ground to cover if ya'll are planning to escape." They shuffled in line, following the others out of the room.

The trek back down to the organ room, as Austin had come to think of it, was uneventful. He noted the energy in the group seemed to have been renewed by the break lunch had afforded them. They wasted no time in demanding the key from Darcy, which she produced from a pocket of her plaid dress and handed over to Lan. They started systematically, trying each door in the long corridor that included the typewriter room. Cam ran to grab the papers from the table and returned quickly.

But they had no luck in the time she was gone. The key didn't match any of the doors on the right-hand side of the corridor. They moved on to the left, Alex insisted on taking over, and Lan rolled his eyes at Cam. "Yeah, because I don't know how to use a key," he mumbled to her.

Cam giggled. "Obviously."

Austin watched them. Cam looked happy and excited, clearly feeling much more into the whole escape room thing than he was. Austin couldn't help but look over his shoulder periodically, as though he expected to turn and see Miranda standing behind him at any moment.

Finally, when they got to the door at the very end of the corridor, the key turned in the lock and there was an audible click. Alex swung the door open, and a few people clapped. "Alright, now we're getting somewhere." He moved through the door, holding it open for them as they shuffled past in a line. It was darker in this space, and oddly, no light switch could be found. Clay pulled one of the flashlights from his pocket and shone it around on the walls near the doorframe, but he found nothing. Then Alex produced a matchbox from his pocket and proceeded to light the candles that stood in elaborate black candelabras on the small tables scattered throughout the room.

They were in a huge library, Austin realized. The little library area in their common room was nothing compared to this. The library appeared to be three stories tall, and had another, larger spiral staircase that scaled its heights. The floor had the same black and white chessboard pattern as the main entrance. Their footsteps echoed eerily on the hard marble.

"Alright," Alex called out; his voice seemed somewhat hushed and subdued, as though he found the room as creepy as Austin did. A loud crack of thunder rolled over them. Austin looked up as he saw a flash and realized the ceiling held a large domed skylight. He caught a glimpse of black-looking storm clouds above. "Remember, we think we're looking for something that looks like a telegraph machine. Why don't we spread out?"

No one spoke in response, but they began to fan out across the room to cover more ground. Austin saw Darcy eye the staircase wearily, as she chose to stick to the main floor. Rahul and Bee climbed the stairs, heading for the second level.

Cam picked up a candelabra and swept it in front of her as she went, shining light along the spines of books. An empty fireplace sat off to the left, with a few armchairs and a low couch scattered in front of it. There appeared to be a bank of what were likely more tall cathedral windows on either side of the fireplace, but there were heavy black velvet curtains drawn shut over them.

Austin moved away from Cam, heading to the far side of the room. He thought about grabbing a candelabra as well; he had stupidly left the flashlight back in the common area. But he found he didn't feel he needed one at all, as his eyes adjusted to the dim lighting. It wasn't long before he found an odd-looking hole in the wall; a rectangular space had been cut out and was lined with molding. It reminded him almost of a doggy door. He thought of the journal, and how it mentioned there weren't any pets in the household, at least not that the brother knew about.

"I found something!" Clay called out from the middle of the room. The others rushed over. Next to a long table, on the floor, sat an odd-looking sort of machine. It was a wooden box, with wheels and gears visible underneath. It had a wooden pole sticking out of it on one side. It looked very old-fashioned, with the exception of what looked like a modern camera strapped onto it. "Look," Clay pointed to the tabletop next to it. Austin turned to see some sort of machine, with an upright handle. Next to it, sat what appeared to be a baby monitor.

"Yes!" Cam said, plopping down in a chair in front of the machine. "This looks sort of like a telegraph don't you think?" She looked over at Austin. "I bet we use this for the code." She set the candelabra down with a clunk and grabbed the sheets of paper from Lan. "Come on." She waved over to Austin, and he moved around the others to join her at the table.

"I saw a hole in the wall, over there." Austin pointed towards the far wall, "It looks like it would be just the right size for this thing to go through."

"Oh my god," Clay muttered, "Please tell me that's what it's for. That last tunnel was bad enough, I am not even trying to squeeze through there." That earned a laugh from the group.

"It looks like this thing has a camera strapped to it... and I bet this is the monitor," Austin continued. He pushed the button on the monitor to wake up the screen and saw the library, but from low on the floor, from the perspective of the odd-looking machine.

"It's an electric dog!" Alex exclaimed; he was kneeling down in front of the contraption, and Austin saw his face suddenly come into view on the camera monitor. Alex grinned into the camera and then up at Austin at the table. "How's my close-up?"

Austin laughed. "What the heck is an electric dog?"

Alex stood up and pointed to the wooden box. "That is. It was one of Hammond Junior's more well-known inventions. Basically, he invented the first robotic dog; it could follow its owner with the use of a flashlight. You had to shine light on its electric eye, which was some kind of sensor, and it would move around."

"Cool," Clay said, kneeling and peering around the wooden dog. "I don't see any sensors or anything like that." He held up the flashlight and shone it around the box, on either side and underneath, but nothing happened.

"Hmm," Alex murmured, looking back and forth between the dog and the machine that sat on the table, "Maybe this one is controlled differently." He looked over at Austin. "Should we try the Morse code?"

Lan spoke up, "Do we move it over to the hole in the wall that you found first? Or leave it here?" Lan looked over at him questioningly. "Maybe the code drives it through the wall to wherever it needs to go."

They debated back and forth. Ultimately, the group decided to move it to the hole in the wall and start the code from there. Clay and Lan moved the dog over to the hole, with Alex over-seeing them. Austin and Cam manned the telegraph machine. Alex called over to them and said that they were ready. Bee, Rahul, and Darcy hovered behind Austin and Cam, watching on the monitor.

Cam read the letters from the code out loud to Austin, one at a time, while he entered each one using the handle on the machine. He tapped out patterns of long versus short taps using the Morse code sheet as a reference. There was a small cheer as the dog began to move forward, moving slowly through the hole in the wall, and whirring its mechanical way down a narrow passage between the walls of the house. There was a moment of uncertainty when they approached a corner, and it looked like the dog might not make the turn, but the code held up, and it turned the corner, switching on some sort of light bulb as it went. The monitor screen, which had grown dim, flooded suddenly with light.

Austin found he couldn't watch along with the others; he had to focus on tapping out the Morse code. He listened as they chattered excitedly. Clay spoke up next to his ear. "Okay, it looks like you've exited into a larger space; this is maybe another room, or a closet or something, I'm not sure. I don't know what the end game is here, but we'll see. It looks like there are boxes and things piled up in here." Austin paused for a moment then continued to tap out the next sequence. "You made it through that area, and now it's in a more open space."

Tap, tap, tap, the machine beat out a tattoo in time with his movements.

"Okay, you're approaching another wall I think. There's something there on the far side of the room."

Austin continued to tap, moving as methodically as he could as Cam read out each new letter to him.

She paused. "You're doing great, Austin; I think we're almost there."

"Yep!" Clay nodded next to his shoulder in agreement. "I see a button, or a switch or something on that far wall. Looks like you're headed straight for it."

"We're almost done with the code," Cam stated, and continued to give him the next letters in the sequence, "E," she said, then paused as he tapped out just one brief tap.

"Got it," he said, prompting her to continue.

"A," she went on.

Dot-dash: one short and one long press.

Then, "And C, final letter."

Austin tapped, dot-dash, dot-dash, and he heard a chorus of cheers go up.

He looked over at the monitor, sitting up straight and stretching his suddenly sore back; he had been hunched over the machine in concentration. The dog appeared to have hit the switch it needed to hit; a bright green light on the wall shone into the camera lens.

They heard a loud creaking sound and turned as one to the far end of the library. Austin could see from here that a set of double doors was slowly swinging open, leading them on to the next room.

"Nice!" Clay clapped him on the back and kneaded his shoulders. "We're moving on, let's go!"

Austin stood gingerly, stretching again, and turned to see Cam holding out a hand to give him a high-five.

"Nice work." She grinned at him.

He smiled back at her. "You too, thanks for reading it out for me; it went way faster that way."

"For sure," Cam agreed. She looked over towards the door, then leaned closer to him, murmuring, "We're going to crush this thing, I can feel it." Her green eyes were flecked with gold, freckles peppered her nose and cheeks. "I can't wait to see Alex's face when we're done early." She grinned wickedly up at him, her full lips parting slightly as they curved upwards.

He felt his gut twist. She really was pretty, especially when she smiled like that. She caught his gaze had drifted down to her mouth. She gave him a long meaningful glance. His heart started to pound against his chest.

"Come on," she said, "let's go." She waved back at him as she turned to follow the others out of the room. The group had swarmed for the next space as soon as the door opened, and he could hear their voices echoing excitedly up ahead.

Austin passed one of the elaborate candelabras on his way to the door; it was sitting on a long low table against the wall. He paused, looking back around the room. They had left all the candles lit. It was probably sort of a fire hazard, especially in an old place like this, with all these books for kindling. He walked over to the table and leaned forward to blow out the candles. As he did, he peered up and gasped, jumping back slightly with a start.

A large mirror hung on the wall above the table; the candlelight glinted off its golden frame. He stared back at his own reflection, his chest heaving with his jagged breaths, his eyes were wide now. But they were their normal blue, and full of fear.

It had been only a moment, just a split second, really, but when he had first looked up, he could have sworn his eyes looked like they were glowing, his pupils reflecting the candlelight back to him.

18.

Cam

Cam smiled to herself, her heart beating a quick rhythm inside her chest. She had seen Austin's expression; the look in his eyes as he watched her lips. The longing in them had been unmistakable.

Lan caught sight of her grinning as she strode into the room. He looped an arm over her shoulder and walked with her. "What are you smiling about?" He leaned towards her, whispering.

"Nothing," she shot back at him, nudging him in the ribs. "Mind your own business."

He made an oof sort of sound and chuckled, falling back away from her and rubbing his ribcage. "Nice." He grinned at her.

Alex walked over to them, arms spread out wide. "Is this cool or what?" He smiled as he surveyed the room. "Do we still think the escape room thing is stupid?" He said out loud to the room in general.

Cam turned slowly in one spot as she took in the vast space around them. They were in a massive hall; it reminded her of the front entrance area, the floors tiled in the same black and white marble, statues lining the walls, and a row of them running up the middle of the room. The room felt like a museum.

She recalled Alex saying the whole castle had technically been turned into a museum by the estate after John Hammond's untimely death, but this was the first time she felt as though they were in some sort of museum at all. There were shelves of artifacts, and she guessed this space must contain the majority of his collection. She saw Bee and Rahul standing over at the far wall, near a second set of large double doors.

Clay and Darcy were wandering over to join them. Lan was walking around with Alex; they were looking up towards the ceiling. She followed their gaze to see a second level. It wasn't clear to her how that level was accessed, though. There didn't appear to be a set of stairs in the room, at least not anywhere obvious.

Cam took in the space. She had no clue where they were going to start. She turned to see Austin lagging far behind them; he was just now entering the room, his eyes sweeping around but hardly seeming to take anything in. She met his stare in her direction and saw with a jolt that his chest was heaving slightly as though he were out of breath. He watched her so intensely, his gaze seeming to lock onto hers. Had she affected him that much? She swallowed, her mouth suddenly dry. Her stomach twisted in anticipation of the evening. Forget the stupid escape room; he had said he would meet her tonight to read the journal and had called it a date.

"Um, Austin." Clay's deep voice reverberated through the open space, setting off a chain of echoes. Cam saw Austin freeze and turn in Clay's direction.

Clay was standing over by a small round, high-top table near the wall. He held a piece of paper up in his hand and stared over at Austin.

Cam watched as Austin made his way over to him. Clay said nothing, just handed the paper to him, a grimace on his face.

Austin took it, giving Clay a long look, before peering down at the paper in his hands. It seemed to take him only a second to read whatever was on it. He set it down on the round table, turned around abruptly, and left the room, heading back into the library.

Cam watched him go, tracking his movements until he was out of sight. She turned back to Clay, holding her palms up and shaking her head at him. "What?" she asked him quizzically.

Clay just shook his head at her, sighing. He crossed his arms and called over to the group huddled at the door. "You guys, I found the next clue."

Alex made his way over to Clay first, followed by Darcy. Bee and Rahul were too busy laughing about something at the door to pay any attention to them. Rahul reached up; he was manipulating a dial on what appeared to be some type of large clock with multiple rows of symbols that stood to the left of the closed doors. Bee grabbed onto his arm, laughing and pulling at it, trying to stop him.

Cam moved towards the table where Clay and the others stood. Alex was holding the single sheet of paper in his hands, staring down at it. Cam moved to his side. "What is it? What's the clue?" She asked.

Alex handed the paper to her, without speaking. He gave her a look as he did so. She couldn't read his expression. Did Alex look worried? That wasn't like him. She took it gingerly and peered down at it, steeling herself. For what, she had no idea. One side of the paper listed the letters of the alphabet, written out from A to Z, each with a dash and then a number listed across from the letter; they were numbered from 1 to 26.

She turned the paper over and found there was a single sentence on the back. It looked like it had been typed out on the old typewriter; she recognized the faint line next to the "e". The paper read, *'What destroyed Austin's marriage?'*

Cam looked up at Alex, a feeling of shock, quickly turning to anger, flooding through her. "What?" She frowned at him, her brow furrowing. She gazed down at the paper, read it again, then again, a third time.

"Why, Alex?" She looked up at him again, "Why would you have them add that to the game? That's awful." She frowned and handed the paper to Darcy, who watched them with wide eyes. Darcy took the paper reluctantly from her.

"It's none of our business why their marriage broke up. How dare you make that a clue?" She felt her hands clenching into fists at her side. Alex was an over-confident prick, but this was low, even for him.

Alex just stared at her, his expression still unreadable. He shook his head slowly. "So, you assume it was me?" he chuckled a bit, shaking his head again and shrugging. "Why am I not surprised?" He looked back at her. "You really do think I'm just an asshole, don't you?" He was starting to look angry now. He pointed toward the doorway, back towards the library. "He's one of my best friends, what makes you think I would do something like that, huh?"

"Oh really, you're what, mad at me now?" Cam glared up at him, her heart pounding. "Who the fuck else would have, or could have, done this Alex?" She spread her arms out around them. "This is your show, sweetheart; you're the big Hollywood director, we're all just along for the ride. Don't try to play innocent."

Alex thought, before nodding at her. He put his hands on his hips. "Okay. Fair enough. But you know what, Cam? It's good to know what you really think of me, once and for all. Noted."

"Come on Alex," Lan spoke up from behind her. "Don't act all hurt, she has a point; you are definitely in charge of this whole thing, it's your crew running this. Don't try to act like this wasn't you. What the fuck kind of game are you trying to play? Huh?" Lan marched over to him, stopping short a few feet away, and turning, he ran a hand over his mouth, cupping his chin. He paced away, his chest heaving. "Fuck," she heard him whisper under his breath.

"No, no," Alex held his hands up in the air. "Fine, you're right. I did instruct them to start incorporating details about us into the game, into the clues. But I never..."

Cam cut him off before he could finish. "Oh, okay, there we go, exactly like I thought. You set this whole thing up on purpose, but for what purpose, exactly, Alex?" She stared him down.

Clay and Darcy stood frozen, watching them with wide eyes. Bee and Rahul had started to drift closer, listening. She turned towards them, and seeing them all watching her, she turned back to Alex. "Why are we all here, Alex? What is this all for?"

He stared back at her silently.

"You're filming us, aren't you?" She shook her head at him in disgust. "You've already admitted to the cameras, implied it was all part of the escape room, but that's not the only purpose of the cameras, is it? You're filming us, all of us, adding in personal questions, stirring up old shit... what is this, exactly?" She paused, waiting for him to offer up some kind of response. But there was only one logical explanation.

Alex just stared back at her, his dark eyes cold and calculating now.

"We aren't just here for a reunion, are we? Getting your old friends together for a weekend retreat." She shook her head, smiling grimly at him. "No, it's much more than that, isn't it?" She paused for dramatic effect and smiled at him. The room had gone dead silent, everyone hung on her words. "We're the stars of your next reality TV show, aren't we?"

Alex stared back at her. He didn't move a muscle.

"Where's those waivers you made us all sign? Huh?" She continued. "I want to see mine. I want to see where I agreed to be filmed for a stupid, mindless TV show so you could take advantage of our friendship and make yourself another million richer."

Alex shook his head at her now, then shrugged. "Wow. You don't know what you're talking about Cam," he sneered at her, "But guess what," he held his arms out away from his sides, "I don't have a copy of your waiver to pull out of my ass for you, and in case you haven't noticed, I'm locked in here, just the same as you are."

She nodded at him, and laughed a little. "How convenient... you don't have them here." She shook her head at the others.

Clay stood with his arms crossed against his chest, his biceps bulging. He glared at Alex. He looked like he was restraining himself, holding himself back from kicking his ass.

Lan shook his head at Alex. "You piece of shit," he said quietly. "I knew it... I fucking knew it. I said so, didn't I Cam?"

He called over to her. "I mean, I was half joking, at the time, but it did seem like just the sort of shitty thing you would do."

"Wow, really, Lan?" Alex turned to him, eyebrows raised and pointed at his own chest. "I'm the piece of shit?"

Lan stood up straighter, glaring down at Alex as he took a few steps closer to him. "Shut the fuck up, Alex."

"Or what?" Alex sneered at him, edging closer.

"Stop it," Darcy called out, she stood with her arms wrapped around herself, shivering almost like she was cold. "Stop fighting. That's enough."

Lan didn't take his eyes off of Alex for a long moment, but he eventually turned to look at Darcy. When he did, Cam saw some of the tension leave him. He took a step back, away from Alex; the two of them continuing to stare each other down. Then Lan turned his back on him and walked away to the far side of the room.

Rahul moved past Lan as he went, making his way over to the high-top table. He picked up the piece of paper, read the sentence, and then flipped it over, studying the numerical code on the back before glancing over at the clock.

Alex watched him, then turned back to face Cam. "Well, like I said," he held his arms out wide, surveying the room, "I'm so glad to know that you all hold such high opinions of me. Absolutely fan-fucking-tastic to hear. Really."

He looked back at Cam, and for a moment his expression was unreadable again. She felt a small fissure of doubt. Was he telling the truth? Was he somehow not personally orchestrating all of this? But if not him, who was?

He held her gaze, and he looked hurt. Had she actually managed to hurt his feelings? To break through the miles-thick wall of bravado and carelessness? Alex had always been so superficial, in a way, so brash and uncaring, that she didn't think it was possible to affect him. She felt herself shrink back, unsure now if she had gone too far. But no, she reminded herself. He must just be acting; perpetuating his agenda for the weekend. She had to be right. There was much more going on here than he was admitting to.

He turned away from her then and made his way back towards the library. "I'm going to check on Austin," he called back over his shoulder.

Cam looked over at Darcy, then at Clay. Clay nodded at her, and approached Darcy, resting a hand on her back. "Come on, Darcy, let's go." Clay said gently to her. She still looked nervous, frightened even. She nodded slowly and let him lead her toward the library.

Cam glanced back at the others; Lan was pacing off by himself. He seemed to be cooling off still. Bee gave her a worried look, and walked over to join her, Rahul following closely behind.

"I hope he's okay," Bee murmured to her. "What a mean thing to do." She shook her head, her eyes heavy with concern. She glanced over at the clock contraption near the doorway. "It looks like we enter the answer on that thing." She explained to Cam. "There are three rings; it looks like the inner ring is numbers, one through 30, maybe corresponding to days of the month." She shrugged, looking over at Rahul, who had joined them.

He nodded at Cam. "Yeah, we aren't sure, but we're thinking those are meant to indicate the day of the month. The second ring contains lines and then numbers interspersed, those go up by fives. And then the outer ring looks like it's made up of letters. But some of them are letter combinations.... or sounds I guess." He frowned slightly. "There's a main dial that spins around. We're not completely sure how it works."

Cam nodded, peering over at the odd clock. "Hmm, maybe the numbers actually correspond to a letter of the alphabet? There are only 26, letters, not 30, though. But maybe we just ignore the last few numbers. Maybe we can spin the dial on the numbers to spell something out?"

Rahul nodded to her. "That makes sense. Yeah, " he said, glancing over towards the library doors, eyebrows raised. "What do you think? Should we go check on them?"

Cam looked back in Lan's direction. He was still pacing. He saw her watching him and just shook his head at her before turning away. "Yeah, let's go," Cam sighed loudly. "Let's head back into the library, I guess."

Their trio made their way slowly over to the library, leaving Lan behind to his pacing. Cam thought it was probably for the best that he kept his distance from Alex for now. Let him have some time to cool off on his own. Lan always did have a bit of a temper.

They entered the library, Cam feeling somewhat reluctant to join the others. They found them gathered around the fireplace. Austin and Alex were both seated in armchairs on either side of the fireplace. Darcy and Clay sat on the low couch. They approached them, weaving their way in between the tables and chairs scattered throughout the room. Cam stopped behind the couch and leaned against the back of it. She noticed Darcy jumped slightly at the movement behind her, turning halfway to see it was just Cam. Cam patted her reassuringly on the shoulder. Clay turned as well and looked at her grimly. Darcy shivered slightly under Cam's hand. No one spoke. Austin didn't look up at them. He stared into the empty grate.

"You cold, Darcy?" Cam asked quietly. "You feel like you're shivering."

Darcy nodded, her jaw clenched tight. "Yeah," she muttered. "Aren't you cold?"

"I'm not too bad right now," Cam replied. She felt warm enough, with her thick sweatshirt and everything that was happening. She felt practically hot now, but she had been freezing this morning.

Darcy looked up at her in surprise. "I'm freezing. I can't seem to get warm in this place."

Austin looked over in her direction. Then he returned his gaze to the area around the fireplace. Cam saw a stack of wood sitting in the black metal holder next to the brick wall.

"I can start a fire in here," Austin murmured. He moved forward onto his knees, grabbing a log from the pile and setting it aside.

"I'll help you," Alex said swiftly, jumping to his feet, and joining him at the fireplace. He sat on the edge of the hearth, studying Austin. Austin didn't look up at him; he just started handing him logs and digging around to check for kindling. He seemed to come up empty-handed.

Austin looked over towards them. "Clay, will you go grab that paper?" He asked gruffly. "The one with the clue."

Clay stared at him for a moment, then jumped up, comprehending. "Yeah, of course. I'll be right back." He made his way swiftly across the room.

Alex grimaced at Austin's words. "Austin," he started, quietly, keeping his voice low, "I'm sorry..." he trailed off. "I... I didn't..."

Austin held a hand up, stopping him. "It's fine," he said, but he looked up at Alex with storm clouds in his eyes, his jaw clenched tightly. "Forget about it."

Alex cleared his throat, nodding. He turned and looked over at the others, his gaze sliding uncomfortably over Cam, and landing on Rahul. "Okay," Alex said, nodding again. "Okay." He paused, looking uncertain how to continue with what he wanted to say. "If you want to tell me, or one of us," he added hastily, as Austin shot him a dark look, "um, what the... answer is, I mean, um... then maybe we could enter it for you, you know? So, you don't have to... have to do it." He finished lamely, looking over at Rahul hopefully.

Rahul shifted on his feet and nodded slowly. "Yeah, man, um, I can do it, if you want. I think I figured out how the clock thing works. I'm guessing it unlocks the next door."

Austin's gaze swung over to Rahul. Rahul met his eyes before looking down, then over at Bee. He shrugged.

Bee sighed, and moved closer to Austin, coming around and sitting on the edge of the couch nearest to him. "Yeah, I can help, Austin, if you'd rather not say it to anyone. I can help you enter it on the clock. There are numbers around the ring; we think they match the letters of the alphabet. I think we would just slide the middle pointer to the right numbers."

Clay returned just then, and made his way over to Austin, handing him the paper with the alphabet code side up. Austin took it from him, thanking him. He held the paper in front of him, studying the code. "Well," he said, "I was going to use this for kindling, but I guess we might want to keep it. It'll be easier to have it as a reference." He paused, looking it over. "Although the code is obviously simple enough. The letters 1-26 correspond to the letters of the alphabet." He didn't sound angry, or sad even, just tired, Cam thought.

She looked over at the table with the telegraph machine on it and saw the pieces of paper still lying next to it. "Hang on," she said to Austin. She made her way back to the table and stood there for a moment. She had been about to grab the paper with the Morse code on it, but for some reason, she thought better of burning that. Maybe they would need it again for something later. She grabbed the typewriter sheet with the music notes typed out on it instead and returned back to them.

"Here," she said, handing the paper over to Austin, "You can use this. We shouldn't need it anymore." She gave him a sympathetic smile as he took it from her. He seemed to avoid meeting her eyes. She knew from experience he hated pity, but it was hard not to feel sorry for him.

"Thanks," he muttered, looking down at the paper in his hand. He stood after a moment, brushing past her, and handed the other sheet of paper to Bee.

Fine. Cam thought. So, he felt more comfortable handing it to Bee for some reason, but she felt an odd flicker of emotion at him passing over her. He proceeded to rip the other paper into large strips and crumpled a few together. He set them in a little pile. Before too long, he had a fire going in the hearth. They found seats again on the couches and armchairs. Austin stood and motioned Darcy to take his chair, so she could be closer to the fire. He remained standing, walking away from them and pacing back and forth off to the side. They sat in silence for a few seconds, no one knowing what to say.

Finally, Cam caught Alex shooting pointed looks at Rahul. Rahul gave him a look back before reluctantly clearing his throat and walking over towards Austin. "What do you think, man?" He asked him, crossing his arms over his chest. "You want to go give it a try? Or..." he let his voice trail off into silence.

Austin looked at him and sighed, then looked away. His face flushing slightly, he said, "Yeah, I guess. It's just... I'm not sure exactly what the right answer is." He finished gruffly, shoving his hands in his pockets.

"What do you mean?" Cam heard Bee speak up from her spot on the couch. She stood, and after a moment's thought, she moved closer, making her way over to Austin. She walked up to him and laid a hand on his arm. Cam could just barely make out her words as she said gently, softly to him. "Why did she leave you?"

Austin looked at her, his expression incredulous, as he raised an eyebrow at her. Cam watched him intently, holding her breath without realizing it, as she waited for his answer. Slowly, he shook his head. "She didn't, Bee. I left her." He swallowed, his voice low and gravelly. "I kicked her out."

Cam felt her eyebrows raise in surprise, unable to help herself from revealing on her face that she was listening. She tried to look away, at the fire, at the others, but she turned to see they were all watching the exchange just as intently while trying to pretend like they weren't listening. Only Darcy faced away from them, staring into the fire.

"You... you did?" she heard Bee ask. "Well..." she seemed at a loss for words. "Well, why, then? That must be the answer, right?" She spoke to him again gently, her hand still on his arm.

Austin sighed, looked away from her, and turned back towards the entrance to the museum room. Then he sighed deeply and turned back to meet her eyes. "She cheated on me, Bee. Okay?" He chuckled, almost laughed, as he said it. Shaking his head and shrugging his shoulders.

"What?" Bee's voice floated over to them. "Oh my god, I'm sorry Austin." She thought for a moment. "With who?"

Austin shrugged again, his voice barely a whisper. "I don't know who. Does it matter?" His cheeks flushed slightly at the admission. He looked away, down at the floor, his hair falling over his eyes, and then he turned and began to pace away from her.

Bee watched him go, letting her arm fall back to her side. She turned and met Cam's gaze for only the briefest of moments out of the corner of her eyes.

"Okay..." Bee said, gently still, keeping her voice pitched low. "Okay then." Cam watched him walk, pacing restlessly back and forth. He ran his hands through his hair. He looked like he wanted to hit something.

"Okay." She heard Bee repeat again. She walked over to him, "Come on, Austin, let's go take a walk for a bit, okay?" She told him. "And when you're ready, we'll go over to the clock, and I'll try that out, okay?"

He didn't nod in agreement, didn't respond at all to her, but he moved his pacing with her guidance and headed for the other room.

Bee looked back over her shoulder. "Rahul," she called out, "Grab the paper, please."

Rahul jumped to grab the paper from where Austin had left it, on the floor in front of the fireplace. Then he followed them out of the room.

19.

Darcy

Darcy shivered from her seat in front of the fire. She wrapped her shawl tighter around herself, hugging her chest with her arms. Why she had decided to wear a dress today was beyond her. She did have thick black tights on, but even still. She felt chilled to the bone. The fire was helping a little, slowly bringing some warmth back to her limbs. She could feel her hands and fingers now at least, and that was something.

But there was something about the cold that seemed unnatural to her. The others seemed to be almost completely unaffected by it, yet she was half frozen. It was very odd. Darcy frowned at the fire. She lifted a hand, laying the back of her hand against her forehead. It felt warm, in comparison, but she couldn't tell if she was feverish. She turned, scanning the room for Bee, before remembering she had taken Austin back to the other room to try to enter the answer to the clue on the odd clock. She would ask Bee to check her when she got back.

Darcy busied herself with thinking about what her next painting would be. She had thought she would gather a ton of inspiration from the castle, from being here and seeing all the artwork, the old furniture and the architecture, and she felt some of that, to an extent. But she shivered again slightly, thinking of the darkness of the place, the foreboding emptiness she felt at the core of the castle. She hated to think of that coldness seeping into her paintings... infecting and twisting the imagery she wanted to capture. How could it not influence her, even subconsciously, without her realizing?

Darcy was startled by Clay's deep voice resonating suddenly at her side. He plopped down next to her, taking a seat on the fireplace hearth. "Hey," he said, "How you holding up?" He looked her up and down and took in the arms wrapped tightly around her middle, like she was attempting to hold herself together.

Darcy gave him a reassuring smile. "I'm fine, starting to feel warmer now."

Clay gave her an odd look. He shook his sweater out like he was fanning himself with the small movement of air. "God, I would hope so," he said, wiping his hand across his forehead, "I've been sitting here for two seconds and I'm already starting to sweat." He looked up at her. "You've been here for what," he looked down at his empty wrist for a second before sighing and looking back at her, "I dunno, an hour or more. I would hope you'd be warm by now."

"An hour?" Darcy asked him, frowning slightly. "It can't have been half that long." She looked around, suddenly taking in the empty couch, and then the empty room. "Where is everybody?" She asked.

Clay raised an eyebrow at her. "They're all in the other room." He waved a hand towards the far wall, towards the museum room. "Although Lan and Cam went missing, a while ago," he added, "I'm 99% sure they went to go find some booze and bring it back here." He rolled his eyes at her. "Normally, I would make fun of them... but in this situation, I feel like a little day-drinking is more than warranted."

Darcy looked at him quizzically. "Okay," she said slowly. "What is everyone else doing?"

Clay inclined his head towards the other room. "Well, most of them are trying to help Austin answer the stupid clue, on the clock thing." He waved his hand in that direction. "Mostly Bee and Rahul." He shrugged, "I mean, they're trying to be helpful, but they're mainly just standing around, watching Austin while he struggles to answer just what the hell exactly ended his marriage." He sighed loudly and ran a hand over his face. "He keeps entering variations of the same thing. Basically, from what I can gather, Miranda cheated on him, and he kicked her out. So yeah, it's been a little awkward." He peered up at her. "You were probably smart to stay in here."

Darcy nodded thoughtfully. "Poor Austin, that's terrible."

"Yeah." Clay nodded, in agreement. "It is. I feel bad for the guy." He looked thoughtfully. "And I don't get what's happening. Alex is acting like he had nothing to do with all this. I mean, how does that make any sense?" He watched her, waiting for some type of answer, but she had none to give him.

Darcy shrugged. "I don't know..." she trailed off, "Most of what's happened this weekend doesn't make any sense to me." She frowned over at the open double doors. They sat in silence for a moment. Then Darcy turned at the sound of voices approaching from the other hallway. She saw Lan and Cam emerge from the doorway. They each held a glass bottle, containing amber-looking liquid.

"How on earth did you get those down the ladder?" Clay called out to them incredulously.

Lan looked over at him stoically. "You don't want to know," he replied. Clay laughed out loud at that.

"Great," Clay said, still chuckling. Lan approached them, unscrewed the cap, and took a long swig from the bottle. He wiped his mouth with the back of his hand and held the bottle out to Clay.

Clay looked at it for several seconds, before reaching up and taking it from him. He took a swig, grimacing slightly afterward. He held it up to Darcy. "Go on, Darc," he said to her gently, "It might do you some good. Help warm you up." He nodded towards the shawl stretched over her thin frame.

Darcy paused, thinking, before deciding he was probably right. She took the bottle somewhat gingerly and took a small sip. She felt it burning all the way down to her chest, where it settled and created a small pocket of warmth within her.

She nodded to him and handed the bottle back. "I'm good, for now. Thanks."

Clay nodded at her, standing and taking one more, longer pull, before handing it back to Lan.

Lan sipped it again. Grimacing and letting out a whoop afterward. Clay clapped him on the back and laughed.

Lan held the bottle up in the air, looked at it for a moment, and then back at Clay. "Liquid courage, right?" he asked.

Clay gave him a funny sort of smile before nodding in agreement. "That's right. That's what they say."

"Alright." Lan nodded to himself. He screwed the cap back on the bottle and turned towards the museum room. "Come on guys, let's go."

The guys began to make their way towards the other room. Cam gave Darcy a small smile and rolled her eyes slightly at their backs. "Men," she said simply. She seemed to be waiting for Darcy to join her, so she stood and fell into step beside Cam, following her to the other room.

They made their way there in silence. Darcy could feel the cold enveloping her as she moved away from the warmth of the fire, entering the cavernous space of the museum room. She held onto the small bundle of warmth in her chest as she followed Cam across the large open space. The group was scattered around the room. Clay and Lan took up spots at the high-top table, passing the bottle back and forth to Rahul and Alex now. Bee was over at the clock, standing nearby as Austin paced in front of it, hands in his pockets and head down. Bee looked over at the girls as they entered, giving them a forlorn, impatient look.

"This is pointless." She heard Austin mutter. "Nothing is working. We might as well go back to the common room."

Bee looked down at the piece of paper she held in her hands. She frowned thoughtfully. "There must be some combination we haven't tried yet."

"Like what?" Austin spat at her, exasperated. Bee's head snapped up; she looked briefly stunned. "I'm sorry," Austin said, sighing loudly, seeing her expression, "It's not your fault." His gaze drifted over towards Alex as he said that last bit. Alex caught his eyes before he looked away, down at his hands on the table.

Darcy studied him, puzzled. He truly did look sorry. He looked... beaten down, somehow. She had thought he was acting, pretending like he had nothing to do with the clue, but maybe he was telling the truth. That thought made her more nervous than she cared to admit.

She stood there, apart from the others at the table. She watched them all. Lan moved away from the group, walking away from them and taking the bottle of amber liquid with him. He took another long pull from the bottle. He was going to be drunk before he knew it if he didn't slow down, Darcy thought. Why did he look so nervous? He looked almost as bad as Austin did. She watched them wearily, the two of them, pacing around the room like caged animals.

Darcy jumped slightly as she heard a step behind her. A soft footfall, then shuffling footsteps approaching on the hard marble flooring. Darcy turned, bracing herself for who she might see, because they were all there already in the room; she had been the last one to enter.

Miranda stood there. She had come to a stop about ten feet away. Darcy was struck immediately by two things. One, Miranda looked nervous. She held her hands together in front of her, twisting them. And two, she was beautiful. Darcy had forgotten somehow just how beautiful she was, in the years since she had seen her last. Her dark, shoulder-length hair fell in large, soft waves. Her dark eyes were solemn, taking in the scene in front of her. Her full lips were a deep shade of purple, almost black. Darcy could never pull off wearing a lip color like that, she thought absentmindedly, but somehow Miranda could.

Everything Miranda did, everything she wore, was effortlessly chic and somehow exotic. You could take the most boring, blandest of fashion trends, but somehow when Miranda donned it, it became cool again. She just had that way about her. She was wearing a dark dress, with a coat that looked almost like a cape, with a hood that fell draped behind her. She surveyed them all and gave them a small smile. Darcy's chest ached, watching her.

Miranda looked at Austin, over by the clock. Darcy didn't need to turn around to know who she was looking at.

Lan turned in his pacing and faced them now. He lifted the bottle to his lips again and froze, his gaze falling on Miranda. She looked over at him, and quickly looked away, her gaze falling to the floor. Lan lowered the bottle, and looked over at Austin, an odd expression on his face. Miranda looked back over at Austin, too, and Darcy felt herself begin to shudder. But it was more than just the cold, this time.

She began to turn towards Austin herself, but she didn't want to look. She felt a feeling like when she was driving and knew she was about to see two cars wreck; that awful moment when everything seemed to slow down, but it was already too late, and nothing could be done to stop it. She turned slowly, reluctantly, her head swiveling towards Austin. And they were all watching him now, staring at him, waiting to see what he would do.

Austin stared at Miranda. Then over at Lan, then back at Miranda. Then he turned slowly to his left and found Alex over by the table. He gave Alex a long look and continued to turn. He walked over to the clock, and time was lagging, as though he were moving in slow motion now. He ripped the piece of paper from Bee's outstretched hand as he went.

As he approached the clock, he glanced down at the paper. He swung the dial back to the top, to zero. Then he swung it to the number 12. Then slowly back around, as though he was heading back to zero, but he stopped at one. Then he swung it back, the dial clicking slowly, echoing loudly somehow in the silence of the room as he clicked through each number, making his way deliberately to 14.

Darcy watched and listened as the numbers ticked by in exquisite slowness. She had no idea what they spelled out, couldn't do that math in her head, but she swallowed dryly as there was a loud clunking sound on the final number. Then a whirring and grinding of gears came from somewhere inside the wall. She shuddered again as a loud low boom of thunder rocked the house. The double doors seemed to shudder in their frame, before they parted slightly, then yawned open, revealing nothing but darkness beyond.

But Austin was already turning away from the doors. He was moving faster now, moving past Bee, the paper falling out of his hands uselessly to the floor as she turned to watch him go. He moved past Darcy next, heading across the room. But he wasn't moving in Miranda's direction.

Then everything happened at once, as he stalked towards Lan, who stared at him, open-mouthed, his eyes wide in fear, his arms down at his sides, as the amber bottle, still half full, slipped from his hand and shattered, just as Austin leapt, from what seemed an impossible distance, and hit him square in the chest, tackling him to the ground.

Darcy was shivering now. Watching helplessly as Austin hit him, again, and again. Blood was spraying, mixing with the liquor on the marble tile; the scent of both in the air.

They scrambled and fought as Lan flipped Austin onto his back, finally gaining the upper hand and slamming him into the ground. Austin landed on shards of glass, crying out with a short yelp of pain.

Lan punched him once, right in the face, before Austin was up somehow, launching them both over, Lan landing on his back again with a thud as the air rushed out of his chest. Miranda was screaming something, her hands over her face, covering her mouth and nose. Tears streaming down.

Shouting mixed with the sound of running footsteps as Alex and Clay brushed past her. Clay, pausing to move Darcy, pushed her farther away from the scrambling mass of violence that was Austin and Lan. Darcy took a step back, then another. Clay's eyes were wide. He said something to her, but she couldn't hear him, couldn't understand a word of it.

She fell in scrambling steps backward until she hit something and bumped into Cam, standing behind her. Cam grabbed her, gripping her arms, watching in horror. Rahul rushed past them, joining the other men as they attempted to remove Austin. He straddled Lan, pummeling him into the ground. Darcy winced at the shards of glass that peppered the back of Lan's arm as it lifted off the floor.

A minute or so later, it was finally over. Rahul, Alex, and Clay managed to eventually drag Austin backward off of Lan. They pulled him away, his feet sliding on the floor as he scrambled for purchase. His shoes were slick with a mixture of blood and liquor. The others must have been, too, as they slipped and slid, leaving red streaks on the marble tiles, scrambling away across the room, and coming to a rest in a heap near the high-top table.

Miranda stood there, staring down at Lan, her expression a mix of horror and disgust.

Alex stood, sighing loudly, panting as he caught his breath. He stared down at the heap of body parts next to him, pointing to Austin. "Hold him," he commanded the other two men. But Austin lay there, weakly, on the floor, half-propped up on the other two. His eyes were closed, and he was panting, his chest rising and falling rapidly. He looked spent.

Thunder cracked again above them, louder this time, reverberating through the open space. Darcy heard the faint rattle of glass as Alex turned to look at Miranda and gave her a lopsided grin. "Well, well, well," he said, gazing over at her, "Look who finally decided to join the party."

Miranda turned her gaze over to him, a look of disbelief on her face.

Alex shook his head. "You always did have impeccable timing, my dear."

20.

Bee

Bee moved slowly, half in a daze, and hardly knew in the end, how exactly she made her way back to the common room.

Rahul had led her most of the way, climbing up the ladder behind her, encouraging her when she paused. The group had somehow made it back, and half of them were a sorry sight, bruised and bloodied.

Bee snapped out of it as Clay approached her, handing her the first aid kit he had noticed earlier in one of the desk drawers. She took it from him gratefully, opening it swiftly and laying it out on the dining table.

Thankfully, it was a large kit and well-stocked. But still, the supplies on hand would only go so far. She felt a flood of relief as she eyed the set of tweezers. She was no surgeon, of course, but she could use them to remove the shards of glass. She would have to assess the damage; hopefully, most of it would be superficial. She turned to find Alex.

"I can treat anything superficial, but if there is anything deeper or if a piece of glass might have hit or be near something vital, we're going to have to call for help." She spoke to him firmly, her tone brooking no argument.

Alex just looked at her blankly before nodding solemnly. "Of course," he replied somewhat numbly. He moved over to the table, eyeing the phone. "I'll call the team and tell them to be on standby." He reached out and plucked the phone from its cradle, holding it up to his ear as he turned to survey the damage.

Lan and Austin sat on opposite sides of the room. Lan was over by the fire, and Austin had been sat down at the far end of the dining table.

He sat hunched over, his head in his hands. Clay and Rahul stood on either side of him, guarding him as though they expected him to get up at any moment and launch himself at Lan all over again.

Alex frowned at her as he held the phone to his ear, listening intently. He pulled the phone away from his ear and frowned down at it, then back at Bee, before saying slowly, "There's no dial tone."

He turned back to the desk, mashing buttons and listening again. He hit the rocker in the cradle repeatedly, attempting to hang up the phone to see if the dial tone would come back. He shook his head at her, turning slowly as he set the phone back down. "Nothing. What the hell?"

Bee frowned at him in consternation. Clay spoke up suddenly. "Well, they can still see us. And hear us, I'm guessing." He nodded to the board hanging over the desk as he spoke. "If we need help, we'll just talk to them, tell them through the cameras."

Bee looked over, up above Alex's head, as he swiveled to look too. Multiple red lights were shining. One was lit up next to Lan's name, one next to Austin's... no surprise there. There was a second light lit up next to Alex's name, too.

"What the fuck!" Alex exclaimed. "What did I do this time?" He asked, spinning back to them, a look of shocked confusion on his face. His gaze landed on Rahul, his expression shooting daggers at him.

Rahul just stared back at him, then looked sideways at Bee and Clay before shrugging. "I have no idea man," he said simply. He crouched down next to Austin. "You hanging in there?" He asked him in a kind, calm voice. Austin didn't look up at him. Didn't move or seem to react at all. Rahul studied him for a moment, his gaze drifting back over towards Bee.

"Lucky for you, we've got a first-class nurse right here with us who's going to check you out and make sure you're okay. Maybe get some of that glass out of your arm, okay man?" He studied Austin's back, looking for a spot that looked relatively glass-free, before placing his hand gently on his back. "Okay, man?" He repeated, dropping his voice lower, speaking directly into Austin's ear. "You're going to sit calmly and let Bee help you out and get you cleaned up, okay?" He waited for a response but received none. "I'm not going to have any problems with you, am I?" Rahul asked, his voice quiet, an edge of a threat to his words now.

Bee watched him intently, studying his manner, his tone. He had done this before. She could tell. He must have some experience dealing with injured, possibly violent, or mentally unstable people. What had Rahul told her he did for work? He had said he was some kind of accountant or something. That didn't seem right, somehow.

Austin moved finally, nodding his head imperceptibly, in agreement.

"Good man," Rahul said. He nodded over at Bee, giving her the okay to get started.

Bee approached Austin, sliding the first aid kit over closer to him. She had prepped some of the supplies she thought she would need, laying them out on the lid in front of her. She lay a hand gently on Austin's arm, letting him know she was there. "Okay, Austin, it's me. We're going to take a look at removing some of this glass, okay? But let me take a look at your face." She slid two fingers under his chin, lifting his head gently.

He sat up for her, putting his arms down on the table, allowing her to turn his face towards hers. He wouldn't look her in the eyes, but he let her check his face for wounds. He had a good gash over his left eyebrow, but it wouldn't need anything much other than to be cleaned properly and bandaged. She was much more concerned about the glass. Thankfully he didn't seem to have much in his face. His back and arms were going to be another story. Bee got to work swiftly.

She did her best to clean him up, bandaging the cut on his forehead. He insisted he didn't need a bandage, but she insisted more firmly that he did.

She had no idea how long it took her to remove the glass from his arms and back. Thankfully the shirt he was wearing was thin, and she could easily see and find the shards of glass with it on still. Once she thought she had all the pieces she could find, she had him remove the shirt carefully, and she searched every inch of his back and arms carefully once more. She cleaned him up the best she could and sent him on his way.

Rahul sent Clay with him, ordering him back to his room to rest. Clay was to sit with him if he'd allow it or move a chair out in the hall outside his room if he wouldn't. Clay agreed readily to this. Austin sat throughout the whole thing, unmoving. He hardly reacted as she pulled shards of glass out of him, and he didn't say a word back to her as she attempted to make small talk. Bee couldn't say she blamed him.

Next, she cleaned up her tools, sterilized the tweezers, and moved on to Lan. Lan's face was in arguably much worse shape than Austin's had been. He had been lying back on the couch with an ice pack. Thankfully, the mini bar Alex had installed for them had included an ice maker. They'd made a makeshift ice pack by shoving ice into a surgical glove and tying it shut.

Lan allowed her to inspect his bloodied face gingerly, wincing as she gently felt his nose and cheekbones. She spoke to him gently as she cleaned off the blood and bandaged him up the best she could. "I think you'll be okay," she told him. "The damage looks pretty superficial to me. You may have some scarring afterward, but I don't think it will be all that bad. I'm more worried about your nose than anything else, but I don't think it's broken."

Lan sighed and nodded grimly. "It's no worse than I deserve," he said. Then amended, "Actually, I deserve a lot worse than this."

Bee sighed, glancing around the room as she worked. She had tied her hair back in a loose bun before she started, but her face-framing pieces had fallen out and kept falling over her eyes. She shook her head and blew them out of her way, catching a glimpse of Rahul. She realized he was watching her work from across the room. The dark look in his eyes made her stomach flip.

He had turned one of the chairs around at the fireplace to face the doorway. He was sitting where he could keep an eye on the door as well as Bee and Lan at the table. Clearly, he was worried about Austin deciding to start round two. She surveyed the rest of the room swiftly. Miranda, Cam, and Darcy were nowhere in sight, only Alex was still in the room. He was lying on the couch, staring up at the ceiling. Bee murmured to Lan. "What on earth happened Lan?"

His gaze shifted to hers, but she kept her eyes on her work as she swiftly began to remove little shards of glass from the right side of his face. He winced as she pulled them loose, dropping them onto a napkin freckled with blood she had draped on the table.

Lan sighed deeply. "I might as well tell you, I guess." She said nothing in response, waiting for him to continue.

"It all started a few months back," he began. "Long story short, Miranda's work took her to New York occasionally. She and I had met up before."

Bee paused and gave him a sharp look.

"Just for a coffee, or to grab a bite to eat, nothing happened." He held his hands up. "Seriously, we'd gotten together a handful of times. It got to where she would let me know ahead of time, you know, give me a heads up when she was going to be in town. It was just as friends. Austin knew about it." Lan met her eyes straight on this time. "He did. And we didn't talk much, in between. Not at first," he added.

Bee sighed. "I can see where this is going." Lan nodded. "Keep still," she said, somewhat more sharply than she intended. He stiffened, and she continued working. He was silent for another moment.

"Eventually, we started just chatting, in between trips. I..." his voice trailed off. "I would start to feel excited when I knew she was going to be in town again." He fell quiet again for a bit. "It was good seeing her again, reminded me of old times, with all of us, you know. It gave me a break, from thinking about work, all the shit I see, have to deal with."

Bee nodded slightly in spite of herself. She could understand that. She saw enough dark things as a nurse. She didn't want to think about the types of things he encountered.

"But it was just that. That was all it was, really."

She waited for him to continue again, moving on to his arms next.

"But then," he swallowed, gulping audibly, "One night... we had been drinking. Had too much to drink. Both of us. And the bar we were at lost power somehow. I don't know how or why, but we ended up back at my apartment." He swallowed again, closing his eyes and wincing in pain as she pulled a particularly large chunk of glass out of his bicep. "It never should have happened, and I'm sorry that it did." He opened his eyes again. "It was never either of our intentions. Miranda felt horrible. Anyway," he said after another long pause, "she left and flew back to Michigan. And I guess... at some point, she couldn't deal with the guilt, and she told him." Bee nodded to him.

He sighed deeply again, looking off into the distance. "But she never told him who. She swore to me she didn't. But I couldn't be sure, you know. When we came out here, and he saw me for the first time. I... I saw his face, and I knew, she had told me the truth. He didn't know."

Bee sighed. "Oh Lan..." she began, then drifted off, shaking her head. She dropped the shard of glass she held in the tweezers and stood to move on to his back.

He grabbed her arm. "I know," he said intently. "Trust me, I know. I have felt awful; you have no idea how terrible it's been. Especially since we got here, being around him, and him not knowing. Then..." he reached up and wiped his upper lip, wincing slightly as he hit a cut on his face. "Then, knowing she was coming here too... I never thought she would, didn't think she was invited at all. I... I never should have come, myself." He finished lamely.

"Why did you?" Bee asked him softly, staring down at him. She couldn't help but pity him, at least a little. He seemed to truly feel awful over what had happened.

She saw Rahul start to stand, his eyes on Lan's hand wrapped around her arm. She shook her head slightly at him, and he relaxed back into his seat, gazing back at the doorway.

Lan took a long pause before responding. "I don't know," he said finally. "I almost didn't. I actually turned around at the airport and started to leave. I..." he trailed off. "It's been rough lately, with work, and everything. I guess I just..." He looked up at her, one eye practically swollen shut. "I guess I just wanted to see all of you again." He swallowed, dropping his gaze back down to his hands in his lap. He slumped forward and fell silent again.

Bee began to remove the glass from his upper back. "Well," she said softly, "I can understand that." She patted his shoulder gently as she worked. "Everything's going to be okay," she told him quietly. "Somehow, it'll be okay," she murmured more to herself now than to him. Utter nonsense, really, she thought. But it seemed like the right kind of thing to say. She looked over to where Rahul sat, guarding the doorway. Guarding her.

She licked her lips and got back to work, telling herself to focus on what she was doing. But her mind kept returning to him as she worked. How he had spoken to Austin, earlier. How he had wanted to talk to her in the typewriter room when they were alone for a moment. *What had he been about to say?* She eyed him wearily across the room. He was talking now, quietly with Alex. They were carrying on a whispered conversation. Alex was propped up on one elbow, gesturing animatedly towards Rahul as he spoke. She couldn't make out anything they were saying from here.

Bee sighed, her mind wandering as she thought about Austin. He must be seething still right now. The look on his face as he had walked past her to attack Lan had been terrifying. Rahul was probably right to be worried. It wasn't the sort of thing you got over after throwing a few punches. Although, he had done quite a number on Lan's face. And poor Miranda, Bee thought. No wonder she had been reluctant to show up this weekend. And she had arrived at the worst possible moment. It was a messy situation all around.

When Bee was finally finished fishing glass out of Lan's arms and upper body, she instructed him to carefully check the rest of his body for any she might have missed. He nodded glumly and shuffled off to his room. Rahul rose and followed him out the door, clearly intending to escort him safely back to his room. He winked at Bee as he left.

Bee made her way over to the couch, sighing loudly as she slumped back, closing her eyes, and then stretching her back, arms, and shoulders. She sat up and rotated her neck as well. She saw Alex get up and leave her. He returned swiftly with two wine glasses in one hand, and a bottle of wine in the other. He set the glasses down on the coffee table, removed the cork, and poured for both of them. He handed her a glass and she smiled wearily up at him.

"Thanks, Alex. That's nice of you." She took a sip and savored the taste. She was no wine expert by any means, but this was good wine. She could tell it was expensive from just one sip.

"You're welcome," Alex said, sitting down beside her and raising his glass to his lips. "You deserve it after that. That was a lot." He lifted his glass to her, and she lifted hers as well, clinking it against his. "Nice works" he said simply, and they both drank. "What a day... huh?" He said after a moment.

Bee just nodded in agreement, too tired suddenly to formulate a response.

Alex sat there thoughtfully in silence. She saw his eyes drift over to the board with their names on it, watched him as he stared at the red lights next to his name. "Well, I'm pretty sure Cam hates me now. Although, to be fair, I think she always has," he said quietly, swirling his glass of wine in slow lazy circles. "Obviously, Austin does now, too. And Lan clearly blames me for that clue being included in the first place... so yeah. That's about half the group at this point. Although I'm hoping Darcy, Clay, and maybe you, don't hate me at least." He gave her a weak smile and took a long gulp of wine.

Bee watched him for a few seconds pause. "You forgot about Rahul."

Alex gave a brief snorting laugh at that. "Rahul. Yeah, I didn't forget about him. He's..." he stopped and trailed off, eyeing her sideways. "I already know what he thinks of me."

Bee sighed and took another long sip of wine herself. She watched the last glowing embers in the grate; most were burnt out, a crumbling pile of white and black coals. But some still glowed orange here or there. "Alex, none of us hate you," she said quietly. "I don't know what's happening, exactly, with," she waved a hand, "Everything, this weekend. But whatever it is, knowing you, I don't imagine you'll tell us until you're good and ready."

Alex looked like he was about to protest, but he stopped himself as she continued. "But the thing is, you can take what everyone said about you today, and you can sit here and feel sorry for yourself, or..." She made him meet her eyes, moving closer to him as he began to chuckle and look away. "Or, Alex, you can listen to them, and take ownership over it, and whatever it is you've done."

He nodded, his jaw tight, as he turned and stared at the rain still beating against the windows.

"Clearly there is something more to this than you've let on. And if you've misled us, well..." she trailed off again, studying his profile. "Then I'll be sorry to hear it. But I won't hate you." She laid a hand on his arm, patting it reassuringly. He just nodded and continued to stare out the window.

Bee heard footsteps approaching from down the hallway and turned to see Rahul entering the room. He waved for her to come over to him from just inside the doorway.

Alex turned and saw him, too. "Thanks, Bee," he murmured, as she stood up. "You're right."

Bee smiled at him. "As usual." She gave a little bow as he laughed, then left him staring out the window and went to see what Rahul wanted.

"Hey," he said quietly as she approached, "sorry to interrupt." He glanced back down the hallway. "Um, so Austin is resting, I hope, at least, but he's locked up in his room and keeping to himself for now. Lan is too; he's taking a break."

"And hiding in shame, I would imagine," Bee added sharply.

Rahul nodded and chuckled slightly. "Well, yeah. That too."

Bee sighed and folded her arms. "What a complete mess. This is unreal."

"Yeah, it's very unfortunate." Rahul nodded grimly. "Um, the girls are hanging out with Miranda, they're in Darcy's room right now. Cam was asking for you."

Cam approached them down the hall, appearing suddenly behind Rahul. "Bee," she said, reaching past him and grabbing her arm. "I need you to come be with Miranda. Please." She shook her head, her green eyes wide and pleading. "I can't do this, and Darcy is basically useless right now."

Bee frowned at Cam. "Why is she useless? What's wrong with Darcy?"

Cam shook her head, tucking her hair behind her ears. "I dunno, she's sitting there, mumbling, talking about how there's something wrong with this place." Cam shrugged. "She certainly isn't interested in comforting Miranda right now, and I... I can't Bee. Please." Cam tilted her head to the side and gave Bee a pleading look.

"Fine, okay, yes, of course I'll come sit with her."

Cam smiled and took her hand, starting to pull her down the hallway into the main foyer. They climbed the stairs quickly, Rahul trailing behind them.

When they reached Darcy's door, Bee stopped before entering. "What are you going to do?" She turned to Cam. She saw Lan stick his head out into the hallway; he turned in both directions until he found them standing there.

Cam sighed loudly. "I guess I'm going to go walk around, maybe look for the next clue." She shrugged. "I know the stupid game doesn't really matter anymore at this point, but I can't just sit here." She folded her arms over her chest and chewed on her bottom lip.

"Can I come?" Lan called out to her softly. Cam turned and gave him a look that said, *really?*

Lan sighed, and stepped out into the hallway, making his way over to them with his head hanging down. "I can't just sit here, either."

Cam shook her head at him and exchanged glances with Bee. "Fine," she said sharply, "You can come along I guess."

"I'm coming too."

They turned to see Alex standing behind Rahul. Cam turned her back to him and rolled her eyes.

"I don't care who wants to come; I'm not stopping anyone from following me. I just need to get out of here." Cam turned to Bee. "I brought some tissues in there earlier." She nodded towards the closed bedroom door. "She's been bawling her eyes out." She squeezed Bee's hand, "Thank you, seriously." Then she turned back to the guys. "Okay, I'm heading out."

Alex and Lan shuffled down the hall after her. Rahul looked at Bee and shrugged. Bee sighed, inclining her head at him. "Go ahead." She gave him a small smile as he grinned at her. "Some of us may as well enjoy the evening."

Rahul's smile widened. "You're a good friend."

Bee chuckled a little. "Yeah, yeah, get going."

"Okay, Clay is across from Austin, he's keeping an eye on his door, just in case." Rahul nodded down the hall. "But Lan will be with us, so I think things should stay calm here while I'm gone."

Bee gave him a smile and nodded as she grasped the handle to Darcy's room. "Okay, sounds good, just be back in time for dinner."

Rahul checked his watch and nodded. "It's about 4:30 now. That gives us a good hour and a half or so. I'm sure we'll be back by then." He started off down the hallway, turning around and walking backward. He winked at her before disappearing around the corner.

Bee grinned to herself as he disappeared, then wiped the smile from her face as she prepared to enter the room. She knew this weekend wasn't turning out to be what most of them had hoped it would be, but she, however, was more than glad she had decided to come.

Bee entered the room quietly, and respectfully, as though she were entering a patient's room at the hospital. She fell into her nurse's role automatically, eyeing Miranda's back warily. She sat in one of the armchairs in front of the small fireplace. Bee could see the crumpled tissues grasped in a tight fist, marked with black streaks from her makeup. Darcy stood over by the bank of windows, staring out into the storm. No one spoke.

Miranda stiffened and turned slightly at Bee's approach, and seeing it was her, she sighed and slumped back into her chair. "Hey Bee," she said, giving her a wobbly smile as Bee plopped into the chair across from her. "I don't know about you, but somehow, this isn't how I pictured it going," she laughed wryly, "Seeing you again, I mean."

Bee gave her a sympathetic smile back.

Miranda sat up straighter in her chair. "How have you been?" She gave Bee a brave-looking smile. "Tell me everything. You obviously already know everything about how things have been going for me." She chuckled and dabbed under her eyes with the wad of tissues. Her eyes sparkled with unshed tears.

Bee smiled again and sat back in her chair, "Well, let me see... so, last I saw you..." Bee began to update Miranda on how things had been going for her the past few years. She told her all about her job, her funny coworkers, and some of the crazy patient stories from the hospital. Miranda laughed out loud at several of those.

She seemed to perk up after a while, and while Bee tried to stay away from talking about anything having to do with men, or relationships in general. The conversation eventually got around to the subject. She told Miranda about some of the more memorable dates she had been on, trying to keep the conversation going, and as lighthearted and funny as possible. Eventually, there was a lag in the conversation, though, and Bee sat back against her chair, feeling a wave of exhaustion sweep over her.

She turned to look over at Darcy. She had been quiet for most of the conversation. She was sitting perched now on the edge of the bed. Holding the brass key on the red ribbon in her hands, playing with it, turning it over and over. She muttered something to herself. Bee frowned at her. *What on earth had gotten into Darcy?* They were all losing it today, it seemed.

"I made a real mess of things, you know," Miranda said suddenly, staring thoughtfully into the empty grate. "I don't know what I'm going to do, Bee." She turned to Bee, her eyes wide and full of tears again. "I made one, stupid mistake. I wish I could take it back... I wish...." she trailed off, staring over at the windows, and the storm was still raging outside.

Bee sat there, watching her, listening to the rain and the relentless pounding of the surf in the distance somewhere below them.

"I tried to talk to him," Miranda continued, "but he wouldn't see me, wouldn't talk to me... I... I thought if I came here, this weekend, where he would literally be trapped." She made a laughing, sobbing sound. "Then he would have to speak to me. And the kids..." She started to sob silently.

Bee got up and went to her, kneeling beside her chair and taking her hand in hers. "Oh, Miranda, it's going to be okay. Everything will work out somehow; you'll see."

Miranda turned to her again, and Bee was struck by how achingly beautiful she was, even when she was crying.

"I have to get him back," Miranda said firmly. "And I will..." She turned back to stare out the window again and added softly, "Even if he hates me now, I'll find a way."

21.

Lan

Lan followed the group, trailing at the tail end. He had a hard time meeting anyone's eyes. His whole body hurt. His back and arms were peppered with dozens of tiny, itchy cuts. The skin around his left eye was swollen, despite the ice pack, and his nose throbbed. He was grateful at least to be moving around, doing something. He couldn't just sit in his room, thinking about what an idiot he was. How much he had fucked up. He couldn't even begin to think about what to say to Austin. He had been terrified, seeing the look on his face as he came after him. But it was no more than he deserved. If he tried to hit him again, Lan knew he wouldn't stop him.

Cam had insisted they grab the flashlights. He carried his loosely in his right hand. Flipping it and catching it again. He pressed the button on the end of the flashlight to turn it on, shining it in dim corners as they went. Flicking it on and off, on and off. They made their way down to the museum room. Lan grimaced at the smell, and the sight of the blood and liquor still swirled together on the marble floor made his stomach churn. Cam dropped behind Alex and Rahul, seeming to sense his discomfort.

"Hey," he said to her, as she fell into step beside him.

She looked up at him briefly, one eyebrow arched. "You're a fucking idiot, you know that?"

Lan snorted a laugh. Then nodded, staring down at his feet. "Yeah, I do, actually."

Cam sighed and faced forward, nodding to herself. "Okay, well, let's distract ourselves with inane puzzles... see if that makes everything better."

Lan laughed again. "Let's hope it does."

Cam flicked on her flashlight as well, shining it into the darkness in front of them. They entered the next room, following closely behind Rahul and Alex; the bobbing circles of their flashlights gave them a glimpse of the space ahead.

Lan squinted in the darkness, trying to make out what lay before them. It took him a moment to realize that they were in a stone passageway. Sconces held what looked like old-fashioned gas lamps on either side of the wall. There was no artwork here, and no doors visible, just a long stone corridor stretching out in front of them, ending in a wall of black. Lan turned to Cam with an eyebrow raised. "Wow, talk about medieval. Now this..." he gazed around them, spinning in a circle, "Is what I think of when I think castle."

"No kidding," Cam replied in a hushed voice. "And talk about cold. Good thing Darcy isn't here. She'd turn into a popsicle."

Lan could feel the cold now, seeping into him slowly. He had the odd sensation of feeling as though they were suddenly underground. Although there was no obvious pitch to the floor, the air seemed dank down here. He thought he could smell the scent of damp earth faintly, mixed with the scent of the ocean.

Alex turned back and moved closer to them. "Now we're getting somewhere, huh? Too bad the others are missing out."

Cam swallowed and looked around, shining her flashlight back the way they had come. "These aren't the tunnels, are they?" She sounded a little nervous, a little less sure of herself than she typically was.

"No," Alex scoffed, "this corridor is definitely not part of the tunnel system." Lan gave him a quizzical look. "What? I saw pictures." Alex shrugged at him.

"Okay..." Cam said, her voice steady. "Well, let's hope this leads us somewhere where we can find the next clue. We're dead in the water at this point otherwise."

They followed the gloomy passageway in silence for some time. Eventually, Lan thought he could see light up ahead. They exited the passage abruptly, and for a moment, squinting against the sudden brightness, Lan couldn't seem to get his bearings. It was as though they had walked out into the open air and had found themselves outside somehow. A large tree stood there; half its leaves had already fallen to the ground, its bare branches twisting up to the sky.

He felt disoriented, but then he realized they must be in some type of greenhouse. Glass walls surrounded them, and a glass ceiling arched high above, culminating in a large dome. Raindrops pattered against the glass. Rolling dark clouds high above moved swiftly past, carried by a howling wind.

Lan realized with a start that the glass dome was bracketed by a thin network of black iron bars, just like the windows elsewhere in the house. He stared out at the webbing of iron. Even in here, if they were to break through the glass panes, they would still be trapped. Unable to escape. He felt a shiver of dread run down his spine as he shuddered slightly.

"Wow," Cam breathed next to him, "I thought we were outside."

"So did I," Lan whispered back. He flicked his flashlight off, remembering they should conserve the battery. Cam watched him and did the same.

She walked over to the tree, reaching out and touching its leaves. A statue of an angel stood against the far wall, framed in roses. Its eyes were full of sorrow. Cam walked over to the statue next and gently ran a hand down the angel's cheek. "This must have been beautiful once." She murmured.

Cam was right, Lan thought. The greenhouse had an air of slight neglect, of being past its prime.

Rahul walked over to the double doors on the other side of the greenhouse. He grabbed the handles and pushed, and the doors swung open. He turned back to them. "Well, it looks like we can just continue right on through." He eyed the decrepit greenhouse. "Should we take a look around?"

Cam began to wander through the greenhouse, following the twisting stone walkway. After a moment, she disappeared around a corner. Lan took the other walkway, moving past a clump of roses, climbing vines, and more twisted trees. "Over here!" He heard Cam cry out. It took him a minute or so to find her; he ended up backtracking and following the path she had taken.

She stood in the middle of the greenhouse in front of a large tree growing out of a circle of worn stones. From its branches hung dozens of antique-looking keys.

Some had different color ribbons attached, some on metal chains or plain keyrings. Cam reached out to touch one of them, turning it in her hands. She looked back at Lan with wide eyes. "There are so many... how will we ever know which one we need?"

Lan sighed, shaking his head. "We must be missing a clue that would tell us which we need."

Cam nodded. "That's what I was thinking. Hopefully, we just haven't found it yet. And hopefully, we didn't skip over it with the room order getting messed up earlier."

Lan nodded in agreement. They did a sweep of the remainder of the greenhouse but found nothing else out of the ordinary. After a few moments, they continued on through the next set of doors.

Lan was surprised to find that they were truly outside, in the next space. Chilly splotches of rain splattered his face as he stepped out into the open air. He breathed in deeply; the scents of fall, damp earth, and saltwater hitting him. They were in a courtyard, he realized, open to the air and the elements. A large rectangular space, with a stone walkway that ran around the perimeter. The middle of the courtyard was filled with water. The water looked deep, with a greenish tint to it. Little shockwaves of circles rippled out from each fat raindrop that landed on its surface.

"Geez," Cam muttered next to him, "It's freezing." She nudged him to keep moving. "Do you think there are any clues out here?" she asked, raising her voice and squinting against a gust of wind that swept through the courtyard, whipping strands of her hair in a swirl around her face. She reached up and brushed her hair out of the way, holding it off to the side to peer at him.

"I don't know," Lan said uncertainly, looking around, "I don't see much of anything out here. " He looked over to see Alex and Rahul already disappearing into the next door, re-entering the house; a gust of wind pushed the door shut, slamming into the frame after them. "Let's keep going," he called back to her over the howling of the wind.

Cam looked around and sighed, nodding. "I don't see anything obvious." She shrugged. "Besides, we can always come back here later, if we think we missed something."

Lan nodded his agreement, and they continued on their way.

They immediately realized they needed their flashlights again. The next room was nearly pitch black. Lan flicked his flashlight on and got to work scanning the walls near the doorway. He came up empty-handed, searching for a light switch. A loud crack of thunder sounded directly above their heads. There seemed to be an answering echoing boom that reverberated through the castle itself.

"Jesus," Cam muttered from somewhere off to his right in the dark. "Good thing I'm not scared of thunderstorms. Some people would be more than a little freaked out right now."

Lan chuckled a little. "Clay," he said back. "He never liked it when it stormed. I forgot about that."

"Well, it's probably a good thing that he's not here, wandering around in the dark, " she replied. "Where are Alex and Rahul?" He saw the beam of her flashlight swing around, scanning the space around them, searching for them.

"I don't know..." Lan replied warily, doing the same. "Shouldn't we be seeing their flashlights right now?"

He saw the light from her flashlight pause. "Alex?" She called out, moving forward. Lan followed her, their footsteps reverberating as they moved through the large empty space.

"I think this must be some sort of ballroom or something," Cam said. "This room is huge and looks like it's practically empty."

Lan spun around, surveying the room. She was right; the room seemed to be enormous and, from what he could see, contained zero furniture.

Lan thought for a moment; something was nagging at him. "Isn't it a little odd that every door has just been unlocked over in this section?"

Cam didn't respond to him, calling out Alex's name again, louder this time.

"Like earlier, we had to unlock every single door we moved through, to get to the next room. Here, they're all just open for us. I don't get it."

He moved closer to her and saw Cam frowning at his words. "It is a little strange, isn't it?" She shrugged. "Maybe the castle is just too big to have a puzzle in every room? I don't know..." she trailed off. "We should keep moving, though; I see doors over that way."

Lan turned to where she pointed with her flashlight beam and saw a set of double doors yawning wide into darkness. They moved over to them quickly, shining their flashlights inside before stepping into the next space.

In this room, Lan found a light switch immediately, to the left of the doorway. He hit the switch gratefully. He didn't mind the dark normally, but this place did give him the creeps, just a little, he had to admit. But nothing happened. He hit the switch again, flicking it up and down, but the room stayed dark.

"Shit," he mumbled. "Either there are no lights plugged in in this room, or we lost power. I'm hitting the light switch, and nothing is happening."

"Great," Cam murmured back. "You've got to be kidding me. We better not have lost power." She spun around, "Alex? Rahul? Where the heck are you?" Her voice echoed back to them, and no response came. "Where the hell did they go?" She said, turning back to Lan. "It's like they disappeared. How have we not caught up to them by now? We were right behind them."

Lan just shook his head in confusion. "I have no idea. We couldn't have been more than 30 seconds behind them, going through those doors. I don't understand where they went."

Cam sighed audibly. "Let's keep going a little further, I guess? We have to come across them soon."

Lan's beam of light shone onto the floor, and he recognized the familiar black and white check marble pattern beneath their feet. He moved forward, sweeping the light back and forth, and came to an abrupt stop as the cone of light revealed a railing off to his right. He shone the flashlight to the left and found another railing on the other side.

"Cam, we're on some kind of walkway or something; there's a short railing on either side up ahead here."

They moved forward cautiously, shining their lights back and forth. Lan moved over to the railing on his right and shone the beam down into the darkness below them.

They were up high, on a raised walkway that led to a twin set of curving spiral staircases twisting down into darkness. They moved to the top of the stairs and chose the left side at random, making their way carefully down the steps. Their echoing footsteps were the only sound in the large open space.

When they came to the bottom of the stairs, they surveyed the room around them. It appeared they were in a main landing area of sorts, with doors on either side of the space and a main hallway leading out of the room. There was a sitting area behind them, past the foot of the stairs, with couches and chairs gathered around a grand piano. A bank of windows gave them a rain-splotched view of what looked like another large courtyard beyond. Lan was grateful for the light that illuminated the space, dim though it was.

"What time is it?" Lan asked suddenly. "Do you have a watch?"

Cam looked down at her wrist. "Shit, no, I don't. I forgot to put mine on. I did bring one, but I'm not in the habit of wearing it."

Lan nodded. "No worries, I was just curious. We've been gone for a while now. And it's hard to tell with the storm, but I feel like it might be getting darker out now. Maybe we should head back soon."

Cam nodded, looking around at the doors lining the room. "Let's try some of these doors, then maybe we can head down the hallway a little bit. Maybe Alex and Rahul went that way."

They split up, each taking a side, and approached the doors, one at a time, trying each handle. The last door on Cam's side of the room was unlocked. She called Lan over, and he joined her quickly. They scanned the smaller room.

It appeared to be a sitting room; they found a fireplace, couches and chairs, and a small desk on the far wall. The desk had a book that lay open, with a magnifying glass lying on top. Some sort of metal globe with circular rings that Lan thought had something to do with astronomy sat on the desk as well, off to one side. Above the desk, on the wall, was an old corkboard. There were pictures, medical-type drawings, and an old-fashioned map of the world. "Check this out," Lan whispered to Cam.

There were little push pins with strings attached to various points on the map. The strings led off to a cluster of photographs connected to each location. There were photos of people. There were more drawings. One of the photos showed what looked like a dead sheep, its flesh in tattered strips, with a matted, blood-soaked coat. Next to the dead sheep, there was an image of a cross.

"What the hell is this?" Cam murmured, shining her flashlight on the clusters of images.

"I don't know..." Lan sighed loudly. "But I'm guessing this room probably contains our next clue, right? This is the first room we've found that has much of anything in it. Besides the keys in the greenhouse, at least." Cam nodded in agreement.

They both turned at a sound, Lan gripping Cam's arm. They froze, listening carefully. It soon became clear what they were hearing was a set of echoing footsteps. They turned and headed out into the main room, shining their flashlights in circles, combing the space. Lan's flashlight landed suddenly on Rahul, as he emerged from the hallway off to the right. He held an arm up over his face, shielding his eyes from the flashlight beam. Lan lowered it, only slightly, keeping the beam trained on him.

"There you are," Cam called out to him. "What the heck happened? We were right behind you guys, and then suddenly you were gone."

Rahul nodded at them. Lan stepped closer, studying him. He appeared to be panting like he was out of breath. "What happened? Where's your flashlight?" Lan asked him, brow furrowed.

"Thank God," Rahul murmured, slumping forward, and putting his hands on his knees. He stood there, catching his breath. "I freaking lost it. Been wandering around in the dark. Bumping into shit. Holy crap," He breathed deeply and stood up straight. "I'm glad I found you."

"Where the hell is Alex?" Cam asked, an edge of anger seeping into her tone.

Rahul shook his head. "I dunno, we got separated."

"How?" Cam asked incredulously, "What happened?"

Rahul explained, "We had just entered back into the house, and the wind slammed the door shut behind us. I thought that was what we heard, at least. But Alex insisted he had heard something slamming up ahead, from inside the house. He took off, running up ahead, and I followed him. I think we were inside some kind of ballroom, that big empty room. Anyway, I followed him, and just as we were coming into this space," he paused and pointed to the ceiling, "Up there, we saw something."

"Saw something? Like what?" Cam asked, shining her flashlight up toward the walkway high above them.

"We saw something moving. Something pale. It had light-colored skin. If it was a person, I don't think it was wearing a shirt."

"What do you mean, if it was a person?" Lan asked, his heart rate starting to kick up slightly.

Rahul just shook his head, a half-apologetic, sort of embarrassed expression on his face. "I... I don't know man. I don't know what the hell it was that I saw. I think it was probably a person, but the way it stood, the way it... moved. I'm not sure. It was half in shadow; we never got a clear look at it."

"So, let me see if I have this right. You found a creepy, pale person, or whatever, with no shirt on, and you followed it in the darkness. And now Alex is... where exactly?" Cam frowned over at him.

"I know..." Rahul shook his head. "I know it sounds crazy, but yeah. We saw something, and we followed it; whatever it was, it didn't seem to like the light from the flashlights. It ran away from us. We chased it down the stairs, down through here, and down this hallway." He turned and pointed back behind him. "There's a maze of hallways back there; they branch off in all directions. I dropped my flashlight, at some point. It slipped right out of my hands, and when it crashed on the ground, the light went out. I heard it rolling away, clattering, but somehow, I couldn't freaking find it." He paused, catching his breath again, and shaking his head in frustration.

"I lost Alex, in that time. I tried calling out to him, telling him to stop, to wait for me. But either he didn't hear me, or he didn't want to stop. I dunno," he shrugged again. "I tried to head in the direction I'd heard him go, but I couldn't find him. I ended up in a dead-end, an empty room with no one in it. I headed back this way, through the hallways in the dark, checking everywhere I could, but nothing. I've no clue where he went."

Lan and Cam just stared at him. "You've got to be kidding me," Lan mumbled, looking over at Cam in disbelief.

"What the hell do we do now?" Cam turned to him.

"I dunno," Lan said, thinking. "We have flashlights now, so let's go back and look for him. Retrace your steps." He turned to Rahul.

Rahul sighed deeply, eyeing the corridor warily. Clearly, he had no desire to go back to wandering the dark hallways, but eventually, he looked back at them and nodded.

"Let's go. We went this way," he said, turning and waving them on to follow him.

Cam and Lan looked at each other once more, then followed him into the pitch black.

22.

Clay

Clay woke suddenly. Jolting upright in his bed with a gasp. It took him a long, disorienting moment to remember where he was. He ran his hands over the top of the unfamiliar comforter that lay beneath him, rumpled and damp with his sweat.

He looked up, out the doorway, and eyed the door to Austin's room. Half of his door frame was visible across the hallway from where he sat on his bed. Clay could see from there that Austin's door was open. It had been closed and locked before Clay fell asleep.

Rahul had asked him to keep an eye on Austin's door, to make sure he didn't try to leave and go looking for Lan. Clay had bristled a little at the request, given who it came from. He had been tempted to tell him to fuck off, but he knew Rahul was right. Austin was in a dangerous frame of mind, and there was no telling what he might do. Clay didn't feel much like interacting with the others, so he hadn't minded in the end, sitting quietly on his own in his room, and keeping an eye on the door.

But clearly, he had let his fatigue get the better of him. He must have drifted off to sleep at some point. And now, Austin's door was open.

Clay vaulted off the bed, moving quickly to Austin's room. He flipped the light switch next to the door, but nothing happened. He flipped it back and forth, brows wrinkled in confusion.

The thick velvet curtains that lined the windows had been pulled shut, but there was enough dim light filtering in through a crack in the curtains to see that Austin's bed appeared to be empty.

Clay entered the room, approached the bed, and patted it to make sure; the blankets and sheets lay in a rumpled mess, but his hand fell on empty bedding. He checked the chair by the empty fireplace; nothing. He peeked into the small bathroom. Austin was gone.

Clay turned and left, heading down the hallway to the main foyer. He trotted quickly down the stairs, moving through the empty foyer into the common room. He paused in the common room, taking in the space. It appeared empty as well, but it was hard to tell in the dim light. The bank of windows by the fireplace area illuminated that space well enough. He could see from here that the couches and chairs sat empty. Clay moved over to the dining table and paused in surprise.

Their dinner was laid out on the table, waiting for them. Each plate was covered in a silver dome that shone red in the faint light. Clay's eyes drifted up to the board over the desk; the red light reflected on the table emanating from the lights next to their names.

Clay stared at the board in confusion. All three lights were lit up next to Alex's name now, the red bulbs shining brightly. He scanned the board, searching for any other new additions, but he didn't think there were any other new lights lit up, from what he could remember.

Clay walked over to the library area, peering up the spiral staircase and calling out softly, "Austin? Are you up there?" He paused, waiting for a response, but none came. Clay sighed and quickly climbed the spiral stairs. He paused at the top and easily ascertained that the small balcony area was empty. "Shit," he muttered to himself. *Where the heck could he have gone?*

Clay turned and bounded back down the stairs, moving swiftly across the common room and back to the main foyer. He stopped abruptly, seeing someone moving towards him across the marble entryway. It was Austin, he realized with a flood of relief.

"Hey man," he called over to him, "You scared me for a minute there, I didn't know where you went." He walked over to meet him. "Everything okay?"

"Yeah, everything's fine," Austin murmured, his voice rough like sandpaper. "I must have fallen asleep. I'm not surprised, I didn't sleep great last night."

"Yeah," Clay chuckled, "I know, I did too, somehow. I just woke up a few minutes ago." Clay eyed him warily as he rubbed his eyes and stretched. He was acting like he had just woken up. "Where were you though? You weren't in your room just now."

Austin frowned at him and looked behind him towards the staircase. It was a long moment before he spoke. "I must have gone for a walk after, just needed to clear my head, you know?" He turned back to Clay and clapped him on the back. "Where's everyone? It should be about dinner time now, right?" Austin peered into the common room. "Not that I'm looking forward to sitting down at a table with everyone." He wiped his hands over his face, then brushed his hair back from his forehead. "Maybe I'll eat in my room or something." Austin blew a stream of air out and paced the floor, moving away from Clay. "God this sucks."

Clay grimaced, unsure of what to say. "I know man, I'm sorry." He looked back towards the common room. "But there's no one in there right now, and the food looks like it's been sitting out waiting for us. I have no clue what time it is." Clay shrugged. "Should we go eat? We can get started without them, at least."

Austin turned back to him and gave him a half-smile. "Yeah, that sounds like a good idea."

They made their way into the common room and found seats at the table. It was only a moment or two before Austin noticed the lights on the board over the desk. They had a good laugh over Alex having three lights lit up. But then Austin's grin faded, and he stared thoughtfully at the board.

"But what does that mean though?" He looked over at Clay. "They said three strikes and you're out..."

Clay stared back at him, then back at the board. "So, does that mean that Alex gets kicked out?" Clay shrugged. They sat in silence for a few seconds.

"Can you imagine how mad he would be?" Austin grinned at him, and they started laughing again.

They ate in comfortable silence for most of the meal, although Clay noticed that Austin seemed to pick at his food, shuffling it around with his fork more than he actually ate it.

"Shit," Clay said after a long pause, "If we had been smart, we could have waited here for them to come bring dinner, made sure they knew about the phone being down." Clay shook his head. With everything going on, he hadn't been thinking.

"The phone's down?" Austin asked him, frowning slightly as he glanced over at the phone. "So, what happens if there's an emergency?"

Clay shrugged. "I mean, it's not great, but like I told the others earlier, I'm guessing they can still see and hear us, and are watching everything that's happening. I'm sure they would know if we needed help, you know?" Austin nodded at his words. "But still, it would have been good to communicate that directly with them, I guess."

Austin sighed, and sat back in his chair, setting this fork down. "Where is everyone else, exactly?" He looked around the empty common area again.

Clay nodded. "So, um, the girls, last I knew at least, were in Darcy's room, I think. Um... Miranda was, ah, upset." Clay felt himself flush slightly. "So, they were sitting with her." Austin sighed deeply, and looked away, crossing his arms over his chest.

Clay continued rapidly, "And I think the others went to continue with the escape room thing. I think they just didn't want to be sitting around you know? Gave them something to do." Austin didn't react. "I heard them talking in the hall before they left." Clay shrugged. "I would think they would be back soon though."

Austin nodded, clearing his throat.

"Did you see anyone?"

"What?" He asked, turning back to Clay, his brow wrinkled in confusion.

"Did you see anyone? When you went for a walk?" Clay watched him closely.

"Oh." Austin's eyes widened slightly. "No, I... I didn't see anyone."

Clay nodded thoughtfully. "Okay then," he said quietly.

Austin stood up, heading over to the fireplace. "I'm going to get a fire going, for tonight," he called over his shoulder. "It's freezing in here."

Austin spent the next few minutes building up a fire. Clay finished his dinner and thought about grabbing a beer from the mini bar. He thought better of it in the end. For some reason, he didn't feel like he should be drinking tonight.

Eventually they heard voices, footsteps echoing in the main entrance. Clay waited to see who it was.

Cam came through the door first, surveying the room swiftly, a flashlight gripped tightly in her hand. "Hey," she called out to them, and made her way over to the table.

She was followed by Lan. He eyed Austin for only the briefest of moments, looking away quickly, and staring down at his feet as he followed Cam to the table.

Rahul trailed behind them. He looked back and forth between Austin and Lan and came to a stop in the middle of the room, standing with his arms folded and feet planted.

"Did Alex turn up back here?" Cam asked Clay, walking over to him.

Clay frowned up at her before shaking his head. "No, it's been just the two of us since we woke up."

Cam had been about to speak, but she paused for a moment. "Woke up?"

Clay shrugged. "Yeah, we both fell asleep for a bit, I guess." Cam looked over towards Austin, then turned back to Clay.

"So, neither of you have seen Alex at all?" She looked back and forth between them as they shook their heads.

Austin had stood up and moved closer to them, coming to stand behind the armchair by the fire. Rahul tracked his movements.

"No, why?" Clay asked her, "What's going on?" His eyes went over to the board briefly, and Cam followed his gaze. He saw her eyes widen as she took in the three red lights next to Alex's name.

"What the heck?" She murmured to herself, before turning back to him. "Rahul and Alex got separated from me and Lan. They thought they saw someone or something, and they chased it."

Rahul moved closer to them. "I dropped my flashlight, and we got separated," he added. "Alex just kept going, and I ended up wandering around in the dark until they found me." Rahul shrugged. "We have no clue where he went but were hoping he made his way back here somehow."

Clay frowned at them. "No," he said. "I mean if he did come back here, he hasn't been in the common room since we've been in here. Maybe we should check his room?" Clay suggested.

They made their way to Alex's room next, but they found it empty. The bed was made. Alex wasn't in the armchairs by the empty fireplace, and he wasn't in the bathroom. They moved out into the hallway. Clay saw Austin had paused further down the hall and stood leaning against the wall with his arms crossed. He seemed to be keeping a distance from Lan, which Clay figured was a good thing.

The door to Darcy's room swung open, sucking a rush of air out of the hallway. Bee stuck her head out into the hall a moment later, and seeing them all gathered there, she frowned slightly. "What's going on?" she asked quietly, moving out into the hallway, and closing the door gently behind her.

Rahul quickly recounted what had happened for her. Bee's eyes went wide when he described losing his flashlight and wandering around alone in the dark. Clay shifted on his feet uncomfortably. His gut squirmed at the look of sympathy in her eyes.

Then Cam spoke up. "The odd thing is, when we got back here, we saw all three lights are lit up now, next to Alex's name." Bee stared at her, uncomprehendingly. "Do you think that means he's out of the game or something?"

"But how?" Lan spoke up. They all turned to look at him. "I mean, how did he get out? He runs after this person, or whatever, and disappears? Rahul came to a dead end when he tried to follow him, and so did we again when the three of us went and looked. How did they get him out of the house, if that's what happened?"

They stood in silence for a moment, shrugging and shaking of heads ensued. No one had an answer to that. Cam sighed and turned to look back down the hallway. "I don't know what to do next, but maybe we should try picking up the phone to ask what's happened. I mean, if something happened to him, obviously they should have seen, and either intervened directly or sent help, right?"

Clay cleared his throat. "So actually, the phone isn't working. There was no dial tone earlier at least. Alex was the one who checked before you guys left."

Bee nodded in agreement. "That's right, he told me the phone was out."

"What the hell?" Cam murmured, gazing back and forth between them.

"But they should still be able to see and hear us through the cameras; I don't think we need to panic," Clay said, holding up a hand.

"The power's out, too," Lan added, running a hand through his hair. "But that shouldn't affect a landline phone."

"So are the cameras even working still then?" Cam looked around at them again, her gaze landing on Austin.

He shrugged and looked away. "I mean, I have no idea, Cam. They could be running off of batteries or have a battery backup. That would be my guess, at least. But I couldn't say what kind of setup they have."

"Jesus," she breathed, "So, is this all part of it, or not? Maybe the power and phone going down are part of the escape room thing..." she trailed off, "or whatever the heck else Alex planned for this weekend."

They stood there for a moment, thinking. "It definitely could be," Clay said. "Of course, now we can't ask him, unless he is still here somewhere, and we can find him."

"I doubt he'd give us a straight answer, even if we did," Cam said with a sigh. "I don't know about you, but how he disappeared doesn't sit right with me."

"No." Lan shook his head. "It doesn't with me either, but you saw what was back there; we ended up in an empty room, and all the other doors were locked, so what are we supposed to do?

Cam shrugged. "The tree with all the keys on it, in the greenhouse," she said, looking at Lan, "Maybe one of those keys opens a door down that hallway."

Lan snorted, "Yeah, maybe, but what, are we supposed to take all fifty of them and try them on every door? And how the fuck did Alex open it and get through in the first place if the door was locked?"

Cam shrugged. "I don't know Lan, okay?" An edge of frustration seeping into her tone. "But we can't just do nothing."

"We go back tonight," Rahul said suddenly, "Keep looking for clues to get further. Cam, you mentioned a room that you and Lan found that might have more clues in it." She nodded to him. "I say we go back after dinner. Keep going. Either Alex will turn up, or he's out of the game. We won't learn anything more sitting around here."

That seemed to be the final word on the matter. They all looked at each other for several seconds, before Austin spoke up. "Dinner is on the table; it's probably been there for a while. Clay and I already ate, the rest of you should as well."

Rahul nodded in agreement and moved over to Bee. "Let's get the girls too, have them come eat something." Austin stood upright at his words and brushed past them, heading down the hall to his room. Clearly, he had no interest in seeing Miranda at the moment. Lan watched him go past, then turned and left, heading for the common area. Clay was glad he had already finished his dinner. What an awkward meal that was going to be.

Cam followed Austin down the hall, grabbing his arm just as he was about to enter his room. "I think we should read the journal tonight still like we planned." Clay heard her whispering to him, although he watched Bee and Rahul, pretending not to listen. "I don't know what they saw, but I don't like the description Rahul gave of this pale person. He said it was avoiding the light from their flashlights. I need to read that journal and see what else it says." Clay felt a shiver down his spine at her words.

He heard Austin reply back. "Okay, we can read it. To be honest, I have zero interest in solving stupid puzzles tonight. I can't..." he trailed off, his voice pitched lower, "I can't be with the rest of them, tonight."

"Then you won't be," Cam said back calmly. "We'll stay behind and read the journal if they go back to look for Alex again. Besides, I don't think they're going to find him."

Clay turned to look over at them, before heading into his room.

Austin saw him watching and nodded grimly to him. Clay nodded back, then entered his room and shut the door. He flopped backward onto his bed. Lying sideways across it. He lay that way for quite some time, staring up at the ceiling. He had no clue what was happening, no more than anyone else did. But he knew somehow, in his gut, that Cam was right. They wouldn't find Alex tonight. He just hoped they wouldn't find anything else, wandering the dark hallways.

23.

Cam

Cam followed the others to the common area and sat with them at the table. They began to eat, mostly in silence, to start. Then, one by one, starting with Bee, people began to bring up random topics, attempting to keep the conversation going to cover up the awkwardness of the whole thing. Cam stared at the food on her plate for a while. She felt so anxious suddenly, just on edge for some reason. She took small sips of water but couldn't seem to bring herself to eat at all. Her gaze kept drifting back to the doorway, to where Austin waited in his room.

Eventually, she stood and quietly exited the room during a peak of conversation. First, she went to her bedroom, grabbing the journal from where she had hidden it under her mattress. Then, quietly, walking on the balls of her feet, she moved to Austin's bedroom and knocked on his door.

She heard movement from behind the door, and after a moment, it swung open.

"Hey," Austin said. His shoulders relaxed as he saw it was just her. She wondered if he had been expecting Miranda, coming to try to talk to him. Her stomach twisted, and she shivered slightly. "Come on in," he said with a sigh. He had a small fire going in the grate, and several candles were lit scattered around the room. He insisted she take the single armchair in front of the fire, and he plopped on the end of the bed.

"Okay," Cam said, opening the journal and shuffling through the pages to find their spot, "Let's try to read the next few entries, just see if we can learn anything else that might be helpful. We're sort of stuck on clues at the moment."

Austin watched her, his arms folded in front of his chest. He nodded, his blue eyes wide and solemn, but he didn't speak.

She felt a current of nerves surge through her. Was he nervous, too, or just quiet for some other reason?

She cleared her throat, picked up the journal, and began to read the next entry.

"We spent several idle days in isolation. John and Marianna had no visitors planned for the next several evenings and no parties to attend. To make matters worse, a storm came rolling in on the third night, and the wind howled against the windows, causing an awful racket. I found I was restless that evening and knew sleep would not find me that night. I paced the

corridors of the castle, taking a candelabra with me to light my way.

I had noticed an odd sort of languidness that had seemed to envelop Marianna. For all her concern about John, I had found her much changed, as well. When she laughed, the musical tones in her voice that I so well remembered were subdued, and her eyes held a sorrow that I could not yet understand the source of. She had spent much of her days in her room. Painting for hours on end, I am told as she was wont to do when feeling particularly distressed. I am afraid I had harassed a poor serving girl into telling me what her mistress had been up to, locked away all day.

I wandered aimlessly through the hallways that night until I came to the overlook room. It is a large space, open to the elements, with stone archways where one can stand and view the most spectacular horizon. I often stood here during my visits, staring out over the ocean. The chaos of the water, the ripples of the never-ending waves, always seemed to fill me with peace. I cannot say what made my steps turn towards that room; with the howling wind and rain outside, there would certainly be no opportunity to enjoy the view this evening.

Yet I found myself wandering there just the same. As I stepped out into the open air, the rain lashing against my face, I was shocked to my core to see a woman standing there; her back was to me. Long, dark hair whipped by the wind. She had stepped through the archway, her arms outstretched to either side. I called out to her, afraid to startle her but wanting to call her back immediately. She turned her head slowly to the side, and I saw with a stab of terror that it was Marianna! She stood there in mortal danger. For below are naught but jagged rocks leading into the sea. My heart was pounding painfully with fear. I called out to her again and begged her to step back. Though what words I uttered, I could not recall now. I only know that I was desperate for her to return to safety and prayed the wind would not cause her to fall.

She only smiled at me, laughed, with the cruelest expression in her eyes. She then flung her arms out wider, and she fell. I could only see her for the briefest of moments as she soared gracefully and sunk below my view. I know only that I cried out, calling her name over and over. I ran to the archway and climbed over the rough stone. I stuck my head over the edge, bracing myself for what I would find. Although the light was dim, with the sun sinking low behind gray clouds, I could not believe my eyes. For I found nothing, nothing at all. Only blank ground, only bare rocks, below the archway she had disappeared through. It was impossible!

I could not, for the life of me, come up with a single explanation for what I had just seen. I stood there, shivering in the rain, shaken to my core. Until I turned, climbed back down, and made my way back through the doorway into the castle. I shoved the door closed, straining against the wind, and collapsed against it for a moment. Then I heard running footsteps, and who should appear in the corridor behind me but Marianna herself!

She ran to me and, grasping my arms, felt and saw that I was soaked to the bone and still shaking in cold and terror. "How?" I demanded of her, gasping for breath. "How are you here? I watched you fall?"

She stared at me in momentary consternation before her brows lifted and she shook her head. She took a deep, sighing breath and asked me to recount for her exactly what I had seen.

When I had finished swiftly, for it was a brief, although startling, tale, she licked her lips, her gaze wandering away from me as she thought to herself. Then she returned to me and said softly, "Yes, that is how it works at first. It can show you what you fear. It can take on any face, the faces of those you love, those you trust. It is an abomination. John does not believe me; he thinks I am going mad. But I tell you, it is real."

She gripped my arms tighter, her nails digging into my flesh. "I have seen it; I have seen it wearing John's face." She whispered to me, her voice sinking low as she looked side to side in the dark corridor. I felt a chill go up my spine, and though I was soaked, the hair on my neck stood on end. "It can only be a demon, an evil, dark thing. I think it feeds off of us. Off of our fear, despair, and rage. You cannot stay here, Garrett. I never should have asked you to come. You must go. You must leave at once."

I could only stare at her in shock, uncomprehending fully what she was trying to tell me. Then I replied, "You cannot think I would leave you here. Abandon you and John to this, this... thing? I'll not leave without you."

"And John will not leave at all," was her reply. "You know how he is. He says he is in the middle of his greatest invention yet, and he refuses to leave the castle. It is hopeless."

"Then you will leave. With me. Let him stay if he is so stubborn of a fool." I'm afraid that was my response, ashamed though I am to admit it. I knew if this was so, she had the right of it, and my brother would not be budged once his mind was made up.

We came to no resolution that night but returned to the library to sit by the fire. We sat up long hours into the night while Mariana told me everything that had come to pass these last few weeks. I felt a sense of hopelessness sink deeper and deeper into me at her words. For what she described was madness. Had I not seen that vision of her with my own eyes, I could not have believed it."

Cam paused as the journal entry ended. She sighed, placed a finger in the pages, and closed the book slightly. She watched Austin thoughtfully. He had stood from his spot at the end of the bed and begun pacing the room as she read.

She watched him out of the corner of her eyes, relishing his movements and the nearness of him as her finger traced the handwritten lines on the page. The journal felt, and looked, undeniably real to her. The feeling of uncertainty, of whether this was all just part of the escape room for the weekend, deepened at each entry she read.

She stared into the fire. She thought they should leave. They should probably just call the whole thing off. The weekend had been a disaster so far, anyway. How convenient it was that Alex was suddenly missing now, just when the phone and the power went out. She didn't believe in monsters, but she did believe in people. In how cruel and awful they could be.

She realized Austin had paused in his pacing and was standing there, watching her. His chest rose and fell slightly. He had a strange, expectant look in his eyes, as though he was waiting for something. Cam cleared her throat. Of course, he was waiting for her to keep reading, she told herself. And she picked up the journal again, opening it to where she had left off. But her voice and her hands trembled slightly.

"I could only hope to reason with John, make him understand that Marianna was in danger. She wasn't safe. Although I knew that his work had always come first, I still could not fathom that he would choose his invention over her. Though she insisted to me, this would be the case. I reassured her I would find a way. We would come up with a plan, and we would leave the castle, all three of us, for safety.

Thus began my work of reaching my brother. Marianna told me that John did not believe in the monster and, in fact, refused to discuss it further with her. He had made her feel as though she were going mad, that it was all made up in her head. He had made her afraid of what he might do.

Would he attempt to commit her to an asylum? I shivered at the thought. One doctor had come to visit her already, had left just last week. He had prescribed rest, and no excitement. She was to have no visitors, I learned. The cruelty of it amazed me. That this would be turned back on her. This is the reason why she had written to me, in dire straits, and had insisted I must say the visit had been my idea. I was to tell John I had come on my own accord, unannounced and planned to stay for a period of a week or two at least.

Now, all made sense to me, at least, as pertains to Marianna's letter. For I had read between the lines such a great sense of urgency, and she had led me to think it was only for John's sake, that he was in peril, to lure me here. Little did she know, it seemed, that she need only say she was in danger, and I would have come to her aid all the more swiftly. But of course, it would turn out, in the end, that they both were in danger and so, in fact, was I, now that I had joined them in this godforsaken place.

Cam paused again as a light knock came at the door to Austin's room. She moved slightly to rise, but he leaped off the bed in one smooth motion, from where he had taken a seat again, and moved swiftly over to the door.

"What is it?" She heard him say, somewhat stiffly. He held the door open wide enough to allow himself to be seen but held it against his body, shielding her from view.

"Hey, um," Cam froze at the sound of Miranda's voice drifting in from the hallway, "I was hoping to talk to you for a few minutes." She paused. "We're leaving soon to go look for Alex, um, we'll probably look for clues, too. Can I talk to you? It would only be for a minute or two before we go?" She paused again, "Please, Austin," she added, her voice trembling. Cam waited, holding her breath, to see what he would say.

There was a long pause where no one spoke, and then Austin turned to the side, looked over at Cam, and nodded in her direction. "I'll be right back," he said in a clipped voice, then disappeared through the doorway, closing the door behind him.

Cam let out a breath and stared at the closed door. She waited for several minutes, but he didn't return. She licked her lips, chewing on her bottom lip, and breathed deeply, calming the nervous energy that seemed to radiate through her tonight. She decided she might as well keep reading in his absence if she was going to have to sit here waiting for him. She picked up the journal again and continued.

"I confronted John the following day, waiting until he was in a good mood to do so. He had been working all day, slaving away in his laboratory. I had actually been called in, by him. He sent a servant girl to find me. He wanted to show me his progress on the latest puzzle he had been chipping away at, as he put it.

I confess, I often struggle to understand him when he speaks about his inventions. He gave me a demonstration, and he was his animated, excited self, laughing and pleased with himself. When in this state, he can be all manner of pleasant, kind, and engaging.

He has infinite patience in these moments, whereas in other moods, he has none.

He showed me a contraption that gives off energy, as he describes it. What form of energy, I cannot say that I completely understood. Though not for lack of his explanation, it is simply a fault of my own mind in comprehending. This was a device that gave off a field of energy. This energy was meant to ward off all manner of illness, using some form of vibration, which he insisted is all that energy in fact is, and with these vibrations tuned to specific frequencies, one could, in theory, treat all manner of disease and dishumors. Of both the body and mind, as he described it to me. I found myself entirely skeptical, I must say, as a physician, that something so simple as a vibration could achieve anything of import.

I watched him as he paced the room, explaining to me how this would change everything. He spoke of hospitals and the sick, but I could not help but think of Marianna. Did he intend to use this device on her? Did he truly think she was going mad and this contraption would save her?

And was he right? A trickle of doubt began to form in my mind, and I shuffled on my own feet, beginning to pace the room myself as the thought discomforted me. I knew what I had seen in the overlook room. I knew it could not have been Marianna who had flung herself over the wall onto the rocky cliff below. But could I be sure, I thought to myself, in the light of day. Could I be completely sure that it was not madness that had overtaken her? In her madness, could she somehow have taken on powers, abilities, that I had not thought possible?

I shook myself, dashing the ridiculous thought from my mind. She had been completely dry when she found me in the corridor, outside the door. No, there is no possible way she had been outside, leaping over the wall, and somehow, what? Flying to the ground unharmed? She was not a witch, I thought and chided myself for doubting her.

John held the contraption up for me, directing me then to hold out one arm. I did so, somewhat reluctantly, and watched as he floated the device back and forth in the air over my arm. It was an odd-looking thing: A rounded handle on one end connected to a wooden box that was filled with wires and metal prongs. I saw tiny mallets, which must create the vibrations, if I had understood him correctly. Attached to the other end, was a wide cone, almost like a gramophone, where the vibrations emanate from. There was a dial, on the side, with tiny numbers around it. He turned the dial, moving it back and forth as though searching for the correct setting by feel.

I felt an odd tingling sensation and watched as the hairs on my arm stood straight on end. I noticed that his did as well. A strange, disturbing sound came to my ears, I flinched and reflexively went to lift my hands to cover them, but stayed myself, keeping my arm held out for him.

He was only able to use the device for a moment, however; his arms began to shudder and then shake. He gasped out as if in pain and almost dropped the device onto the ground. He set it down frantically on the table and, jumping back, he retreated across the room, a hand over his chest.

He breathed rapidly, his chest rising and falling, and he looked over at me with wide eyes as I stood there, unaffected in the slightest.

"I cannot understand it," he muttered, staring at me in confusion. "I cannot understand why it affects the user, so." He shook his head as though to clear it and turned away from me. "I must keep working," came his low and gruff voice. He kept his back to me, and I knew that I was dismissed, so I began to exit the room.

I turned back to him, for my plan had been to confront him on the issue of leaving the castle. Though I felt my moment of opportunity, with his passing mood, had been lost, I knew I must begin to try to reason with him.

"John," I spoke softly, in a kind voice. "You are making wonderful progress," I paused, thinking of an angle, "Perhaps you might take a break, perhaps a brief rest even, would do you good. Come with me," I urged him, "Come with me, and bring Marianna as well, if only for a few days... a week," I continued, but I could already see he was shaking his head. "Get out of this castle, get some fresh air, and perhaps a new perspective."

He turned on me, his shoulders raised, and he loomed over me as though suddenly he was taller, his shoulders broader. Muscles bulged beneath his thin white shirt, and the buttons on his chest appeared strained. His face was changed, his features more raw somehow, the angles to his face sharper and in shadow. And his teeth... how had I not noticed his teeth? The two front canines appeared elongated and sharper than usual.

He spoke, and his voice came out as almost a growl, low and reverberating through his chest, into mine, as though I could feel it. "What has she told you?" He stepped towards me, and I fell a step back, his voice penetrating me, "She has gotten to you, hasn't she? Inside your head?" He eyed me in anger, his chest rising and falling more rapidly. I held my hands out, attempting to calm him as he continued to approach me.

Then he stopped abruptly, studying me, and I am sure, seeing the fear in my eyes. "You fool," he muttered. And then he turned away from me, retreating across the laboratory to the dimness of the shadows. "Stay away from her." Was all he uttered, and I turned and fled the room."

Cam stopped reading there, lifting her head from the journal. She shook herself, looked around the room, and found the doorway. The door remained closed. *How long had he been gone?* She wondered. What were they talking about? Were they making up? Her chest ached painfully at the thought.

She stood and set the journal down, face down on the chair, and began to pace the room, following in Austin's footsteps. She moved back and forth, coming to a stop eventually in front of the tall bank of windows on the opposite wall.

She stood next to the velvet curtains, running a hand down the tassel fringe that lined the edge. Her heart beat jaggedly, rapidly, in her chest as she pictured him returning to her, entering the room, and telling her it was over. It was over between him and Miranda. He realized he'd never wanted her in the first place. That it had always been Cam. He'd just been too stupid to realize it.

Her face flushed as she stared out over the grounds through the rain-splotched windowpanes. She laid a hand on the cold glass, then rested her forehead against it as well. She was a fool, an idiot. Ten years later, she was still pining after him. Aching for him. And for what? He was married. Had a wife. And yes, she had cheated on him, but clearly, it had been a mistake. She obviously regretted it. Had told Cam as much. She knew Miranda still loved him and wanted him back.

Cam had listened to Miranda carry on for several minutes after the fight as she cried, and had felt herself overheating, suffocating in Darcy's room. She listened until couldn't take it anymore, couldn't listen to her a moment longer.

She had found Rahul in the hallway, just outside the room, and sent him to find Bee, and bring her back. She hadn't wanted to leave Miranda alone, she was her friend, after all. But she couldn't bear to hear it, to commiserate with her. She had wanted to scream at her for being such a careless fool as to hurt him, to cheat on him, and with Lan, of all people, a friend of his. For just throwing away something she wanted so desperately it hurt, as though it meant nothing to her.

Cam jumped back, startled at the sound of the door opening behind her, as a rush of air was sucked out of the room. Several candles flickered and went out, leaving one lit on the nightstand. She reached up hastily and wiped her forehead with the back of her hand, where it was damp from condensation.

Austin stood there, his figure framed in the light from the lit candelabras lining the hallway behind him. The fire had burnt low in the grate. She squinted at him. His face was in shadow, his eyes just barely visible, peering at her. They stood there like that for a long moment. Then he turned and shut the door behind him, saying, "She's gone with the others."

He cleared his throat and moved further into the room, moving around the bed, he came around and leaned on the edge farthest from the door, facing her. He crossed his arms over his chest, studying her. She breathed evenly, trying to calm her heart pounding in her chest. "They all left," he continued, "to go look for Alex."

Cam nodded at him and eyed the journal lying upside down on the chair. "I read a little more while you were gone, I..." she shrugged. " Sorry, I was waiting for a while."

"I know," he said, his voice low and gravelly, "I'm sorry," he added, "that you were waiting."

She licked her lips, chewing on her bottom lip for a moment. "It's fine," she said abruptly, and she turned and walked past him, grabbed the book off the chair, and sat back down. Her heart raced in her chest now. Nothing was happening, she told herself. So, the others left, she had known that was going to happen. And they were going to stay behind to read the journal. That was the plan.

But there was something in his manner, his movements, and the way he watched her. Why did she feel as though he were waiting? Waiting for something to happen? Was he waiting on some sign from her? She felt herself starting to tremble again, anxiety flooding her, as it had when she sat at the table earlier, thinking of being here, with him, tonight. She was glad she hadn't eaten anything.

"Should I go back?" She asked him calmly, looking over at him. He remained in the same spot, staring down at his feet.

"No," he replied quietly, "It's okay, just keep going." She nodded to herself and raised the journal again, steadied herself, and kept reading.

"I now had a better understanding of just how dire our situation was becoming. For John refused to leave the castle, and Marianna refused to leave without John. I struggled through dinner that evening. Sitting down to my plate, I eyed it warily, my stomach twisting and turning slightly at the thought of putting anything in my mouth.

I told myself this was just nerves. Knowing the task that lay before me and not knowing how I would accomplish it. I eyed Marianna across the table. Did she appear paler this evening? As though more of the life had been drained out of her. She wore a gauzy scarf tied around her throat in a bow that draped down over her shoulders. It seemed uncharacteristic of her, somehow. Not being a fashion I had seen her wearing previously. Nor in fact, being a fashion, I had seen any young ladies wearing out in society. I wondered at it until she caught me staring at her neck, which brought a flush of color to her otherwise pale features.

I looked away promptly, not wanting to draw John's attention between us. For already he eyed us both suspiciously, I thought, whenever we were all together. Since that moment in the laboratory, when he had told me to stay away from her, I labored now under the weight of his suspicion. And along with it, the growing sense of unease and guilt that blossomed in my gut, like a budding flame of foul origin that could not be extinguished.

We spoke little at dinner, maintaining a light, civil conversation about mundane topics such as the weather. We commented on the extended storm we were experiencing, as the castle seemed shrouded in rain, and thunder and lightning pounded the castle walls, only furthering my sense of dread.

John stood abruptly, about halfway through the meal, and announced he would retire to his study for the evening. He was in the midst of attempting to resolve the puzzle of why his latest invention affected the wielder so. He bid us a gruff goodnight and stalked from the room. *Almost immediately after his departure, Marianna turned to me, speaking quietly, with her eyes downcast; she explained she was suffering from a headache and would plan to spend the remainder of the evening in her chambers. She left even more abruptly than John had. I stood, pushing my chair back from the table, and called out after her, but she only shook her head at me and rushed from the room.*

I paced the length of the dining room, startling a young serving girl who happened upon me. She gathered a tray and curtsied to me, explaining in a halting voice that she was taking some things to Mrs. Marianna in the library. I waited for a length of time after she left me, continuing to pace and muttering to myself under my breath, which, naturally, was not normal behavior, but I found myself rehearsing what I would say to her. I was starting to feel as though I were the one going mad.

I eventually made my way to the library, my feet carrying me there almost of their own accord, while I continued to attempt to discern a way out of this mess. I found Marianna in the library, just as the girl had said she would be. She stood before a large table, empty with the exception of the tray, and a large tome, which lay open before her, its dusty pages smelling of must. I approached her cautiously but deliberately as I continued to formulate what I must say to her in my mind.

She was startled by my appearance, nonetheless. And I saw her hand go to her throat for a moment, in what must have been a subconscious movement, before she caught herself and lowered her hand to her side.

I paused in my recitation of my thoughts and stared at the scarf tied around her neck. It was of such a light and flimsy material that it had begun to slip. In so doing, it had revealed what it was clearly intended to cover up: a raw red marking that stood out starkly against her pale skin.

I am ashamed to say I reached for the scarf, pulling it down lower, to see the extent of the damage that had been done to her. I gasped, and, raising my eyes to hers, saw they were filled with tears, which glistened in the candlelight. "Did he do this to you?" I demanded of her, my voice barely able to remain even and steady as I trembled in anger.

"Garrett, please," she murmured, drawing away from me, appearing to shrink into herself. "Leave it be. You mustn't be angry. There is nothing to be done."

I stared at her in disbelief. "Nothing to be done?" I shook my head, stepping closer to her. "Oh, there is much that can and should be done. Marianna, you cannot stay here, I am begging you. Please, say you will come away with me, even if John will not."

She watched me, her eyes wide, as I pleaded with her. I would go down on my knees before her if that were what it took. She shook her head, "How would that look, Garrett? I cannot leave with you, not without John. And besides, I won't abandon him here, to that creature."

"Marianna, I care not how it would look or what anyone would say. Do you know what they say now, in town, about this castle? About the creature?" She shook her head again, eyes wide. I moved a step closer to her, "For I have asked. When I left the castle today, I went for a walk, yes, but I stopped in town. I learned of what talk the servants have spread amongst each other. They say a creature, a demon, stalks the castle at night. They say it feeds off of heartache, malice, and cruelty, just as you have said. But they say more. They say it can take over a man. Possess him. Become him. They say it can cause a man to commit all manner of evil deeds. They say that it cannot be killed. That it feeds off the helpless."

She shrunk back further again from me, her eyes wide in horror this time. "No," she murmured, "They cannot know that."

"They can, and they do," my voice rose higher as I trembled with frustration. "You don't know that he leaves? He leaves the castle, Marianna. There are people, young women, that have gone missing. One of your own servant girls. He... he took them. Tell me you didn't know that." My voice shook with emotion.

"The creature?" Marianna replied, her voice barely above a whisper.

"No, Marianna. It's John. It's been John for some time now, I think. I don't know when or how, but-" She began to tremble then. Visibly shaking in front of me. A sob released from her throat, and she covered her mouth with both hands as she wept, as though she could keep the sobs in.

I went to her and then took hold of her arm to comfort her. "Marianna please, leave. With me. Before he does worse to you." I brushed my hand down the length of her neck, past the open red wound at the base of it. "I *love you, Marianna. I think you know that I do. I've always loved you. I will not let him hurt you."*

She raised her eyes to meet mine, her sobs subsiding as she listened to my words, as she finally heard me. I looked her straight in the eye and repeated again: "I swear to you, I will not let him hurt you."

She shook her head, beginning to sob again. "Oh Garrett, I cannot... please, you must know..." She stopped, letting out a gasp, as though startled suddenly by something she saw in my face, in my features. But by what, I did not know.

Marianna turned and ran from the room, fleeing from me. My instinct was to follow her, to run after her and chase her until I caught her. And then... and then... what? I asked myself, pausing in my pursuit of her, for I knew not what I had planned to do in that moment. Only that I must have her.

I left the library, shaken by what had occurred, and returned to my room. I locked myself inside. It was long before I slept that night. I stood there, staring out my window at the rain, at the storm lashing the castle. And in it, I felt all of the pain, all the rage that was bubbling and burning deep inside me, as though it had been unleashed upon the world.

For though it shamed me to admit it, I loved Marianna, my own brother's wife. And I coveted her, wanted so dearly, for her to be mine. Since arriving at the castle, the thought had consumed me. Until it had become my every waking thought, my only desire. I burned for her, and yet I knew that she never would love me back."

Cam paused again, her voice trembling involuntarily as she read the last paragraph. Her eyes began to fill with unshed tears. She blinked rapidly, dispersing them, and took a deep breath, attempting to calm her nerves. She felt almost suddenly ill. Her gut churned, sick with dread and longing, as she read those words.

She felt, rather than saw Austin get up, moving away from the bed. She refused to look at him but continued to read.

Attempting to hide that more than just her voice was trembling now. She was shivering in minute little jolts as though her anxiety, being bottled up inside of her, had found a way to release itself.

He stood before her, reached down, and placed a hand under her chin. He tilted her face up towards his, away from the book. She felt her arms lower as the book landed in her lap.

His blue eyes were dark, with something like pain mixed with desire. She felt a white-hot heat sweep through her as he stared down at her. Then he leaned in closer and kissed her.

She felt his lips on hers and parted her own, opening her mouth to him as he kissed her, first gently and then deeper, more urgently. She could feel herself trembling, and she shivered now with desire for him. She heard the journal fall to the ground as he grabbed her arm, pulling her to her feet, one arm sliding around her, enveloping her, and pulling her to him. She melted into him, allowing him to move her closer to the bed as he continued to kiss her.

She fell backward onto the bed, and he climbed over her, pressing himself against her. She sighed in relief at the feeling of his weight on top of her. He kissed her more frantically now, fumbling to pull her shirt off, sliding it up over her head. She threw it on the floor, as he quickly removed his own. Then he looped his arms beneath her, removing her bra as well, flinging it away. His mouth moved down to her neck, to her chest, until finally, he took a nipple in his mouth, sucking and pulling, his hand kneading her as she moaned with pleasure.

He moved back to her mouth, kissing her deeply again. Suddenly she felt a sharp stab of pain, pulling back away from him slightly, a hint of the iron taste of blood filling her mouth. She touched her lip gently and her fingers came away with a wash of red. "God, sorry," Austin murmured, lifting himself up on his arms, looking down at her lips, and then at her fingers.

"It's okay," Cam said breathlessly, her heart pounding against her ribs.

"Are you sure?" he asked her, between panting breaths. She felt him, hard against her thigh, pressing into her, and she writhed slightly against him, pulling him back to her, she kissed him this time, claiming him with her mouth.

After another moment or so, she felt him start to slide her pants down, past her thighs, and finally to her ankles. He moved off of her as he went. He had left her panties on, she noted with amusement. He leaned back over her, kissing her again, moving once more to her neck, as he slid one hand down her stomach, tucking under the band of her panties until he caressed her at her core, flicking and teasing her as she writhed against him. She moaned again, louder this time. Biting down on her now puffy lip to stop herself from making too much noise. She reminded herself the others were gone, off searching for Alex. No one would hear them.

She felt a shiver down her spine at the thought, as his teeth grazed her neck. She was driven to distraction again quickly as his fingers moved against her. "Austin," she murmured, she couldn't take it much longer. She reached down and fumbled with his belt, undoing it clumsily, and pushing his jeans down. He stood and removed them, along with his boxers, tossing them on the floor. She moved backward, away from him, towards the head of the bed, until she felt pillows behind her.

She lay back, watching him in the dim glow from the coals that now burned low in the grate. The storm raged outside, a crack of thunder pealing somewhere nearby as he scaled the end of the bed, crawling towards her across the mattress. The muscles on his back rippled as he moved. His eyes locked on hers, unblinking, as he came for her.

She shivered in anticipation, and froze for a second, catching her breath as a sliver of fear danced through her. The light from the candle next to the bed caught his eyes for the briefest of seconds, but then he was on her again, the feeling of his skin against hers was like velvet. She trembled in his arms. He slid his hand over her again, teasing her once more, until she was panting, begging him to take her.

He slid her panties off, moving his mouth to her throat as he finally pushed inside her, pressing into her as he moved against her while she exploded with pleasure. His kiss became rougher, harder at her neck, as he nipped her slightly. She moaned, and her skin broke out in goosebumps. He chuckled, kissing and licking her neck, then moving up until his mouth brushed over her ear, sending a cascade of shivers down her spine. She moved against him now too, wanting him urgently deeper. He moved back to her neck, and she felt him nipping her again, in what started as pleasure, but grew steadily sharper, slowly edging towards pain. He rode her harder until she cried out as the caress of his tongue ended in a sharp, stabbing pain.

Cam squirmed backward, away from him, shoving her palms against his chest. He moved back, releasing her, leaving her suddenly cold as the warmth of his skin against hers disappeared. She lifted one hand to her neck, and this time, she could see even in the swiftly darkening room, the bright red smear of blood that stained her hand.

"You..." Cam trailed off, looking up at him in horror. "You bit me." She murmured.

Austin stared at her, unblinking, saying nothing. She felt herself shrinking back against the headboard. Her heart was racing now with an edge of fear.

"I... I'm sorry," Austin mumbled, running his hands through his hair as he stared back at her, appearing equally horrified now. "I... I didn't mean to." His voice came out in low, guttural tones. She felt his voice reverberating in her chest. "I'm sorry, Cam. Are you okay?"

She wiped her hand down her neck and attempted to peer down at it, but of course, she could see nothing. "I think so," she said. "I can't tell how bad it's bleeding, but I think I'm okay."

"I'm sorry," Austin murmured again. Climbing off the bed and turning his back to her, he grabbed his boxers and pulled them on.

"Okay..." she said, her voice strained. She watched him dress. "So that's it then, I guess." Her cheeks flushed red with embarrassment and disappointment.

"I think we should stop," he said, half turning back to her. "I... I can't do this."

"What do you mean you can't do this?" His words reverberated, echoing hollowly within her. Her chest filled with a bubble of anguish.

"I mean, I can't do this Cam." He said louder this time, turning to her and flinging his arms out. "What do you think that means?"

She shook with fear and anger. Sitting there cold and naked, bleeding in front of him. She was silent for a long moment. Then she heard her own voice, shaking and weak, "Do you have any idea, any idea at all, how long I have wanted this to happen?"

He just stood there, silently, watching her, his face half-hidden in shadows. She swallowed dryly, continuing, "Any idea at all what you just did to me? What you've done to me? For years, Austin. Years."

He didn't move a muscle, stood there waiting for her to continue, his unblinking eyes locked onto hers. She moved to her knees. "Do you understand, Austin?" Her voice broke on his name. "I was in love with you for years. The entire time we were at State. For four years, I was head over heels for you. Obsessed."

"I'm sorry, Cam," Austin said again, stiffly this time.

"Oh, you're sorry? Are you? Is that all you can say? Are you sorry that you led me on? Flirted with me, shamelessly? Made me think you cared about me?"

"I didn't," he mumbled, then trailed off, "I didn't do it on purpose."

"Oh, you didn't? Well, that's good to know." She slid over to the far side of the bed, climbing off, putting the bed between them. She searched for her underwear in the dark, finding her scattered clothes, always keeping one eye on him, not letting him out of her sight. She gathered them in her arms and set them on the bed as she began to dress herself.

"I didn't mean for you to think..." he continued, but she interrupted him.

"You didn't mean for me to think what? That you loved me back? Do you even remember the things you did? The things you said? The stupid poems you read to me?" She stared at him in disbelief. "What about the mixed CDs you made me? Huh?" He just stared back at her. She found she had picked up his shirt, along with her things, and she threw it at his face. He caught it, in one hand. He didn't even flinch. He held it in a crumpled ball, his eyes never leaving hers.

"Why did you do that, Austin? You made me those stupid CDs, filled with songs that were ours. Our inside jokes, the ones we sang together in your car. The rest of them were love songs. Obvious, blatant love songs." She shook her head at him. "What was I supposed to think that meant, Austin?" She shook her head at him. "Can you name a single song now? Because I can. I remember every word of every stupid love song you burned for me." He seemed at a loss for words. She found her bra and put it on, turning her back on him, until she was fully dressed. She kept her head turned to the side. *Why was she afraid to look away from him?*

"And that night, at Henley Park." She turned to face him again, "I finally worked up the courage to tell you how I felt. To tell you I was in love with you. And your response? Two words. 'I can't.' What was that supposed to mean?"

He just stared at her, as though he were frozen. She waited, her heart in her throat. She had asked the question out loud that she had asked herself over and over in her mind. For ten years, she had longed to know the answer. She had to know.

But Austin remained silent. Staring. He didn't seem to move a muscle. She couldn't even tell if he was breathing. *Was he ever going to answer her?* She watched him. Studied him, searching for the minutest clue. *Was he ever going to blink?* Ten years later... he still couldn't give her any answers. Still couldn't even admit whether or not he actually ever cared about her. She wanted to scream at him.

"Do you have any clue what that did to me? How devastated..." She broke off, trembling, shaking now with cold, rage, and a tiny flame of fear that burned in her gut. Cam moved to leave the room but turned back to him. "And apparently, I was too young, too naive, and too hurt to demand any kind of explanation from you. I just..." she trailed off. "Walked away."

"Cam," he murmured, finally moving. He moved closer to her, his hand outstretched.

"Don't," she gasped, her voice sharp as she took a step away from him. She stared at him, studying him again in the faint light from the remaining candle. The coals now just an orange glow in the grate. "What's happening to you?" she asked in a whisper, her voice quivering. Austin only stared back at her. Cam swallowed audibly. "You're going to take her back, aren't you?"

He stared at her for a moment longer, uncomprehending. Then his eyebrows raised, he sighed and looked away from her, finally unable to meet her eyes.

"I knew it." She trembled with rage. "You fucking coward," She whispered.

She turned then and walked away from him, but she paused mid-stride, her eyes catching on the journal. It lay where she had dropped it, in a heap on the floor. She scooped it up, closing it carefully, and tucking it into her arms.

Cam moved to the door, put a hand on the handle, and turned back to find Austin. She half expected him to have moved. To have closed the distance between them silently, but he was still standing there, his crumpled shirt in his hands. She waited for half a heartbeat to see if he would say anything, if he would try to stop her. When he didn't move, she opened the door, stepped into the hallway, and slammed it shut behind her.

She moved down the corridor and hated the part of herself that listened, that waited, to see if he would come after her. Because he wouldn't, she knew that now, with sudden certainty. She finally understood. He had every opportunity, back then, ten years ago, to tell her he wanted her, to come after her, to make her his. Instead of hints, signs... notes, and CDs, there should have been dates, kisses, and I-love-yous. And there hadn't been. Nothing had stopped him then, and nothing was stopping him now.

But he didn't want her. Not truly. Or she would have been his.

She had given herself over fully to him, back then. And like a fool, she had done it again, tonight. And she hated herself for it. Hated him, too. A deep tide of anger rose in her. Starting in the pit of her stomach, it rose to her chest, expanding until it burst out of her, consuming her. She let out a scream of rage, trembling in fury, that echoed through the main foyer. She stalked down to the common area, her footsteps slamming on the ground. She moved blindly through the room, grabbing a flashlight that had been left on the dining table. She stopped long enough to look over at the board, at the red lights now lit up next to her name.

Her shoulders rose practically to her ears as she turned, restraining herself from ripping the board off the wall. She left the room, flicking on the flashlight as she went.

24.

Austin

Austin stood there for a long time, in the dark. As though he was frozen. He couldn't seem to wrap his mind around what had happened.

He jerked suddenly, hearing a cry echoing from somewhere in the castle. The noise seemed to wake him from his stasis, unfreezing his limbs and allowing him to move again. He pulled his shirt back on and stepped out the door, pulling it shut with a soft click behind him.

He looked up and down the hallway, moving noiselessly to Cam's doorway. Her door stood open, the room inside flooded with darkness. He let his eyes adjust to the dark, scanning the space. He moved on, silently and swiftly, until he found himself in the main foyer. He paused at the top of the stairs, peering through the doorway to his left, down the corridor that led to the rest of the castle. He saw nothing, he heard nothing. He turned and headed for the common room.

Entering the large space, he oriented naturally to the only real source of light in the room: the board that hung over the desk, flooding the desk and dining table below with red light.

Austin approached it, his head moving back and forth, eyes sweeping through the gloom, but he could already sense that the room was empty. He stopped by the board, staring up at it. There were now two red lights next to his name. He was a little surprised to see there were two next to Cam's name now as well.

He kicked himself internally, licking his lips, then running the tip of his tongue gingerly over his teeth. He tried to tell himself that it must have been just his imagination. His canine teeth no longer felt oddly elongated, as though they were too big for his mouth.

But he knew they had been, as he stood there in his bedroom, staring down at Cam. He recalled the feeling, with a shudder of pleasure and agony, watching that trickle of red moving slowly down her neck.

How had he done that, otherwise? He had bit her. He still couldn't believe it. He reached up now with his hands, running his fingers over his teeth. Finding nothing out of the ordinary, he sighed deeply. He felt suddenly wracked with guilt at what he had done. Not just the bite.

He hadn't meant to hurt her. There was no way to make her see, make her understand that.

He had been an idiot, back then. Not wanting to be tied down. Then after, when they were graduating, when he knew she would be leaving, moving away out of state for law school, he had almost gone to her and told her how he felt. But that sense of losing something, of missing out on everything, all the possibilities that lay before him, had been too strong. He couldn't give it up. Not then. Not for her.

So, didn't that make her right? he asked himself. Hadn't he led her on with no real intention of being with her? Made her think he loved her. He felt an odd mixture of disgust, rage, and desire. His ears pricked, sensing motion down the hallway, back towards the stairs. Had she gone back to her room? He felt himself tensing, his muscles preparing to propel him forward. To go after her, find her, in the dark. He breathed deeply, calming his heart as it raced in his chest.

He had been so angry lately. Angry with Miranda first. And now, angry with himself. Because part of him *had* wanted to hurt *her*. Miranda. Wanted to get back at her. That was part of it, wasn't it?

Yes, a part of him had wanted Cam tonight, too. Had needed her. But, hadn't he used her, in the end? Perhaps he hadn't meant to. Not really. But what did that matter, at this point?

He went to the phone, plucking it from the cradle. He held it to his ear. There was no dial tone—nothing but dead air.

He moved over to the fireplace. Stared down at the empty grate. Slowly, he began to build a fire, to occupy himself. He was going to leave, he had decided. As soon as the others got back. Hopefully, they would return with Alex. He'd demand he let him go.

Austin crouched before the fire, listening to the howling wind, the pounding rain and surf... and farther away, the movements of the others... their footsteps echoing through the castle. He listened. And he waited.

25.

Darcy

Darcy moved through the hallways, following the others, as though she were in a dream. They had been searching for Alex for what felt like hours now.

She clung to Clay's arm. Pulled on by the bobbing flashlight beams up ahead. It was getting harder for her to stay focused. To feel as though she were in the present. She was tired, she told herself. That was all it was. Had she slept since she got here? She had been wracked by dreams, by a sort of waking nightmare. Of course she hadn't slept. Not really. Not well enough to feel rested.

The feel of Clay's arm was reassuring. She gripped his bicep tightly in her hands, trusting him to lead her where she needed to go. She wanted to get out of the castle, wanted to leave.

She heard one of the others call out from up ahead, flashlight beams moving faster now in the darkness. They gathered in front of a small room. A door stood open in front of them. They moved into the room; Clay brought her over to the wall beside the doorway. She watched as Rahul bent down over the desk on the far wall. The beam from Lan's flashlight shone over his head, illuminating a corkboard on the wall above. She could make out photographs and drawings from here. Strings led from the images to points on a map. Secured with push pins.

They were chattering excitedly, their voices pitched too low and too fast for her to follow. Clay's face appeared in front of her. "Darcy, are you okay?" He frowned at her. His face became blurry for a moment, as he swam in and out of focus. Darcy heard a crack of thunder then, in the distance.

She didn't think they could hear the waves from here, deep in the castle, hadn't noticed them the last few minutes, but she heard them now; a crashing sound, but also like static, like a radio being tuned in and out. She opened her mouth to speak, to answer Clay, but she swayed slightly on her feet, her eyes going wide as she reached out for him. She felt his arms around her, catching her as she fell. Then she surrendered to the darkness.

She moved through the common room, drifting towards the entry to the foyer. She could barely hear the waves pounding here, over the sound of the rain. It pelted the roof, cascading down in a sheet of water.

She moved through the doorway and felt her feet on solid ground again. The black and white marble floor was covered in several inches of water.

Darcy gazed up at the ceiling and had to close her eyes, squinting as fat raindrops landed on her upturned face. She continued on, walking through the freezing rain towards the main staircase. As she approached the first step, the ticking started. It was like a clock, but it was loud—so loud that it moved closer and closer to her until it surrounded her, until it was in her head.

She lifted her hands to her ears, covering them, as she ascended the stairs. The door at the top of the stairs was closed. She turned and continued on towards the guest wing, the ticking somehow growing even louder.

It was there, suddenly, before her. Like a dark shadow in the night, it was growing and stretching, becoming impossibly tall. "Tick-tock, Darcy." She heard it chuckle. She screamed then, surrounded by outstretched limbs, long claws encircling her, caging her, and a pair of glowing eyes.

Night. The darkness was safe, comforting, and pure. They moved through the hallway like shadows, pausing to listen, to sense, and to feel. It was as though they had a direct lifeline, plugged into all that breathed and moved in the castle. The slightest movement, a rustle of fabric against skin, the twisting of sheets. The ones who slept were dreaming, longing, and wanting.

The want. The aching need, the constant demand for more. It was incessant. How he loathed that ache. It reminded him of the familiar need to feed, old as time, that plagued him. It filled him with rage, and he shuddered with it.

But it wasn't food or sustenance that they wanted. No, it was a million other things. Some that had no names. And it was each other. Mostly each other. That was the part that drew him out, filled him with rage. The need they had to own, to consume, one another.

He passed silent as a shadow through the first door. This one slept sideways on the bed, his feet and hands splayed, hanging over the edge. He was filled with hunger for her... the small one whose head was filled with dreams of more. But it was an old ache, fading and less intense than some. But it was edged with frustration, and there was anger underneath. Yes, he might do.

But he turned and continued on his journey, pausing as he passed by the door with two heartbeats behind it. He slid inside and slithered below the bed. Lay curled beneath them as he stared up into them.

The one on the right had so much potential. But she was strong, this one. A fighter, like *he* had been. Yes... but she was so filled with want, with a thirst, and the anger... the self-loathing. She would be delightful to devour, slowly, until she was his. He slid a long white hand up, up, over the edge of the bed, until he found hers. The touch of her skin against his made his skin crawl, all while it filled him with need. His teeth elongated and drool dripped down his chin. He held her hand for some time, listening to her heart whirring and ticking above him. The blood pumping in a steady rhythm.

But there were more, so many more, with potential. So he moved on, eventually. Sliding sinuously out from beneath the bed and back to the corridor. There was the one who was lying, playing a role. The one who had lied, cheated, and caused so much pain. She was paying the price for her lust now, though, wasn't she? These fools. They never realized that every debt would be paid.

The detective... oh how exquisite his thoughts were. The ones he hid from himself, in the dark corners of his mind. The stuff nightmares were made of. He would be a nice little snack. But he would put up a fight, too.

Then, there was the one with the big dark eyes, who stared back at him. Saw him immediately, somehow. He didn't like that one. She needed to leave.

He turned then, cocking his head to the side. He had heard something moving in the dark, floating down the corridors with no footfalls. And it reeked of her. He hissed, low in his throat, looking back at her closed door down the hall. How could that be?

He turned, moving through the next door. This one was going to be his. This one was perfect.

He climbed onto the bed, one appendage at a time, moving over his prone body until he sat perched on his chest. He chortled and chuckled to himself, delighting in his meal.

One claw held out, he stroked his bare chest, his cheek. His tongue slopped loose from between his teeth, and he slid the tip up his neck, over to his lips. He clamped his mouth over his and breathed in. Gently at first, then harder, sucking as he felt him loosening. Felt them begin to combine, to merge. His edges dissolved and swirled like smoke, opening to let him in. He waited as they mixed. And then he let the breath out, in one large rush, as he entered him, molding to his form.

Austin gasped and choked, sputtering, as he sat up in bed. His eyes were wide, taking in the room around him. Blinking in confusion, he gasped for air, grabbed at his throat, and slid a hand to his mouth. The hand came away damp, and he stared down in confusion, turning it and squinting in the dark.

Then he lay back down, panting. Until his breathing calmed, his heart rate slowed. He lay there, teetering on the edge of sleep, falling deeper and deeper. And while he slept, the thing inside him stretched and curled and made itself comfortable. And Darcy could only watch, her soul writhing in terror as she screamed.

26.

Lan

They were finally starting to get somewhere, with the clues. Studying the board over the desk and the manuscript that lay next to the funny-looking metal globe with rings. Lan whipped his head around at the commotion that started up over by the door.

Clay stood there, holding Darcy, propping her up. She hung limply in his arms, her head lolled back at an unnatural angle. Lan knew immediately that she was unconscious.

Bee got to her first, of course. Checking her pulse. Pulling back her eyelids, one at a time, she borrowed a flashlight, checking her pupils. "We should bring her back to the common area," Bee said a moment later. A few people groaned.

"That's really far, Bee. Is it safe to move her that far?" Clay asked her. He looked down at Darcy. "I can carry her," he said, glancing back up at them, surveying the group.

"It should be safe," Bee said gently, "I think she's just fainted. She's unconscious for now." Bee looked over at Rahul. "Why don't some of us head back, bring her back to the common room, so she can rest and recover. I'll go, of course," she added. "The rest of you can stay. Keep looking?" She seemed uncertain.

Lan shook his head, speaking up, "I don't think that's a good idea, for just the two of you to go." He didn't want to insult Clay, but he continued. "It's farther than you think, carrying someone like that. I think a few of us should probably go and take turns carrying her. Then we can head straight back, keep working." He looked over at Rahul, who nodded to him in approval.

Bee smiled grimly at Clay. "You're probably right. Why don't we all go? Take a quick break, and then a group can come back here."

The others agreed readily, and they turned and began to make their way back to the common room.

Clay carried Darcy first, and Lan trailed at the end of the group. He eyed Miranda's back; she was walking beside Bee, up near Clay, at the front of the group. Which was good. Lan was making sure he kept his distance from Miranda. Not only because it was awkward, but because the last thing he wanted to do was further piss off Austin at this point. He didn't need to give him any other reasons to want to come after him again.

They shuffled along in relative silence, only speaking occasionally when someone needed to clarify which turn to take. About a third of the way there, Lan moved to the front of the group, laid a hand on Clay's shoulder, and suggested he take over for a while. Clay nodded without speaking, his mouth a thin line.

He transferred Darcy over to Lan, and he slid his arms under her shoulders, and below her knees, lifting her and settling her against his chest. He didn't like the way her head hung, bobbing limply on her neck. He tried to move her as gently and evenly as possible, to disturb her the least. He was surprised initially at how light she felt in his arms. Like he was carrying a child. Thankfully, she was petite, and he was able to carry her quite a ways before he started to tire.

As they made their way back towards the organ room, Lan came to a sudden halt, Clay almost slamming into his back. "God, we're so stupid," he groaned out loud. "We can't carry her back to the common room." He turned towards the rest of the group. "We forgot about the ladder."

"Fuck," Clay murmured, running his hands over his head. "I completely forgot." He shook his head, turning to Bee. "What are we going to do?" They all stood there in silence for a moment, no one quite sure what to do next.

Finally, Miranda spoke up, her voice soft. "I brought my coat with me," she said, starting to shrug it off. "I was cold, earlier." She held it up. "It's huge though, more like a cloak really. We can use it for something soft, to lay her down on to rest."

Bee smiled at her and nodded. "Good idea. Let's bring her over here, I guess." She gestured over to the side of the room.

That's as good as anywhere else." She supervised as they spread out the cloak, gently lowering her to the ground on top of it. Miranda used the hood to make a little pillow for her.

"Alright, well," Bee looked up at them, as she sat on the floor next to Darcy. "There's really no point in all of us staying here with her. I'll stay." She shrugged. "I may go grab the first aid kit, but that will only take me a minute or so if someone else can stay with her. I doubt we'll need it, but just in case."

"I'll stay too," Clay said swiftly. Bee nodded and smiled up at him.

Lan cleared his throat. "I'd like to head back for a few minutes, grab something to drink, and take a bathroom break. What do you guys think?" The others began to nod in agreement.

"I'll go back with you too," Rahul said.

"A bathroom break would be good," Bee said thoughtfully.

"You go too, Bee," Miranda said. "Clay and I will sit with Darcy; we'll take care of her until you get back." She looked over at Clay. "Are you okay to stay, Clay?"

He hesitated. "Yeah, I mean a bathroom break would be good. Depending on how long it takes until she wakes up." He looked down at Darcy uncertainly.

"Go ahead," Miranda said, "Just leave me a flashlight." She chuckled. "I don't want to sit here in the dark."

Clay protested for a moment, saying he would stay, but Miranda insisted he go, that she would be fine for a few minutes.

"Bring me back a bottle of water, will you? If you see any?" She asked. "Maybe grab some for Darcy, too, when she wakes up." Lan nodded in agreement.

They left a flashlight with Miranda, and Lan continued on with Bee, Rahul, and Clay, making their way over to the ladder on the far side of the room.

Lan stuck his flashlight into the top of his pants, tightening the belt another notch to keep it in place. Bee giggled a little at the sight, but it allowed him to climb up the ladder first, with at least some light to guide him as he neared the top. Rahul stood below, lighting his way at the bottom of the ladder for as long as he could as well.

They made their way up the ladder, one at a time. Bee breathed a sigh of relief as she made it to the top and was back on solid ground. She chuckled slightly. "That is one thing I am not going to miss when this weekend is over."

They moved quickly back towards the door at the top of the stairs leading into the foyer. "What are we going to do if she doesn't wake up soon?" Lan heard Rahul ask Bee in a low voice.

Lan peered up ahead, seeing movement—someone coming towards them in the darkness. He shone his flashlight towards the dark figure moving down the corridor. He saw Cam pause and take a step back as she held up a hand to shield her eyes, squinting at them.

"Jesus," she murmured, and Lan dropped the beam to her feet, and off to the side. "What's going on?" Cam asked. Her voice sounded oddly strangled and horse. "Did you find Alex?" She peered past them, trying to see who else was there behind him in the dark.

"No," Lan sighed. "Unfortunately, we didn't. There was no trace of him. We started working on the clues again, though. We were just getting somewhere, but then Darcy fainted."

"Darcy fainted?" Cam asked, surprised, "Is she okay?"

"I think so," Bee said. "We're heading back to grab water and the first aid kit. She's down in the organ room, resting, with Miranda watching her."

Cam nodded. "Well, hopefully, she's alright then."

"Come on," Lan said. "Let's get moving. We're heading back to get the supplies and then heading straight back down to them. We forgot we couldn't carry her up the stupid ladder," he chuckled. "We were planning on bringing her back to the common room."

Cam laughed a little at that and turned to head back with them. They moved as quickly as they could now. Lan pictured Miranda sitting there alone in the dark, Darcy's unconscious body next to her. He didn't envy her and had to give her credit for being brave enough to sit there alone.

They entered the common room, and Bee headed straight for the desk, opening the drawer that held the first aid kit and pulling it out. Clay searched the mini bar for water bottles.

"Okay," Lan said, "Let's stop back at our rooms quickly to pee and then we can head back down." He turned and stopped, staring at the board; the glow of red lights was stronger now. He noted the two red lights that beamed next to Cam's name, where there had been none before. There was a second next to Austin's name, as well.

Lan turned, a quizzical look on his face, searching for Cam. He froze at the sight of a tall figure shrouded in darkness, silhouetted in front of the fire. The figure moved towards them, and something about the way it moved caused Lan to take a step back. Then another. He realized with a start that it was Austin. Lan braced himself as he approached.

But Austin moved closer and called out, "Hey," eyeing Cam for a split second and moving past her towards Lan. "Did you find Alex?" He asked. His voice was low and gravelly. Lan eyed him up and down. He looked like he was on edge.

"No, man," Lan replied as evenly as he could, "Unfortunately, we didn't. We looked everywhere but found nothing. We were just getting somewhere with the clues though, when-"

Austin cut him off. "Who cares about the clues?" He said. He moved restlessly, walking in a circle and then turning back to him. "I need to leave, " he said abruptly.

Cam snorted, and his head swiveled over to her momentarily. Austin continued, "I'm leaving. Tonight. Now." He walked over to the board, peering up at the ceiling, where the crown molding met the wall. "I don't know who's listening right now," he said, his voice rising, "But I'm done. I'm out. Send a car, or whatever, and someone to unlock the goddamn door."

"Austin," Bee started, her voice tentative, "Is everything okay?"

"No, Bee, it's not. But thanks for asking." Austin's voice was dripping with sarcasm.

"Hey, it's not her fault man," Rahul began, walking over towards him."

"I didn't say it was, did I?" Austin said, eyeing Rahul. He stood up straighter and didn't move as he approached him. They met each other's gaze, Austin staring him down, unblinkingly. "It's my fault, actually," he said dryly. "Everything is my fault."

Cam made another half-snorting laugh and slammed the journal she was holding in her hands down on the dining room table. "Oh, look at that. Did you finally grow a conscience?" She said to Austin's back.

Lan held his hands up. "Whoa guys, what's going on? Did something happen?"

"You could say that," Cam began.

Austin turned towards her, and snapped, his voice almost a growl. "That's enough Cam."

"Oh yeah?" Cam raised an eyebrow at him, her features tight with anger. "Fuck you, Austin."

"Hey, hey." Rahul took another step closer to them, holding his palms up in the air. "Why don't we all calm down?"

"Why don't you stay out of it?" Austin turned on Rahul. "Who the hell are you, anyway?" He held his arms down at his sides, and Lan could see from here that his fists were clenched. Whatever had happened between Austin and Cam, had clearly put him over the edge.

The group fell silent, waiting for Rahul's response. Then Lan cleared his throat. "Yeah, I mean, let's get that out in the open because you weren't at State, man."

Rahul stood there staring Austin down for another long moment, then he pulled his gaze away backed up a few paces, turning to Lan. "Yes, I was," he started.

"Nah man, you weren't," Clay spoke up suddenly, moving closer to them. "See, two brown guys," he gestured between himself and Lan, "wouldn't forget a fucking third brown guy hanging out with us. You weren't there. I'm positive." He crossed over closer to Rahul, planting his feet. "I wasn't at first." He shrugged. "Figured you might have lived on another floor and maybe you didn't come around as much. But I'm sure now. You weren't there. So." Clay folded his arms over his chest. "Just who exactly are you?"

Rahul sighed, looking down at the floor. He shoved his hands in his pockets. "Fine," he said, looking up at them all. "You're right, I wasn't there."

"Then why are you here, now?" Clay pressed him, eyebrows raised.

"I'm an actor, okay?" Rahul sighed again, running a hand over his mouth, and down his goatee. "I've worked with Alex before." Murmurs and groans of protest rose from the group. Rahul continued, "He wanted someone on the inside, who could have some knowledge of the clues. Help the group out when you got stuck. Since, you know, there wasn't going to be an all-powerful facilitator, or whatever, who we could call up for a hint, like there are in most escape rooms."

Lan turned to look at Bee. She stood over by the desk, her jaw dropped open as she stared at Rahul in disbelief.

"An actor," she repeated. Shaking her head at him.

"Bee-" he started, but Clay interrupted him.

"How come we've never seen you before then? Obviously, none of us recognized you."

Rahul shrugged. "I've been in a few things, probably nothing you've seen. My first big movie, we just finished filming a few weeks ago." He shrugged again. "It hasn't hit theaters yet."

"Is Rahul even your real name?" Bee asked weakly.

"Yes, it is." He turned back to Bee, his dark eyes wide and pleading. "Look, Bee, I'm sorry, I wanted to tell you-" she cut him off, shaking her head and chuckling.

"Forget it," she mumbled. She turned to Clay. "This is taking too long; we need to get back to Darcy."

Clay nodded at her. "Let's go, I'm ready when you are."

"Wait a minute," Lan said, his mind going back to the escape room. "You mean to tell me, you've known all the clues all along?" He held his hands up. "Then let's fucking go, man." He pointed back down the corridor behind them. "Let's head back down, and you can tell us exactly what to do, and we can get out of here tonight."

Rahul was shaking his head. "It's not that simple. I did memorize a lot of the puzzles, yeah, but not everything. Not to mention, something got messed up like Alex was pissed about earlier. Things are all..." he trailed off for a moment, searching for the right word, "Out of order. I can do my best, but it's not going to be as simple as you think. I'm not sure what happened." He shrugged.

"So, what actually happened to Alex then?" Lan asked. "Did he get flown out of here on a helicopter or something? I mean, I'm assuming he's not actually missing, then."

"I'm really not sure, honestly," Rahul replied. "I know at one point he was saying he would be ready to take himself out of the game if needed, to... I dunno, 'keep things more interesting', was the way he worded it. But he never discussed specifics with me. I am just as in the dark as you are on that one. All I can say is, there was something, or someone there, running from us in the hallways. That part was real."

Lan sighed, ran a hand through his hair, and turned to Clay. "Fuck. All right, let's get going then."

"What about the clues?" Clay asked, his voice holding a hint of anger. "The clues, about us? How did he know about..." Clay trailed off, glancing over at Lan. "Obviously, he was responsible for those clues being in the game after all."

"He hired a PI," Austin interjected suddenly. The group turned to stare at him.

Clay frowned. "A PI?"

Rahul sighed and nodded, looking down at his feet. "Yeah, uh, like a private eye, you know? A private detective, to like, dig up dirt on all of you." He held up his hands as murmurs of protest rose from the group. "And before you ask, I don't know the extent of what else he found out."

"That fucking bastard." Clay looked away, turning and pacing.

Rahul turned to Austin. "But how did you know that?" Silence fell as they watched Austin pace back and forth, back and forth. Lan sighed deeply. He had a guess.

"He told me," Austin grumbled. "I called him. Said I wasn't coming." He stopped pacing, folding his hands over his chest, his gaze dropping to the floor. "He told me I should change my mind. That there would be... information, revealed, this weekend, that I would want to know." Austin peered over at Lan from beneath his brows. "He basically implied that he knew the truth about Miranda." Austin grimaced. "He refused to tell me ahead of time, to force me to come here. I've been pissed at him for weeks."

"Jesus Christ..." Clay murmured under his breath, "What kind of game was he playing... that's fucked up, man." Clay shook his head at Austin.

Lan turned away, pacing himself for a moment. He could hardly meet Austin's eyes. He struggled to maintain his composure, taking deep breaths as he walked.

"I don't know, man..." Rahul sighed, "Alex does what he wants though. I do know that. He has his own agenda..." He trailed off. "He's super intelligent, but he's devious too, he..." Rahul stopped and caught himself suddenly, as though he had forgotten about the cameras watching them, recording everything.

He cleared his throat before he continued. "There's one more thing." He pointed to Austin. "That, right there. What just happened... that should have gotten some type of response. If someone wants to quit, opt-out, and leave, I mean, you're allowed to do that. Someone should have responded, or..." he looked over at the door that led outside, "be showing up soon, or something." He looked around at them. "If nothing happens, I... I'm not sure what that means. I'm not sure if anyone is hearing us right now."

They all stared at him in silence for a moment. Then Clay shook his head, saying, "Are you saying you think we're actually trapped here right now? With no one watching us?" He looked around at them all incredulously, "So if something happens, there's a chance no one is coming to help us?"

Rahul swallowed audibly and nodded. "Yeah, that's what I'm afraid is happening. Yeah." He looked over at the phone. "The phone is down, and we know the power has been out for a while now. Maybe they don't have eyes on us anymore? I really don't know."

Clay eyed the door across the room. He moved over towards it and shook the handles, pulling hard on the door with his body weight. It hardly budged in its frame. "Hey," he called, turning and looking up towards the ceiling. "Whoever's listening right now, we need you to come let us out. Send a car..." he looked around the room. "You know what, why don't you just send Alex himself back here? We have some questions. And we're done. We want out, now." They stood there awkwardly, waiting, but nothing happened. "Fuck it," Clay said, turning back to them. "We'll break down the door if we have to. There's got to be some tools... a crowbar or something. Maybe back in the lab room?"

Lan held up his hands. "Okay, let's not panic." The group turned to him. "I'm sure we can come up with a way to get out of here if needed. It might not be a bad idea to look for some tools. But let's keep in mind, they're going to come back, right?" He pointed over at the table. "I mean, they're going to come back and bring us meals, right? Let's just stay calm. We're not actually trapped in here. There are people, presumably a lot of people, who know exactly where we are. And besides," he shook his head, "someone is still lighting up the board." He pointed over to the red glow on the wall. "How do we know this isn't part of it, right? Part of the whole escape room weekend thing? Maybe the phone was supposed to go down, and the power was supposed to go out? Maybe they're watching, to see how we respond. What we do next."

Bee sighed loudly and turned back towards Clay. "Either way, this is taking too long. We need to get going. I'm heading back down to Darcy."

"Bee, let me come with you." Rahul started moving towards her.

"No," she held a hand up. "I'm good, thank you," she said in a clipped tone. Bee turned to Clay and Lan. "Are you coming?"

They nodded. Clay ran off to use the restroom. "I'll meet you at the top of the stairs," he told her as he left.

Austin stood there for a moment. "Yeah, okay, then," he said, turning to leave the room, slinking off into the darkness.

"Where are you going?" Cam called after him.

"Don't worry about it. I'm done with this shit," he called back over his shoulder, before disappearing through the doorway.

Cam sighed and walked past Lan to the fireplace. He watched her walk by. "What the hell happened between you two?" He asked her, eyebrow raised.

She looked at him bleakly. "Trust me, you don't want to know." She shook her head and sighed. "I can't talk about it right now." She moved over to the couch, and sat down sideways on the end, her back to him. She faced the wall of windows. Turning her head to the doorway, she seemed to peer through it, as though making sure she had a line of sight.

After just a second, she stood again and began to make her way out of the room.

"Where are you going?" Lan asked urgently.

"I'm staying here. I'm just going to grab the journal from my room. I need to finish the rest of it. There's not much left now."

Lan turned back to Bee, shaking his head. They shrugged at each other and began to leave the room. He had been afraid she was going after Austin. It was best if she stayed away from him, kept a distance at the moment. Lan made sure he had his flashlight and grabbed the bottled water from the table. He eyed Rahul as he walked past him. He was still standing in the middle of the room.

"What are you going to do man?" Lan asked him in a clipped tone. He felt a little sorry for the guy. Just a little.

Rahul shrugged. "I don't know." He watched Bee's retreating back. "I guess I'll stay here." He looked around him.

"Hang out here for a while." Lan nodded to him. "If you guys need anything, let me know."

Lan turned, walking backward, and replied, "Yeah, we'll come to get you when we're ready to figure out the next clue. We'll be back after we check on Darcy, I guess."

Rahul nodded and stood there, watching him go.

Lan backtracked, moving closer to him. "Hey," he said, keeping his voice low. "Keep an eye on Cam, okay?" He said. "Something must have happened with her and Austin. Just make sure she's okay, alright?"

Rahul nodded, seeming to perk up slightly at being given a task to do. "You got it," he replied, nodding.

Lan turned back and hurried to follow Bee across the foyer, and down the hallway leading towards the rest of the castle. He didn't know what to think about everything they had just learned. It was a lot to process. But he did know one thing; he needed to keep everyone calm. Keep the group from panicking; maintain order.

He also knew that he was getting them out of here tonight one way or another. He didn't like the way any of this was going. He would break down the front door himself if he had to.

27.

Clay

Clay ran to his bedroom and used the bathroom as quickly as he could. He ran back down the hallway of the guest wing and spied Bee waiting in the dark up ahead for him at the top of the staircase.

"Hey," he called out to her, as he jogged the last few steps over and came to a stop.

"Hey," she said, smiling weakly at him. She nodded down the stairs, back towards the common room. "Just waiting for Lan to catch up." She chewed her bottom lip. "I think we should all stay together from now on, don't you?"

Clay looked at her solemnly for a moment before nodding. "It's going to be okay, Bee," he started.

"I'm scared Clay," she breathed out, blinking her eyes rapidly against the tears that were starting to build. "Something's wrong, I just know it. I don't know what Alex had planned, but I don't think this is all just part of his stupid show anymore. I'm scared we're actually trapped here. I..." her breaths came faster; he could see her chest start to rise and fall rapidly. "I... I can't do this, Clay; we have to get out of here."

Clay moved forward, taking her hand in his, "Hey," he said, struggling to keep his voice calm and even as possible. His own heart was pounding in his chest now, too.

Clay had always hated being closed in, especially in tight spaces. He knew the others were aware he was mildly claustrophobic, but in reality, it wasn't a mild case at all. He was terrified of being trapped in a small space; underground, on an airplane, a car. He had a history of having panic attacks when he wasn't able to leave.

He was good at hiding them, on the outside. But on the inside, his heart would race, and his hands and fingers would go numb and tingle. He would have to fight not to puke. He felt some of that old, familiar panic starting to creep up on him now, at her words.

He had been a little worried about coming here this weekend, given it was an escape room theme. But it was a castle, he had told himself. A massive castle, with wide open rooms. He would be fine. It was a silly, pointless fear anyway. And high time he faced it. And beat it, once and for all. He was sick of waiting for the next attack, never knowing when the irrational fear would strike him. He could do it. He knew he was capable of it. And he would be strong, now. For her, if for nothing else.

So, Clay took her hand in his, and squeezed it firmly, moving closer to her and waiting until she met his gaze. Her eyes flickered back and forth between his and she stilled. "Hey," he repeated, "take a deep breath, with me." She nodded, breathing in deeply with him, as he did the same. "Good," he murmured, nodding, "That's good."

She nodded back to him, but her eyes were still wide and panicked, and her nostrils flared with each breath. She squeezed his hand tighter. And he could feel her, on the edge of her panic. It was easy to recognize the signs in someone else. "Repeat after me, okay?" he continued, his voice firm and calm, "I am stronger than my fear."

She nodded again, her bottom lip trembling slightly. "I am stronger than my fear," she said softly, her voice shaking.

"Good, deep breath again." Clay nodded, and they breathed again together. "And this time, you're going to mean it, okay? Because you are Bee, you're strong. And I promise you, we are going to walk out of this castle, tonight. We will get out of here, together, okay?"

She sobbed slightly now, nodding again, and he saw her shoulders relax slightly. Her death grip on his hand eased a little.

"I am stronger than my fear," he repeated, nodding encouragingly at her.

"I am stronger than my fear," she said back to him, her voice stronger this time, more confident. She took a deep, shuddering breath afterward and gave him a small smile at the end.

He smiled back and reached up and tucked her hair behind her ear. "Good. You got this Bee." He nodded again to her, taking in her beautiful eyes, sparkling slightly with tears. His gaze dropping to her lips.

"Hey," Lan called out to them, and they turned to see him taking the last few stairs two at a time. Bee dropped his hand from hers. And Clay sighed deeply.

"Let's go guys," Lan ran up to them and clapped a hand on Clay's shoulder. "We need to get Darcy to wake up," he said, looking back and forth between the two of them. "If we can't rouse her, I want us to split into two groups, okay? One or two of us can stay with Darcy, and the others continue on with the clues." He paused, studying their faces. "I think we need to start working harder to get out of here, tonight."

Clay nodded, eyeing Bee warily. He didn't want to upset her again, not just after she'd managed to calm down. "We were just saying that. Let's start taking this seriously. We're going to be okay," Clay said firmly, looking pointedly at Bee. "But we need to work on getting out of here. Take matters into our own hands at this point."

Lan eyed Bee at Clay's pointed glance; taking in her still heavy breathing. He nodded swiftly. "That's right, we're going to be just fine." He gave them a reassuring smile. "We don't need the others to solve these stupid riddles; we can do this all on our own. Right?"

Bee grinned weakly back at him. "Right," she repeated, nodding.

"Hey," Lan said, patting her on the back. "Let's get you back down to Darcy, okay? Let's go see how she's doing."

Bee nodded, seeming to feel better immediately at the thought of Darcy needing help. "Yeah, let's get going," she said, turning and leading the way.

Clay and Lan paused for a moment and exchanged a look. Lan nodded to Clay grimly, and they turned and followed Bee down the dark corridor.

28.

Darcy

Darcy woke with a deep gasping breath, sitting upright in one smooth movement as she clutched at her throat.

She panted, a sobbing sound escaping her lips as she patted her body, a hand to her chest, then both hands on her legs. She took in the plaid pattern of her dress and her dark tights. Her gaze moved upwards, and she saw Bee, sitting next to her, a rag held up in one hand.

"Hey," Bee murmured reassuringly, placing a hand on her shoulder. "It's okay. You're alright Darc. You just fainted, that's all. No harm done." Bee set the rag down on the first aid kit that lay open next to her on the floor. "Here." She turned and grabbed something from an outstretched hand. Lan stood over them. A water bottle. Bee twisted the cap off and handed it to Darcy. "Drink some water, Darc. You're probably just dehydrated."

Darcy lifted her hands up, weak and shaking, to grasp the cold plastic of the water bottle. She noticed Bee didn't let go of it; she helped her guide it to her mouth and kept it steady while she drank.

Darcy drank several large gulps of water. Then she stopped and moved the water bottle down, letting Bee take it from her.

"You okay, Darcy?" She heard Clay's voice, off to her left. She turned towards him, nodding, as he came closer and kneeled beside her.

"I'm fine..." Darcy said, still taking rapid breaths. She moved to stand up, but Bee placed a hand on her arm.

"Take it easy, there's no need to rush," she murmured.

"Really, I'm okay," Darcy insisted. Moving again to push herself up, she took Clay's arm and let him help her as she struggled to her feet.

Darcy turned and searched the room around them. The others watched her closely. She saw Miranda had been standing back behind her, and that was it. "Where's everyone else?" Darcy asked, her voice coming out a little hoarse. "Where's Austin?"

Bee gave her a strange look for just a second, before replying. "We aren't sure where Austin is." She cleared her throat, eying Miranda. "He was upset, earlier. He tried to leave."

"What?" Miranda asked, her eyes widening. "When?"

"Just now," Clay replied easily, "It didn't work. I tried too." He shook his head.

"What do you mean you tried? What did you do?" Miranda asked.

"Called out to the cameras, or the people behind them, at least. Asked to leave." Clay shrugged.

"What happened?" Miranda asked breathlessly.

"A whole lot of nothing." Clay shrugged again. "We don't think anyone is listening anymore. Or watching... whatever. Or if they are, they certainly aren't responding, at least. It looks like we're on our own."

Darcy and Miranda exchanged glances. Miranda swallowed nervously. "You can't be serious," she said. "There was a whole crew, a team of people. How can they just be ignoring us? You think that what, they just left us in here? Without any way of contacting the outside?"

"That's what it sounds like, yeah." Lan stepped forward, a serious expression on his face. "But look, panicking, is not going to help us find a way out of here."

"But what are we going to do?" Miranda demanded, holding her hands out.

"We already know what we have to do," Lan replied evenly. "We have to keep going, solve the escape room puzzles, find our way out of here."

"But everything got messed up, remember?" Bee pointed out, her voice trembling just slightly. "Alex was pissed the order was messed up. Even Rahul agreed; he mentioned it earlier." She turned to Miranda and then Darcy, "He's an actor, by the way."

She blew a breath out her nose and squared her shoulders as Miranda's eyes went wide. "You're joking?"

Bee shook her head. "I wish I was. Alex hired him to play a part, help us with the clues if we got stuck."

"And who knows what else," Clay murmured under his breath. Loud enough that only Darcy seemed to hear. *Thankfully*, she thought. She gave him a look, and his gaze dropped to the floor. It wasn't like him to be unkind.

"Anyway," Bee continued, if she had heard Clay, she was choosing to ignore it. "My point is that Rahul knew all about the clues, at least many of them. And presumably knew the order. He mentioned earlier that something must have gone wrong or been changed. So, how do we know anything we do right now will actually work? How do we know solving the clues will lead us out?"

They all turned to look at Lan, for an answer. He looked around at them. "We don't." He shrugged. "I don't know how much the order matters, any more than any of you do, but I do know it's our best chance of finding a way out of here."

They were quiet for a moment. Then Miranda took a deep shuddering breath. "Okay." She nodded slowly. "What are we waiting for, then? Let's get going."

Bee nodded grimly, turning to Darcy. "Are you feeling strong enough to come with us, Darcy? If not, you and I can head back to the common area; let the others keep going."

Darcy shook her head. "No, I'm fine, really. I want to help. Let's find a way out of here." Bee nodded, and Clay patted her on the back.

"Okay, good," Lan said, "Let's head back to the chessboard room. "There were a bunch of items lined up on the table. At least we know what we need to work on next." They followed Lan as he led them out of the room.

They were quiet as they made their way back through the spaces they had already unlocked. No one seemed to be in the mood to chat. When they entered the open courtyard, Darcy paused, at the back of the group. She breathed in deeply, relishing the fresh, cold night air filling her lungs. It was a small taste of freedom, but she noticed the others slowed their pace considerably in the courtyard as well. A light mist fell on Darcy's upturned face as she gazed up at the sky. The fresh air was short-lived, and all too soon, they returned to the interior of the dank, dark castle.

They had reached the marble walkway when a faint sound hit Darcy's ears. It sounded sort of like a door slamming shut, but it happened a fraction of a second after the door just behind them swung shut.

Miranda spun back to the door. "That must be Austin," she said, her voice low. She turned to look at Darcy for a moment, thinking.

"Miranda, no." Darcy shook her head, her heart sinking. "Don't-"

Miranda stared at her, eyes wide, before turning to the others. "I'm going to go look for Austin," she announced to the group. They came to a stop. Lan turned back to Miranda with an eyebrow raised. "I heard him, just now."

"How do you know that? All I heard was the door slam shut." Lan shook his head.

"No, there was another noise, just after that; it sounded like a different door," Miranda insisted. "It has to be him, who else could it be?"

"Miranda." Bee shook her head, "That could have been just an echo. And besides, I don't think it's a good idea for you to go off on your own. We really shouldn't split up."

"I'll be fine," Miranda insisted, shaking her head. "I need to talk to him." Her eyes flicked briefly in Lan's direction. Darcy saw him grimace and look away. He turned and walked a few paces ahead as Bee and Miranda continued to argue. Lan distracted himself by shining his flashlight up ahead of them and then down over the side of the railing.

"You have no idea where he is Miranda," Bee continued, "he could be anywhere right now. You're just going to be wandering around in the dark alone. It's not safe. We don't know what's-"

"I'm going, Bee. I'm not going to lose my chance to talk to him."

Bee moved closer, shaking her head, looking to Darcy for support. Darcy's chest felt tight suddenly, as if she couldn't breathe properly. She took deep breaths, trying to still herself.

"Just wait, you won't lose your chance. No one is going anywhere at the moment," Bee added, looking at Darcy again. When Miranda's back was turned, she gestured with a waving hand toward her, urging Darcy to say something.

"Miranda," Darcy began, sighing, breathing deeply again as she turned towards her. "Bee is right. You have no clue where to begin looking for him. Not to mention, he's..." she trailed off, uncertain of what to say. "He hasn't been acting like himself, lately. I think you should give him some space, keep a distance from him. Don't go off by yourself like this." Darcy swallowed; her tongue felt too big for her mouth, her throat dry. "Please, Miranda..." she trailed off, "I'm asking you, please, don't go after him."

Miranda turned to Darcy, her expression incredulous. She stared at Darcy now, only her eyes moved, flickering back and forth, studying her. But Miranda's mind was made up; she could see it on her face.

"I'm going," she said slowly, a half-apologetic expression on her face. "I've wasted too much time already."

"And taking one of our flashlights with you, apparently," Lan added grimly.

Miranda looked over at him. "Really?" She said, her eyes wide, lips pressed in a thin line.

Lan looked away hastily, peering back over the railing. Miranda sighed and shook her head in disbelief. "I'll catch up with you later. I'll come find you in the chessboard room," she reassured Bee. She gave them a small smile, her eyes meeting Darcy's once more. And with a nod in her direction, she disappeared through the doorway before they could argue further.

The group continued on, down yet another member. Darcy couldn't help but turn to look back over her shoulder several times as they went, her brows creased in worry.

29.

Austin

Austin wandered the halls, moving through shadows. He walked blindly through the castle. It didn't matter where he went. It wasn't that he was unafraid, it was just that he realized now it didn't matter where he was, the danger was already there with him.

His chest rose and fell rapidly. He felt like he wanted to run. If he weren't trapped here, he would have. Running had always helped to calm him and soothe his frayed nerves, release the pent-up energy that threatened to boil over inside him.

He continued down the hallway, his head whipping to the right as he caught movement out of the corner of his eye. But it was only the moonlight filtering in through a nearby window, illuminating his reflection as he passed by a large mirror. He stepped closer, homing in on his reflection, placing a hand on either side of the ornate gold frame.

He peered closely into his own eyes, searching for any hint of a difference. But he saw only his own familiar features staring back at him. His chest rose and fell rapidly as his heart hammered below his ribcage. He just needed to calm down. He needed to relax, and he would be fine. Everything was going to be fine.

He paused, muscles tense, head-turning. The faintest of footfalls in the distance, back down the corridor, moved towards him.

"Austin?" It was Cam's voice calling out to him. He waited for a moment, meeting his own gaze once more in the mirror. He heard her call out to him again, and he felt a ripple down his back at her voice; his pupils dilated, his teeth, suddenly too large for his mouth, pushing past his lips as the hair on the back of his neck stood on end.

His reflection shook his head. "No..." he mumbled, "no, this can't be happening." He blinked rapidly, tears pooling in his eyes. He lashed out suddenly; unable to keep the rising tide of rage from bubbling over, he slammed a fist into the mirror. His reflection stared back at him, fractured and distorted now. Knuckles slick with blood. But the action had calmed him momentarily. His breaths came slower and more even now. He turned slowly to face Cam as she moved closer down the corridor before melting back to blend into the shadows in a corner.

He waited there, alone in the dark, still as a statue, a tingle of anticipation in his gut. She turned the corner, flashlight in hand. He watched as she moved it with a sweeping motion. She paused at the sight of the broken mirror; the pieces scattered below on the floor. Then the edge of the beam caught him for a second, and she jumped back, startled.

"Austin," she repeated again with a sigh. "What are you doing?" She moved closer to him, lowering the flashlight beam. "Why are you standing in the corner like that?"

His chest rose and fell. His pulse was pounding as he watched hers, the blood pulsing in her throat. She swallowed and moved another step closer to him.

"Austin," she sighed, looking away. "Look, maybe I wasn't being completely fair. Back there." She murmured, turning back to him, her eyes flickering back and forth over his, trying to read his expression.

His head hurt. He was so hungry, so thirsty. The light from the flashlight irked him and put him on edge. Even though it was pointed away from him now, it was too bright and too loud in this space. And he was angry. *Why was he so angry?*

He shook his head slightly, trying to focus. Trying to focus on her words. But he watched her mouth, her lips moving. And all he could think about was her lips; the taste of her. His eyes drifted to the hollow in her neck. To her chest, rising and falling. Austin clenched his fists. The muscles in his arms straining. His entire body screamed. He needed to move. To run. To hunt.

"It's not all your fault," Cam continued, "Some of the blame is mine." Austin heard something then; it was faint, in the distance. But it began to grow louder. To swell. A ticking clock.

Tick-tock, tick-tock. It was incessant, growing louder and louder until it echoed in his brain. Until he couldn't hear her voice anymore.

He watched her lips move but heard nothing—nothing but the ticking of the clock. He watched her lips as he moved forward, closer and closer. Her features began to shift, then to change. Her face shuddered at first, then melted, ran, and churned, her body shaking and convulsing.

Austin took a stuttering step backward, watching in fascination. His hands were over his ears, and he squeezed his head, trying to block out the sound.

And then it was Miranda, standing there, in front of him. Staring at him in horror. And the noise stopped. He was blanketed in silence. So quiet, he could hear his ears ringing. A high-pitched tone that grew and then faded.

Miranda's eyes were wide, wet with tears. "Austin?" she whispered. "What's happening to you?"

"I..." he began, then cut himself off. His chest heaved as he breathed in and out in a steady rhythm, still trying to maintain control. "I don't know..." he murmured eventually. Watching her as she studied him, eyes wide, flickering back and forth across his.

Then she smiled—a slow, knowing smile. "I see," she said softly. "I know what you want," and she turned away from him, putting her back to him and moving off down the hallway.

Austin followed her, always keeping several paces behind. He took in her every movement.

The flashlight was gone. Her hands were empty now, somehow. The rational part of his brain noted this and then dismissed it immediately. She led him down empty corridors. A door that had been locked before opened at her outstretched hand. He felt a flicker of surprise at that. She moved through the moonlight filtering in through the windows to their right; the pattern of light from the iron bars making it appear as though she were walking through a jail cell.

She turned a corner ahead of him, and he picked up his pace slightly to keep up. She looked back at him, a wicked smile on her face. And it was Cam's face, this time. He felt a tightening in his gut. His skin crawled along his shoulders and neck. A cascade of shivers at her voice.

"Always so predictable," she murmured. Her voice was heavy with amusement. "Of course, you can't admit it; even to yourself. Your fragile little ego couldn't handle that," she mused. Her back to him again; moving faster now. He lengthened his stride naturally to keep up. His pulse tattooing an excited thrum in his chest. "No, you have to rationalize, compartmentalize. Come up with your excuses. Make up a story for yourself and repeat it enough times; until you believe it. Until you can almost forget it was a lie. But deep down, you'll know." She smiled again at him, half-turning. "And I'll know. I always know."

She stopped at another closed door, grasping the handle and pushing it open. It yawned into darkness. Into a void. She stood there, waiting. For what, he didn't know. She began to chuckle after a moment, then laughed harder, reaching up to pat the tears from her eyes. His gut twisted slightly, and he felt his chest tighten in anger. Her laughter died down, and she tilted her head to the side, watching him now in an almost pitying way. "Oh, come on, Austin. This will be a lot more fun if you just let go."

He eyed her warily. She sighed deeply, clasping her hands together. "Oh, I see; I've confused you, haven't I." She shook her head. "You know, it's really all very simple. For once, in your pathetic life, you're going to admit what you want, and you're going to take it." She moved closer to him, her voice dropping low. "See, I'm going to run..." She sidled closer until her mouth was just inches from his. He felt himself leaning forward slightly, involuntarily. Then she tapped him lightly on the chest with the tips of her fingers, "... and you're going to chase me." She smiled at him, the slightly mischievous smile he loved. "And do you know what happens next? Hmm?" she hummed, and he felt the vibration in his chest, even though her voice was barely a whisper.

She slid her hand down his stomach, lightly brushing her knuckles over his abs. Her eyes trailed after. Her dark lashes bobbed. He felt a throbbing between his legs. "Then, you catch me." She peered back up at him from beneath her lashes, a smile curving the corners of her lips once more. "Then you take what's yours." She stared at him meaningfully for a moment, then turned her back on him and disappeared through the doorway into the darkness.

He stood there, panting slightly. He could hear her footsteps, pitter-pattering away from him. He held himself back. Paused. He wouldn't follow her, wouldn't chase after her. It wasn't really her, he tried to tell himself. It couldn't be Cam.

But he could smell her still, the scent of her lingering in the air in front of him. He closed his eyes and breathed in deeply. He felt himself letting go, the muscles in his back rippling, his limbs stretching and elongating, his teeth protruding. He could feel every sense heightening, and everything felt sharper, better, and clearer.

He opened his eyes. He could hear her still, running from him up ahead. He could hear voices far away, below him. And somewhere up ahead, a second set of footsteps—slower, more tentative. Austin smiled then. It was a good night, to hunt.

30.
Cam

Cam sat by the fire, letting its warmth flood her, hoping it would remove some of the chill she felt. She sat hunched with her knees up, the journal resting on top, angled so she could just make out the script by the light of the fire. Her stomach clenched tightly, and while she had stopped shivering, she felt herself hovering there, on the edge, feeling that it could start again at any moment.

"Anything good so far?" Rahul asked her. He leaned forward, hands clasped together, elbows resting on his knees. She looked him up and down and shrugged coldly. He sighed in response, leaning back in his chair. "Ah, so you're pissed at me too, huh?"

She gave him a look. "For Bee's sake, maybe just a little." He had the decency to wince at her words. "But otherwise, I'm indifferent." She shrugged again. Glancing back at him. "It sounds to me like you were just doing your job." His features relaxed. He gave her a small smile.

"Thanks." He nodded, looking over at the fire. "Yeah, I was," he added simply.

"So, Alex was filming all of this? After all?" Cam watched him, one eyebrow raised. She wished now that she had pushed harder when she confronted him.

"No." Rahul turned to her. "Well, yes," he broke off. She gave him an amused look. "I mean, yes, there are, or were, cameras like he said, and they are filming for the escape room thing, but it was never going to air anywhere. Alex was getting ready to pitch this to networks, either as a reality TV show or as a pilot." She stared at him blankly. "He wasn't sure," Rahul continued, "if he wanted to turn the concept into a reality show, using a group of friends, just like this," he swept his hand in a circle, "You know, bringing them back together again, throwing them into an escape challenge. Making it about their old history and issues, but with an element of danger." She glared at him now. "That was the concept, at least," Rahul said hastily. "Versus, you know, a scripted version, with actors."

"God," Cam sighed, "that asshole." She shook her head, "So he was using us as guinea pigs essentially, is what you're saying."

Rahul grimaced a little again, nodding. "You could put it that way, yes."

"Perfect." Cam sighed resignedly, turning back to the journal. "Well, I have bigger problems to worry about right now."

"Yeah?" Rahul asked curiously, raising an eyebrow. "Like what?"

"Like getting out of this fucking castle," She replied. "And figuring out what the hell is wrong with Austin." She sighed more deeply.

"Yeah, what's his deal? He seems to be wound up tight at the moment." Rahul shook his head, his gaze straying over to the board above the desk. Cam turned to follow his gaze, the glow of the red light bulbs casting the room below in an eerie ambiance.

"I think I know what his deal is..." Cam drifted off in thought. "Well, part of it is that he's just an asshole and a coward. But the other part... I hate to say it, but I think there's something wrong. I think maybe something is happening to him." She looked over at Rahul, suddenly serious. "I think it has to do with this house. With the demon..." her voice dropped to a whisper. "The Besomar thing."

Rahul shook his head, starting to chuckle. "You can't be serious; you don't really think-"

"It's all right here." She held up the journal. "In this journal. The same things the brother, Garrett, describes happening to John, I think maybe they're happening to Austin."

Rahul stared at her now, open-mouthed. "Like what?" His eyes flickered to the doorway, to the darkness in the hallway beyond.

"Like…" Cam trailed off. "You didn't see him earlier, but he… he was scaring me, a little." She stopped again, flushing slightly. "And he bit me."

"What?" Rahul sat up straighter, his tone incredulous. "What do you mean, he bit you? Like a freaking dog?"

"Or a wolf." Cam eyed him warily. "Or a vampire… or a possessed demon mixture of the two. Yeah. Pretty much." Rahul snorted, and she glared at him. "Oh okay, go ahead and laugh, but weren't you the one claiming he saw a pale… something, running through the hallways, scared of light?"

Rahul stopped chuckling and paused, staring at her thoughtfully. "I mean, yeah," he admitted. "I did see something. It looked human, but… not, at the same time." He shrugged. "I dunno, I guess I started thinking maybe it was fake, you know? Another actor, in make-up, that Alex had set up for his disappearance scene."

Cam nodded at him thoughtfully. "Yeah, that could be. You're right." She thought for another moment. "Anyway, the thing with Austin," She chewed her lip, gazing into the flames in the grate, "I don't think he meant to do it. Not intentionally. And there was a second, when his eyes… I dunno…" she looked back at Rahul. "I think he's dangerous, right now. And maybe, he's in danger," she finished in a soft voice.

Rahul watched her for a long moment as they sat silently, thinking. "You said you had more left to read earlier."

Rahul nodded to the journal. "Maybe you should read the rest of it, see what else it says."

Cam looked at him solemnly, then she nodded, taking a deep breath, and she began to read out loud to him from the final journal entry.

"I had not known that the days leading up to my receiving the letter from Marianna, prior to my hurried flight to the castle, and the few days we all spent there together, were to be my last days of true peace. Would I have done anything differently had I known? I suppose it is human nature to think so. But there is no way to know now, in hindsight.

Dawn broke that next day, finding me in a state I struggle to describe in these pages. I felt as though a fever of some sort had come over me. Although being a physician, I was more than familiar with the classic signs and symptoms of fevers of all types and causes. And yet, nothing in my repertoire prepared me for the suffering I experienced that day.

I felt a growing sense of doom hanging over me like a cloud. I was filled with rage, anger, and despair. I stalked through the castle in ill humor, finding fault with all before me. I felt as though I would break apart at any moment.

My skin crawled, and my spirit itself felt ill to the core and restless. I could not take any food, nor drink, but that it turned my stomach, burning through me like poison. Yet I felt a deep hunger, unsatiated by anything I tried. Moreover, my muscles ached, feeling as though I had run for miles in my sleep, although I, of course, had done no such thing.

I attempted to leave the castle to go for a walk on the grounds as the rain let up in the afternoon, the storm leaving behind only a light mist in its wake. But I found I could not bear the sunlight. It was painful somehow, hurting my head and my eyes. I found I preferred the cool dark corridors of the castle to the outdoors. I spent the remainder of the afternoon pacing through the tunnels far below the castle proper.

I kept my distance purposefully from Marianna, for I did not wish her to see me in such a state. I feared what it would do to her already fragile countenance.

I did not appear for dinner, for I was wont to have to explain why I could take neither food nor drink. I asked one of the maids to let John and Marianna know I had taken ill and would keep my distance from them.

That night, however, as I wound my way aimlessly through the corridors of the castle, having emerged from the tunnels now that it was dusk and the sun had sunk below the horizon, I heard voices drifting to me from somewhere further up ahead. I heard the shuffling of footsteps on the stone floor and a woman's voice cry out as though in pain. I did not pause to think but ran towards the source of the noise; my ears pricked to what I could now hear was clearly a struggle.

I emerged into the cool night air in the overlook room. By the moonlight filtering through the clouds above, I could make out the two of them, limbs locked together. Marianna stood there, cowering, arms out, pushing back with what little strength she had left. And there, I realized with a start, must be John.

John appeared now unnaturally tall; he towered above Marianna, and his broad, muscular shoulders were hunched over. He was shirtless, his bare skin pale in the moonlight. But his face... never have I seen such a sight. His face was that of a monster, a demon from hell. Half covered in a fine coating of fur, his eyes appearing to be that of an animal, reflected the moonlight, seeming to glow even of their own accord. He snarled down at her, his teeth sharp and dripping with what I knew had to be blood. He held his machine, his contraption, in outstretched hands, pointing the cone at Marianna as it began to emit the most awful noise I have ever heard.

My stomach lurched at the sight, and I covered my ears instinctively. Marianna seemed somehow unaffected by it, but John staggered back a step, and I heard him *gasping in pain. The muscles and tendons in his arms stood out as he strained, shaking, trying to hold onto the machine. He dropped it as though it were hot and burned him, and it slid on the wet stone, coming to rest at my feet. The noise stopped abruptly as it hit the ground.*

He did not seem to see me, to notice me, standing there, so fixated he was on Marianna as she crumpled in a heap at his feet. He moved forward with a speed I did not think a man capable of and grasped her by the shoulders. He lifted her frail frame easily, his mouth opening wide, revealing sharp, elongated canines. He hovered over the delicate pale skin at her throat, before his teeth sank into her. I saw her eyes rolling back in her head, and she whimpered pitifully as she began to lose consciousness.

I stooped to pick up the machine that had landed before me. Examining the dial, I turned it all the way to the right, as I had seen John do. I grasped the handle in one hand and held it aloft in the other. Shaking with rage and malaise, I pressed the button next to the dial and aimed the machine directly at John, stepping closer to him.

He noticed me finally as I approached nearer, pausing in his depraved meal to peer up at me. And it was not my brother's eyes that watched me, for he was fully gone, lost to the demon now. He sprang back, dropping Marianna. She fell limply to the stone floor.

I moved closer, pressing him back, pushing him away from her. Though he snarled at me, writhing in pain, he still moved to press forward as though he would grab her again and carry her away with him. His hands pressed over his ears, and I resisted the urge to do the same. My whole body trembling now with the effort of holding onto the machine, when every fiber of my being wanted to let it go, to dash it on the stone floor.

He hit the archway, his back glancing off the stone, and I saw his feet start to slip out from under him, noticing for the first time, the nails that had turned into claws.

He scrambled for purchase, removing his hands from his ears, to grasp for the stone columns on either side of him, but the stone was slick, still wet with rain, and the fine mist that fell even now. And it was too late for him. I watched in terror as I saw him fall, the snarl on his face the last thing I saw, and the echoing cry of rage the last thing I heard.

I dropped the machine instantly and fell to the ground myself. My body spent, and my spirit broken, all at once. I crawled on all fours to the edge of the stone wall, pausing momentarily to check Marianna's pulse. And once confirming she still lived, I moved closer to the edge and hung my head over the side of the wall.

I half expected to find nothing, once again, as the whispers of the villagers had told of how the demon could not be killed. But I looked down at the body, crumpled on the jagged rocks below, and I saw nothing of the demon remained. It was my own brother, my dear brother John, who lay there, unmoving. Still, I cannot fully explain to this day but can only surmise that the demon's spirit must have left him, exiting his body as he fell, to be dashed on the rocks below.

We spent the following days in a cloud of grief and shock as we recovered slowly from all that had taken place. I watched, growing more hopeful. Marianna seemed to recover her strength, little by little, with each passing day, until the color returned to her cheeks, and she appeared once more returned to health and good humor. She spent long hours painting in her salon. Though now not in a spirit of agony so much as a spirit of calm, and reflectiveness. I heard her humming and singing to herself as she painted, and smiled to hear her sweet voice and knew she was now at peace.

It was not so simple for me to return to what I once was. I continued to feel weakened and ill at times, although the joy of spending time with Marianna seemed to act as a sort of salve to my battered soul.

I slowly, over time, found that I could stand in the sunlight—first as it shone through the windows, and then eventually, I could return outside during daylight hours. While I still found the sun unpleasant, it did not have the same ill effects as it once had.

I began slowly to eat and drink, tolerating only small sips or a morsel of food at first. I studied in the library, using a book Marianna had found for me, amongst others. I took notes, documenting all that I had seen and knew of the demon that had taken hold over my poor brother. I sat in his study and laboratory often, distraught that his genius had been destroyed, taken from the world far too soon.

I sat there often with the machine that he had worked on up until his death. I started by absentmindedly turning it on and soon found that I could tolerate it, as well. At first, in small doses, indirectly, and then for longer periods, and directly, until I became accustomed to being around it. Or perhaps I developed some sort of tolerance to it. For while I still found the noise to be noxious, I was able to remain in its presence for longer and longer periods.

We eventually decided to leave the castle. Marianna agreed at my continued insistence. We discussed that we might leave the castle in the hands of the estate. There was talk of turning it into a museum to showcase my brother's collection of curiosities from his foreign travels and inventions.

I did my best to discourage this, though. For I could still hear something at night, moving around deep down below the castle, in the stillness of the tunnels. A pale figure haunted my dreams. I followed it at night, as in fever dreams, stalking the corridors. Sometimes, I even seemed to peer out through its eyes.

I thought of taking the machine with us, but in the end, I left it there, sitting on the worktable, in the lab. I leave this journal behind now, too, that it might serve as my confession and provide perhaps a warning and record of the evil that haunts these halls. For we are on to *better things, I hope. And while I still feel as though I am not fully recovered, I hope to be, soon. Once outside of these god-forsaken castle walls.*

Cam looked up, meeting Rahul's eyes, and closing the journal. "That's it," she said quietly. "He signs his name here at the end and dates it." She stroked the cover of the journal with one hand. And looked back at him. "I don't know what to think."

"I don't know, it's almost..." Rahul trailed off, cringing a little, "Over the top... with the old-timey language. Almost kind of cheesy, isn't it?" Rahul said with a grin, running a hand over his chin. "I dunno, I find it obviously hard to believe any of this is real."

"I know," Cam said quietly, dropping her head and propping her hand on her chin. "I do, too. But, like I said, something seems off with Austin. Maybe I'm being silly; maybe none of this is real." She shrugged. "But either way, the castle, this place, something, has gotten to him." She shrugged again. They were silent for several moments. Rahul stared into the fireplace, appearing lost in his own thoughts.

Cam settled back against the couch, curling around a pillow. She felt suddenly exhausted. She stared at the fire as well, thinking. They spent several minutes in a comfortable silence, and she felt her eyes starting to grow heavy. Her eyelids fell and then rose again as she jerked herself awake. She would close them for a moment, she thought—just for a moment—to rest.

Cam felt herself jerk suddenly awake. She felt disoriented, unsure when or where she was. She had been dreaming about Austin. She tried to recall the details, wanting to hold onto the feeling of the dream, but it was already fading. He had found her alone in a dark room somewhere in the castle. It had been raining. She had made him admit that he wanted her. Her heart was still pounding. She felt a throbbing between her legs. She rubbed her thighs together slightly, cheeks flushing.

She glanced towards the chair and found Rahul still sitting there, a nearly empty beer glass cradled in his hands. She hoped he hadn't been watching her sleep, watching her while she was dreaming... But he was frowning, glaring into the fire, seemingly oblivious to her presence. She shivered and sat up, then turned her head slightly to the side as though listening to something.

"What is it?" Rahul asked, frowning as he watched her.

"Someone's coming," Cam said back quietly.

It was only another moment or two before the sound of voices and footsteps echoed clearly down the hall—the sound of more than one set of footsteps, moving quickly, heading towards them.

Rahul stood, and Cam set down the journal on the couch, doing the same. Clay appeared first through the doorway, followed closely by Lan and Darcy. Cam waited, watching the doorway behind them, but no one else emerged from the darkened hallway.

"Where's Bee?" She heard Rahul ask behind her.

"And Miranda?" Cam added, frowning. "Everything okay Darcy? I'm glad to see you're up and about." Darcy gave her a small smile, her lips tight. Her huge brown eyes creased with worry. Cam felt the smile fall from her own lips. "What's happened?"

"It's Bee," Clay said, and Cam noted he was breathing rapidly. "She's missing."

"What do you mean, she's missing?" Rahul moved forward, coming around the couch to meet them as they approached. "Wasn't she just with you? What happened?"

Clay nodded grimly. "Yeah, she was. She was right there." He gestured with both hands to his side. "I swear, one minute she was right there, next to me. The next..." he trailed off shaking his head. "I heard her screaming, and it sounded faint. Like it was coming from far away."

Lan nodded in agreement. "We could all hear her, but we couldn't figure out where she went. And then we found her; she was underneath us. She somehow ended up on the other side of the floor. How she got there, I have no idea. Maybe a trap door opened up, or something like that. But we could hear her down there, yelling up to us."

"Where?" Rahul asked urgently.

"The room with the chessboard," Lan replied. "We made it that far. It's next to-"

"I know where it is." Rahul cut him off. He turned and headed back over towards the fireplace. Sliding the armchair over next to the grate, he climbed onto it, stood on his toes, and reached out over the mantle. Rahul tugged on the handle of one of the crossed swords that hung mounted there. Cam heard a loud clanging *'zing'* as the sword came loose, sliding against its twin.

Rahul leapt down off the chair and moved back around the couch to the group by the doorway.

"Holy shit man," Lan said, chuckling a little. "What is that for?"

Rahul shrugged, glancing over at Cam. "I dunno... demons, I guess. I'm going to find her."

"I'm coming too," Clay said, eyeing both Rahul and sword suspiciously.

"Demons?" Lan chuckled nervously. "You don't really believe there's a Besomar, or whatever, do you?"

Rahul eyed Cam out of the corner of his eyes and shrugged. "I dunno, all I can tell you is I saw something, with Alex. Either that was an actor... and if so, I mean, "Rahul chuckled slightly, "they did an amazing job, it was pretty darn convincing. The way it moved... I... it was fast, and..." he trailed off. "I don't know what that thing was," he said more seriously. "But yeah, I'm not ruling out that there isn't something... some kind of creature, maybe? Maybe it was a person, but they were deformed or something?" He shrugged again. "Either way, I'm not taking the risk of going out there in the dark again without a weapon."

Lan sighed deeply, thinking. "I saw an old-fashioned lever-action rifle in the library, over the fireplace. I wonder if it still works." He fell silent for a second. "And whether it's loaded.

"Wait, where's Miranda?" Cam asked suddenly, frowning. "Did she stay behind in the room where Bee disappeared?"

Lan sighed, "No, actually. We heard something, just before that, and Miranda insisted it must be Austin. We told her how he was trying to leave, earlier, and she was worried about him. Anyway, she went to go look for him." Lan shrugged, "She didn't come back, so I'm guessing she found him."

Cam's frown deepened. She looked over at the couch, at the journal. "I'm coming with you, too. I just need to grab something first. I'll meet up with you guys, okay?"

Rahul started to jog backward lightly towards the hallway. "Sounds good, I'll see you down there." He nodded to them and turned, disappearing into the darkness. Lan flicked on his flashlight and turned to follow him. Clay turned to leave as well, but he paused and turned back to Darcy.

"You okay to come along Darcy? Still feeling okay?" He looked back through the doorway and then back at Darcy, hesitating but clearly worried he was falling behind the other guys.

"Why don't you go ahead?" Cam asked him. She moved over towards Darcy. "Darcy can come with me, and we'll catch up to you in a few minutes." She looped her arm through Darcy's and smiled at her. Darcy smiled weakly back, nodding.

Clay nodded to her appreciatively and turned to leave without another word, taking off at a jog after the others.

Cam turned to Darcy, and said, "We'll meet up with them soon. There's just something we need to find, first."

31.

Bee

Bee trembled, alone in the dark. She stood there for several moments after the voices above her faded. She knew they could hear her and realized where she was, but it was hard to make out exactly what they were saying.

She was soaked to the bone and freezing cold. She realized immediately that she had landed in one of the tunnels that ran below the castle. She had fallen suddenly, the floor opening up noiselessly beneath her, and landed hard onto rough stone, covered in a few inches of standing water. She was lucky she hadn't hit her head when she fell.

Bee had been standing next to a small table in the middle of the room, playing with the chess board on the table. She had been moving the pieces around as though she were playing a game against herself when she felt the ground fall away beneath her. She stood there, shaking in the cold, and cursed her bad luck.

If only she had been paying more attention to the puzzle the others were working on. But since learning that Rahul was actually an actor, which made a whole lot of sense, in a way, but left her feeling confused and hurt, she had found it difficult to focus or think about anything else. She had been playing with the chess pieces absentmindedly, while she thought about him. Went over every interaction, every conversation, in her head. Seeing the obvious clues for what they were. Well, she had known something was off, at least had been aware of that much. *But had any of it been real, then? Was he just acting the whole time?* A little voice in her head asked her. And she didn't want to answer it.

Her only saving grace now was a grate a few yards away, set high in the ceiling. It was open to the air and allowed moonlight to filter in. Without it, Bee imagined the tunnel would have been pitch black. She was without a flashlight. She stood there, frozen with indecision, waiting for the others to return. Her ears strained for any sounds up above, for a creak of a floorboard, but she heard nothing.

After waiting several minutes, she realized she had to make a decision. Either stay there, waiting for the others to return, for help to arrive, or head down the tunnel, and try to find her way out on her own.

She worried she would never find this spot again if she moved. Bee searched the area around her for any landmark she could use. She studied the ceiling of the tunnel and realized immediately that this section of the ceiling ended just past her, with floorboards overhead. Off to her left, the tunnel continued on with an arched stone ceiling above.

She had no way of knowing if there were other similar sections that switched to floorboards overhead, but at least this obvious difference gave her a chance of finding the spot again.

She decided, ultimately, she should start moving if only to try to stay warm. She set off down the tunnel, heading for the grate several yards away.

She made it there and peered out of it as best she could, but all she could see was the night sky above, pale clouds racing past. A fine mist drifted down onto her upturned face. She shivered again and continued on. She made it to the end of the length of the tunnel that she had seen from the spot where she fell and realized she had come to a wall straight ahead, with the tunnel continuing on in both directions to her right and left.

Bee tried to picture the orientation of the room above her when she had fallen. It was difficult for her to say, but her gut told her turning to the left would likely take her back towards the part of the castle they had already explored, while the right branch would likely take her farther away, deeper into the unexplored areas of the castle.

Bee couldn't help but think about the warning from the escape room prompt; it had specifically said to stay out of the tunnels to avoid the Besomar. She steeled herself, taking a deep breath, and said under her breath, "I am stronger than my fear." She forced her legs to move forward, picking up one foot after the other. She moved through shadow, heading down the tunnel on the left.

32.

Darcy

Cam led Darcy down darkened hallways, shining her flashlight up ahead to light their way. For a few minutes, she could still hear Clay and Lan, their voices echoing in the distance as they called out to each other, racing after Rahul.

She hoped they would find Bee quickly; she didn't want to think about how Bee must be feeling right now. All alone, and likely lost in the dark, somewhere below their feet. Darcy wished they had never come here.

She had no clue where they were going or what Cam wanted to find, but she hoped desperately that it was something that would help them escape—maybe a key to unlock the front door, allowing them to walk out into the cool night air.

Cam led her back to the room with the Ouija board. Shining the flashlight for her as she descended the ladder into darkness, through the hole in the floor once more. She waited, shivering with cold at the bottom, for Cam to make her way down. They looped arms again, Darcy shivering against Cam, as they moved swiftly through the organ room, through the double doors, and down the hallway to the room with the typewriter. The laboratory room: filled with machine parts, tools, bottles, pages of notes scattered about.

Darcy stood in the doorway, arms crossed tight, pulling her sweater around her, as she watched Cam move up and down the workbenches that lined the space; shining the flashlight beam over the objects that littered the tabletops, searching for something. Darcy sighed deeply. She was so tired. She had passed out, somehow, been unconscious for a while, but she had awoken feeling just as tired as before, if not more so. She was weak, nearing the edge of exhaustion. Something about this place was draining her. She needed to rest.

"What are you looking for?" Darcy called out to her after a few minutes of this, clenching her jaw slightly to stop her teeth from chattering. She saw the flashlight beam pause, as Cam turned at the sound of her voice. Almost as though she had startled her. Had Cam forgotten that she was standing here?

"Something that will protect us," Cam said back to her after a long pause. The flashlight beam continued its sweep.

"Protect us? From what?" Darcy asked, her eyes wide, and already filling with unshed tears of fear. She felt a spike of terror at Cam's words and a shiver that went down her spine. She already knew the answer, but she needed to hear someone else say it.

Cam stopped suddenly, the flashlight beam backtracking over the workbench. "Yes." She heard her murmur, and she reached and picked up a device that sat there in the pool of light. It was a plain wooden box with what looked like a small cone from a gramophone sticking out on one end.

Cam grabbed it by the rounded handle and held it aloft in the light, turning it from side to side. She quickly brought it over to Darcy and urged her to hold the flashlight for her. "Keep it steady," Cam whispered in a hushed voice.

She watched as her hand found a dial on the side of the wooden box. She turned it all the way to the right. Then she pointed the cone away from them, off towards the wall, and hit a small button next to the dial. Darcy watched as Cam seemed to brace herself, stretching her arms out stiffly, holding the box as far away as she could. She turned her head over one shoulder, as though in an attempt to shield her face.

At first, nothing happened. Then Darcy thought she could hear something, the faintest, high-pitched hum, on the very edge of her hearing.

Cam gasped beside her, releasing the button after a few seconds and dropping her arms down. She nearly dropped the box itself, as it practically slipped out of her grasp, ducking below the flashlight beam. "It works." She heard Cam mutter to herself. She turned to Darcy with wide eyes. "Come on, we're taking this with us. We can't let it out of our sight."

Darcy nodded solemnly to her. Cam paused and seemed to think for a moment, then she held out the box to Darcy. "Here, you take it. It will be safer with you."

Darcy frowned at her in confusion, but Cam reached and gently took the flashlight from her with one hand, placing the box in her open palm. Darcy grasped it. "Let's get going," Cam said, turning abruptly and heading out of the room. Darcy pulled the box closer to her, hugging it against her chest. She followed Cam out into the darkness of the hallway beyond.

33.

Austin

It was a pleasure to move, to feel his muscles stretching and straining, finally given free rein. He ran through the dark hallways, following the twists and turns based on instinct alone. He trailed behind her, tracking the sound of her footsteps until they stopped suddenly. But he was close enough at that point, knowing she was near.

His own footsteps fell in splashes as he moved through water, flooding the floor and hallways. Rain fell on him, and he lifted his face and smiled. The feeling of the raindrops warm against his cool skin. He felt the castle groaning around him as wood sagged and swelled. And the feeling of decay, inevitable destruction, and chaos left him feeling strangely calm. As though the storm around him soothed and quieted his soul. A flash of lightning illuminated his surroundings briefly, and he turned and entered the room to his right, melting through shadows into the dark maw of the doorway that opened before him. He moved to the center of the room, then stilled. Listening, waiting, ears straining for the sound of a heartbeat in the dark.

He felt her presence behind him, then her breath, hot on his neck, his ear, as she whispered to him, her scent washing over him.

"Admit you wanted me," she crooned to him, "admit you wanted to own me, consume me... until there was nothing left." Austin shuddered, a chill running down his spine. "You wanted me to want you, to beg you to want me." Austin frowned, shaking his head slightly. "No," he started, but she cut him off.

"Don't deny it. I know your deepest thoughts." He could hear rather than see the upward curl at the corners of her lips. "You wanted to own me, so you could discard me whenever you wished. Throw me away like trash when you were done with me."

He started to shake his head again, to deny it, but he felt the sharp curve of claws pressing against his neck. The pressure was just enough to make him freeze, muscles taut. He took a breath, his heart starting to pound. "No, I cared about you. I..."

She chuckled, her voice low and with a strange quality, an underlying distortion he couldn't remember being there before. "Let go of your shame, your regrets," she whispered, her voice trailing off until it was almost a hiss on the last syllable. "Embrace what you are; who you are. The darkness here..." she crooned against his ear, one hand wrapping around his chest, "can't you feel it? It embraces you, welcomes you."

Her grip on his neck slackened and released, and he turned to face her. Nestled against her body. She was warm against his chest. Her breasts pressed to him as he slid an arm around her waist, his newly elongated fingers slightly clumsy, a talon snagging on the fabric of her shirt. His lips hovered over hers, and she smiled as he leaned in and kissed her. Roughly, without holding back. Without fear of judgment or the need to restrain himself. Her smile widened as she opened to him.

He pulled back after a moment, his eyes meeting hers. They breathed in together as one. And he felt a smile tug at the corners of his mouth.

"Admit you wanted to own me, consume me..." She murmured against his lips, her hands moving to his waist, sliding beneath his shirt. The feel of her skin on his was exquisite.

"I wanted to eat you whole," he growled against her mouth, kissing her once more, and he could feel her laughter echoing around them and through him. His soul smoldered with pleasure as he let it all go. The burden of what could have been and what was. The fear over what could be. It evaporated from his shoulders, the weight of it falling away like mist. Then she was naked, in his arms, and nothing existed except the feeling of skin on skin. He lifted her with ease, moving to press her against the wall. Claiming her as his, as the rain fell on them, and the sky above them boomed, and the walls shook. It was as though they were one and had never been separate. As though he was finally whole. For the first time, in a long time, Austin felt like he was home.

34.

Clay

Clay took off at a steady clip. He could hear Lan somewhere up ahead still, calling out to Rahul to slow down. They met up at the ladder; Lan was just starting his descent to the organ room. They moved down the ladder in silence, moving as fast as they could.

At the bottom, Clay paused to catch his breath. Lan eyed the doorway on the far side of the room. "Come on," Lan turned to him, "We're going to lose him if we don't keep up." Clay rolled his eyes. Lan certainly didn't seem as out of breath as he was.

"Okay," Clay murmured and followed Lan as he took off again at a light jog. "I don't see how we could lose him, though," Clay added, trying not to breathe too heavily as he spoke. "He's going to hit a dead end in the chessboard room anyway, just like we did."

Lan shrugged as he jogged, half-turning back to him. "Maybe he knows another way? Who knows what kind of information he has, about the layout of the place." Clay had to admit that Lan was right; maybe Rahul knew of a way to get down to wherever Bee was.

They made it to the library, and still hadn't managed to catch sight of Rahul somehow. "Damn, that guy is fast," Lan called back to him, finally showing signs of being a little out of breath. Lan paused to catch his breath for a second, and Clay saw him eyeing the rifle that hung over the fireplace. He hadn't even noticed it was there earlier. But Lan was a detective, and a cop before that; it made sense he would have noticed it.

"Hang on a second," Lan called to him. He moved over to the fireplace. He was so tall that he could reach up and pluck the rifle out of the brackets that held it in place. He took a moment to examine it, popped it open, and checked for bullets.

"Is it loaded?" Clay asked him curiously.

Lan looked over at him and nodded. "Feels like a full chamber, actually. It's a Winchester, should be six rounds," he answered with a grim smile. Clay stared at him. "I don't plan to use it, but everything Rahul just shared..." He trailed off, looking away from Clay. "I don't like it. Any of it. This whole thing is making me nervous."

Clay nodded his understanding. "I don't like this house, castle; whatever you want to call it." Clay shrugged. "I've had a bad feeling since we got here." He sighed. "And I know Darcy has, too." He gazed in the direction Rahul had headed moments before them. "We need to find Bee and come up with a plan for getting out of here." Lan met his gaze, his expression serious, and nodded once.

"Let's get going," he said. "We'll find Bee first, gather the group together back in the common room from there, and figure out how we can break out of here." Lan glanced around the room. "I don't give a shit if they can hear us or not; clearly help isn't coming, and clearly, we don't have the full picture of what's happening here." Lan tilted his head back the way they had come. "What I said earlier, back there? I was just trying to keep everyone calm. We can't have people panicking, making bad decisions, or hurting themselves. But I agree, we need to get out of here, tonight. And get some answers."

Clay took a deep breath and felt himself growing calmer at Lan's words. At least someone else agreed and was taking this seriously. They would work together, stay calm, and find a way out.

They continued forward and made it all the way to the greenhouse before finally running into Rahul. He stood at the door on the other side of the greenhouse and was just opening it as they stepped inside.

"Hey!" He called over to them, pulling the door open, and gesturing with his head to the side. "I grabbed the key..." he breathed rapidly, his chest rising and falling, "from the tree." He looked down at the large brass key in his hand. It hung from a long chain. "At least I think this is the right one," he murmured, staring down at it. "Come on, we're heading for the room with the walkway. There's a door that leads off of that space."

He didn't explain further, and they didn't ask. He took off at a run once inside, sword held to the side, stabbing back in their direction as he ran. They kept their distance behind him as they followed him.

They eventually made it to the marble walkway, and finally, Rahul slowed his pace. As they approached the twin spiral staircases, Clay called out to him. "So, where does this door lead exactly, that we're looking for?"

Rahul turned back to him. "Let's take the left staircase, I think it's on this side of the room." He peered over the railing. "It's one of these doors, near the little study room." Rahul paused at the top of the staircase and turned back to face Clay. "We're looking for a door with a set of stone stairs. They lead to the tunnel system. That's where I think Bee ended up, down in the tunnels."

"Okay," Lan said, breathing heavily. "And are you familiar with the layout of the tunnels?" Rahul raised an eyebrow at him and started down the stairs.

"No man," he chuckled a little. "I mean, they showed us a map, at one point. But God, I mean, I wish I had that kind of memory. But there's no way."

"Right," Lan said, trading a look with Clay. "So, once we go down there, we're blind, so to speak. We'll have no clue where we are, or how to get back out?"

Clay saw Rahul shrug, his flashlight trained on him. "I mean, I guess that's right. We'll have to do the best we can, right? Try not to get too turned around, get lost ourselves."

Lan looked back at Clay again. He shook his head. "I don't like this man. I mean, we need to find Bee, but we won't be much help if we can't find our way back out again."

"Okay..." Rahul said, then trailed off. "So, what are we going to do?" They had reached the bottom of the stairs.

Lan sighed loudly. "Okay, um, I've got nothing with me that we can use to mark our path. Ah, why don't we head down, and one of us can hang back a ways, like at the first fork in the tunnel or something, that we come to. Hopefully still in sight of the door. That way, we can wait for Cam and Darcy and at least let them know where we went. If we all go now, they won't have any clue where we are."

Clay thought over Lan's idea. It made sense, he decided. That way, the girls could tell the others where they were, in case they didn't come back or got lost down in the tunnels themselves. Clay nodded his approval, and Rahul agreed readily as well.

"I'll hang back, I guess," Lan said as Rahul made his way to the second door in the wall ahead of them. He inserted the key into the lock on the door and turned it, then turned the handle. There was a groaning sound from the hinges, and the door swung open.

Clay stepped to his side, shining his flashlight through the doorway. They could just barely make out a set of stone steps, descending into darkness. "God..." Clay murmured, then trailed off. He felt a pang of guilt. No way did he want to go down there. The top side of the castle had been bad enough. He hated to think what the tunnels would feel like. But they would have to go. They couldn't leave Bee down there all by herself. She didn't even have a flashlight. He pictured her crying down there, in the darkness all alone.

Rahul looked at him and took a deep breath. "You ready?" He asked, holding the sword aloft. Clay would have laughed if he wasn't about to enter a creepy pitch-black tunnel. Rahul looked like he was playing some kind of hero in an action movie. As it was, all he could manage was a nod. Rahul turned and began to descend the stairs, and, after only a second's hesitation, Clay followed him.

35.
Bee

Bee continued forward, placing one foot after another. She headed towards the next grate, keeping her eyes trained on the pale light up ahead.

When she reached the grate she paused, peering through and trying to see anything that could orient her. She didn't hear the footsteps until she stopped moving. The faint sound of water sloshing had been covered up by her own movements. Her head whipped to her right, and her eyes strained as she peered down the tunnel, trying to see what was coming towards her in the darkness. She moved several paces back until she was just outside of the pool of moonlight.

Bee held her breath as a figure moved closer through the gloom of the tunnel. She breathed a sigh of relief as she saw it was Rahul. "Oh, thank god," she called to him, taking a step forward into the light. "It's awful down here. I'm so glad you found me." She took another step towards him, then paused, remembering. Her face fell a little. She studied his dark brown eyes. "Why didn't you tell me the truth?" she asked quietly.

He stared at her for a moment, then shook his head, looking away. "I dunno Bee," he sighed, running a hand through his hair. "I mean, I wanted to. I didn't find the right time," he finished lamely. "I hope you can forgive me," he said, smiling at her tentatively.

"Well," Bee sighed. "I suppose it was all just... part of your act then. Huh?" She bit her bottom lip, peering up at him with wide eyes as she waited for his response. Her cheeks flushed. She wished she didn't care so much what his answer would be.

Rahul chuckled and shook his head. "No, of course not, Bee. Everything was real." He met her eyes. "I swear." He held his hand out to her. "Come here," he said, gesturing to her to come to him. "Let's get out of here. I can show you the way out." She noticed as he reached for her, he didn't let his hand cross that line, between light and dark.

Bee moved to take a step forward, then hesitated. Rahul watched her, so intensely. He had almost started to smile as she moved towards him. The corner of his mouth twitched. She stared at him. He was empty-handed, she realized. He had come down here to find her, and he hadn't thought to grab a flashlight? Instead, he had walked through the tunnels alone, in the dark. And why had he stopped just where he had, just outside of the pool of light?

Bee's stomach clenched, and she began to shiver harder, but she smiled at him, giving him her best winning grin. "No," she said, "why don't you come here?" She held a hand out to him this time; her voice pitched low. She smiled at him seductively. He stood still. Bee's heart pounded in her throat. He should have no problem walking over to her. He shouldn't even hesitate.

Rahul lowered his head, his eyes piercing into hers, and time seemed to slow down. To freeze. Then he smiled. And the smile was the most terrible, horrifying thing Bee had ever seen in her life.

She screamed then as he moved towards her. He was so fast that it startled her, causing her to lose her balance. She nearly fell but managed to stumble backwards. She turned and sprinted as fast as she could back up the tunnel the way she had come. Her arms and legs were pumping as though her life depended on it. She didn't look back to see if he followed her. She could hear it; it was like the sound of claws, scrapping against wet stone. The sound of his laughter came then, low and cruel, echoing through the tunnel, reverberating around and through her.

36.

Cam

Cam and Darcy exited onto the walkway. Their footsteps were the only sounds in the silence surrounding them as they traversed the black and white marble tiles. They still hadn't managed to run into the guys, somehow. Cam figured they would make their way to the room with the chessboard and hoped they would figure out where they went from there. As they descended the spiral staircase, she felt Darcy grab her arm suddenly.

"That door, there." Darcy pointed over to the right. "It was closed before."

Cam looked over to where she was pointing and saw that the door next to the room with the corkboard and photos was now standing open. Darcy was right, it had been closed and locked earlier, but now it yawned open into darkness.

"Good eye Darc," Cam murmured. "Maybe that's where they went. Maybe they found another route to get down to a lower level."

They made their way swiftly over to the open door. Cam shone the flashlight inside, then took a step back, looking back at Darcy with raised eyebrows. Rather than opening into another room, a set of stone stairs descended into darkness below them, leading down below the floor.

"The tunnels," Darcy whispered, looking up at Cam with wide eyes. She took a step back. "I... I don't know Cam," Darcy murmured. "I don't know if I can go down there." She shook her head. "I'm just... I'm just so tired. And there's something," her voice dropped to a whisper, "Cam, I think there's something wrong with Austin." She looked from the hole in the ground that threatened to swallow them, back to Cam. "We don't know where he went..." she trailed off, looking around as though she might find him suddenly lurking behind her.

Cam turned away from her and looked down into the tunnel mouth. "I know, Darc. I know." She sighed. She lifted her flashlight beam and scanned the space around them. The beam fell on the chairs gathered near the grand piano that stood in front of the tall windows off to their right. "Why don't you go sit over there, Darcy? Go rest for a bit, okay? I'll head down the tunnel a ways and see if I can find any sign of the guys, okay? Then I'll come back here to you."

Darcy started to shake her head, but she looked back into the darkness of the tunnel and her face crumpled a little. She looked like she might cry.

"Really, Darcy, it's totally fine; come on." Cam led Darcy over to a chair. She made her sit, and found a blanket draped over a loveseat and brought it over to her. "You stay here; I'll only be gone a few minutes."

Cam turned to leave before she could protest. "Cam," Darcy called out to her. Cam turned and saw that Darcy held the machine up to her, arms outstretched. Her arms were trembling, trying to support the weight of it. That concerned Cam more than anything, at that moment. *We need to get Darcy out of this house*, she said to herself. Cam moved back to her and took the wooden box from her hands, turning it so she could grasp the handle and carry it with one hand while holding the flashlight with the other. Cam nodded to Darcy and turned away from her.

She moved to the open doorway, stared into the tunnel mouth, and turned back to Darcy. Darcy nodded solemnly, and Cam took a deep breath as she moved forward, heading into the dark to look for the others.

37.

Darcy

Darcy sat there alone in the dark for several minutes. The moonlight, filtering in through the tall bank of windows beside her, comforted her only slightly.

She could feel herself getting weaker. Thinner, somehow. Like she wasn't really part of the world. Of her surroundings. It felt like either nothing was real, or... she wasn't. Like she was starting to disappear. She shivered against the cold. It was useless, trying to stay warm. The cold of the castle had seeped into her bones now; it was inside her. Nothing she did would get rid of it. She had known that for some time now.

But she felt the cold starting to intensify as she sat there. She shivered harder now, rocked by spasms. She could see her breath exiting her mouth, a white cloud swirling into the air.

She heard him then as he walked towards her, melting out of the shadows. His footsteps were deliberate, but she detected something cautious in their pattern.

He stood over her now. And it was an effort, to open her eyes, to raise them to meet his. Blue eyes stared down at her. They were Austin's eyes, but not, at the same time. And a smile.

A dangerous smile. *The smile of a predator*, she thought. And that felt right. That was what he was.

"My my," he murmured, whispering, as he leaned forward. He moved back and forth, swaying side to side in languidly lethal movements, like a snake, as he studied her from multiple angles. "Just what do we have here?" He asked, with a chuckle deep in his throat. "I don't believe I've ever seen anything quite like you before."

His voice was so soft. So dangerously seductive. Almost a pur. "You're going to make this a lot harder for me, aren't you?" He chuckled. "Too bad you're running out of time."

Darcy began to shake violently now, convulsing. Her head fell back as her eyes rolled back into her head. She heard his laughter echoing in her ears, as she sank under.

38.
Clay

Clay was truly out of breath now, huffing as he tried to keep up with Rahul. They had left Lan behind; at the first juncture they came to. Clay watched as Rahul's flashlight beam bounced up ahead. God, that guy was really starting to get on his nerves.

Clay was just passing a branch off of the main tunnel when he heard something. He paused, and moved back a step, peering down the tunnel in the darkness. He could have sworn he had heard a voice cry out. "Rahul!" He called out to him, but Rahul must not have heard him. He continued to run forward; the flashlight beam never pausing.

Clay shone his flashlight down the tunnel as far as he could, hesitating. He should keep going, or he would lose Rahul completely. "Clay!" He heard it then; faint but coming from further down the tunnel to his right. God, he could have sworn that it sounded like Darcy's voice. He frowned, looking back up the tunnel the way they had come. *But how was that possible?* Shouldn't she be behind him, with Cam? Clay hesitated a moment longer, then turned to his right, heading down the tunnel towards the voice.

"Darcy? Is that you?" He called out to her and waited for a response. But he heard no reply. He continued forward. He could always backtrack and return to follow Rahul up ahead or go back to Lan, he told himself. He moved at a slower pace, walking now, and he kept his eyes peeled for any movement ahead.

Clay froze as the far end of his flashlight beam illuminated a pair of shoes in the water straight ahead. He slowly raised the beam, traveling up, revealing a pair of legs in tights and then a plaid dress.

Darcy stood there, shivering in the cold, a blanket wrapped around her shoulders. She squinted in the light, peering around with wrinkled brows. "Clay?" She asked, her voice trembling and weak. He realized her teeth were chattering. "How?"

"Darcy?" Clay asked, starting to shake slightly himself, still panting. "How... how did you get down here?" He turned and looked behind him. "How did you get ahead of me?"

Darcy shook her head at him, frowning. "I... I don't know. But Clay, you need to leave. You need to get out of the tunnels." Her already enormous brown eyes went unnaturally wide with fear. "Get out, now," she begged him. He stared at her, a cold sliver of fear spreading in his chest, as she whispered, "He's coming for you next."

Clay shook his head, taking a step back. "W-who, Darcy? Who's coming for me?"

"Clay?" He heard Bee's soft voice behind him and practically jumped as he whipped his head around, turning his back on Darcy. "You came after me," she said, smiling and moving towards him. "You found me."

"Bee?" Clay murmured in confusion. "How did you get..." he turned back again to find Darcy, but she wasn't there. He scanned the tunnel with his flashlight beam. "What the hell..."

"I'm sorry, Clay," Bee continued, seemingly unfazed by his odd behavior. "I'm sorry for everything. That I never realized how much I care about you. I know I can't go back, can't make up for it, but-" she paused, as he turned back to face her, eyes wide, "you're the only one I want now." She shook her head, smiling at him. "I hope you can forgive me."

Clay frowned, raising the flashlight just a fraction, so he could see her face better in the gloom. Bee seemed to shrink back slightly, taking a small step back from the light. His frown deepened. "Bee, I..." he shook his head, he wanted to believe her, wanted it more than anything. But his gut twisted, and his heart raced. Alarm bells were going off in his head. "I... I don't know, what to say..." he trailed off.

Bee moved closer to him, reaching out an arm. She rested her hand on the end of the flashlight, pushing it down and off to the side as she slid her hand up its length, then up his arm, until her hand rested on his shoulder.

He watched her, eyes growing wider, heart thumping so loudly in his chest he thought she must be able to hear it. She smiled up at him, a wicked sort of smile on her face. Then her expression grew serious. "You don't need to say anything at all..." She slid a hand behind his neck, pulling him closer to her. Her lips curled upwards. He stared at them as she smiled, seductively, all the while pulling him steadily closer. Closer to her mouth, until she was pressing her lips against his neck. He felt them cool and damp against his skin. He sighed, despite himself.

But he pulled back slightly, trying to peer down at her. "What..." he breathed, "what about Rahul... why..." his brow creased in confusion. "Why all of a sudden? You didn't seem... I don't-" He cut off abruptly as she pulled him back to her, as she kissed him, sucked on his neck. He felt himself start to relax, his body beginning to go limp; he felt the sharp points of her teeth grazing his skin as goosebumps prickled and the hair on the back of his neck stood on end.

She moved suddenly, with a jerk, pulling him tighter to her as she sank her teeth into his neck, and he howled in pain. It was a pain unlike anything he'd ever felt before. Her teeth were like two sharp daggers, stabbing into him. And she was strong. Impossibly strong. He tried to pull away from her, to push her off of him at the same time, but nothing happened. He couldn't move.

His heart hammered in his chest now, and he started to panic. This couldn't be real. This couldn't be happening. Had he passed out in the tunnel a moment ago? Was he dreaming? Hallucinating? He felt her pause, suddenly, releasing his neck. She peered over his shoulder, looking at something behind him.

"Let. Him. Go." He heard Darcy's voice again now, from just over his shoulder. Bee laughed, and her voice wasn't normal; it was distorted and dark. Tears of pain and fear gathered in his eyes.

There was a sudden blast of light then. It was blinding, even with his back turned. And he felt her release him; felt her writhe and scream in pain. Clay fell to his knees in the tunnel, gasping for breath. He managed to turn, as the light began to fade. And he could just barely make out Darcy's figure, as though she were hardly there. He saw her face fading, her image surrounded in a sort of fog before it disappeared entirely.

39.

Cam

Cam moved slowly, following the winding tunnel. She stepped gingerly through several inches of freezing cold, standing water, quickly soaking her socks and shoes. She trained her flashlight beam up ahead, peering into the gloom of the tunnel that stretched before her.

Thankfully, it wasn't too long before she came upon Lan; he had been hovering around a corner at a juncture in the tunnels. He moved around the corner towards her suddenly; his flashlight beam caught her for a second before he saw her and lowered it. She closed her eyes instinctively and shrank back from the light, calling out to him, "Jesus Lan, are you trying to give me a heart attack? You scared the crap out of me."

"Easy enough to do down here," he replied evenly. "You run across anyone on the way down here?" He asked.

Cam shook her head. "No, not a soul. I left Darcy upstairs, by the piano." Cam gestured back with an elbow. "She looked like she was terrified to come down here. Plus, I'm not sure what's wrong with her exactly, but she seems to be getting weaker. She could barely lift this earlier." Cam raised the wooden box, showing him.

"What the hell is that anyway?" Lan asked, frowning at the machine.

"I'm not sure what it's called, but I read about it in the journal," Cam replied. "It's some sort of device that John Hammond was working on right before he... died. He was trying to invent something that could cure all sorts of illnesses. But I guess this worked against the demon thing too." Cam shrugged, as Lan snorted. "I figured it can't hurt right? Might as well have it with us." Cam frowned at him. "Nice gun, by the way."

Lan shrugged and chuckled a bit. "Yeah. After Rahul grabbed that sword, I guess I figured a gun might be effective against demons too, or whatever it was he saw, anyway."

Cam studied him for a moment before nodding. "Where are the other guys?"

Lan nodded down the branch of the tunnel to the right. "They went that way; they took off to go search up the tunnel a ways for Bee. We figured I should stay here to let you guys know where we went, but also so we don't lose the way back to the exit." Lan shrugged. "That's the hope, at least."

Cam nodded. "Okay, well, I guess I'll walk after them for a bit and see if I can catch up to them." She looked Lan up and down. "You good hanging out here by yourself?"

Lan nodded to her. "I'm fine. But are you sure you want to go after them? I would stay here if I were you." He nodded to the right again. "Let them look for Bee. She couldn't have gone that far. I'm sure they can find her."

Cam hesitated, peering down the tunnel to the right and then looking to the left. "I'm sure," she said after a moment. "But I won't go too far. I'm just going to... look around, for a bit." She smiled at him. "I have a pretty decent sense of direction. I'll try to memorize the turns I take. Work my way back here."

Lan gave her an odd look, then nodded slowly. "Okay, well, that sounds like a plan, I guess. I'll keep an eye out for you returning. See you in a few."

Cam nodded to him and turned down the right-hand tunnel, moving slowly but deliberately through the water. She looked back only once before she got too far from Lan. She could barely make him out waving to her in the distance. She waved back and continued on her own.

Eying a grate, set high in the ceiling, Cam made her way over to it. She stood beneath it, staring up at the night sky. Then she clicked her flashlight off, tucked it in her pocket, and continued on her way.

She had made it about a hundred yards or so away from the grate when she heard a sound up ahead. She continued straight until she came to a wall dead ahead. She turned and peered down the tunnel to her left, then to her right. She stood there for a while, uncertain which way to go. Then she thought she picked up movement to her left. Very faint, but it was there.

She chose the left tunnel, repeating *left* to herself over and over again in her head as she went.

He came to her a minute or so later, suddenly moving into her field of view, stepping out of the shadows. She gasped slightly, in spite of herself, and took a step back.

He moved closer, watching her. He circled her, in the tunnel, eyeing her up and down. *When had he stopped blinking?* She asked herself. It was so noticeable now. But she really couldn't say.

"What are you doing down here?" His voice came out rough and gravelly. She felt it reverberating in her chest. Her heart pounded against her ribs. He had always sounded like that, in a way; he had always had a deep voice. The change was subtle, but it was there.

"I came looking for you," she responded, keeping her voice as calm and even as possible. "I had a feeling I would find you here," she murmured.

He moved closer to her until he was only inches away. Cam tried to slow her breathing, trying to hide her fear. He studied her. She saw his eyes lingering on her neck. "That...was a very silly idea..." he murmured, his gaze moving back to meet hers. "Wasn't it?" He leaned closer, his cheek sweeping just past hers until his lips hovered over hers. She trembled slightly. "When are you going to learn to stay away from me?" He whispered to her.

Cam let out her breath slowly, shaking her head. Her gut clenched, and she tried to ignore the throbbing in her core. She gripped the cold metal of the machine handle tighter in her right hand. Then she reached with her left hand, sliding it carefully between them, to support the bottom of the wooden box.

He smiled, his lips close enough to touch hers. "*Autumn's Monologue*," he said softly. Cam felt a jolt of surprise and froze. She could hear her own heartbeat in her ears. "I remember every song too, Cam."

Austin leaned closer, closing the space between them until he was kissing her. The gentleness in the kiss surprised her. It was enough to make her pause, for just a fraction of a second.

He moved faster than she had anticipated, knocking the wooden box and slamming it out of her hand. She heard it crash to the ground. He grabbed her by the neck, shoving her against the cold stone at her back. He held her there, pressing her against the wall. She gasped for air, cringing down at the machine where it lay in the water, useless on the ground.

"Nice try..." the voice was different now, cruel and distorted. "I've seen that nasty thing before. Did you really think you could fool me so easily?" The thing that held her there laughed, and the laughter echoed up and down the tunnel. Cam shuddered as she turned to face it.

Its features were coated in fine hair, the open mouth sporting long fangs. Its breath reeked. She gagged slightly, and it clenched harder around her neck, its claws digging into her. "You're too late, anyway, you fool..." the thing laughed again, cackling in satisfaction, as her vision began to swim. She saw two of the hideous things, moving apart then back together again as her vision blurred.

But a third face was there suddenly; over his shoulder. Cam stared, trying to focus on it, as she realized it was Darcy's face somehow, her eyes wide in the gloom. Her brain couldn't make sense of it. Didn't understand. Why had she followed her down here? He would destroy her next. She began to panic then, attempting to twist out of his grasp.

She tried to call out to Darcy, to scream at her to run, but only a rasping moan escaped her lips. Her eyes began to shut down then; it started like a dark fog at the edges, in the periphery first. Then the darkness spread until she was blinded completely. She remained conscious long enough to hear it whisper, its mouth right next to her ear, "You're already mine..."

40.
Bee

Bee ran as hard as she could for as long as she could. Careening through the tunnels until she came to a juncture and hesitated for only a second before choosing the right one at random. She was starting to slow, her breaths coming in huge gasps now.

She turned back to look behind her and saw nothing, at least as far as she could see in the dark. Then she suddenly heard a sound in front of her and yelped, coming to a halt and jumping back. She scrambled against the stone wall, pressing against it in fear, as though she could somehow sink through it. She closed her eyes tight and waited for the monster to grab her.

"Bee!" She heard Rahul's voice call out to her and opened her eyes instinctively at the tone of surprise. She was blinded by his flashlight as she screamed at the top of her lungs. He jumped back a step. "Jesus Bee, what?" He looked behind him, swiveling to see what she was screaming at.

Bee's mind couldn't comprehend what she was seeing. Rahul held a flashlight in one hand, and an old-fashioned sword of some type in the other. "Is it really you?" She gasped, wiping tears out of her eyes, peering at him. He just gaped at her. "Say something!" She demanded, pressing harder back against the wall, panting in fear. "Say something only you would know."

He stared at her, his eyebrows wrinkling in confusion. "Something only I would know?" He looked around the tunnel, as though it held the answer he was searching for. "Okay... um... ah," he shrugged and looked at her, studying her face.

"For fuck's sake Rahul," Bee screamed at him.

"Okay, okay!" He put his hands up, nearly dropping the sword. "Um, you ah..." His eyes went to her hair. It was a sodden, damp, tangled mass from when she had landed in the water. She had slicked it back to get it out of her eyes. "Ah, your hair." He pointed with the flashlight towards her. "Your hair looks..." he trailed off, trying to come up with the right word, "really, really good right now. Just perfect." She frowned at him for a moment, her brows drawing down. "You know." He shrugged. "A white lie."

Bee's brows cleared after a second, and she let out a rush of air, sighing and wiping her hand over her face. "A white lie," she repeated, nodding, remembering their conversation on the boat when they first met. That felt like half a lifetime ago now. "Yes," she said, smiling a little and nodding again. She no longer pressed herself into the wall. "Okay... um, give me your flashlight." She held a shaking hand out to him.

He gave her a look, but he turned the flashlight around and laid it against her palm. She took it from him, and shone it directly on him, right in his face. He squinted, raising an arm to shield his eyes, but attempting to peer at her still.

"Okay, Bee, what's going on?" He asked. "Is everything okay? I mean," he sighed, "I know you're not okay, you've been trapped in the dark down here, and I know you're mad at me, about the whole, you know... acting thing. But," he frowned, "did something else happen?"

Bee sighed, lowering the flashlight. She moved away from the wall towards him. "Yes, you could say that. Something happened." She nodded. "And yes, I am still mad at you, about the acting thing." She looked at him, panting a little, her heart racing still. "And I'm hoping that it wasn't *all* acting." She continued. "But right now, I'm just really, really glad you found me. And I'm really glad it's you."

He smiled broadly at her, moving a step closer. "Well, I'm glad I found you, too. And I can confirm it wasn't all acting." His expression turned serious. "None of it was, actually, when I was with you." He held the sword out to the side for her to see. He smiled and shrugged. "Plus, I mean, I did come down here to rescue you from the tunnels and the demon thing. I even brought a sword." He grinned down at her. "That counts for something, right?"

Bee smiled up at him, nodding, unshed tears gathering in her eyes as she half-sobbed, half-laughed. "Why yes, I do believe it does."

He reached up, tucking her damp hair behind her ear. Then he tilted her chin up and kissed her deeply. She smiled against his lips, as he wrapped one arm around her.

Rahul pulled away slightly after a moment, grinning down at her. "Good. Now, let's get the fuck out of here."

41.

Cam

Cam moved gingerly; every limb, every muscle screaming in agony. She opened her eyes, scanning the tunnel for the monster. For Darcy. But she saw nothing but darkness. She attempted to get her bearings, slowly propping herself up on one elbow and resting for a moment. Then she pulled herself to a seated position. She was surprised to see the wooden box still lying there, in the water in the center of the tunnel. She had landed slumped against the wall, on the raised lip of stones that lined the tunnel walls. It was a good thing she had landed the way she did, she thought. Otherwise, she might have drowned in just a few inches of water. What an embarrassing way to go.

Cam got carefully to her feet, using the wall behind her for support. She walked a few paces over to the wooden box and plucked it from the water. Thankfully, she saw it had landed with the exposed inner wires and metal tongs facing up. She checked the dial and pressed the button, confirming a few seconds later that it was still working. Then she turned, and stood stock still, listening.

She made her way to the right and continued to follow the tunnel until she came to a door on her left. It was near enough to the next grate that she could see the open space yawning next to her; she thought she spied the doorframe. She slid a hand against the wall next to it until her hand hit open air, then made her way carefully through the doorway.

Her toes hit a stone step, and she nearly tripped, pitching forward. She made her way more carefully up the steps from there. As she climbed, she saw a faint light up ahead, moving closer and closer.

Finally, she made it to the top of the stairs, stepping into an empty, narrow corridor. She eyed the gold candle holders attached to the wall across from her. She paused again here, listening, then continued forward, until she came to another door. The door stood open, revealing a spiral staircase that wound in a tight circle upwards. Cam climbed, holding onto the railing for support.

She stepped out into a wide-open space, breathed deeply, and scented the fresh night air. The salt smell of the sea was strong up here.

Part of the overlook room was drenched in moonlight, filtering through clouds high above. The rest remained in shadow. She turned to her right and saw Austin. He was already aware of her presence, head turned to her. Miranda stood there, across from him. She gripped the sides of the stone archway; her fingers scrambling for purchase on the smooth stone pillars that formed the walls of the arch. Her hands slid slowly, almost imperceptibly.

Something hovered there, between her and Austin. Cam squinted, trying to process what she was seeing.

It was Darcy, she realized with shock. She floated there, covering Miranda and the space between her and Austin in a moving, swirling dark cloud of fog. Miranda's eyes fell on Cam, and they were wide in fear. She lifted one hand, attempting to grasp the pillar again more firmly.

And that was when she fell. She was there one second, then gone the next, her scream echoing shrilly as she plunged down into the night.

Austin turned fully to face Cam as she stood there in shock. His head came forward, shoulders hunching slightly, as he locked onto her. His eyes flickered, catching the moonlight, and reflecting it back to her. He practically growled at her. "Leave, Cam." He looked back at the doorway behind her. "You should go." He lowered his gaze to the machine in her hands, frowning slightly. "You need to stay away from me." He met her eyes again. "I don't want to hurt you." The last part came out barely a whisper. But she heard it.

She took a deep shuddering breath. "Of course you don't, Austin." She moved forward, taking a step closer. "According to you, you never did." She moved again, one slow step at a time. "But that's what you do, isn't it?" She laughed, but it came out more like a sob. "You can't seem to stop hurting me, actually."

Darcy's face turned towards her, watching her, eyes widening, as Cam moved closer to them. But she was fading now, the fog thinning and starting to dissipate.

Austin turned slightly, following her gaze, and Cam used the split second, while he was distracted. She lifted the machine, pressing the button, and aiming it towards him. She moved forward, one step at a time, as he curled in on himself, hands over his ears, crying out in pain.

Cam's arms were shaking with the effort, but she held onto the handle, turning her head to the side as she moved ever closer to him. She was screaming herself now, crying out as she used the last of her strength, closing the distance, the last few feet to the archway. Austin rose up, his face changing, his teeth elongating, body contorting, and then he lunged.

42.

Lan

Lan didn't like it, he decided. He didn't like how long she'd been gone, and he didn't like the thoughtful look on her face as she debated entering the tunnels. His gut told him she wasn't going after Rahul and Clay, wasn't looking for Bee.

He waited a few minutes, peering after her in the dark, before he muttered, *"Fuck,"* and took off after her. He attempted to follow her the best he could through the tunnels. He came upon nothing but further stretches of empty tunnel. It seemed that he had chosen the wrong route, after all.

He ended up deciding to double back. Finally deciding to head back to the mouth of the tunnel, he backtracked all the way back the way he had come. Or at least, he thought he had. After several minutes of wandering aimlessly, he had to admit to himself he had lost his way. He had gotten turned around somehow.

Lan continued to tramp rapidly down the tunnels, his feet sloshing through the freezing cold water. His toes were numb at this point. He muttered curses under his breath.

Finally, he caught movement up ahead. He froze, bringing the flashlight up and pointing it down the tunnel ahead. But as far as the light reached, he saw nothing. He waited, frozen and listening, his muscles tense. He almost called out, but something made him pause. His ears strained, but he heard nothing but his own shallow breathing.

Still, he waited and eventually heard water sloshing. Someone was moving towards him. He stilled, holding his breath, to see who would appear out of the gloom ahead.

To his surprise, it wasn't one of his friends. No. It was a child. Lan frowned at the small figure that materialized out of the darkness, stopping just a few feet beyond the bright cone emanating from the flashlight.

He could have sworn his heart stopped when he saw its face.

Lan would have recognized that face anywhere. His jaw dropped open, going slack. He stared, his heart racing now, and his mind trying to catch up. "H-how?" He murmured. "That's not possible. How?"

The small, innocent face peered up at him, eyes wide. The little boy was trembling, he saw, either with cold or fear. Lan shook his head. It was the little boy. The one he had found hiding in the cupboard after they'd raided that apartment. He would never forget that day or that face; he couldn't erase it from his memory. Not with all the booze and women in the world. Lan began to shake then, trembling himself.

He stared at the little boy, waiting. Nothing happened for a long moment, and Lan took a shuddering step closer to him. He moved back a step in tandem, moving at nearly the same instant. Lan stepped forward again, and the boy moved backward yet again, just a fraction of a second slower. The cone of light still feet away.

"What, are you?" Lan whispered, his voice shaking, his breath coming out in ragged pants.

The boy tilted his head down, smiling as he did so. And now it was Lan's turn to take a step back, moving slowly at first, then more rapidly as the boy approached, moving faster and faster. "I have many names...." He half spoke, half hissed. Then he was sprinting, racing forward.

The thing ran at him at an impossible speed, and it was scaling the tunnel wall somehow, going down on all fours, then leaping at him, lunging in the dark. Lan had dropped his flashlight in his haste. Heard it hit the stone floor. He brought the rifle up, twisting away at the last second and ducking down at the same time.

The thing landed just past him with a splash. Lan didn't bother to turn to look back. He ran.

It followed him. He could hear it clawing closer. Gaining on him. He ducked around a corner and sprinted hard, pumping his legs and arms as hard as he could. Then he turned, bringing the rifle up. He'd put just enough distance between him and the thing that followed to allow him to swing the end of the rifle up between them. The thing lunged, suspended in mid-air; he caught a glimpse of pale arms ending in claws, stretching out for him, a face coated in fur, and an impossibly wide mouth with a set of pointed teeth.

He aimed square at its chest; pulling the trigger once, then cocking the lever forward and spinning the rifle 360 degrees, like he had seen in countless Westerns; he let off a second shot in rapid succession. The force of the bullets was enough to knock it off course slightly.

Still, momentum carried it forward, and it slammed into his left side, taking him down to the tunnel floor as it went.

He landed on his back in the icy cold water. Barely noticing the temperature in his shock and panic. He held the rifle up in his right hand, keeping it out of the water. He thought he had shot twice; four rounds left.

The thing made a screeching, sort of keening sound, and it shuffled away from him, scrambling backward, pushing itself with its legs.

It snarled at him in the dark. He saw it gathering its legs underneath it again, readying itself for round two. It was injured, clearly. But those shots would have killed a man. It seemed to be... recovering, somehow. Lan shuddered, scrambling to one knee as he watched wearily, bringing the end of the rifle up again and aiming at its head. He took the shot while he had it and hit true.

The thing's head jerked backward, and it was knocked off balance, falling onto its back. Lan lowered the rifle slightly, watching in shock as the thing kept moving, scrambling backward in the dark. It made a skittering sort of sound that sent chills down his spine. He watched in horror as the mass of limbs and fur seemed to melt into a pile of flesh; seemed to pulse and vibrate in the dark.

Then he saw a back rising, pale and glistening, as limbs seemed to separate in the gloom. It stumbled to its feet. He watched in terror, eyes wide with disbelief. Austin's face stared back at him, a wicked, curling smile on his lips. Austin leaned forward, locking onto him again. He moved a step closer, baring his teeth at him, and laughing maniacally. Lan scrambled to his feet, moving backward. "What the actual fuck?" He gasped.

And the thing with Austin's face laughed again, moving steadily closer, one step at a time. "You ready to finish this, Lan?"

"Wh-what?" Lan stumbled backward, water sloshing and splashing his legs.

"There's no one here to pull me off of you this time," the thing growled. Lan shook his head, continuing to move backward, matching Austin step for step.

"You can't be... you're not really him. This isn't real." Lan insisted, shaking his head as though to clear it.

"I am him, and he is me." The thing moved down onto all fours, front limbs seeming to elongate before his eyes. Its canines were longer and sharper now, too. They fell past his bottom lip. Austin grinned at him again. "I may let you live for a while... you've seen so many things. So much to be afraid of."

Austin grinned at him wickedly. "We could have fun, you and I."

Lan pumped the lever, aiming for his chest, and pulled the trigger again. He hit him in the upper shoulder this time. And the shot barely registered; didn't slow his pace. Lan stopped, planting his feet, he pumped the lever again, aiming directly between his eyes. He paused for just a fraction of a second, before pulling the trigger again. As Austin fell back, he pumped the lever a second time, moving a pace forward, and hitting him square in the chest. He was out of bullets now. He let the rifle fall limply to his side. He didn't think it mattered.

Lan waited, then heard a low, deep chuckle, echoing through the tunnel. He watched with a sinking feeling as Austin pitched forward; one hand on the tunnel wall as he pulled himself back to his feet. He stared over at Lan, panting a little, a too-wide grin on his face. Lan was out of options. His only hope now was to keep it talking. Move to a junction in the tunnel and try to make a run for it. He eyed the tunnel behind him briefly and turned back to Austin, keeping one eye on him.

Just then, he saw him pause, cocking his head to one side, just like a dog... listening. Then Austin turned, looked back down the tunnel behind him, then momentarily back at Lan. Without warning, he took off like a shot in the darkness, quickly moving out of sight.

Lan stood frozen, panting, staring after him in the dark. He was flooded with relief for just a second, but the relief quickly turned to dread. With a jolt of terror, he realized that the thing could only be going after one of the others now. He groaned inwardly, cursing himself for losing the flashlight earlier, and he took off after the monster, following it into the dark.

Lan continued forward, taking turns at random, moving at a steady pace, while trying not to make too much noise. He strained his ears, listening carefully for the faintest of movements up ahead in the darkness. Eventually, he turned a corner and paused. He thought he heard something. Was it a voice? A movement? He stood frozen until he was sure. He could hear water moving, sloshing slightly up ahead.

He moved forward more carefully now, trying to make as little sound as possible. Lan hopped up onto the flat stones that lined the tunnel wall. Walking at an awkward crouch that made his back, and calves scream after just a minute or so.

He saw the faint light streaming in from a grate up ahead of him. And he paused with a small gasp as he realized a figure stood nearby.

It was Cam, he realized with a start. He had finally managed to find her somehow. He watched from a distance as she made her way down the tunnel. She seemed to have lost her flashlight too, from what he could tell. Or maybe it had stopped working. He was about to jump down off the ledge, to move closer and call out to her, when he saw her freeze, her head cocking to one side. There was something in the movement that was so eerily similar to the demon thing, that his blood froze for a moment, moving like ice water through his veins.

He watched her with bated breath, attempting to control his breathing, which sounded loud in the silent tunnel. He hung back. How could he be sure it was really her? Was this another trick?

She kept stopping, standing still, as though she were listening. At first, he thought she was listening for him, and he forced his breathing to slow, taking deeper, more deliberate, but quieter breaths. But her attention seemed to be focused up ahead.

He followed behind her, maintaining the same distance. Eventually, she led him inexplicably out of the tunnels, up a staircase. He waited at the bottom, listening to her footsteps on the stairs, waiting until they disappeared into the distance. He paused another moment or so, and he followed her up the stairs then, his heart hammering in his chest. Just as he was about to reach the top, he thought he heard a faint scream. It sounded like a woman's voice.

He exited into a hallway and found it empty. He moved forward swiftly, turning and looking behind him as he moved, keeping an eye out in all directions. He moved past an open doorway and peered in, clearing the space. It looked to be another set of stairs, climbing in a spiral, so he couldn't peer up the stairs. He continued down the hall until he came to a set of closed double doors at the end of the hallway. He hadn't heard any doors open, but it was possible she had done so quietly. He tried the handles though, and found the doors were locked.

He moved back to the spiral staircase. He waited at the bottom, listening. His ears strained to pick up any sounds from above.

He realized he could smell the ocean here, the fresh cold air wafting down to him as he climbed halfway up the staircase. He heard shuffling steps, and then a voice crying out again up above. He knew with certainty this time that it was Cam.

Lan took the stairs as quickly as he could, exiting into the cold night air, his heart in his throat. He spied Cam immediately. She was standing over by the stone archway, her back to him.

For a long moment, he watched her, as he began to shiver slightly with cold and adrenaline. There was no one else up here, he realized. But Cam was looking down, leaning out over the edge of the stone wall. She turned and looked back at him. Her face was pale in the moonlight.

"Cam?" He asked quietly, stepping towards her. "Are you okay?" He looked over at the edge. "I thought I heard you cry out..." he trailed off. But she only shook her head, covering her mouth with one hand and pointing down past the edge of the wall. Lan moved slowly like he was in a dream. Or some terrible nightmare, that he couldn't wake up from. He leaned over, holding on to the stone column with both hands, tilting slowly until his upper body leaned out over the edge, and peered down. He could barely make out in the gloom, two bodies lying there, crumpled on the ground below.

He moved back from the ledge, turning towards her. She held her hand over her mouth still, shaking in silent tears. Lan moved to her, pulling her into his arms, he rocked her back and forth as she cried, her breaths coming in shuddering gasps.

"It's going to be okay," he murmured against her hair. "It's all going to be okay."

43.

Darcy

Darcy woke up, after what felt like an eternity. She had been drifting, again. Down in the tunnels. She had managed to find Clay, to warn him. She had forced the monster away from Cam somehow, too. Blasting him with every ounce of rage and energy she had left within her.

And then she had drifted once again, floating aimlessly. Just as she had in her dreams, that first night. Until she found Miranda and Austin.

She saw Miranda's face again before her; the fear in her eyes, just before she fell. Darcy sat there perfectly still for several minutes after she woke up. Tears streaming freely down her cheeks. She shook with grief and rage.

And then she waited, to see what would happen next. In this nightmare that wouldn't end. She didn't expect to see floodlights illuminating the walkway high above, shining down the stairs. Men in what looked like white crime-scene-style suits and several police officers galloped down the staircase, rushing over to her. All in a hurry.

They approached her cautiously, as they got closer. Shining their lights in her face. Asking her where the others were. How many of them were still in the house? Did she know what had happened? Did she know that people had fallen? Two people had gone over the edge of the castle wall. *Two?* Did she know of anyone else that had been hurt? Had anyone been killed?

Darcy sat there, mutely. Shaking her head no. She cried harder, then. In great shuddering sobs. And she heard one of them saying that she was in shock. One of the officers picked her up, like she weighed nothing at all, and carried her out of the castle, blanket and all.

They set her down in the back of an ambulance. Wrapped her in a thin silver blanket, like softer tin foil. And she waited again.

There were a lot of people outside. Coming and going. She sat numbly for a long time, watching. Her eyes were unfocused at times. But she scanned their faces occasionally. She found Austin. He was on a stretcher at the back of another ambulance. Several paramedics swarmed over him, monitoring him.

Austin saw her and watched her from where he lay reclined. He raised a weak, shaky hand in her direction and nodded slightly. She nodded back to him. He looked like himself, she observed in some aloof part of her mind. He looked like Austin. But Darcy shook, even with the blanket and the silver blanket they added tucked tightly around her.

Clay eventually found her. He came and sat with her. He murmured to her, the sound of his voice reassuring. He promised her that somehow everything would be alright.

He explained that Rahul and Bee were here somewhere, too. They had made it out of the castle. They had gotten lost in the tunnels and wandered around until they managed to find an exit. They had emerged onto the castle grounds, somewhere out in the gardens, and had gone immediately for help.

Miranda had been taken away already to the hospital. She was in critical condition. But Clay reassured her that he believed she was going to make it.

Lan was here somewhere as well, he said, talking to the police and trying to explain what had happened. Clay explained gently to her that the police were going to have a lot of questions for all of them.

"I have a lot of questions, too," Clay growled, "for Alex in particular." After a while, he left her and went off to talk with Bee and Rahul. He promised her he would be back.

Snippets of conversation carried over to Darcy as she sat resting with her eyes closed. She heard a gruff voice asking, "What happened with the cameras?" And a female voice answering a moment later, her words lost to the surrounding chaos; "...some sort of malfunction...technical difficulties..."

Darcy saw Cam a few minutes later. She was carrying the wooden box in one hand, the gramophone-like cone dangling almost to the ground. Cam searched the faces around her, too, looking for anyone she recognized.

Darcy moved to try to get up and go to her. But she watched, eyebrows raised, as Alex beat her to it. He was dressed in different clothes than he'd been wearing earlier. A small knot of people followed closely behind him. Clearly, his entourage. One held a camera. A police officer approached, speaking angrily to the cameraman, covering the lens. Alex spoke to Cam for some time, and she appeared to listen, interjecting occasionally. Then she reached out suddenly and slapped him across the face.

Alex reached a hand up to where she had struck him and watched her go as she walked away from him. She had seen Austin, Darcy realized, and was heading his way. Darcy moved then, forcing herself to action. She half jumped and half fell off the back of the ambulance, making her way over to Cam on wobbly legs.

Darcy intercepted her before Cam could reach him. Cam saw her and turned to her; eyebrows raised in surprise. "Darcy," she breathed, cupping her face in one hand. "There you are. You made it out." Cam pulled her close, hugging her tightly in a one-armed embrace. She pulled back to look at Darcy again, and Darcy shot a hand out from the folds of her blanket, grabbing Cam's arm.

"Cam," Darcy breathed, "It was Austin. It was Austin the whole time." Darcy shook her head. "I... I don't know, but

I..." she trailed off, "It's all my fault," she broke down, sobbing. "I should have tried to stop it earlier... I-"

Cam's brow wrinkled in confusion. She grabbed Darcy by the shoulder. "Darcy, none of this is your fault. How could it possibly be?" Cam frowned at her.

"You don't understand..." Darcy insisted, dropping her voice low. "It was Austin." She glanced over in his direction. He watched her from his stretcher. Watched her as she whispered to Cam. "I knew from the beginning. I knew something was wrong. I saw his face..." Darcy continued, trembling. Tears of fear streamed down her cheeks. "That first night, in the common room. I saw his face... on the stairs. I... I didn't understand what I was seeing. It didn't make any sense at the time. But it was a warning. Cam, the demon is inside him; it's done all of this. He's the reason Miranda is hurt. It's controlling him." Darcy paused, swallowing.

Cam shook her head, stood up straighter, and released her shoulders. "Of course it is," she said, her voice oddly cold. She looked over in Austin's direction. "That's because Austin is weak. He always has been." Her gaze turned thoughtful, and she murmured, almost to herself. "But I think it's gone now. It worked. I think it left him when he fell."

She turned back to Darcy and met her gaze again. Cam's eyes flickered strangely, reflecting the flashing lights surrounding them until they seemed to glow.

She stared down at Darcy, and a small smile came to her lips. "You just have to be strong, Darcy. You can't let it take control."

An ice-cold sliver of fear ran down Darcy's back, and she stumbled away from Cam, moving backward with a gasp.

Cam smirked slightly in Austin's direction, shaking her head once more. Then she turned and looked off in the distance towards the ocean. She breathed in deeply, smiling to herself. "Take care of yourself, Darcy. Maybe I'll see you around." She grinned in her direction. Then she turned and walked away. Darcy watched her go, weaving in between cars and people until she disappeared, into the night.

THE END

Visit A.C. Hessenauer's Author Website:

Sign up for A.C.'s monthly newsletter for updates on
new releases,
special content, free ebooks & more!

https://achessenauer
.wixsite.com/author